JUNK LOVE

ABILENE POTTS

MISFIT SAINTS

JUNK LOVE

Copyright 2023 by Misfit Saints Publishing LLC

FIRST EDITION

ISBN Paperback: 979-8-9881223-1-9

ISBN eBook: 979-8-9881223-0-2

Book designed by Mark Karis

Printed in the United States of America

FOR MARA

CORA

A couple of minutes ticked by in mostly dead silence. The sand itched Cora's cheek. *We have to get moving.*

"Julie?" she whispered.

Silence could be a hospitable thing. Cora often gifted people with it, making space and allowing the other person to take the spotlight. But this silence from her older sister—her role model, her leader, her hero—this silence was like being shoved off a cliff.

Cora tried not to panic and turned as little as she could to show obedience.

Julie was gone.

"Julie?" she whispered. Up from behind the scraggly shrub, crouching in case she was watching, Cora called again, hushed, "Julie?" Then she straightened tall and yelled, "JULIE!" Was she behind the rocks? Past the ledge? She couldn't have gotten far in that short time.

She can hear me. The thought twisted tight, wringing out her gut.

The desolate expanse widened and closed in as Cora's world shifted. Her misery didn't just love company, it required it for survival. Her head shot forward, and she dry-heaved, her hands bracing her knees. A tear landed in the patch of sand within the perimeter of her hanging red hair.

Cora scanned the desert clearing. Julie was probably past the ridge, running in one direction or the other in the streambed.

Deeper in the sandy field stood a barren tree. Its round crown of spindly branches did not offer much shade, but it was something. Surveying the gleaming landscape, she padded toward it in her socks. Because the sun shot up from the ground in a sneak attack, she held out her hands, squinting, navigating around the clusters of spiky, sprawling plants.

"Ow!" Balancing at first on one stocking foot, Cora limped over buried thistles like eggshells. Even the sand wasn't safe.

From the tree, she surveyed her surroundings. Once more, she called, "Julie?" As her cupped hands dropped away from her face, not even her echo replied. Cora sank to the earth. The bottoms of her socks peeked between her crossed legs, filled with thorns. She picked at one, but it pricked her finger and refused to yield. When a tear pooled in the corner of her mouth, Cora pressed her lips to take in the salty moisture and tried to swallow. She coughed instead and then curled into a fetal position, sobbing into her hands. *I'm going to die here.*

Eventually too exhausted to cry, Cora flopped onto her back and squinted through the twiggy branches to the blinding blue sky. Tears rolled off her face and into the dust. The harsh filtered sun heated her skin. She waited. *Maybe I'll just fall asleep and not wake up.* Would it hurt?

A bird trilled above her. Its chipper chirping seemed insensitive given her impending death.

Wait a minute. Cora's head throbbed; her thoughts blurred. It hadn't been three days without water. They didn't finish their bottled water and pretzels until the end of the first day. And the campers Cora had found this morning gave her that grapefruit soda and the turkey sandwich. Her stomach grumbled as if trying to eat the memory. She wasn't going to die—not right now, anyway. She could move. Her heart ached for Julie, and tears came again. Maybe she would die of heartbreak.

The bird repeated itself, insistent, then fluttered down amid its chittering, melodious lecture. Cora's round, little bird friend was speckled brown. Its black-and-white lined owl eyes took her in, and she couldn't help but smile at it.

"Hi."

The tiny desert bird hopped toward the ravine, then flew off. It was like a gift, like God was trying to cheer her up and coax her to move. Was that crazy? Her parents would think it was. Cora didn't know what to think anymore. She used to believe in God, but then after Julie came home, having barely graduated from Berkeley, the family stopped going to church...

While she took in the blue sky, a faint and familiar something hovered just outside her consciousness. She stilled, listening as she would to catch a fleeting dream.

Was God up there? Was He rooting for her? Would He help?

A chemical surge akin to apathy flooded her like the lye bath Julie had used to create the cat skeleton for her high school science project. The flood of anti-feeling stripped away her anxious muscles and all the vestiges of Cora—the daughter, the sister, the ambitious student, the shy girl—leaving just bones of a being in a big, indifferent world that would keep going without her. The thing that used to be Cora had been dropped in a pitiful pile on the doorstep of an old friend, someone powerful and kind who could rescue her.

A foreign thought interrupted: *Pathetic, making up an imaginary friend.*

No. She had been living in fear; she had been chasing after someone being chased by imaginary things. God was different. He was real.

A bird broke into song again. The melody was beautiful and all over the place like her dad's jazz records.

Early mornings at the summer lake house came to mind: wrapped in a robe on the elevated deck, taking in the fog that shifted while the sun half-heartedly tried to melt it, in no rush. Only the swallows rushed, pelting from the madrones to the cabin down to the lake and up and around, zipping into the round hole in the birdhouse that hung from the porch.

Cora wanted to go home. This was not her doorstep. If she was on a doorstep, it was death's. The blue heavens were in charge here, and as scary as death was, the thing she felt most was guilt. A tear rolled down her cheek. It felt like God might be sad, too.

He was there. How could she deny Him under His heavens, on His turf?

"I'm sorry," she whispered.

A breeze kissed her skin.

Get up. It was an invitation to move forward, like a protective hand on the small of her back.

Peace spread over her like a comforter, lulling her heavy eyelids into rest.

HOLLY

Ding.

Holly flopped open the toaster oven door, whacking the brown speckled granite countertop. The hearty warmth made her smile while she spread the toast with basil pesto aioli, topped the melted provolone with a pile of roast turkey, and wrapped the big, browned beauty in aluminum. She set the hunk in Keith's insulated lunch bag on top of the Caprese salad and sliced orange and reached for her mug. That would warm her up.

Nope. Holly's nose wrinkled before she slipped the tepid coffee into the microwave which beeped, accepting its orders. On a Post-it from the junk drawer, she wrote:

10 min @ 350. Love you!

The sticky note refused to adhere to the foil.

"See you at the gym!" Keith called.

"Hang on!" She scooped up the cream cheese brownie as the front door slammed, dislodging her jaw. He knew she was making his lunch. Frowning, Holly dropped the brownie into the bag and sped barefoot across the hickory laminate, her teal robe flying behind her black babydoll nightgown.

Skidding on the gray-and-white entry rug, she reached for the lever, but the door swung open toward her. When she leaped back, the open lunch bag ejected her precious parcels.

Keith paused under the entryway's high ceiling. The scattered food containers could have been dismembered body parts by the sound of his "Oh god!" Balsamic vinaigrette oozed onto the diamond-print rug while he stormed to the master bedroom.

"I've got it," Holly called, kneeling and locking down the Caprese salad's lid. She refilled the bag and used the napkin to blot the oily brown beads.

He whisked to the doorway; she held up his lunch.

"Can't forget this." Waggling his phone, he patted her blonde head. "Or this!"

"I'll pick up something." He raised his suited arm and waved, gracing her with the back of his hand while he marched through the patchy snow. The car door slammed. As his red Audi left her sky-blue Mini Cooper in the driveway, the scraping snow tires grated like gnashing teeth.

She stood to approach the vexatious lever, ready to make amends.

Across the street, the older neighbor had frozen beside her cookie-cutter lawn, holding a newspaper and staring.

"Good morning!" When Holly waved, her silky, sliding sleeve exposed her cold arm.

The neighbor spun away as if one of them should be ashamed, even though there hadn't been a nip slip.

Gripping the handle of Keith's front door, Holly swiped left.

* * *

Exam Room 3

Holly halted at the closed door. *Focus up, Samuelsson.* The new client deserved more than half-assed attention and a fake smile. *What am I grateful for?* The brilliant linoleum shone back at her.

My job. And her tan-and-white houndstooth checked pants, as comfy as yoga pants but somehow appropriate for work. *Win-win.* And her soft, creamy cashmere sweater that clung like a hug. She double tapped the door and entered.

A stunning Latina woman in a navy suit sat in an upholstered client chair on the far wall. When she looked up from her phone, her brown tortoiseshell glasses framed darker brown eyes, which stayed huge while she smiled. She had the same effortless grace as Holly's friend Meena.

"Hi. I'm Holly," she said, extending her hand and now feeling underdressed, "One of the dietitians here."

"Pleasure to meet you. I am Renata." Her long dark hair waved over her shoulders like glossy liquid reflecting light. That's something Keith didn't understand: if she dyed her hair like he wanted, it would look flat and fake, not like this. Why did he start dating her in the first place if he didn't like her as is?

"Your gastroenterologist referred you for your celiac diagnosis?"

"Yes." Renata tucked her phone into a little black purse.

"When I found out I was lactose intolerant, it was a game-changer." Holly perched on the white wheeled stool at the computer, tempted to spin in it like a kid. "At least there's an easy fix, right?" She clicked open the electronic file. "What do you do for work?"

"I practice juvenile dependency and delinquency law at the Public Defender's office."

"Like juvenile delinquents?"

Renata nodded, offering a closed-lipped smile. "I am appointed to youth who commit what would be criminal acts if they were adults. And when DCFS, Department of—"

"Child Welfare?"

"Child and Family Services. That's correct."

"My friend Courtney's a caseworker," Holly smiled.

"Courtney Wakeman?" Renata was even prettier when she really smiled, and brilliance poured out like she'd been nomming on pearls.

"You know her?" For a split second, Holly braced herself for some over-the-top story of Courtney being Courtney, but she was sure

Courtney saved her lascivious humor for her down time.

"She is wonderful."

Of course she is. Holly smiled through her fleeting disloyalty and said, "I'll tell her you said that," then turned back to the computer screen. "That must be challenging work."

"Some days are harder than others. Caseworkers like Courtney help."

"Aww." Her smile drooped when she read the hemoglobin A1C test result from 2014. "Have you checked your blood glucose levels recently?"

"Should I?"

"Nothing to stress about. Your blood work showed prediabetes two years ago. Your doctor didn't discuss that with you?"

"I am prediabetic?"

"Two years ago. Those results were close to normal, only a tenth of a percent over. That's probably why he didn't mention it."

Renata fidgeted with her gold watch band on her lap.

"You look healthy. Prediabetes is actually common. One out of three Americans has it." Resting a foot on the stool's base, she said, "Ninety percent of those people don't even know."

"I have company, then." Renata frowned and adjusted her wedding ring.

She did have company: she had a husband. She should be grateful.

"Let's do new labs! Your blood sugar could be normal."

"Please." Renata's doe eyes still looked mournful, which made her less perfect and Holly less sympathetic.

"Fantastic. I'll get that in. Then we can talk about gluten." She clicked open a lab request window. "You can prevent diabetes through diet and exercise. If your blood test shows prediabetes is still a concern, we offer medical nutrition therapy."

"Should my daughter be tested for celiac since it is genetic?"

"Autoimmune diseases are tricky. Her pediatrician would be the one to ask."

"She said not to bother until she has symptoms." A twinkle of hot copper in her eyes sparked with Mama Bear energy.

"Hang on." Smiling, Holly kicked the white padded stool to the cabinet and returned with a pamphlet that sported a green-and-purple double helix. "These guys do genetic testing for hereditary health issues. That promo code will give you 30% off. You spit in a vial, and voila!" She grinned and handed it to her. "If we have leftovers when the promotion's ending, I'm doing it. Knowledge is power, right? Do you have other kids?"

"Only Isabel."

"She's how old?"

"14."

"You don't look old enough to have a teenager!" She checked the screen. The black "37" leaped from the two-dimensional blue light like a ninja slashing swords through her consciousness, leaving her stunned and split like a three-layer cake.

In the base layer, Renata's muffled womp-womp voice said, "Isabel keeps me young. We had her right before law school."

In the middle, Holly wore a professional, possibly creepy smile.

Topping it all was a piercing, eerie tinnitus. Holly's biological clock had exploded. This woman, only a couple of years older than her, could be a grandparent before she even had a baby.

* * *

As Holly thrust her feet against the asphalt, every step in her bright blue running shoes stung like a slap in the face. She could usually hold her own with beautiful women. *Other beautiful women.* Life wasn't a competition. A memory popped up: teenage Holly posing with a bouquet of red roses in one arm, Seraphina's reins draping from her other hand. *I should visit Dad.* He had a gift for snapping her out of a funk.

This funk wasn't just from Renata. The lonely insignificance had been creeping up for months. Keith was a common denominator. Like last night at the gym when he left her waiting while he chatted up another pretty stranger, looking happier and flirtier than he ever did with her anymore.

What had happened to them? They had moved fast, which suited her fine. After only a couple of months, he'd given her a drawer and closet space in his rental house. She'd met his kids, started cooking family dinners, and their sleepovers were no longer limited to the nights Keira and Liam were at their mom's house. Then last summer, he asked if she'd take his name if they got married.

Was it her? Had she gotten impatient when the honeymoon phase was over and Keith was pulling back, slowing down, when she was itching to get to the finish line and have a family?

Sing it, Jessie J. Holly's thighs hummed like they were made for this, pumping endorphins, launching her body through her cold universe like hot pistons. By the second seductive chorus of "Bang Bang," the lyrics hurt. Keith didn't want "it" anymore. His back was better since he was doing his regular workouts again. She was getting tired of initiating.

She was tired of being a lower priority than his fricking phone. Her stepdad Charles would never disrespect her mom like this. *Even Brett's better to Danielle—and he's a meathead.*

The snow-covered path through the park opened and she took it, grinning at a snowman's Olaf carrot nose. *Let it go.* If marrying Keith was meant to be, it would happen. The first thing was to get grounded, to feel like herself again. Take her power back.

Holly hummed like a machine: arms rocking in rhythm, blonde ponytail swishing like a metronome, feet happily tapping. Her minty lip balm converted each inhale to radiant heat as the ladies sang, "Bang bang—"

Smack! Pain and blindness jerked her back to standing.

"Sorry!" The boy sounded young.

Her palm pressed her cold eye. The icy impact shocked her, but after a beat, she had to laugh.

When she pulled out an earbud and wiped her face on her yellow hoodie sleeve, another boy behind her called, "Are you okay?"

More boys stood on the bank, one holding a forgotten snowball. His friend elbowed him, and he dropped it.

"Yep!" she called, tempted to scoop up a snowball and join them. "Be more careful, okay?"

"Okay!" "Sorry!"

"No problem." She smiled at them and charged ahead.

At the end of the park, a girl in a pink coat flopped on her back, making a snow angel like Holly and Keira had after watching *Frozen* for the five hundredth time. *Let it go.*

Turning the corner onto the boulevard, she passed Harmon's grocery store and a Dutch Bros. Coffee stand. The digital clock on the bank read 12:41. Around the McDonald's, even the fry-old-laden air smelled unhealthy, but the drive-thru had plenty of victims.

Junk food hurts so many people.

Feeling feisty, she shook her fist at the golden arches, but an employee appeared from behind a nearby car and took her seriously.

The teen's sneering side-eye was asking to be laughed at, but that would have made him even grumpier, and the poor guy was probably having a shitty day, so Holly channeled her bubbling energy into a smile and called, "Have a nice day!" while serving up an extra-large wave.

Fort Herring Medical Center took up the next two blocks. Across the boulevard bisected by the planter of dormant trees sat her favorite Starbucks and the parking lot where the food trucks gathered.

After veering into the driveway of Peak Functional Wellness, she pulled her lanyard from her yellow hoodie, swiped her badge at the side door, and went in. The door closed behind her as she checked her watch. Time to change back into her work clothes and scarf down her salad.

* * *

On her way to the exam room, Holly tugged the hem of her thin white sweater over her hips. She wished Vicki's insurance would cover more frequent visits; she enjoyed their quarterly chats.

Holly knocked, stepping in. She had expected clear sailing to the client chairs on the far wall and almost face-planted into a maroon-sweatered man chest. Above the brawny torso camped a shaved and handsome head.

The statuesque man stared, probably because she'd removed her eye makeup, smeared from the snowball, and now her eyes were naked. His were green—more evergreen than kryptonite, color-wise. They were steady, self-assured, and maybe a little selfless. She couldn't back out of them.

"Holly!" Vicki's champagne-bubbly voice carried from her seat across the room. "This is my son, Jacob. Jacob, meet the best nurse ever."

"Not a nurse." She held out her hand. When his warm hand encased hers, she was glad she had gotten the words out first.

"I'm not her son. Found her in the street." He gave a side nod to his mother. "Clearly a mental health case. Do you do that here—help crazy people?"

A glance at Vicki, beaming brighter than usual under her feathery gray and brown hair, confirmed she was enjoying her son's joke, so she played along.

"Absolutely." Her face was deadpan, her body, not so much. "If you want her committed, there's a ton of paperwork." By dropping Jacob's electric hand, she had cut off the cable to temptation. Now she just needed the sparks on her skin to die out.

"Commitment's good." His voice was charged, too.

Her eyebrow twitched. "Vicki." She turned away from him and took the client chair with the black leather jacket over the back. "You look hot. Did you bring your son in for a wellness consultation?"

"He drove me. I hate driving in the snow."

"I was going to say he doesn't look malnourished. Your husband must be tall."

"These pants make me look fat." Jacob smoothed his sweater over his flat waist.

"Excuse me," she said, averting her gaze from his ridiculous biceps. Dodging his orbit, she settled on the white stool and jiggled the mouse at the computer. "Okay. Catch me up."

Toward the end of Vicki's appointment, Holly handed back the quartz pink logbook.

"Your blood sugar levels look fantastic. You nailed your nutrition and exercise goals. Anything you want to change up? I'm thinking, 'If it ain't broke, don't fix it,' but it's your case plan."

"Can I try a longer fast?"

Holly asked Jacob, "Has your mother always been an overachiever?"

"I can only vouch for the last thirty-some years." Then he shook his head, scrunching his dark eyebrows. "Belay that. She has a ton of incriminating 4-H awards from her childhood. Good instincts." He held up his palm.

She couldn't leave him hanging so she stood, high fiving him. *Smack.*

"Okay, Vicki. If it feels right for your body, you can fast 18-20 hours if you w—" Sitting back, her hips bumped the edge of the wheeled stool, which shot toward the door. "Woah-o-oh shit!"

Jacob tried to catch a flailing arm, but she was down like Bambi on ice. Splayed on the linoleum, her ass, palms, and pride stung a bit.

"Mom, we need to find you a new dietitian. This one's broken." Smiling, he offered his hand.

His open palm was other-worldly, like a key to a hole from another time: that morning. In her mind's eye, she was back on the diamond-print rug, and this kind, manly hand reached for her and connected and pulled her up where she belonged.

Nope. Chuckling, she waved off Jacob, whose hand would have felt like cheating. She got up on her own.

"You okay?" He stood close.

The smell of him—pheromones and soap—hit her like coffee. Even with the adrenaline from the fall subsiding, her heartbeat upticked.

"I'm good." While she brushed herself off and retrieved the rogue stool, she smiled at Vicki. "Where was I?"

Jacob pointed at the floor.

The smirk was tight in her cheeks. *Brat.* At least she kept the laugh contained—the giddy energy bubbling up felt loud.

"Fasting," she said. "If you want to add a few hours, you can try bone broth instead of lunch. Make sure you're hydrating and getting your electrolytes. Sound okay?"

"Great!" Even smiling, Vicki's face appeared thinner.

"When can she eat birthday cake?"

"Anytime. We want sustainable habits. Food is fuel, but it's also fun. I have recipes for healthy swaps, too. Even chocolate cake."

"Iron will, this one." He patted his mom's leg.

"If you do have a processed treat, help your body out with some protein. Be prepared to ride out some detoxing. Evolution designed us to eat foods in nature, so the more processed something is, the less we're adapted to it."

"Would living on burgers and beer speed up the adaptation process? I'm happy to help out—for humanity."

Holly was starving for playful banter, but she didn't bite.

Leaning in, he asked, "How does a mindless force design something? Doesn't design require intent?"

Vicki chuckled, "Don't start."

"I'll update Dr. Anderson." Before rolling to the computer, she smiled and said, "He'll probably reduce your metformin."

"What does that do?" Jacob's eyebrows drew down in concern.

"Metformin?"

He nodded.

"It's commonly used for Type 2 diabetes."

Vicki smiled. "Can you show him Sully?"

"Sure thing." Hesitant to reveal her silly drawings, she retrieved her glossy white binder and laid it open on her lap. "I like Dr. Jason Fung's suitcase analogy."

When Jacob leaned close, she wished she had brushed her teeth after she'd inhaled her garlicky salad. The first page showed a thick-outlined bubble man with an oversized, round head, a pear-shaped belly, and big mitten hands. His only detail was a bow tie, and he held a folded item over an open, orderly suitcase.

"Meet Sully, your friendly neighborhood hormone, insulin. He's your body's valet—an old-timey manservant who takes care of your stuff."

"*Downton-Abbey* style?" Jacob smirked. "Cute. Go on."

"Sully packs your cells with glucose so they have the energy they need. If there's a reasonable amount of sugar in the bloodstream, everything's dandy."

On the second page, Sully squatted on a partially closed, overstuffed suitcase with a downturned squiggle mouth. A conversation balloon full of bleepity-bleep expletive symbols hovered overhead and messy piles littered the page.

"The trouble starts when there's too much glucose from our diet. They call it 'insulin resistance,' but I'd be resistant, too, if someone gave me an impossible job."

She had to stop looking at Jacob. When their eyes met, his were sweet and supportive and sort of intense.

About to turn the page, her watch showed she was late.

"I'm sorry," Vicki said, checking hers.

Holly waved her off. "It's my job to keep track of time."

As they stood, Jacob reached for the binder. "Can I see that?"

"Sure. That's something I made up. If you want more information about metformin or Type 2 diabetes, we have professional pamphlets I can send home with you."

What did Jacob's home look like? He didn't wear a wedding ring. Did he live with someone? Did he treat that someone better than Keith treated her?

"I'm not trying to sell you on metformin as some magical cure with the fairy thing," she continued. "Quick, easy fixes don't last like things you earn the hard way over time, the way nature intended." She smiled at Vicki. "Which you're doing!"

"I couldn't have done this without you."

"You're Rocky. I'm just your trainer."

"You're too pretty to pass for Mickey Goldmill," Jacob said, turning a page.

"Should I schedule another appointment in three months?"

"Please!" Holly strode to the door. "And talk to Dr. Anderson about titrating off your metformin. It might be time to ditch the training wheels!"

In the hall, Jacob handed her the binder. "I like your work."

"I'm just a visual person."

He nodded.

Was he a visual person, too? *Men tend to be visual, sex-wise.*

He offered his hand. "Glad to meet you, Nurse Holly."

"I'm not—"

His hand distracted her, but the flash of a smug dimple gave away that he was joking.

"Thank you, random citizen." She maintained a straight face. "The receptionist can give you the commitment paperwork on your way out."

"C'mon, Mom," Jacob said. He slung his arm over Vicki's shoulders. "Let's get you home before the snow redesigns your driveway."

CORA

The red TRIPLE LETTER SCORE square beckoned like a button flashing to be pressed.

"You're not going to believe this." Cora grinned, checking the Scrabble tiles in their wooden tray.

"Let's see what you've got." Her dad smiled from his high-backed chair at the end of the dark distressed wood kitchen table. The night had turned the picture window behind him into a mirror, offering a view of Cora and her parents instead of the wooded Mountaindale neighborhood. Because her dad's face usually looked grumpy, thanks in part to his peaked reddish eyebrows, his smiles were precious.

Still in her apron, her mother raised the pen above the scorepad. Electric guitar drills dropped muffled through the high ceiling from Wes' bedroom upstairs.

Leaning forward, Cora covered the red TRIPLE LETTER SCORE with a Z tile, turning the horizontal QUART into QUARTZ. Beneath it she slid E, B, R, and A into the square divots.

Her dad lifted each tile as he counted. "Ninety-three points. Well played." He braced his hands against the table's edge, stifling a proud smile. "Game over."

"C'mon, Dad. You guys can still catch up." They probably couldn't, but it had been a long time since she'd won.

But the landline rang from the black granite counter behind her mom, who popped up.

"Saved by the bell." His brown eyes grinned.

Putting the phone beneath her salt-and-pepper curls, her mother said, "Hello?" After a moment, her mouth went limp. "Just a minute, please." She walked toward Cora's dad, phone first.

The first thing to disappear was his smile. "Hello?"

Then her mom disappeared, flying to the phone in the master bedroom.

While her dad paced, glowering at the mystery caller, Cora slid her paperback closer and fiddled with the barcode sticker. *Everything I Never Told You* would have to go back to the Fort Herring library unfinished. Real life was sad enough.

"How could the judge find she isn't a danger to herself?" her dad demanded. "She was on the Golden Gate Bridge, hearing voices!"

My voice.

The ballistic dread in her dad's voice hurt. It hurt knowing that Julie had told the police she was meeting Cora when they found her loitering, maybe suicidal, a few nights ago.

She pushed aside the book and scavenged Scrabble tiles from the maroon cloth bag. The third tile was a J, as in Julie. A J was worth 8 points; a C was only 3 points.

I should be with her. But the thought brought a memory.

The hotel bed isn't as comfortable as the hospital bed was. The deep red comforter is tucked too tight over my toes, and I can't get warm.

"Do they have B&G?" Wes is such a bottomless pit. "Or eggs Benedict." Tugging his suitcase through the doorway sounds a scraping alarm.

"Careful." Dad's stern voice carries from the hall.

The hotel room door slams over Wes' apology before their muffled muttering fades.

When their melodic almost-argument is out of earshot, I fill my lungs with glorious silence. It's glorious because it's temporary, like a musical rest. My pulse throbbing in my Frankenstein feet picks up next, drumming for a homecoming parade. Julie is alive. My family is back together. The nightmare is—

Wait a minute. My eyes snap open. The door to the adjoining room is open, too. Where's Mom?

Bedsprings creak from the room behind me. Denim scuffs denim with a first, a second step. Mom was wearing slick khakis, so that must be Julie. The psychiatrist said I'm not supposed to be left alone with her.

Then Julie's profile appears through the door frame. Her cropped sandy brown hair is clean, just tweaked from being slept on.

"Good morning!" I force a smile.

She pans to the window and walks past the queen beds.

"Did you sleep well?" My smile strains—not that she sees it.

After she reaches the window's edge, she tucks her hand behind the thick open curtains. With each zip of the vertical cord, the heavy material closes in, shrinking the rectangle of morning light until the room is shrouded.

I blink in the dim light as she turns to face the room. Faint scraping of ribbed denim matches Julie's steps toward me. I freeze. She steps into the slit of space between the wall and the queen bed and stands above me. Her brown eyes bearing down are darker in the half-light.

Trying to smile but not too big, trying to breathe but not too quickly, I revert to my childhood strategy for coping with nightmares: if I don't see the monster, it can't hurt me.

Her voice booms loud enough for an audience. "Won't it be nice to get home?"

"Yeah." I mean it.

When she sits on the side of the bed, her body pushes down the mattress and pins me under the dried-blood-red blanket. Before I can shift away, she grabs my shoulder and hisses hot air in my ear.

"Act normal. The FBI has bugged this room." She jabs her

finger toward the ceiling light. Her demeanor is sincere now that her words are weird. "We'll talk later."

Julie still expects obedience.

I can't. I can't help her. Cora's pulse pounded in her temples while she shuffled tiles in the tray.

"Well, she's out. What a joke." Clunking down the phone, her dad resumed his seat at the table.

Her mom appeared at the entrance to the open kitchen where the hardwood met the carpet of the lightless living room. "You can finish the game without me," she muttered.

"No worries, Mom." Cora left the table and went in for a hug.

But her mom tensed and pulled back. Cora loosened her hold and fought tears of rejection while her body tremored. It was her mother sobbing in her arms. She hadn't been refusing Cora; she'd been trying not to cry.

The squeal of chair feet preceded her father's swift, weighty footfalls and his arms around both of them, tight.

CORA

FRIDAY, DECEMBER 18, 2015

All Cora wanted was to go home and sleep. Other Mountaindale University students were going out to celebrate the end of finals week, but she had not been invited anywhere, which was fine.

The only thing energizing her was the coil of nerves floating to her throat as she traipsed across the sprawling student union's coffee shop toward the table at the wall of windows where her showstopping teaching assistant lounged.

Walsh's long denim legs stretched into the walkway. His deep brown hair dangled close to his eyes as if it were just as smitten with them as most of the women in her Philosophy class. His red pen poised over the paper spread open, vulnerable before him, reminding Cora of his notes on her first paper: cutting, insightful, challenging. His ruby-red scrawl praising her later work had made her heart skip. But not as much as it was pounding now while her steps brought her closer. She fingered the buttons of her gray wool coat, all closed.

When Walsh spotted her, his frowning face turned radiant. "Cora!" Up from his seat, he waited for her to reach the table and then cupped her arm below her shoulder.

"Hi Walsh."

"I told you. Call me Aiden."

She didn't want special treatment—if it was special treatment and not something he offered every female. He was too beautiful to be trusted.

"Did I get an 'F' on my final paper?" she asked, hefting her backpack.

His hand dropped away. "Would that be so bad, having class with me again?" His gleaming smile softened while his eyes grew wider, revealing more of their devastating blue. "Actually…" Backing up to his chair, he lifted an open palm toward the opposite seat. "That's what I want to talk to you about."

As Cora sat, she lowered her bag to the floor and tried not to panic.

"Your paper was excellent, as usual."

Oh, thank God.

"Did you have any last questions for me as your T.A.?"

Cora shook her head.

"What are you drinking? My treat."

Her head was shaking, bewildered.

"Later then. No questions? Last call."

"I didn't have any until you asked to meet." She wished his smile weren't so charming. She knew better.

"I never want to be your T.A. again."

"Thanks a lot!" she laughed.

Walsh stretched back, smiling. "I don't hear that enough."

"Thanks?"

"That laugh. It's nice to see you smile, too."

He's a flirt.

"Are you still flying off to University of Washington next fall?"

Cora nodded, trying not to be flattered that he remembered.

"Do you know anybody there yet?"

Her shoulders tightened. That's what this was: social-butterfly graduate-student pity for the lonely freshman girl.

"I know someone starting a job there this summer. Come to dinner tomorrow. I'll introduce you."

CORA

When Walsh parked at an upscale apartment building instead of the Ethiopian restaurant he had been raving about, one of Cora's fears felt validated. Until she remembered his friend. Maybe they were picking her—or him—up.

He unbuckled and smiled. She waited for him to tell her whether to stay in the car, but he let the quiet hang thick.

"Oh! Your friend can have shotgun." She unclipped her seatbelt and followed him out.

"You're sweet." Walsh smiled over the roof of his sporty black Subaru, locked it, and waved for her to come, stepping away.

Cora had to talk down her nerves while she ascended the wood steps behind him. He had told her mom he would have her home by nine o'clock. Besides, he could have about any woman he wanted; he didn't need to entrap anyone.

At the top, he knocked on the apartment door and grinned at her. "He's probably fixing his hair. I told him how cute you are." He crossed his arms and leaned on the balcony railing.

"What?"

He grinned.

She wasn't sure what flustered her more—embarrassment or envisioning the banister breaking and Walsh falling to his death. "Can you please…?" She reached out but didn't touch him—just waved for

23

him to step away from the edge.

"This?" He grabbed the banister and tried to shake it. "This isn't going anywhere."

When his hip pushed back against it, Cora sighed.

"Sorry." Walsh stepped close and dug in his pocket. "I love that look—you worried about me. But that's selfish." His long fingers flipped through keys on a ring.

Wait. He lives here? Could his friend be his roommate? But why wouldn't he have gone straight in?

"Want to know what else I'm sorry about? Come in, and I'll tell you."

As she hesitated at the threshold, what she could see of the apartment was sleek and modern. To her left, the evening sun beamed through a two-story wall of windows, highlighting an M.C. Escher-type staircase of floating steps in the far corner. A small, simple table and chairs below it fostered the only color in the room: a thin vase with a handful of red flowers. To their right, the room was darker: blocky charcoal kitchen cabinets topped with stained wood counters that matched the earthy floor.

Heading toward the distant stairs, he called up. "Aiden, buddy. Come on. Don't keep the lady waiting."

There's no friend. To her left lurked a light gray sectional with sensuous pillows and blankets offering a view of a fireplace with a flat-screen above it. How many women had been lured to this couch?

After flicking on lights, he returned. "Do you forgive me yet?" His smile was sheepish, but his eyes were playful and maybe predatory.

"For being you?"

"You sound like Mr. Rogers," he beamed. "I freaking love that."

Cora laughed and shook her head. Her temples were as tight as her heart, her throat, and the grip of her crossed arms around her ribs.

"Can I take your coat?" He closed and locked the door.

"Are we staying?"

"I hope so," he said, plopping onto the gray sectional. "Here's what I was thinking. You're a private person, right?"

She shrugged and nodded.

"And you don't know me that well."

Exactly. Why are we here?

He stretched his arms open toward the ends of the apartment and said, "This is me," and then clasped his hands. "I think you're fascinating, and I want to get to know you better. Isn't this more comfortable than a restaurant? And you can remind me how to play Scrabble after dinner." Nodding at the box near the fireplace, he said, "I just bought that."

"How did you know I like Scrabble?"

"The tile on your keychain. And…" From the kitchen, he said, "You can tell me how this is." A carafe of dark orange juice came from his black refrigerator. "It's my first time making Tej." It clunked on the block island.

While his back was turned to retrieve a glass, she wandered closer. The flowers on the compact table below the gravity-defying staircase were roses. This wasn't a date, but it looked like one.

Walsh locked his crystal blue eyes on Cora's and handed her a glass.

Instead of a citrus flavor, the sweet, yeasty drink was more like funky beer. The second sip was better.

"I like it."

"May I?" His hand was touching hers, so she let go. After he licked his lips and returned her drink, she told herself that alcohol might kill his germs before taking another sip. "Don't hit it too hard. It's Ethiopian honey wine."

"Honey. That's what I'm tasting."

"It's slammable, so go easy." When she set it down, he said, "One more," and smiled over it. "Don't worry—I'll be sober to drive you home."

If she looked concerned, it wasn't about that. Did he think this boundary violation was sexy, or was he just crass and inadvertently attractive?

"Not yet though, I hope. Will you stay? I bought loads of Ethiopian food and can't possibly eat it all by myself."

The plan was to have dinner with his friend; the friend was just him. She could use more friends. Cora unbuttoned her coat.

"You wore that the first day of class."

Trying not to blush, she let him take it.

"You were looking for an open seat—away from as many people as possible, right?" Walsh hung it in the closet. "When I saw you standing there, I wanted to throw a blanket over your head."

She stiffened.

"You know how some people wear their heart on their sleeve? You're worse." Returning to the kitchen, he said, "You wear your heart like an exoskeleton. When you walked into class that day, I thought, 'This woman is either incredibly brave or stupid.'"

Cora felt stupid for staying and stupid for being attracted to him and too stunned to step back.

"You're the farthest thing from stupid. Sorry. I meant it as a compliment. You radiate something. Like goodness. Like nuclear energy. It…" He grinned and shook his head. "Hungry?"

She took tiny sips of honey wine while he set out to-go boxes.

"So, why didn't you go straight to UW?" he asked, opening the microwave.

"It's a long story."

Walsh hesitated but didn't push.

"What about you? What made you choose Mountaindale for your master's?"

"It's a long story." He winked. "I wanted to be close to family."

"Your family lives in Mountaindale?"

"Close. Fort Herring. My dad owns this building, so I get a break on rent."

"Wow." Cora surveyed the apartment. She liked everything except the stairs. Aesthetically, they intrigued her, but they weren't safe. "How many siblings do you have?"

"A younger brother, about your age. How old are you?"

"Nineteen. Almost twenty."

"You seem like an old soul. Has anyone told you that?"

She shrugged.

Once the food was hot, he handed her an ivory china plate with a dove gray rim and introduced her to each dish with a warning for the spicy ones.

They sat on opposite sides of the square table. Walsh moved the vase of roses to the side and offered his hands.

"I've seen you pray before lunch. You're hard to miss with that hair."

Cora placed her fingers over his. She didn't want to overshare, but since the desert, God had been kind of like her secret boyfriend as her parents hated Him.

"Hit it." He bowed his head.

"Dear God, thank you for this food." Heat rushed to her face from his silky hands. "Please bless the hands that made it. Thank you for sustaining me—us—through finals and for this time to rest. Amen."

"Amen. That was nice. I like the part about blessing the cooks' hands. Does that include beverages? I want my hands blessed." Since Cora didn't have an answer, Walsh unfurled his napkin in his lap. "We stopped praying after my mom died."

She stared. "I'm so sorry."

"If heaven's real, she's there now," he said, lifting the plate of giant holey crepes. "She had good taste in china, right? My stepmom wanted new stuff when they got married." He took the top piece and passed the dish.

"When did she pass away?"

"Three years ago. Fuck cancer," he said, ripping off a corner of his Injera bread. As he scooped up the reddish Doro Wat stewed chicken, he smiled. "I guess that story isn't too long after all."

When he took a bite, his eyes met Cora's: vulnerable for a moment before they pinched into a wincing smile.

"That's got a kick." He sipped his water. "Your turn. Why are you at Mountaindale?"

"It started with mono."

"The kissing disease?"

Ignoring his wiggling eyebrows, she said, "That would make sense with my luck—I literally had one boyfriend in high school. But he never got sick. My sister came home from Berkeley with Chronic Fatigue Syndrome, and I got sick right after that."

"Kissing's more fun." Walsh chewed, smirking.

CORA

Get up.

An alarm was going off in Cora's head like she had hit snooze and was late for something important. She shuddered, sitting up at the base of the scraggly desert tree, about to rub her eyes with sandy hands but stopping just in time.

How long had she slept? The sun had dipped toward the hill frontier. Cora imagined it on fast-forward, sinking behind the distant hills and pitching her into black.

"God, please help me." A tear rolled down her cheek. Could she make it back to the car before darkness set in? That first night under the stars had been terrifying enough when they had heard the mountain lion scream. Without Julie, she might look more like dinner.

The trail map from the campers was in the car. Maybe she could sleep there and follow the ATV trails to the road. *Too far without water.* Cora shook her head, hoping the fear would fling out. She lifted herself from the sandy dirt, brushed grit off her arms and legs, and stepped out from beneath the tree.

"Ow!" Either thorny thistles were everywhere lurking below their sand camouflage, or she had terrible luck.

Returning to the streambed was comforting because it was the path to the car. The downside was the temptation to drink. The last time she had cupped the cloudy water, after the silt settled, her palms held

29

tiny red wriggling worms.

The mud beneath the water looked more hospitable, so she slipped off her floppy ankle socks and walked toward it, but the sharp rocks jabbed. Socks were better than nothing. Cora pulled them back on and splashed into the atomic waterway. As her feet sank into the muck—a heavenly balm on her broken skin—the water's surface reached her ankles, awakening predatory swirls of disturbed sediment. When the cool afternoon breeze reminded her to move, she did. The socks didn't.

Cora backtracked through the narrow orange ravine carrying her mud-caked degenerate socks which now refused to stay on. She walked in the shadow of the gigantic stone wall, surveying the location of each step. Her skin only exuded prickly heat now, no longer absorbing the sun's blasting rays.

If she could have thrown a rock at the sun, slapped its cheek, insulted its mother, done anything to get it to come back and fight, she would have. Night was terrifying. And it was coming. The first night under the stars, she had had Julie. The second night, they had slept in the car. This coming night was like a doomsday Door #3.

The break in the ravine she was searching for where flatter desert became accessible, leading to the ATV trail and the rocky road where Julie had parked after she had fled the campers who were only trying to help, was not too far ahead.

But then what? Cora's cut and swollen feet were killing her and this dusty, spiky terrain was nothing compared to the gray gravelly rocks that had crunched under her Birkenstocks on the way down the hill when she had pled with Julie to reconsider, tried to make her feel safe about driving another way, begged for the keys, pleaded with her sister to stop walking farther and farther from the rental car and from her.

The pain was one thing. The distance was another. She would have to backtrack down the rocky road in the morning to get to the ATV trails leading out. Along with the map the campers had given them, Julie's untouched "probably poisoned" sandwich and soda were there. Cora wished there were an extra pair of shoes. She shivered. She wasn't going to make it there before the darkness. Tears rolled faster and her chest squeezed tight.

The sharp masochistic melody of her physical pain trumpeted over the bluesy, hopeless notes that would have otherwise demanded the spotlight: eardrum-rupturing panic.

"Please, God, help me." What was that old saying? "God helps those who help themselves." She whispered it, scratchy, like a mantra, "God helps those who help themselves." When her throat got too hoarse, she just formed the words with her mouth.

The shadow grew.

Click.

Cora froze. She lifted her eyes, then her head. On a ledge at the base of the orange ravine wall stood a man in a slouchy hat, hunched over, facing away from her. She blinked at the mirage man. He was real.

"Thank you, God!" With the whisper came a cough. "Hello?" She called louder, 'Hello?' and waved.

The man straightened and turned from a tripod. "Hi," he called, waving back.

"Can you help me? My sister and I got stranded."

"Where's your sister?"

"She..." Her heart pushed into her throat like a trumpet mute.

"Be right there." He collapsed the tripod. After crossing the narrow ravine, the photographer, built like a football player, stood in front of her and stared at her bare feet. "Where are your shoes?"

"I gave them to my sister."

His dark eyebrows huddled. "She didn't have her own?"

"This is going to sound crazy. She said she gave them to a man in a cave."

"That does sound crazy."

Cora nodded. "She thought a stalker was following us. That's why she drove us out here. She's getting worse, hallucinating."

"How long have you been out here?" His puzzled stare fixated on her button-up floral blouse and rolled-up jeans, rusty with smeared dirt.

31

She wasn't dressed for a hike.

"Almost three days, I think? Yeah. Two nights and three days."

"Here." From his small khaki backpack, a plastic water bottle appeared, and he cracked open the spinning button cap.

"Thanks so much!" She gulped liquid life until her stomach lurched.

"Take it slow."

She stared at a cluster of spiky plants while her insides cramped.

"You okay?"

Nodding, Cora ventured another sip.

"Where did you last see your sister?"

"She was in a clearing—back that way."

"When?"

"A few hours ago, maybe? It's hard to say, I'm sorry."

"Any chance she came this way?"

"I don't know. I kept trying to get her to." She pointed. "Our car's parked up there."

"How far?"

"Not too far, I don't think."

"I'll take you there. In case she changed her mind." He held out his hand. "Jacob."

"I'm Cora. I can't thank you enough."

Jacob pulled a cell phone from his utility vest, said, "No service," and picked up his tripod. "This way. Can you walk?"

She followed him, focusing on the ground and not the pain.

When she noticed him way ahead, she flashed to midnight scurrying after Julie when her clunky Birkenstocks kept slipping on the shale hills. She wanted to yell but couldn't, like one of those dreams when you try to scream, but no sound comes out.

He stopped, stooped, found a long stick, and turned back toward her, breaking off branches. He wasn't Julie; he wasn't leaving her.

"Here."

While she tried it out, they inched forward side-by-side.

"Better?"

She nodded. "Thank you."

"Why'd your sister take off?"

"She thinks the FBI is after us."

"Not a stalker?"

"Not anymore. Sorry. It's so weird. I thought he might be real at first. But the night before we got stuck here, she said he'd switched cars from a red car to a white one."

"Classic spy move."

"It was pitch black, so all you could see was headlights." Cora sighed. "Apparently, she and the stalker are besties now. When I found her barefoot earlier, she said she'd talked to him in a cave and he told her to take off her shoes, so she did. They were expensive shoes."

"Lucky stalker."

"If you see an imaginary man in Mephistos…"

The stubble around his smile brightened it. "If you're a fugitive, I'll have to turn you in."

"I wished the FBI would track us down. I'd take a ride, even to—" Her heel didn't tell her brain it was being invaded until the thing cut deep. She screeched like nails on a chalkboard and doubled over the walking stick, dangling her freshly stabbed foot.

Jacob held her shoulder. "Keep that up, okay? Hold still."

A yelp slipped out with whatever had been in there. When she shuddered, her arm with the walking stick buckled.

"Let's get you off those." He squeezed her shoulders. "You okay for a sec?" Once he set down his backpack, camera bag, and tripod, he said, "I'm a police officer," and raised his palm to swear. "Not FBI. Mountaindale P.D."

"I'm from Mountaindale, too. We aren't close to home, are we?" Cora swayed, so he braced her arms again.

"Home's a few hours north. Piggyback?" He looked super fit, but she had smelled like a zoo the last time she had squatted to pee.

"I'm afraid I'd break your back."

"Gym membership's finally paying off. Leave the stick."

"What if your camera gets stolen?" She let him take the socks. "I'd feel terrible."

"Theft by invisible man? I'd file a report. Maybe we'd get those shoes back." When he winked, close, she flushed. "Easy paycheck for the sketch artist." He crouched in front of her.

Cora hovered her swollen hand over his giant shoulder.

"You'll need to lose the stick."

Thunk.

"Here," he said, and wrapped her arm around his neck. "Just don't choke me."

Her body pressed against his back, and she didn't have time to process all the ways it felt wrong before he stood, and she had to cling harder. Even with her thighs.

Blushing and glad he couldn't see, she said, "I found campers not too far from here this morning, but I don't think they'd steal your stuff if they came this way. They were nice."

"They didn't help you?"

"No, they were a big help. They tried to be."

"Not following."

"I'm sorry. I just—I don't know where to start."

"Try three days ago."

"Julie got the car stuck above the stream, high-centered on a mound we couldn't dig down." Her bare feet passed over the rusty dirt as if she were a ghost. "We tried to hike out and hit a dead end, like a cul-de-sac in the rock, so we slept under the stars. Then we had to backtrack to the car the next day. We slept there the second night. This morning she told me to stay put. She said she was going to climb a hill to see better and find a way out, that she could go faster without me."

Jacob veered toward a rocky bank.

"My shoes sucked for climbing. I waited, but when she wasn't back when she said she would be, I followed the road out to try to find help."

"Why didn't you do that in the first place?"

"Right? That's what I wanted to do when we couldn't push the car free. But Julie said the stalker was waiting there. She wouldn't come. She said we had to find another way out."

He tramped up the ridge.

Cora clung tighter. "I couldn't just leave her." But she had left her finally after calling and calling with no response. "When I was on the trail, I heard voices and found the campers." Seeing that pickup truck and the yellow tent had been the best thing ever. "They gave me grapefruit soda and sandwiches and drove me back to our car. Julie got back when they were tying their pickup to our rental car to pull us off the mound."

Ahead, parked sensibly beside an ATV trail, was an old white SUV. The orange dust clung to its creamy body.

"Did she overpower them and tie them up? That would be the Sheriff, not the feds."

She smiled. "At first, driving away from them, I thought we were good. I had the map and her sandwich. Julie said I shouldn't have eaten mine, that it was probably poisoned."

It hurt picturing that again: sitting beside her sister, realizing that Julie hadn't joined her back in reality. She should have hurled herself out of the moving car and run back to the campers. But her ride was here now.

"Prepare for landing," he said, stopping beside the angelic off-road instrument of salvation.

Cora planted her hand on its fender to make her wretched descent. "At a fork in the trail, she turned the opposite way he told us to go."

He opened the door. "You okay there?"

"Mm-hm." Standing hurt more than before, and she was tempted to climb into the seat while he rattled around in the back. Her taut ankles were ready to pop like balloons—ironic given all the pricked holes in her feet.

"Here." He wrapped a gray blanket over her shoulders. "I'm going to pick you up, okay?"

"I can—" she started, then gasped as she took a step.

"Do you always have trouble accepting help?"

Speechless, dazed, throbbing in pain—instead of answering, she shivered.

"I'm picking you up." Then he deposited her on the cushioned seat, set a second, folded blanket on the dash and patted it. After she eased her feet onto it, the seat back jerked, reclining. "Sorry. That okay?" When she nodded, he slammed the door and said, "Be right back."

In the moment of quiet, she relished the elevation of her feet. But the sight of her ankles, bloated and cracked like damaged pottery…

"Kitchen's closed." Jacob smiled through the open window. "Best I could do." Three plastic water bottles formed a pyramid in his hand. He gave her one; the other two went on the roof before he held out two granola bars.

"These look incredible." She took the slick, bumpy things. "Thanks so much!"

Her swollen sausage fingers failed to twist off the bottle cap, so he took over.

"Thanks."

"Here." He shook a pill bottle over her palm. "Ibuprofen. It'll help with the pain and swelling."

"Thank you." But the thing sitting there was an oval white tablet. Not Advil or the generic brand her mom bought sometimes, which were both brownish.

As Jacob crouched to the dusty earth and clacked open a neon orange plastic toolbox, she rolled it over: Motrin 600.

That made sense. She popped it in her mouth, took a swig, and closed her eyes. The sounds of ripping paper, crinkling, and then swishy shaking water weren't enough to tempt them open.

Click. A switchblade, close.

Cora knew she shouldn't run, but her pulse ticked up like she should consider it. He took the weird tinted water to the hood where he hammered down onto the water bottle, jostling the SUV, then returned with the knife in one hand and the bottle in the other.

"This might sting." His fingertips were bloody orange. "Betadine antiseptic. Quick rinse before we wrap your feet." Shaking his head, he frowned at the granola bar. "You better eat something. We'll do this after the pain pill kicks in."

After she crinkled one open, peanut butter goo melted from the oat brick, coating her tongue and yielding starchy, hearty goodness, then subsided into crunching echoes. The back door thumped closed, and Jacob returned, gripping shoulder straps.

"I'm off. Get my gear, maybe pick a fight with a boogeyman. If your sister shows up, tell her that her stalker friend said to sit tight."

Her feet throbbed while she watched him leave, toting a bulky, black backpack. Faint metallic noises clinked like fading jingle bells as he trudged away.

CORA

SATURDAY, DECEMBER 19, 2015

"I can't compete with that." Walsh leaned back from his empty plate. "Did this guy save your sister, too?"

"He was part of the search party that did the next day."

"Cool."

Cora laughed, looking at all her food. "I never talk this much."

"My plan worked. So did you and this Jacob stay in touch?"

"We wanted to send him a thank-you present, but his business card went through the wash. When we called Mountaindale Police Department, they said a Jacob Daniels used to work there, but he'd retired."

"He was older?"

"Not that old. I might have gotten his last name wrong—I only saw it once—but they didn't have any other Jacobs there either."

"Are you done? Scrabble?"

"Sure."

Cora picked up her plate and teacup and followed him around the island. Her skin crawled like the desert sun all over again; he probably thought she was crazy.

When he turned from the far side of the kitchen, she was afraid to meet his eyes. They were sweet, though—intimate—and his smile tugged her heart like a secret handshake. Off-balance, her grip on the delicate saucer relaxed, and the cup slipped off. Her gasp met shattering porcelain, then quiet.

"I'm so sorry!"

"I thought you were Irish, not Greek." Smiling, he picked up his empty plate and nodded to the fireplace. "You're supposed to throw plates, though, right?"

"I'm Spanish," Cora mumbled, feeling dumb for correcting him. "I'm so sorry."

Walsh shrugged. "Accidents happen. But if you don't stop looking like you ran over my dog, I'm going to drop this." He held the dish over the tile.

"What? No! That won't help!"

"We'll be even."

"No!"

He pointed a circling finger at her face with one hand and extended the plate with the other.

"I can't help my face! It was your mom's. Come on." Trying to step over the broken porcelain, she secured the dish from his hand and set it behind him. "I'm sorry—"

When she turned, she had just a moment before he closed in, reached around her head, and kissed her.

CORA

WEDNESDAY, DECEMBER 23, 2015

"What do you think?" Aiden clicked the mouse on his bedroom desk and opened another photo of Belltown Suites. In this one, the picture window in the modern white living room offered a view of the Space Needle.

It felt like an insult—like he was trying to remind her he was temporary, that the last five days had only been a fling and that she should be a good sport about it. Cora didn't want to be a good sport. She wanted to get off his lap and get out of there.

"It's nice." Leaning forward, she swiped the empty mug from his desk.

"I can keep looking if you don't like this one. You'll visit, right?"

Her heart twitched. Why was he doing this? She shifted her weight to her feet, but Aiden squeezed his arm around her.

"I'll pay for half your plane tickets." Finally, he released her. "Who am I kidding? I'll pay the whole thing." He stood with her, taking her free hand. "I could invest in a private jet?"

Cora still wanted to get out, but she studied his face instead.

"You're right," he said. "I can't afford a jet. You know...you'd be helping me out if you came to Seattle a little early. Do you have summer plans yet?"

A horrible suspicion clouded everything: he was reading her mind, telling her what she needed to hear to fall for him. She already had, but it wasn't too late. At this point, she could dust herself off like all the times she scraped her knees as a kid. She would have to put on her own

Band-Aids because she wasn't about to confess to her mom that she hadn't been completely honest about where she was spending all her waking hours during her Christmas break.

Cora couldn't breathe, not with Aiden offering a future that probably wouldn't happen. Castles in the sky aren't that appealing for someone with a fear of heights.

"I'm a one-day-at-a-time kind of girl." She withdrew her hand and cupped it around the mug.

"No, you're not."

Being known felt warm and wonderful but also dangerous as if she were a frog in a beaker of water coming to a slow boil. *Time to get out. Politely.*

"It's beautiful." Before she could say something about meeting for coffee when she came to Seattle in the fall, an image of Aiden making out with someone else on the sleek white couch drove her to the stairs.

"Cora," he called.

While she pattered down the slick steps in her stocking feet, she ran her hand along the wall.

"Hey." He followed her into the kitchen.

She rinsed her mug in the sink.

"I knew that might freak you out a little, but I didn't think you'd be mad." He waited by the island.

"I'm not mad."

"Right."

After putting her mug in the dishwasher, she scanned the floor for her shoes.

"Not mad, huh?"

"I'm not." She met his eyes to prove it.

"Then you won't mind me hugging you." He stepped closer. "Before you go." Once his arms surrounded her, he put his chin on her head. "I thought you were staying for dinner, but whatever you have planned is fine. You do have your day planned, right, since you're a one-day-at-a-time girl?"

Cora pulled away.

"Sorry," he said, squeezing her snug again. "I'll understand if you need to be somewhere else this summer. I'll just miss you."

"Please don't."

"What?"

"Who knows what you'll want by this summer."

"Me. I know."

She sighed.

"You're the one with the knowing-what-you-want problem." He took her hand. "We could work on that." Stepping with her to the kitchen drawer, he fanned take-out menus across the counter. "What do you want for dinner? Let's start there."

"I'm not hungry."

"Okay." He leaned against the counter.

"What do you want?"

Aiden beamed and wrapped her in a hug again. "You."

Her head was grateful for the support of his chest, but the rest of her was ready to let go at any moment. Any minute now. He wasn't letting go. His hands weren't moving, and he wasn't trying to kiss her. His stillness infected her. Her body betrayed her first, melting into him. Then her mind started in: *He actually cares about me.* Another part of her fought back: *Or this is a ploy to seduce me.*

"You know what helps overthinking?" Releasing her, he loped to the walk-in pantry and reappeared with wine and a square clear bottle. "A little reset courtesy of Mr. Ethyl. Wine is the classier option, but vodka's more efficient."

He was only holding them out, displaying their labels, but he may as well have hit her over the head with one. She backed up a step. The five days of making out had been working up to this: convince her they had a future and get her drunk.

"I have to drive," she said, heading for the closet. "You go ahead. I should get home anyway." She tensed at his steps behind her, but he was past her when she turned.

"I'm sorry." He patted the couch. "Come sit with me for a minute?"

Cora draped her coat over the shorter section and sat adjacent to him instead.

"I shouldn't have said that." Aiden's smile was sad. "You don't have a knowing-what-you-want problem. Although sometimes it's like pulling teeth to find out. I need to grab something upstairs. Will you wait here?"

She nodded.

When he came back, he sat closer. "Here." Papers—her philosophy papers—were on her lap. "I kept copies. Please don't freak out."

The scrawls in the margins that used to be red were gray now. But there were more notes in blue that she had never seen before: a question mark, a smiley face, an arrow with a note at its end:

Ask Cora about this.

"It hasn't been just a week for me."

"Five days." She stared at the photocopied sheet.

His chuckle was a little tight. "Counting days, huh? Anyway, I'm sorry if this feels fast. I shouldn't have sprung summer on you yet. No pressure." He rested his hand on her arm. "Okay?"

As Cora flipped pages, they were too blurry to read.

"Please don't think I'm a serial killer." His voice had a cringe in it. "I just love your brain. It was hard waiting to ask you out until I wasn't your T.A. You can have those back if you want, but if you're going to run out the door screaming, let me give you your Christmas present first."

"We agreed not to buy presents for each other!"

"I didn't buy you anything. Are we okay?" He pulled her to stand. The papers slid off her lap.

She considered what to say, but she was off the hook since he kissed her. His kiss was soft like their first kiss in his kitchen, marking a beginning.

In a corner of her consciousness, Cora acknowledged the game she had been playing with Aiden as an unwitting participant. Like kids with toy blocks, she would build a defensive wall and then watch as he came and knocked it down, surprised by her delight. She didn't want to play that anymore.

"I need to run upstairs," he said. "Want to come with me?"

Her mind was jumping to conclusions; her body was wishfully thinking. If they spent more time in his room, would they have sex? They always made out on the couch, or lying on the rug by the fire, or standing in the kitchen.

Her only point of reference was her boyfriend from youth group. The day they made out in his bed before his parents got home, he asked if he should get a condom. She got mad and asked what he was talking about since he knew she was waiting until marriage.

If Aiden did want to have sex, she wasn't sure she would say no.

"I'll be right back." He patted her shoulder and trotted up the floating steps.

The space helped, sitting alone on the couch. Cora remembered her first impression of it: a luxurious lure to seduce stupid women. Or at least willing women. At the time, she had not considered herself either of those, but here she was.

The Scrabble board sat by the fireplace. They'd only played half a game before they started kissing. She focused on the label. To "scrabble" was to struggle toward a goal. She smiled to herself; she hadn't thought about its meaning before.

That's who she was: someone who liked smart things. *Not a slut.* Her dad had asked her if she wanted to be one or end up like one, almost spitting in rage in his bathrobe when she came home late after youth group—hours late after youth group—after she and her boyfriend had lost track of time in his backseat.

Aiden's footsteps padded down the stairs.

"Merry Christmas." From behind her, he lowered a thin gold thread and clasped it at her neck.

"What?" She pressed it to her skin. "You said you didn't buy me anything."

"I didn't."

The delicate chain had a small pendant. It felt like a cross.

"It was my mom's."

"What? No!" Cora spun around, standing.

When they met at the end of the couch, he smiled. "There's a mirror in the bathroom if you want to see."

"I can't possibly."

"I don't wear it," he shrugged, then led her into the downstairs bathroom. He stood behind her at the mirror. "It's perfect on you."

Shaken by the love bomb, she desperately needed a boundary. Maybe she could tell his reflection.

Pressing the cross pendant, she said, "I'm really touched."

"Uh-oh. There's a 'but' coming, isn't there?"

"I'm afraid I've given you the wrong impression."

Aiden's smile vanished.

"I like you. We just might have different expectations." She sighed. "Are you assuming we're going to have sex?" Cora couldn't read his wide eyes. "Sorry, is that rude to ask?"

"No—I mean, it's not rude."

Prompted to run, instead, she lifted her hair off her neck. "Could you take this off, please? It's beautiful, but…"

"I want you to have it." He rubbed her shoulders. "There are no strings attached. If I used my mom's necklace for evil, she'd have to haunt me. Which would be hard for her since she didn't believe in ghosts. And because she loves me. But it would be tough love. She did believe in that. She would have liked you."

"Do you think sex is evil?"

"She did—outside marriage. Not evil, but sinful. Is that the same thing?" he asked, adjusting the chain. "I'm thinking you two might feel the same way about that."

Cora couldn't find words. "Virgin" was a word. "Waiting" was a word. But her heart was pounding in her ears so loudly she couldn't string any together.

He put his lips to her head. "So…?"

She nodded, watching his reflection.

"I should have known. It's not an insult. Look at you. You exude purity." His face was sweet. Playful again, not predaceous.

Her joy bubbled up into a smile. "Skin cancer runs in my family. Pale is the new…whatever."

After a kiss, he said, "It does kind of feel like I'm making out with the arc of the covenant sometimes."

"Thanks," she laughed.

While he fondled the necklace, he said, "This might help, too. A little reminder. Remember the Nazis in *Indiana Jones*, opening the arc when they weren't supposed to?"

Cora hadn't seen any of the series, but she smiled.

"If I went and got my face melted off, you wouldn't kiss me anymore."

HOLLY

The perfect yule log swirl in the pork roast, which had taken some work, transfixed Holly as she put the leftovers in the glass container. Eight days later, she was still replaying every moment with Jacob. *Design does have to be intentional.* She carried the roasting pan to the sink. *Design might be the wrong word, then?*

The soap bubbles multiplying in the pan reminded her of *The Love Bug* when the haughty villain poured Irish coffee into Herbie's gas tank before the big race, leaving Herbie bubbling, broken, and drunk. *We do malfunction on fuel we weren't meant to use.*

When she slipped the maple bacon Brussels sprouts onto a cold clear shelf, Liam's construction-paper Santa on the stainless-steel refrigerator greeted her. She missed believing in big, benevolent beings. Her Unitarian Universalist roots might be showing. Or it could be Nat King Cole, crooning about a weary world rejoicing from her iPad on the countertop, making her brain all squishy.

Picturing Jacob's mock-serious smile inviting a comeback sent a thrill up her spine. She frowned. Her mom would say she was thinking about another man because she and Keith weren't having enough sex.

Closing the dishwasher door, she caught her violation of Keith's dishwasher protocol. Left to right stood three white dishes, three pink plastic monkey plates, three blue plastic whale plates, then the white dishes she had put in, distant from their counterparts and facing the wrong way. She left the plates as is and opened the refrigerator. Warm spiced cider sounded yummy.

Be loving. Sighing, Holly returned to the scene of her petty crime, let the dishwasher door flop toward the hickory laminate floor, and pulled out the rack. Not only were the plates segregated by color and oriented left, but the juggling monkeys' topmost balls were exactly aligned—same with the whales' spouts of water. After she'd incorporated the rogue white stoneware, she nudged the kids' plates to approach Keith's precision. Did lack of exactitude disturb Keith as much as his uber-order unsettled her?

*   *   *

While Keith clunked around in the master bathroom, Holly lounged against the upholstered headboard, sipping lukewarm apple cinnamon tea and smiling at a candy cane cookie recipe on her iPad. The bedroom glowed with just the light of her bedside lamp.

Because his hair was wet when he appeared, it was darker brown and spikier.

"How's your back?"

"Fine." He eased himself into bed.

Plunk went her iPad on the little table. She clicked off her light, about to scooch down under the downy silver comforter.

Click. His lamp went on.

Keith sat tall, nestled his phone in his lap, scanned her sparkly corset, asked "Aren't you cold?" and then devoted his attention to the blue glow.

Holly considered asking Victoria's Secret for her money back while she retrieved her iPad, but the cookie photo cheered her up. Keira would enjoy making them—she was so detail-oriented.

"You get Keira and Liam at noon tomorrow?"

"Mm-hm."

He had a handsome face, a baby face, which bugged him. She knew his profile well.

Either the silence or her stare won her a glance, a smile, and a question. "What time do you head to your brother's?"

"I'd love to see the kids first. We could make Christmas cookies." She turned the iPad toward him.

"You don't need to do that." He didn't look up. "You should get an early start, especially with snow coming. Your family doesn't get much time with you."

No trick-or-treating, no Thanksgiving, now no Christmas with his kids.

Keith patted her thigh over his comforter with its Moroccan-trellis pattern, exposing a text chain with Katelyn, Keira's friend's mom.

Holly threw off the blanket and stomped to the dresser, glad she was mooning him in her thong.

"Is everything okay?"

She flung open her drawer, pawed to the bottom, and grabbed her coziest, dumpiest sweatshirt.

"I'm sorry if I missed a hint." He sounded put out at the thought of putting out.

She faced off with him and tossed her gray sweatshirt on the bed, fighting the corset's top hook with her arms tucked back.

"I guess it has been a while." Keith set his phone on his table.

The clasp unstuck, and she proceeded down the back until the sparkly pink corset fell away from her breasts and onto the floor.

"Isn't that my job?"

"I'm just gonna say it." She planted her fishnet-stockinged foot on the bed and grabbed a garter clasp. "It feels shitty to have you texting another woman when you're in bed with me."

"Katelyn? Holly. We've been over this. We're just friends. You don't have any reason to be jealous."

"Do you want to tell me what's going on?" The stocking dropped to the carpet.

"Nothing's going on."

"It's not just Katelyn," she said, tugging the heather gray sweatshirt over her head.

"I can't have any female friends now?"

Her head popped out, cocked. *What the fuck, Keith.* "I'm sleeping in Keira's room. Merry Christmas Eve."

"Holly, come on. I'm sorry!"

She turned.

"I should have remembered how sensitive you are about Katelyn."

Seriously?

"Holly!" His patronizing tone didn't help. "Come back."

She did, back to the tall doorframe.

"Come back to bed." He patted it.

"I'm too pissed to sleep here."

Keith sighed. "Promise you won't get mad."

Her arms crossed over the long sweatshirt.

"Can you at least put some pants on? It's Keira's bed."

CORA

FRIDAY, JANUARY 1, 2016

Cora was glad the New Year's fireworks were over; she preferred the quiet of the night sky. Leaning back against the hot tub jets, her arms wanted to float. Her legs wanted to float. Her heart was already buoyant, laughing at her brain for ever doubting Aiden.

It was more than a New Year: it was a New Everything. Her body was like a chrysalis she was simultaneously exploding through and finally truly living in. Remembering their countdown kiss made her euphoric.

"What do you say to New York next year? We can watch the ball drop in person."

New York sounded dirty and crowded, but anywhere with him was Yes.

She basked in warmth and memories from the enchanted evening. His dad and stepmom had been so welcoming. Even though she usually got anxious at social gatherings, being at Aiden's side made everything delightful. He had guided her to common ground with new people, directed their steps, helped her feel safe to explore.

When she gazed at the star-speckled sky, a memory nudged her: shivering beside Julie, lying in the shadow of a rock wall with blue moonlight bathing the desert floor.

Cora was warm now. She batted away that memory and reached for her champagne flute. Her pruny fingertips had just reminded her she had been waiting a while when she heard footsteps on the deck stairs.

Aiden came around the corner, rubbing his nose, and slipped into the water, sniffing a little.

"Sorry for the wait." He pulled her onto his lap, harnessed her wet curls, and moved them aside. "Neil's crew finally took off."

"I feel bad." Her body felt great since he was kissing her neck, but guilt lingered about his brother wanting them to join the after-party, a tradition he was missing due to her.

"I feel bad for the limo driver, but Neil's a good tipper, especially when he's high."

"He's high?"

Aiden stroked her naked neck. "Do we need to fish for the necklace?"

Cora's hand went over his. "I took it off so it wouldn't get hurt."

"Of course you did, you brilliant, beautiful thing. Here." He spread his legs and sat her on the edge of the seat.

"Are you worried about your brother?"

"No. That's why they have the limo," he said, massaging her shoulders. "Lauren is usually friendlier. The four of us should get together when they're sober."

"You could have gone out with them."

"No fucking way." He nibbled her ear. "Your celebrity crush Edmond is a moron."

"Who?"

"*Mansfield Park*. I've seen your face reading that."

About to argue, she remembered him coming up behind her before class without saying anything, just slowly turning her paperback to reveal the cover, then smiling and walking away.

"If you were Fanny Price, I'd be up those stairs every fucking night." After he pulled her hips into him and slid his hands over her bikini top, he asked, "Can I sleep in your room?"

She laughed. "Your parents would think I'm a slut."

"Step right up, ladies and gentlemen. The eighth wonder of the world: The Celibate Slut." He kissed her neck while his hands explored her torso.

For a couple of minutes, Aiden seemed intent on stroking every raised hair on Cora's skin, releasing each infinitesimal air bubble that clung to her.

"You believe in destiny, right?"

Trying to rally her besotted brain, she said, "Predestination, I guess. But there's free will, too." Shame was edging in.

"What about love at first sight?" His fingertips feathered over her covered nipples.

"Hell no," she chuckled.

"I didn't used to, either." Aiden unclasped her bikini top.

Maybe it was the champagne or the jets, but something was making her effervescent besides his fingers, which moved like divining rods, sliding down to her suit bottoms. She hesitated but then bent her leg in compliance and leaned back on his chest.

The physical rocking was slight: the hot water lapping her skin, his hands moving her body. The emotional rocking was harder, flinging her into the summer she was sixteen when she would lie on the lake house dock, bobbing over boat wakes, her flushed face covered by a sunhat and her skin slathered in sunscreen, sizzling with hormones and daydreaming about romance.

Cora's younger self's fantasies were realized. Grounded in cosmic ecstasy, held and caressed by Aiden and the toasty bubbles, her future looked beautiful.

Aiden's prickly jaw rested against her temple. "I love you." Even though his eyes had whispered it before, they hadn't spoiled the surprise. It was like Christmas again as the words echoed in her heart like a bell.

She said, "I love you, too," twisting back to receive a kiss on her forehead, and then she hugged his hugging arms back. But his clairvoyant hands got busy again, and soon she was transforming into light. She caught herself, caught hold of his whirring hand. "Are you sure this is okay?" she whispered.

"Oh yeah." Aiden's fingers hit a dimmer switch that lowered her eyelids. "We have sluts in here all the time."

She spun to confront him, splashing and disoriented.

"Gotcha," he smiled, seizing her slick, naked ribs.

Sputtering blissed-out fury, she said, "Come on."

"You first."

"This isn't fair," she laughed between kisses. Her breasts skimmed over the spritzing liquid heat. "You have me completely naked."

After his hands disappeared into the water, he deposited his wet trunks on the side near the folded towels. When he took her hand, she pulled back, hugging the periphery.

"This is a bad idea."

"It was your idea." Stronger, he hauled her into his lap. "We'll be careful. I'm familiar with the mechanics. I'm clean, too—I got tested before I asked you out."

"What?" Cora floated over him, but her knees grated against the rough surface of the seat.

"I need to feel you."

She clutched Aiden's shoulders. In the light of the half-moon, his eyes were different. At first, the feathering, sliding skin below distracted her, and then his mouth took all her attention while he deposited her onto a safe landing strip.

"Oh my god," she gasped. She felt bad for taking the Lord's name in vain, but it just slipped out.

Aiden slipped his tongue in around hers and rocked her by inches. Her world became dark with only senses. Her mind was tricked back to the lake house dock where she used to rock with the bobbing water, longing, kissed only by the sun.

"I should get off you."

He wiggled his eyebrows. "Get off?"

"No." She tugged away, smiling, nervous.

"Kidding," he said, holding fast. He stared like he was angry or sad while he dragged her crotch across his lap, debilitating her.

But he knew she was waiting. This felt more intense, more dangerous, than the other ways they made out, but maybe it was okay to be scared together, to be starving together—

His feral grip around her hip bones dropped her jaw. Aiden had more control over her body than she did, which alarmed her. His broken eyes scared her more. She tried not to see it, but they were looking through her.

Leaning in to kiss him and return to togetherness, trying to get her love's lips back, get his eyes back, she was shoved.

In her mind, the corpse of sixteen-year-old Cora lay splayed with her chest arched back, impaled by the tooth of a great white shark, skewered up through the lake house dock.

In the hot tub, her tortured eyes asked Aiden's dead ones, *why*. His eyes were invaders now—not only strange but a stranger's. She was a house of pain, and he was in it, beholding it—but not with empathy. With hunger.

Sharks couldn't live in fresh water. That's what her parents had told her to help with her phobia, but logic hadn't kept her from peeking over her shoulder while she waterskied behind the family boat, scouting for a gray dorsal fin.

Aiden shuddered.

CORA

The note on Aiden's letterhead was written in blue ink instead of red.

Mi Corazón
Is gone
I'm not sure how I'm breathing
Death is slower than I expected
Pleasure is gone
Colors are gone
Except for the red of your hair
Around your eyes, more heat than green

I'm sorry
I want to tell those eyes I'm sorry again
Make them love me again
It can't be a forever kind of broken
My heart is stronger than that
She can fix them
Even if I can't
But I want to
I need to

I need you

Cora knew the poem by heart. She should throw it away, but she couldn't. She was making progress, though. She had followed Dr. Fairbanks's recommendation to tell Aiden not to contact her anymore.

Leaning to her bedside table, she placed the poem next to the Christmas necklace, which lay in a glinting heap. Wasn't it manipulative, him having her "keep it or throw it away"? Cora closed the drawer on it, clicked off the lamp, and tugged up her covers. Maybe tomorrow would be better.

Please, God, don't let me see him on campus.

Sighing, she checked her alarm and then opened Aiden's text from February 9th after their final conversation.

> **I'll honor your request, but please reconsider two things. You're right about everything else.**
>
> **I didn't need a drug to feel good with you. You always felt amazing—even stone-cold sober. Doing that coke with Neil was idiotic and something I'll regret forever.**
>
> **Your pain didn't make me come. I understand your perspective—and it kills me—but I was operating on pure sensation. Our first time—your first time—was supposed to be so different, and it's all my fault.**
>
> **The only thing left is to honor you by leaving you alone. I'm going to earn your trust back, even if you can't see it. At least become a man who comes closer to deserving you.**
>
> **I love you. I am so sorry.**

Thirteen days. That's how long they had dated. The phone went back onto her bedside table.

Maybe this was how Lucy Pevensie felt coming out of the enchanted wardrobe, back from Narnia to her old, dreary life where only minutes had passed instead of years. Cora pictured Aiden like the Fawn, Mr. Tumnus, turned to stone by the White Witch after he had befriended and betrayed Lucy.

Cora liked Lucy. But she was naïve. Cora pressed her palms to her eyes, curled into a fetal position, and groaned. When she opened her eyes, the utter blackness beneath her hands intrigued her. Lucy might not have seen it coming, but Cora had known—with Julie, with Aiden. She had known something wasn't right. Why hadn't she trusted that? The darkness had no answers, so she sighed, stretched, and wrapped the covers over her shoulder.

She had never liked Valentine's Day.

HOLLY

FRIDAY, FEBRUARY 19, 2016

Even the extra garlic powder hadn't helped. Keith set his dinner plate on the glass-topped wicker coffee table on his back patio. Every kernel of brown rice was gone but the broccoli was untouched.

Holly pushed a chunk of teriyaki chicken into her remaining florets. Her appetite was gone. The heat lamp wasn't enough with the blood going to her stomach, and the sweat wasn't dry beneath her workout clothes. She put down her dish and turned to face him, tucking a cold foot under her thigh.

"Do you want to start, or should I?"

Keith shrugged.

"I've been thinking." She grabbed his hand. "I have faith in you. Someday, you'll be totally healed from your divorce and be an amazing partner to a very lucky woman. Here's where I am." She waited for him to look up. "I feel like I've been trying to give my heart to a wonderful guy whose hands are tied."

When he had come late to the gym that evening, exasperated about his forever-taking meeting, he'd vented about his boss repeating something "*o*-ver and *o*-ver." Across the eleven months of their relationship, Keith had warned her repeatedly about his brokenness, so she tried to lighten the mood.

"You've told me," she said, imitating his venting session, "*o*-ver and *o*-ver…"

He squinted, raising an eyebrow.

"…that your heart's still healing." She released his hand. "I need to protect my own heart. I don't know how to stay in a relationship with you and do that. Having sex with someone who might not love me anymore seems seriously unhealthy. But for you, I get that not having sex could trigger issues from your marriage. Do you have any ideas for how we can navigate this?"

Keith slumped. "I don't know what's wrong with me. It's just…I don't feel the excitement I did when we started dating. But my counselor said, 'Love is a choice, not a feeling.'"

The mound of beautiful broccoli was getting cold on his plate.

"I'm sorry," he said, stabbing a floret on the periphery. "I appreciate you cooking." He chewed, begrudging.

Am I his broccoli now? "I don't want you to choose me. I want you to love me."

"I'll work on it." He stared at his hands.

"It's okay." She rubbed his firm shoulder.

The backyard fence blocked naked deciduous trees that were waving, swaying in the slight evening breeze. Holly picked up the dishes and went in. She left the patio door ajar since Keith would probably follow soon.

In the kitchen, she dabbed her eyes with a napkin, threw it in the trash, and clattered everything into the dishwasher. The plates were facing the wrong way.

Get out.

Her heart surprised her. It was right. She didn't belong here.

Burgling her belongings, she grabbed grocery bags from the walk-in pantry and popped in her vitamins and probiotics. In the bedroom, she collected the few remaining clothes from her drawer.

She hurried to the bathroom. When she locked eyes with herself in the mirror, she saw Keith on Sunday, Valentine's Day, looking past her naked body bent over the countertop, staring at himself.

Ending it was the right thing. Their relationship wasn't healthy anymore—if it ever had been.

Was that a noise? Her pulse pounded. If he were to come in and express any genuine emotion, give her hope that love could be salvaged here…

Her part of the walk-in closet had been emptied since their talk last week. Her shoes, purse, and coat were at the front door. That was it.

Get out.

At the entryway, her bags thumped loudly onto the diamond-print rug, but the picture window still showed the back of Keith's spiky-haired head. He faced down, which meant he was either sad or tired—or reading his phone.

Holly's untied bright blue running shoes took in her feet. Her white puffer jacket and turquoise purse unhooked from the coat tree. Catching up to her racing heart, she slipped his house key off her keychain and left it on the bench.

Get. Out.

She heaved open the heavy door and obeyed.

CORA

SUNDAY, FEBRUARY 21, 2016

Cora's eyelids flew open like spring-loaded curtains. She leaped from the twin bed, sprinted from her bedroom, grabbed the banister like grim death, and yanked herself forward, flying past the titanic chandelier that topped the foyer below.

The toilet seat over-cooperated with a clattering ceramic slam and she barely had time to hold her hair before she heaved.

The sun's rays had shifted on the shower curtain in front of her. Cora's pajama pants drooped in sage green rippling pools around her ankles and her frizzy curls hung over her face. Her sinuses burned. Above her bare legs, two lines confronted her from the white plastic stick's oval window.

The wrapper moved over the stick like a body bag zipping up over proof of life. Mummifying the evidence in toilet paper, she buried it in the trash, topping it with used tissues, a snotty disincentive to any investigation.

With her hands braced against the marbled granite, she studied her reflection. Her eyes didn't show she had been crying. They also looked kind of dead. She combed through the drawer until she found the translucent orange, white-capped cylinder. Her stomach gave the all clear, but food might be a game changer. Did she have to take it with food?

Wait a minute. Clicking off the light, she headed to her room, retrieved her phone from her bedside table, and Googled: **taking Effexor during pregnancy.**

A CDC link popped up:

Use of the Antidepressant Venlafaxine During Early Pregnancy May Be Linked to Specific Birth Defects.

Sitting on the bed, her hand trembled above the screen in her attempt to close the article. Her feet were cold. She pulled them up and tucked into bed.

Even though she didn't want to think or feel, her logical brain was dragging thoughts out like water from a well, which scared her given all the nightmares lurking in the depths. Each bucket being drawn, hand over hand on the rope, could have one smuggled aboard. She hoped her overachieving mind would spot the gleaming eyes through the dark before it was too late, and the thing was up in her consciousness where it could launch itself forward and devour her.

She would stop taking Effexor. That was easy. Maybe the small accomplishment would be enough, and her brain would shut off.

She had to tell Aiden.

No. She didn't have to tell him. Dr. Fairbanks said no contact.

But she was having his baby! Didn't this change everything?

No. Cora couldn't trust him. He had undoubtedly lied to her. Who only snorted coke occasionally? And if Neil really "dabbled" in it more than Aiden did, he should have been a positive influence, not participated in his little brother's corruption on holidays.

Regardless, she couldn't trust herself with him. Like with Julie, she needed to be strong to withstand his will, and she could only get stronger away from him. But she was nowhere in the neighborhood of strong.

As a tear slid onto her pillow, a ghost of Aiden spooned her, transporting her to the rug by his cozy fireplace, so she tuned out the watching part of her mind and relaxed into the memory for a taste—a dream of a taste—of being safe and wanted and loved.

But a mental Polaroid of Aiden's fiendish face in the hot tub slapped close. She couldn't look away. Even when her eyes snapped open and she registered her aloneness in her own bed, his dead and ravenous eyes remained.

Something like a firework popped off in her abdomen, gutting her in memoriam. The second one she heard coming, whizzing up to her heart. *Unlovable.* Cora crumpled around her shredded chest. Number 3 rapid-fired in her brain. *Stupid.* She groaned, hoisted on a phantasmic petard. A second round began, and she clutched her seizing belly.

Stress was not good for the baby. *A baby. Inside me.* With her hands on her stomach, she took in fresh oxygen and fresh thoughts to help with the havoc: she was safe now. They were safe now.

After a few minutes, her emotional skies were clearer. Through the window, the morning sun bathed her bedroom in goodness. *Sorry,* she told the baby, holding a hand there.

It feels like a girl. She sighed, smiling a little. *I know I can't know that, but it feels like a girl.*

HOLLY

From her perch on the white countertop, Holly soaked in the bright, beachy blue walls. The pictures her sister-in-law had texted hadn't done the new paint justice. It wasn't that she hadn't liked the color, the same color as her beloved old purse, it had just seemed a bit much for a whole kitchen. But as usual, Danielle's judgment was flawless—with the obvious exception of choosing her big, bratty brother as a life partner.

Holly wouldn't have missed her nephew's 6th birthday, but the visit wasn't helping her get over the breakup. Brett and Danielle deserved to be happy—well, not Brett. He had some karma to work off. But it hurt. She shouldn't compare, but it hurt.

The salad bowl went into the stainless-steel refrigerator in exchange for the sparkling Moscato. Danielle's blonde pixie cut worked perfectly with her elfin face, and she looked pert and breezy in the apron Holly had given her last Christmas: black with white polka dots and spring green satin for the sash and ruffled edging. She hoped Danielle really liked it and wasn't only wearing it because she was visiting.

While her sister-in-law opened the wine, Holly dismounted from the countertop, kicked aside a stray white balloon, and rambled to the sliding glass doors where clouds rolled in, pushing out rosy sunlight.

On the back deck, Brett stood at the smoker, facing the darkening sky. He looked like their dad from the back with his tall, lanky build, only with their mom's blond hair. The clinking of glass and a glugging sound brought her back into the kitchen.

"Does your husband realize it's not spring yet?"

"He's excited about his new tuna marinade," Danielle said, extending a stemmed glass of barely bubbling wine as if it were a flower. "Cheers!"

"What are we toasting?"

"How strong and lovable you are." Her blithe brown eyes smiled.

"Aww. Cheers."

Clink. Its luminescence reminded Holly of string lights, and when she sipped, the effervescent liquid exuded sunny energy. Savoring the pineapple and apricot flavors and the resulting warm glow it imparted, she tried to tune out the whoosh of the sliding door.

"This is good." Danielle sniffed her glass.

"A friend turned me on to this winery," Holly smiled.

"Not a new boyfriend?" Brett stood by his wife and eyed her wine, which was offered and accepted. "A little sweet."

"Not a boyfriend—Meena."

"The Indian girl?" Returning the glass to Danielle, he said, "I need a pan for the fish."

Holly scowled. "You mean the missionary and physical therapist? From England?"

"She's cool." He nodded. "Thanks." And he took the pan.

"No more boyfriends for me." Boosting herself onto the countertop, careful not to kick the white cupboards, she said, "I'm becoming a nun."

"Better get off your agnostic fence. You won't get past the interview."

When he helped himself to a slug of Danielle's wine, she said, "I can pour you your own."

"Please." With a smooch and a nod, he left the kitchen.

The feeling of sitting on a fence, looking over the green grass of her brother's charmed life, wasn't new. But today she felt benched more than anything, like she wasn't good enough to play adult—a married adult, anyway.

"Can I talk to you?" she asked Danielle.

"Absolutely! Let's sit." Grinning like a tall Tinkerbell looking for mischief, she set down Brett's wine, slipped off her polka-dot apron, and led the way to the family room, ducking under the "Happy Birthday" banner.

The square corners of the off-white sectional mirrored the grids in the windows, bright and orderly.

After sinking into the cozy sofa across from Danielle, Holly sighed. "I'm allergic to dating."

"You and Keith were together about a year, weren't you? Your heart needs a rest."

"Nope. It's a pattern. I need to cut men out of my life. Make a clubhouse with string lights." She presented her unseeable sign in the air. "No Boys Allowed."

"Sign me up." But then she shook her head. "I would miss Brett and Owen. I'll visit."

While Holly stroked the closest leaf of the floor plant living happily in the corner, she said, "More like a sensitivity. I crave being in a relationship but feel messed up afterward—like what ice cream does to me."

"Dang it!" Danielle's reaction was a bit much. "I forgot to make tartar sauce. Can we talk in the kitchen?" When they relocated, she said, "Ice cream," and rummaged in the refrigerator

Brett breezed in with the pan. "Fish is ready."

"Help me with the tartar sauce?" she asked, handing him a jar of pickles. "Go on, Holly. You were talking about relationships making you feel gross like ice cream."

Pop. The lid twisted off the pickle jar. "Doesn't that Lactaid stuff work?"

"It helps." Holly couldn't help smiling. Her brother acted oblivious sometimes, but he was actually a pretty perceptive guy. "I still try to avoid it."

Grinning, he opened a cupboard. "The ladies at the nunnery should help you avoid sex."

She hopped back up on the countertop. "Ha. Ha."

"Lust-aid." He speared a pickle. "There's your answer. It comes in little red packets." With his free hand, he held an inch of space between his finger and thumb. "Be careful you get the women's one. The men's version is a low dose of the drug they use to chemically castrate sex offenders."

His wife busted into a laugh like a beautiful goose.

Holly smirked. "You should do a commercial for them."

"Having an irresistible hunk for their spokesperson." He nodded, attempting a smolder. "Smart."

"No," she said, stifling a laugh. "For dramatization. Warn unsuspecting women what horrifying husbands they could end up with if they give in to their lustful natures." Past her sweeping hands, the invisible screen appeared across the kitchen. "You in a dirty wife-beater, scratching your crotch, leaving the bathroom with the toilet seat up..."

"And don't take it too long." Slapping the round black lid of the hand-held food processor, he explained, "Side effects include mental health haircuts and drum circling."

* * *

"Keith was a tool." Brett ended his proclamation from the head of the dining room table with a decisive salad bite.

Her brother had his moments.

Towheaded Owen stopped stabbing at the cherry tomato spinning across his plate. "How can a person be a tool?"

"You know, sweetie." His mom rested her fork hand. "Like your toolset from Gigi and Papa. Tools fix things like people fix things."

"Or screw them over." Brett chewed.

Danielle's fork clinked on the china as she gave him laser eyes, but Brett just nodded at his son as if imparting grave wisdom. Owen nodded back, then popped a tomato into his mouth.

"Fork, please," his mother said.

"Man Boy was right about one thing." Brett wiped his lips on the ivory napkin. "Or his therapist was. Love is a choice. Dating's all fireworks and adrenaline. Other hormones, too, but that medical stuff is your deal. Sparks either light something lasting or fizzle out. People like Man Boy are crappy kindling."

His wife shook her head at "crappy."

"You have to be mature to offer real love," he continued. "Love requires sacrifice, putting the team before the self. That's the choice."

While Holly searched for an Owen-appropriate way to tell her big brother that he was evidence against his theory, being an immature butt-head, Owen asked, "Aunt Holly?" with his mouth full of greens.

"Swallow first," his mom said.

He gulped. "You never answered me about God."

Brett and Danielle studied Holly.

"We were working on his Lego police station, and Owen told me about Sunday school."

"What was the lesson, honey?" Danielle asked.

"Miss Elaine shook up the box of Legos." He demonstrated with his little hands. "She asked how long we had to wait before it came together."

Since the lesson still annoyed her, Holly cut to the chase. "Owen asked if I believe in creation." She plopped a dollop of tartar sauce on her plate, allowing time for redirection.

"Don't leave the boy hanging." Brett took a tuna bite.

Seriously?

Danielle smiled, waiting.

Turning to her nephew, she asked, "Where did we leave off?"

"You said we could have been made on purpose."

Brett grinned.

She hoped her brother wasn't getting his hopes up. *I'm not buying any golden tickets to heaven today.*

"You have an excellent memory," she said. "I don't know whether God created us or not."

"You don't know?" Owen dropped his oily fork on the tablecloth.

Nodding, she scrunched her mouth. "It's more fun to be sure about something, huh? Creation makes sense to me in some ways. Ask your mom to teach you about entropy next time you clean your room."

Danielle was still smiling, not giving her a signal to rein in her corrupting commentary. Owen's perpetually inquisitive brow was low and certain. Holly was proud of him for thinking through important things. Remembering what had happened when she was eight, only two years older than him, she wanted to bubble-wrap him or hand him a sword.

"Question for you, bud," she smiled. "If you could make animals, would you make them stiff and unchangeable? Or would you make them flexible, so they could adjust to new things and change if they needed to?"

* * *

The beachy blue kitchen was even sunny at night, glowing beneath the recessed lights.

After Danielle rinsed a wine glass, she said, handing it over, "I didn't want to talk about this in front of the boys, but the hormone talk reminded me of something I realized back when I was breastfeeding Owen."

"That God didn't give newborns teeth for a reason?" Holly cradled the glass in the fluffy dishtowel.

She smiled. "Would you agree that people can be selfish jerks?"

"Of course."

Danielle meditated on the bubbly washrag. "God rigged us to not be complete jerks because we need each other."

That was a stretch, but Holly was still curious.

"Like that African proverb," she continued, setting a wet glass in front of Holly. "'If you want to go fast, go alone. If you want to go far, go together.'"

"I like that." *Sort of.* She saw truth in the sentiment but having a lonely slog ahead of her as a single woman, which might be the only way she could be healthy, sounded unhappy. Even if she could go fast.

"Putting your desires aside for your baby is hard. Same with marriage."

Danielle rubbed the soapy cloth around the last wine glass.

"I'm surprised you only realized people can be selfish jerks after you had Owen. You'd known Brett for years by then."

She cracked a smile while she rinsed.

"What was your big realization?" Holly sighed. She was happy for Danielle, who had all the answers, but her answers didn't apply well to Holly's life. Still, she asked, "God designed us to stick together? Needing the pack, all that?"

"Why I had such a hard time trusting your brother."

The glass slipped in her hand. "What?"

"God's rules are for our protection. Including sex outside marriage." Her eyes twinkled, teary, but she smiled. "Thanks for how you handled Owen."

"Of course. I meant it."

"I think that's what you're feeling—unprotected. In your relationships. Before your brother, I had so many boyfriends I felt like an overused piece of tape."

It took a second for her to register the wet pan Danielle was holding out.

"God designed us to connect despite our innate selfishness. Hormones are one way He does that."

"Oxytocin."

"Exactly." Danielle eased the salad bowl into its bubble bath. "One purpose of sex is to bond a committed couple. We're not designed to attach to someone, rip apart, attach, and rip apart... That's what I mean about tape. I was so jaded from failed relationships, I..."

"I feel you."

"It sucks." She gave Holly a sweet, sad smile. "I'm sorry you're going through that."

"Thanks."

"It's not forever."

"For you, maybe," Holly muttered, depositing the dried bowl on the countertop.

"Would you be up for a challenge?"

"If it's Brett's idea, I need to hear it first."

"Your clients try elimination diets sometimes, right? If something is making them ill, but they don't know what it is?"

"That's why I'm swearing off men."

"What about just sex?"

"Dating without sex?"

Danielle nodded.

"At my age?"

"Some men are up for that."

"Gay men looking for a beard, maybe."

"Brett can grow his own beard just fine."

Holly stared. "You waited?"

"Technically."

"Nice job. Not for you. It can't take much self-discipline not to touch my brother. He's gross."

CORA

"I think you're damn lucky to be alive, kiddo." On the ginormous flat-screen TV, the sneaky villain, Burke, with his dark poofy hair faded into the background as the camera panned to the hero, Ellen Ripley, sitting in the spaceship's hospital bed.

As Ripley stared down toward her feet, Cora inhabited her shell-shocked brown eyes, haunted by solitary horror—solitary because the aliens had killed her entire crew in the first movie. Cora's ears stayed on the couch next to her mother, whose knitting needles clicked like metal heartbeats. Her mind went back to the desert hospital.

> *"You and your sister are lucky to be alive."*
> *Are all social workers like this, trying to be your friend from the end of a 10-foot pole? He can't catch crazy. He doesn't need to hold his clipboard like a chest plate, standing far away at the foot of the bed.*

Jonesy's green cat eyes pulled back with his orange pointed ears, transforming him as he hissed, fangs out. Ripley stared forward.

It's only a movie—a nightmare in a movie. Cora slid her hands into the pockets of her pale green fleece vest, clenching the thin phone brick within.

Ripley groaned, curling in as if she carried an alien parasite about to burst through her abdomen.

Chemical currents tore through Cora's skin like lightning-fast worms. She yanked her feet off the ottoman, clutched the back of the ecru couch, and wobbled, grabbing the fuzzy back of Wes' chair behind his tousled brown head before she dragged herself away from the dominating TV and hell-bent speakers.

Her dad's balding red head turned from his armchair.

"Are you okay?" her mother called as Cora staggered into the beacon of kitchen light.

"Want us to pause it?" Wes yelled.

"No!" As she slipped in her socks to the hall bathroom, her answer was drowned out by Ripley's guttural projectile scream.

The toilet seat clicked up and she clenched her curls to her neck. She waited.

Her mom tapped the door. "Are you okay?"

"I just need a minute," Cora called through it.

"Your stomach again?"

"Mm-hm."

"I hope it's not from dinner."

"Dinner was great."

"Iron supplements can upset your stomach. Maybe you should stop taking that?"

She should have hidden those like she hid the folic acid. A cramp hit lower, so she dropped the hollow seat and her jeans.

"Go ahead and watch the movie," she said. "I'll be out soon." Another cramp.

"I'll be in the kitchen. Will you call if you need me?"

"Mom. You don't have to do that." Cora could still hear her at the door. "Fine."

While her mother's footsteps receded, she pressed her forearms over her lurching gut. The broad mirror above the sink reflected her wild red hair around sunken green hazel eyes. Picturing Jonesy, she wanted to hiss at herself.

When she wiped, the toilet paper had a streak of blood. She stared at it, then released it into the water. There was quiet. Like the charged calm before a thunderclap. Like a moment of silence.

"Did we lose her?" Wes' voice bounced off the hardwood floors of the kitchen. The pantry door squeaked.

"Tummy trouble," their mom told him. "She said you don't need to wait."

"But she'll miss her boyfriend." After a pause, the pantry door clicked closed. "Not A-hole."

"Wes."

"I didn't say the word. Or his name." The microwave buttons beeped. "Mom. Michael Biehn. The Marine? In the movie?"

Cora pulled her phone from her pocket and typed in the Google search bar.

"The age difference is kind of disturbing if you think about it," he added. "Ripley's half a century older than him."

A *"fully formed baby"*? The article's illustration showed a pink, bean-shaped baby in a human palm. Had she killed it? She had wished that the pregnancy might not last. She hadn't made a prenatal appointment yet.

Gunshot popping came from the kitchen. Wes was making popcorn. *The dead baby's going to come out of me.* A tear ran down her cheek.

"You alive in there, Raco?" Wes' voice ricocheted off the door.

Cora gulped air. "Watch the movie."

"We're watching this for you."

"Watch what you want."

His feet thumped away. "You still want to watch *All of Me*, Mom? I've seen *Aliens* a hundred times. Dad doesn't care."

She cramped again. Was the baby going to just fall out? She couldn't let it drop into the toilet. She would have to bury it. The idea of a bloody baby in her hand was too much. The idea of a secret burial—*in what, a shoebox? Like a dead bird?*—was too much. She would have to tell her family. She couldn't bear this alone.

The pain moved up from her abdomen to grip her head and chest. Was it her fault? She hadn't aborted it. She had quit Effexor, taken the right vitamins…but she was wishing it away. *Maybe it felt unloved?*

After a while, the cramping was over. Instead of using the word "miscarriage," she Googled: **10 weeks pregnant bleeding.**

The top article read:

common occurrence…not necessarily cause for concern… normal pregnancy…birth to healthy babies.

* * *

When Cora walked to the family room, Steve Martin had replaced Sigourney Weaver on the TV.

"You're alive!" Wes held popcorn in a pincer grip, ready to throw it at her.

"I'm going to bed."

"Already?"

Their mom left her knitting and came to her. "Good night." When she hugged her, her curly salt-and-pepper hair tickled Cora's cheek. "Do you need anything?"

"I'm okay."

Her dad gave her a little smile as he came in for a hug. "Good night," he said, patting her back.

"Good night, Dad."

"'Night!" Wes yelled from the couch.

Cora got a glass of water and cut through the regal navy-and-gold dining room. Light from the old-fashioned streetlamps woke the shimmering wall hangings. The *Tree of Life, Stoclet Frieze* print hung sectioned in three gold frames across the midnight blue wall. It was elegant and palatial. Her mom used to say the swirling branches were beautiful like Cora's hair. But it was creepy.

Before Aiden, she had been anxious for the hugging couple in the far-right frame because the jealous woman on the left leveled such a menacing stare at them, like she was gearing up to vault through the golden frames and attack them.

During the blistering season of Aiden, she was the woman being hugged.

Since New Year's, she identified more with the lone, glaring woman. Cora padded closer to her. Maybe it wasn't jealousy. Maybe the woman was judging the hugging couple. Maybe she knew the guy and was watching out for her naïve friend. And the man bent forward, making the woman in the hug tweak her neck back and face the sky. That did not look comfortable.

Headlights from the hilly street hit the scowling woman and, for a moment, she appeared to hold a bundle. *A baby?* She scrutinized the upturned hands. The woman wasn't holding a baby but the mental picture stuck. Would that be her someday? If she kept the baby, would she ever find love? She wanted nothing to do with love right now. But someday, maybe...?

Sighing, she took the stained wood stairs beneath the gigantic chandelier that topped the open foyer and glimpsed her family—most of her family—watching the movie. Upstairs at her bedroom door, the slick slope of the brass lever was cool under her fingers. To her right, the door to Julie's room was closed, too.

It was dark inside her big sister's room except for moonlight. The trio of angled windows showed shadowy evergreens. The wooden king-sized bed took up most of the room, inherited when their parents upgraded bedroom furniture. It was only occupied in Cora's mind: she remembered Julie there almost a year ago.

Julie's cropped head is puny in front of the giant sham pillows. "Close the door."

I do it.

"Can you keep a secret? Even from Mom and Dad?"

"What is it?" Something's not right. Not the "not right" I'm used to, us shut in like invalids—something's worse.

"I need to know whether I can trust you. You need to promise. Promise you won't share what I'm going to tell you—with anyone."

"Okay." I sit on the side of her bed.

"I can't stay here. If I stay here, I am going to die."

Is she saying she'll kill herself? Chronic fatigue syndrome isn't terminal.

"I have to leave. We can't make it on our own because of our health. My CFS is worse than your mono, but we need each other. We can call Mom and Dad once we're gone so they know we're okay. But they'll try to stop us if they know we're going."

The gigantic pines rustled in the gloom, uncharacteristically ominous, but Cora sat down anyway. She used to covet her big sister's room, but now it was morbid. The gold Berkeley pennant glowed. Julie's miniature globe stood still. The frames holding memories of her high school cheerleading, her semester at Oxford, her European vacation with her old boyfriend—she couldn't see them well in the dark. Maybe they had darkened for Julie, too.

Her parents laughed downstairs, which made Cora smile a little. They didn't laugh much anymore—even less since the private investigator had reported last month that Julie was living in a homeless shelter in the Tenderloin District. Tight, exhausted, defeated, she sighed. Then she clasped her hands and bowed her head.

God, please protect Julie. She opened her eyes. *Am I just as bad as Julie, praying? Is God a figment of my imagination?*

The room felt full of ghosts. Grateful she wasn't carrying one, she held her belly. She should make a doctor's appointment. The doctor would keep her secret, but she couldn't hide the baby forever.

Cora imagined her parents, aghast: *"You're not thinking of keeping it?" "What about UW? You want to be a single parent with a high school diploma?"*

She needed a plan. Maybe University of Washington would let her defer her admission one more year? *Probably not.* She had been lucky to get the first deferral when they suspected she had chronic fatigue syndrome, too, and they scheduled her to see the immunologist.

Mountaindale University was a blessing keeping her on track for UW, but it wasn't competitive. Her dream of getting out of small-town Utah, living in Seattle, spreading her wings, and leaving home—the right way, like Julie had done when she went to Berkeley and made the family so proud... Was that over?

Maybe she should rethink the med school plan. She didn't have to be a doctor. She wanted to help people, but her parents might want another M.D. in the family more than she did. Maybe a nurse. That still required a lot of school. *High school diploma. A single mother with a high school diploma.* That's who was going to bring this poor—literally poor—baby into the world.

Cora wanted to throw up. She wished her mom could comfort her in her misery, like how she used to hold back her hair when she had to puke as a child. But she wasn't a child anymore. If she were a child in her parents' house, she would need to obey them. And if they were in charge about the baby, she would be getting an abortion.

She would have to start apartment hunting in secret. A faint, familiar bell jingled in her mind: this was too close to what she had done with Julie. *I won't run away. I'll tell them what I'm doing. But not until I know what I'm doing.*

Cora hated secrets. When was she going to tell Aiden? Having him back in her brain, in her heart, stabbed her with shame and guilt and grief. Not anger anymore—she was only angry with herself for forfeiting the driver's seat to him, for living out her lusts. He might have loved her as much as he could. Maybe he was just broken and therefore dangerous.

She would have to tell him at some point, but not yet. He was like a magnet messing up her compass. Once she got her bearings, had a plan—if she was strong enough—she could tell him then.

HOLLY

FRIDAY, APRIL 1, 2016

The matador's eyes glint, grimly gleeful.
Everything goes black. His cape must be over my face.
I tense for the stabbing blade.

Everything was brown: the brown of Holly's comforter. Her alarm chimed from her bedside table.

"Ung!" Fighting off the downy girth, she registered the cold in her bare leg poking out. When she clawed for her phone, she brushed her water glass, which tipped onto its side.

Clink, splash. She clutched in its direction, but the comforter had her trapped, so the empty ridged glass tumbled, rolling over the bedside table while she wriggled to free herself, hauled off the chocolate-brown thing by its scruff, and lunged—

Holly hit the deck of her lavender-blue sheet, her arm reaching out to the sound of shattering glass on the white oak floor. For a moment, splayed like a corpse, she froze, her hand limp and impotent. Then she smacked the mattress and sprung to her knees.

"Seriously?"

The alarm chimed brighter, louder.

"Shut. Up." Her stupid phone was dry, thank god, and she turned off the alarm. Tucking back her intrusive hair, she angry crawled over the bed, snatched a towel from the bathroom, and reapproached Ground Zero. On the bedside table, the glossy white folder with the green-and-purple double helix lay, drippy. She hesitated before swiping off the horrible thing and throwing it onto the pile of covers.

Coffee.

In her compact kitchen, Holly seized the black mug her realtor had given her two years ago when she bought her house.

The caffeine got neurons firing. *When should I tell Mom I know?* In person, so on a weekend. She hated the drive to Vegas. She checked the calendar on her white refrigerator.

It's April Fricking Fools' Day. She was standing in the same place she'd been last year when she got Keith's text.

It's a new month. I love you.

My heart's racing, and I haven't even made coffee yet. I stare at the empty countertop across from me wiggling my toes in my fuzzy slippers.

My gut is churning. Butterflies? Makes sense—it's the first time he's told me he loves me. He loves me! But it's the first time he's told me he loves me—and it's a fricking text. Incompatible things curdle inside me like that cement mixer shot of Irish cream and lime juice Courtney and I once took on a dare.

Hang on. It's April Fools' Day. I key back:

Are you serious?

I watch the screen for a second, but that's stupid. I need coffee. Of course, the second I set down my phone, it beeps, so I check it.

I'm sincere. Just a fool for love.

Ew. I set down my phone and cinch my bathrobe. Keith isn't usually cheesy. Is this a side of him I haven't seen yet? The cement mixer shot comes to mind again, so I open the coffee grounds and inhale. Toasty, magnificent dirt. I love YOU, coffee!

I get it now—I told him in March it was too soon to use the "L" word since we hadn't even been together a month. He's being funny. And romantic.

The coffeemaker clucks to itself like Dad's chickens. The mug up front is the red "GRATEFUL" mug my client gave me full of chocolates last Christmas with an evergreen tree in place of the "A." I should be grateful. It can't be bad that Keith loves me—or thinks he loves me. Yeah, it sucks that he texted it. But this is good. Nothing's perfect. Nobody's perfect.

I type back:

I love you, too!

The black coffee mug was an upgrade from the phone with the idiotic texts—hers included. She hadn't been in love with Keith. In lust, yes, and hopeful, but it wasn't love.

Sighing, she clicked on the morning news. The white noise from the TV didn't help.

Her shower didn't help. It made it worse: memories of shower sex left her feeling dirty and dumb and sad. A pitiful, whorish, not-the-marrying-kind of sad. Danielle had gotten her shit together, so Holly tried to muster up some hope. But they were so different. And Danielle had her God. *That must be nice.* Like having an omnipotent version of her dad. *Dad.* Tears turned into sobs, and she braced herself on the wet tile wall.

* * *

Somber piano chord pairings filled Holly's car as she jerked into the Peak Functional Wellness employee lot, parked askew within the painted lines, and punched at the radio's off button, missing. A sultry "Hello" went goodbye when her last hit met its mark and shut Adele up.

Holly flipped down the visor. Its shiny rectangle revealed two eyes—pink and very puffy.

"Fantastic." She prodded the swollen flesh, then smacked the mirror against the ceiling, snatched up her travel mug and her purse, and froze, staring at the empty passenger seat. Her gym bag still waited on her sofa. "Fan-fricking-tastic."

* * *

Her University of Utah travel mug had seen better days. Holly fingered the worn "U," swiveling in her cubicle's chair, itching for her computer to wake up.

"'Morning, Holly!" The receptionist, Anita, strode behind her.

"Good morning," she mumbled, jiggling the mouse.

Clink. A white ramekin appeared on her desk beside the digital frame, now showing a photo her dad had sent of Seraphina, her Palomino, galloping just for fun with the Colorado hills in the background. It flicked to a selfie of Brett, Danielle, and Owen from a football game.

"I remembered your dish today. Thanks again!"

"How was it?" She turned.

"Oh, Holly! Are you having an allergic reaction? You look awful."

Thanks. "I'm okay."

"Are you sure?"

"Totes." With two thumbs up, she spun back to her computer, which had finally decided to make itself useful. While Anita moved on, Holly clicked open her calendar.

9:00 a.m. – Vicki Davis

Jacob. The thought of him hit like lightning: the initial flash was excitement, hitting brittle dry fuel in her heart. Then shame sputtered as she remembered him popping up in her mind intermittently, at first uninvited in her dreams, but after Keith, she'd let him stay for a few fantasies. Objectifying strangers was not cool. But the fire had gained strength. She checked her reflection in the windowpane mirror on her workstation wall. The puffy pink eyes were payback.

An idiot in a body cast hobbling through caution tape to get back on a broken roller coaster with a swath of missing track—that's what she was. *Just as well that I look like shit.* She shuffled to the door.

Exam Room 2

Knock knock. Her double tap was so weak it was almost inaudible. *Please don't let Jacob be with her.*

He was, relaxing beside his mom, his arm stretched over the back of Vicki's chair and his ankle propped on his knee. Jacob's smile caught her breath as he stood, being a gentleman. Had she ever dated a gentleman? A real gentleman—not someone showy like Dave, who was a selfish prick in private.

"Good morning, Vicki. Nice to see you again, Jacob." Her hand remained with the door, guiding it like a Boy Scout foisting his help on someone perfectly capable.

"Good morning," Vicki beamed.

Jacob stepped to Holly with an intimate intensity that made her want to get back against the wall. She stayed put, suffering through his sweet scrutiny. *Damn his eyes.*

"You okay?" The concern in his soft, deep voice melted her. He knew she wasn't okay, but he was too polite to impose reality on her without her consent.

"My eyes?" she asked, patting the bags. "New wrinkle cream." Lying to him was sickening. "Benadryl would help the swelling, but it makes me sleepy." His expression stuck at suspicious. *Who am I kidding?* She took the stool at the computer while Jacob sat by his mom.

"You don't need any creams," Vicki smiled. "You're too young."

"I'm almost thirty-five." *So, if I ever get pregnant, it will be "high risk."* "How've you been feeling?"

"A little poorly." Her voice was flat. "It's probably a cold bug."

"What are your symptoms?" Holly caught Jacob looking at her. She was talking, so of course he was looking at her.

"I've been tired a lot."

"Anything else?"

"Some pain down here." She rubbed her abdomen.

"How long have you felt this way?"

"A couple of weeks?"

"Longer than that." Patting her knee, he said, "She's not a complainer. Hard to say."

"That's right." She nodded to herself. "Early March. Some days are better than others."

Holly clicked through the electronic file. "You met with Dr. Anderson?"

"In February."

She studied the screen. *What?* "He didn't decrease your metformin?"

"No...?"

"No need to be concerned," she said, smiling assurance. "Dr. Anderson knows his stuff." She thought he did, anyway. "I'll chat with him. Make sure he understands how well you're doing, kicking your insulin resistance. Your symptoms could indicate your metformin dose is too high."

"Really?" Her hand flew to her heart. "It could just be a mistake with the drug?"

"You're tripping over your training wheels, Mom."

Although Vicki's smile was contagious, Holly lifted a cautioning hand. "I'm not a doctor. That's only my theory. Can I see your logbook?" Wheeling her stool to their chairs, she pointed at its seat and told Jacob, "I'm keeping my butt planted this time."

"Give me a chance to redeem myself." He raised his palm to swear. "I won't miss this time. Promise."

"I'm taking zero chances."

While Vicki rooted around in her pink tote, something smelled fresh and yummy like a garden. The way Jacob was smiling, Holly wondered if her nose had been twitching like a rabbit's.

"You have to smell that," she said.

His smile widened. "We have something for you."

"Oh!" Vicki said. "Yes."

A tiny tomato plant in a white ceramic pot appeared from under his chair. "A little thank-you for helping Mom."

"It's adorable."

As she took custody of it, he sandwiched her hand between the smooth container and his calloused free hand. "Got it?"

If it weren't so hot, she might have been insulted. While his skin slid away from hers, blood rushed to her face and everywhere else, so she focused on the plant. Its vines relaxed outwards, supporting leaves like basil with dolled up edges. Holly lifted the tomato plant to her nose and breathed in its tangy, almost piney bouquet.

When she peeked at him through the furry green stalk, magic felt perfectly possible. If Jacob was the giant at the end of Jack's beanstalk, she wanted to be the goose that laid his golden eggs.

"Thanks. I love it." Holly blushed harder, hearing herself use the "L word" in front of Jacob. She'd meant it like she loved chocolate, but everything was serious with this guy.

"You can move it outside next month," Vicki smiled.

I can finally start that garden!

At the end of the appointment, Holly typed up a message to Dr. Anderson about the metformin, trying to avoid all caps and insults.

"Do you have weekend plans?" Vicki asked.

"That's right." She smiled at the screen, juggling assertive typing and small talking. "It's Friday. I'm going out with friends tomorrow." Picturing Jacob sitting behind her, she asked, "What about you guys?"

"Gardening." Vicki sounded happy at the prospect. "Cleaning, watching the grandbabies."

"That sounds like a perfect weekend. It's supposed to be sunny." She considered whether "I look forward to hearing from you" or "Please advise" was a better way to end her demand note to Dr. Anderson. At least they wouldn't see her face if Jacob announced having plans with his girlfriend—or fiancée. Just because he wasn't wearing a ring didn't mean some lucky woman wasn't wearing one from him.

Please advise.

Vicki spoke up. "Where are you and your friends going?"

Holly clicked "Send" and spun in the stool.

With his elbows on his knees, Jacob shook his shaved head at his mom—a quick, tight shake, constrained like a twitch. The ridge of his scrunched eyebrows topped an irritated scowl.

As Vicki glanced from her son to Holly, her energy was different, like shaken and shameful champagne. Then it hit, like a cork firing into Holly's eye—Vicki's face matched her mother's when she'd set her up with her best friend's son in high school. Did Vicki like the idea of Jacob meeting up with her over the weekend?

Jacob sure didn't seem to.

"It's a birthday surprise." Holly plastered on a smile. "Sort of a consensual kidnapping."

"Happy birthday!" Vicki beamed. "You're turning 35 this weekend?"

"Tuesday." *Thirty-fricking-five.*

Upright off his elbows, Jacob said, "Happy birthday," friendly again.

"You two didn't go to high school together, did you? Jacob's 37."

And the prickly look was back. Was being set up with her really that intolerable?

"I didn't grow up around here."

"I forgot you're from Colorado." Vicki's bubbly smile seemed pressured. "This is a wonderful place to raise children."

"Mom." His deep command voice startled her.

"My friends with kids think so." She stood. "But I might become a nun." Carrying a bomb in her chest with only a few seconds on the clock, she opened the door and told the hallway, "Nice to see you both again," then bent her head toward her hazy wristwatch when she faced them. "Vicki, can you schedule your next appointment on your way out?"

"Yes. I'm sorry if—"

"No problem." Holly smiled in their general direction and bolted.

* * *

A beige cafeteria tray slid onto the tall round table beside Holly's.

"Hiya babe!" Stately Meena with her lyrical British accent rocked her purple scrubs. She didn't have to hop up and shimmy like Holly did to mount the spindly-legged chairs. "How lovely to see you."

"She forgot her running gear." Their friend Paige looked wise with her dark-rimmed glasses. Even though on her, the white lab coat registered more mad scientist than doctor, especially at times like this when her wild and willful chestnut hair wasn't reined in. "But she might need an intervention more than a run. Our girl's in crisis."

"Nope," Holly grumbled, toying with a red pepper strip in her stir fry. "Just had a shitty morning."

Crossing her arms over her hefty chest, Paige muttered, "IVF again."

Meena's brown eyes widened beneath her bangs. "Surely not. You're just free of Keith."

"Talk to my ovaries."

Paige chuckled, "Thanks."

"You have Rob," Holly said. "You can start whenever."

"There's no need to rush." Meena's polished tawny hand on her wrist reminded her to do her nails. "The man for you is out there."

"Nope." Her ponytail tickled her neck, then she turned her Red Delicious apple in the light. "Did I ever tell you the first time Keith told me he loved me was in a text?"

Paige's eyebrows went high and mighty. "You know you didn't."

"You're joking." Soup dripped from Meena's suspended spoon.

"On April Fools' Day."

"What?" Paige slammed her plastic cup and sloshed her Coke.

Holly snuck a side glance at the low table by the window. Nurse Shelly, the self-proclaimed hall monitor, was probably glaring at them again for being too loud; the profile of her asymmetrical blonde bob had shifted to a face. Not that Holly cared, but she liked to keep an eye on potential sources of bitchiness or assholery—a survival instinct from growing up with Brett.

"A year ago today?" Meena lowered her spoon.

She nodded.

Paige shook her head. "No wonder you had a shit morning. What an idiot." She raised her sandwich. "Him, not you."

"Yes, me. One of many red flags."

"Which you hid from your friends." Paige stared her down. "Next time, keep an eye out for that."

"Nope. No next time. This single lady doesn't want a ring on it. I do want a baby, though."

"Holly," Paige said. "Sweet Holly. You know how I beat you at poker, consistently?"

"Shameless cheating?"

"No, my friend. You have no poker face."

"I'm not bluffing! I'm over it. I'm an idiot when it comes to men, a Mendiot."

"I know you're not bluffing."

"Thank you," she said, crunching into her apple. It was not delicious.

"That's a different tell. You do this when you have a garbage hand and you're trying to convince yourself it can work. You don't have a garbage hand." The apples of Paige's cheeks rounded above her slim smile. "You had a garbage boyfriend, and now you're free of him—"

"Thank God." Meena rolled her beautiful eyes, sipping soup.

"—and you're going to show yourself some kindness—"

"And some grace."

"—and give your heart some love and time to heal."

"Amen," Meena beamed.

"But I'll be too old to have a baby soon." Holly set the bitten apple on her tray.

Meena's eyebrows scrunched. "That's not true."

"Maybe we should table this until next week," Paige told her. "We won't lose her to a manhunt with Courtney this weekend if she's sworn them off. Tell her how much work it is to be a mom."

"You'd think it would get easier when they become more

independent," she said, pushing her loose dark ponytail behind her shoulder, "but the challenges just change."

"See?"

"It's without question the best thing I have ever done." Meena smiled, winsome and defiant.

"Meena!" Paige's arms flew into a shrug. "Come on!"

Shelly's head twitched across the room.

"It's true." She was remarkably honest, although she would hedge, in her lovely British way, when her words might hurt someone. "Please don't rush. Find peace. Go from there." Squeezing Holly's hand, she added, "I'll pray."

"I wish I had your faith." Holly ran a finger down her plastic water glass, moist with condensation.

"That's an excellent thing to pray for." The serenity of her smile seemed incompatible with her belief that her two friends were going to hell, Paige being Jewish and Holly being agnostic. Holly ached for spiritual solid ground, but she couldn't hold that kind of cognitive dissonance.

While Holly drank, Paige said, "Hey. What if you gave new men that same skepticism you give religion before you drop trou?"

Pfffft! Her spit take misted the entire table.

Paige busted out with rumbling laughter and Meena's melodic giggle joined in. Holly coughed windpipe water into her elbow. It took a minute.

"Are you okay?" A hand pressed her shoulder blade.

She gave a thumbs-up and nodded, still coughing.

The hand disengaged and a hot guy in a lab coat appeared.

"You're looking well, Scott," Meena smiled. "This is my dear friend, Holly. She isn't dying."

"No better place to need a doctor." Paige grabbed a carrot stick.

"I've seen you around." His eyes were grayish blue. "Not as often as these two."

Meena nodded. "Holly's a runner."

"Kind of a fair-weather friend," Paige smirked.

"Left her trainers at home today."

Scott transferred his paper coffee cup and extended his hand. After Holly shook it, nodding, he ducked closer and whispered, "Heads up. Shelly's on the warpath, so…"

"Shelly can mind her own business," Paige scowled.

"No." Meena frowned. "She can't."

"It's a medical condition," Holly said, clearing her throat. "Very slow, painful death."

"Can't say I didn't try to help." He had a kind smile. "Talk to you later."

While Paige and Holly nodded goodbye, Meena called, "Be seeing you!" Then her grin grew in direct correlation to the distance between his feet and their table.

An invisible veil of mourning cloaked Paige's slowly shaking head. "You poor piece of man bait."

"Scott's lovely." Meena glowered at her.

"I don't want him!" But it was nice to feel wanted.

"He was awfully eager to give you CPR." Paige crunched her carrot. "Just saying."

"He was being kind."

Meena shook her head. "He's sweet on you. He asked after you a few weeks ago when we met for lunch. Say the word and—"

"You guys! No more men. I'll only get hurt."

"It's okay." Paige patted Holly's hand. "We're here to help. Let's practice you learning to say 'No.' I'll be Scottie. What do you say when I offer to beam you up?"

Laughter erupted at their table and Shelly with the sharp hair stared daggers.

CORA

Her mother clunked the deadbolt behind them.

The neighborhood isn't that bad. The homeless guy digging for cans in the trash hadn't helped sell Cora's mom on the apartment in Fort Herring. She had been expressing her disapproval since Cora broke the news last Saturday, most recently during the silent twenty-minute drive from home.

Striding to the main room, Cora planted the baby Chinese evergreen on the glass-topped, gold-trimmed coffee table. The cylindrical white container matched the larger pot holding the fiddle leaf fig in the corner and the lampshades on either side of the cobalt blue couch. The apartment looked cheap and tiny compared to Aiden's, with everything but her bedroom and bathroom in one cramped space, but she needed to be careful with her money.

"Doesn't this look better, Mom, now that everything's organized?" A cardboard box beside the white armchair outed her. "Almost."

Her mother scanned the living room and adjacent kitchen in a moment, then set her purse on the beige vinyl counter, which hung over three brown barstools Cora had found at a garage sale.

"I'm happy for you."

"But...?" She wanted a glass of water, but her mom was in the way.

"I'm sorry," she said, but sounded like Cora should be. "We just don't like to see you waste your money. And your father's hurt that you didn't include him in your decision."

"With my financial aid, this is within my budget. And it's just until I move to Seattle. I'm being careful." She backed up to the couch. "Being careful" made her think of her poor judgment in the hot tub, a private train of thought that her mother had no reason to share. She pulled the box closer over the pale laminate-wood floor and withdrew the wrapped frame on the top. "This was the cheapest thing I could find that was safe."

When she removed the newspaper wrapping, the family photo from the lake house displayed The Double Martinis: her dad and his brother with their wives and kids surrounding them. The nickname was a misnomer because when the Mountaindale Martins got together every summer with the Bozeman Martins, the adults drank margaritas and beer, never martinis.

"Home is cheaper and safer than this." Her mother took the white armchair. "You have to think about medical school, long-term. Financial aid isn't the answer. You'll rack up debt."

"I know. But it's time I grew up."

"You can be grown up at home. If you wanted to be in the dorms meeting people, I would understand."

Stick to the plan. She would tell her about the baby after finals.

"Are there any new boys you're interested in?"

"No." She escaped to the kitchen.

"What happened with Aiden?" Her mother sighed, looking earnest. "I've been trying not to pry, but…"

"Breaking up with him was just the right thing to do." She gripped an off-white overhead cupboard by its yellow stained edge, and the door clunked open against its sister.

"You broke up with him?"

Cora nodded, filling the glass in the sink.

"You got so depressed." Her mom relocated to a stool across the counter. "I thought he broke your heart." The phone rang from her mom's purse. "It's your brother." She put it on speakerphone. "Wes?"

Cora sipped her water.

"Hey, Mom! We're on our way home."

"Thanks for the update."

"Can you set two extra places for dinner?"

"I'm sure Eli and Keegan's parents want them home, too."

"Not for them. I'm sick of those jerks. For my sister wives."

Cora flinched. Was Wes bullying Eli for being Mormon?

"Say 'hi,' you're on speaker," Wes said.

Keegan and Eli sang in falsetto voices, "Hi Mrs. Martin!" and "Hullo, Mumsie!"

Cora leaned over to the phone, glad Eli was part of Wes' joke and not the brunt of it. "That's a charming accent. You found these ladies in Sun Valley?"

"Raco!" Wes said. "I didn't know you were there. Want me to pick up a husband for you?"

"I'll pass, thanks."

"Suit yourself. Mom, my wives can't wait to meet you. Can you teach them how to cook?"

"Ye dinnae like the haggis?" Eli's attempt at a Scottish accent wasn't bad—but it wasn't good either. "Och! Mrs. Martin, dinnae Wes give ye the braw news: we're both pregnant!"

What the... The glass in her hand slipped and almost toppled as she set it down, staring at the phone in her mother's hand.

"I'm having twins," the first boy-bride said.

"Three bairn! You're a lucky grandmother, Mrs. Martin, if I do say so."

Oh, thank God. They're not talking about me.

From the barstool, her mom's face pointed straight as a hunting dog at Cora's belly, where Cora's hand had planted. As her hazel eyes rose to Cora's, icy-hot shame and adrenaline shot out to Cora's pores and every inch of goosebumped skin.

Her mother renounced the stool, rounded the counter, and swaddled her in a mama-bear hug.

"Mom?" Wes asked. "Aren't you going to welcome your new daughters into the family?"

"Wes." Her tight voice was loud in Cora's ear. "I'll have to call you back."

"Jings!"

"Drop it, Eli."

"Nae, eejit. The lassies can still hear me."

"Dumbass," Wes said. "She hung up."

"Your bum's out the windae. See for yourself."

"Shit. Shit!" He ended the call.

Cora took deep breaths in her mother's arms.

After a couple of minutes, her mom sniffled. "Do you have Kleenex?"

"I don't think so," she said, and retrieved a roll of toilet paper from the bathroom. "Here."

"Let's sit. This is the mystery, then. I thought it might be adjusting to the Effexor."

Settling on the couch beside her, Cora let that go without discussion.

"How far along are you?"

"Thirteen weeks today."

"Thirteen weeks? Why did you—? Earlier would have been better, but we can still take care of it."

She did want to take care of it, and not in the Mafia sense. "I'm not going to kill the baby, Mom."

"It isn't a baby yet. There's still time."

"I'm sorry. I had to decide this on my own. After everything with Julie, I've been struggling to get my compass back."

"Exactly. You're just getting back on your feet. You don't have to— you shouldn't handle this alone."

Cora sighed.

"Does he know? Is that why you broke up? I never did trust him— why couldn't he find someone his own age?"

The two times her mom had seen Aiden, she had fawned over him like she was proud her daughter had caught the interest of such a handsome, successful man.

"He doesn't know I'm pregnant." *It was kind of why we broke up.*

"The New Year's Eve party?"

She nodded.

"Weren't you at his parents' house?"

"It's not their fault. We drank too much." It wasn't a lie, but she walked to the kitchen to evade her mother's gaze.

"I thought you were waiting until marriage?"

Aiden smiles at the cross pendant on my neck. "This might help, too—a little reminder. Remember the Nazis in Indiana Jones, opening the arc when they weren't supposed to? If I went and got my face melted off, you wouldn't kiss me anymore."

He couldn't kiss her anymore.

Her mom sighed. "This is my fault."

"What? No, Mom—"

"I didn't prepare you. We should have talked more about safe sex." She shook her head. "Those old religious ideas do more harm than good. I'm sorry, honey."

"Mom, no—"

"And he should have been more careful!"

Cora had assumed her dad would be the force for Aiden to reckon with, but as her mother's face reddened, she realized it could very well be her.

"Let me take you to a clinic. That thing needs to go."

HOLLY

FRIDAY, APRIL 15, 2016

"Holly!" Meena called, extending her hand from the boulevard's crosswalk, looking ready to explore something with her dark brown hair cascading over the furry collar of her long cloudy gray coat.

Abandoning her GIF search for the Seinfeld Soup Nazi, Holly sent the text to Paige and stepped off the curb.

Okay. No soup for you! ;-)

When she slid her phone into the pocket of her short white puffer jacket, her elbow hit a man zooming past.

Meena slipped her hand in Holly's arm. Sometimes when they walked like that, citizens of their conservative town stared as if pondering whether they were a gay couple. The looks could have been directed at Meena because she was exotic for Northern Utah, but if anyone did think Holly had the honor of making out with her beautiful friend, she'd accept the compliment.

The scent of yeasty dough and garlic greeted them from the scattered food trucks.

"You're going to love this." Meena stopped them at the end of a line of people. "I'll fetch a menu."

The nutty aromas emanating from the truck hinted at onion, beef, paprika, and cumin.

"Holly?" A whiff of artificial musk smelled like Keith. It was Meena's friend from the cafeteria.

"Scott, hi," she smiled, relieved.

Scott's smile was sort of long, and he didn't say anything. Even though he was handsome, he only sparked tension.

"Hello Scott!" Meena was back, thank goodness, and she handed Holly a flimsy, trifold menu.

"Hi Meena."

"That looks scrummy," she beamed.

His transparent plastic box contained steamy teriyaki chicken—Keith's go-to meal.

As the line moved, he stepped with them, watching Holly's face. "How are you ladies today?"

"Doing well, thanks," she smiled. "You two catch up for a sec. I'd better figure out what I'm ordering."

"I should head back." He lifted the bento box. "Wolf this down. See you around."

She nodded.

"Take care!" Meena called.

Scott's walk was capable, not cocky, and he had humble shoulders. When he passed the Japanese food truck, Holly realized he'd gone out of his way to greet them.

"You didn't have a minute to speak with poor Scott." Meena's pouty lip made it hard to take her angry eyebrows seriously.

Holly shrugged. "He feels like Keith 2.0."

"Pretty boys off the menu, then?"

"Boys, yes. No boys."

"I'll have Paige update your Tinder profile."

She stared her down until Meena smiled and shook her head.

Ahead of them, a red-haired woman in a gray peacoat drifted from the food truck's window.

Holly nudged Meena. "Look at that hair."

"Lovely," she muttered, either peeved about Scott or hangry. She nodded at Holly's dangling menu. "You have your order sorted, then?"

The redhead smiled at the dark-haired woman joining her, who carried a paperboard box in front of a big, beautiful baby bump that popped past her open purple puffer jacket.

"I'll have what she's having." Holly nodded at the pregnant woman. "Hey, that's my doctor's receptionist."

"The ginger girl?"

"No, the pregnant one. Doesn't she look happy?"

At the food truck window, Meena stuffed bills in the tip jar while Holly scanned for seats. The chairs under the canopies were mostly taken, but three men in matching blue jackets were leaving a far picnic table. Meena outstripped Holly as they headed toward it.

Dr. Rigby's pregnant receptionist and the redhead were huddled in conversation at a table for two by the walkway.

"Aren't you scared?" The younger woman's hair blazed down her back in golden carrot ringlets.

Olivia shook her head, but playfulness spilled out from her undulating blue streak. She broke into a grin and leaned forward. She whispered, "I'm terrified," before she winked and nodded encouragement. "We can do this."

Holly had to stop at their table. "Olivia, right? I'm a patient of Dr. Rigby's. Holly."

"Hi." Her fork hovered.

The redhead sat back and focused on her food.

"Congratulations!" Holly nodded at Olivia's pregnant belly.

"Thanks." Her smile was a distant sort of friendly.

"When are you due?"

"May 9th."

"That's soon!"

"Not soon enough." Olivia rubbed her abdomen with one hand and raised the other toward her friend. "Cora's going to help part-time while I'm on leave. She's training today, learning all my secrets. You might see her next time you're in."

"Cora. I love that name. It suits your hair. I'm Holly." She extended her hand.

Something about the redhead was like a feral cat. Only her fingers made it into the handshake as though she were offering as little as possible of her paw.

"Hi." Her upturned eyebrows asked a question she was too polite to voice.

"Your hair reminds me of coral, but softer."

Cora seemed afraid she might reach out and squish it, so she laughed herself out of the hole she was digging.

"Women with stick-straight hair get sort of obsessed when we see someone as blessed as you in the body department."

Now the poor girl looked like she thought Holly was talking about her body—cute, petite, she could tell, even with the peacoat—but not what she meant.

"I'm with you," Olivia rescued her. "My hair would never do that."

Cora smiled and touched her hair. "It's kind of crazy today."

"It's beautiful." She took mercy on the girl, who acted allergic to attention, and turned to Olivia. "You know what? I might be due for a pap. I'm glad I ran into you. Hey! Does Dr. Rigby do IVF?"

"She can give you a referral."

At the distant picnic table, Meena lowered her head over her food.

"I better go. So happy for you! Good to meet you, Cora."

"Likewise." As Holly left, Cora whispered to Olivia, "What's IVF?"

"*In-vitro* fertilization."

Grateful Meena had found them an end spot, Holly climbed over the bench.

"I forgot," Meena said. "Did Paige want anything?"

Holly opened her food box. "She already ate. She's feeling better."

Nodding, she said, "I have a brilliant plan you'll quite possibly hate. Gary and I could throw a little soirée—just a casual get-together, really—dinner—for you and a few friends..."

"Like Scott?"

Her smirking brown eyes, cocked head and shrugging shoulders answered before she took a bite of empanada. Then she chewed, satisfied with herself.

"Come on." Holly shook her head and removed the fork from its napkin roll.

"Are you still mulling over your sister-in-law's idea of waiting?"

It was hard to believe, but she must have a higher sex drive than Danielle and Meena. Holly always thought of Meena as a sensual person. She didn't kiss and overshare like Courtney, which she appreciated, but she thought Meena and Gary had a healthy sex life. Her happy, sated blushing when she had labeled their wedding night "an absolute disaster" had been precious. Holly shrugged.

"It attracts a different sort of man." Meena dabbed her mouth with her napkin.

A nearby man held still, likely tracking their conversation.

"Like Scott? He's just like Keith." She wasn't going down without a fight. "Attractive, fit… Same haircut. Same cologne, even." *How superficial is that?*

Meena smirked.

"Dammit." It might not be fair. Scott's eyes were less flirty than Keith's. He was probably looking for a meaningful relationship and might even be emotionally available. "Okay, fine. But why are you so Team Scott?"

"I'm Team Holly. I'll stop pestering if you need more time."

Her plastic fork was shitty at cutting through the empanada; its white tines were all bendy. Did she want more time? *Not really.* She wanted a man in her life. It still hurt, picturing Jacob's irritated face.

"It's worth a go, isn't it? Diverting the less desirables? A man worth fathering your children would respect that boundary." Holding her hand flat near her head, Meena said, "Like a post at an amusement park: you must be so tall to ride. Speaking of tall, there's a charming single man at my church, Bobbie. Beautiful inside and out. He's a bit older. He's a counselor. And he cooks!"

"I can cook for myself."

"You two have a similar sense of humor. Dancing around the dark places, finding bits of light and fun."

Holly shook her head.

"It also helps you think straight."

"Not having sex? I call bullshit. If I get too hungry—for anything—that's all I can think about."

"That may be." Meena frowned. "But you can't really assess someone's character when he's lighting up your nerve endings like Christmas. Like Courtney's beer goggles."

"Courtney didn't make up that term, you know." Holly took her bite before she tried to take away that pleasure, too.

An eyebrow fled into her dark bangs before she smiled and said, "Sex goggles," with a satisfied nod.

"Isn't the sex part after the clouded judgment?" Holly said, covering her full mouth. "That's how Courtney does it."

CORA

"You're so welcome. We'll see you then. The 12th at 10:30." Cora's smile persisted after she hung up the phone. Maybe this was why Olivia was so happy. Your mouth got into a habit.

A photo of Olivia and her husband beamed from a ski slope on the reception desk. Olivia seemed to have a fulfilling life. *Maybe this isn't a bad job.* Could she raise a child with this salary?

The bell on the glass door jingled: it was the blonde woman from lunch the other day. Cora glanced at the calendar:

Holly Samuelsson

Holly was nice. A little intense, but nice. *Confident.*

Smiling from the clinic's entrance, Holly wiped her tan boots on the doormat. Cora smiled bigger, possessed by a weird impulse to try on being as happy and normal as Holly.

"Hi Holly!"

"Hi Cora!" In all black but her boots, she tramped across the lobby like a slumming-it celebrity, equipped for the rain they were having but ready to jet to a tropical island whenever her gallant leading man was available. Her leather jacket lounged open, unrestrained and snappy like its owner. "Glad I ran into you ladies. I was late for my pap smear."

"Did we forget to send you a reminder card?"

"You didn't even work here!" she laughed, then shrugged. "I probably lost it. Dr. Rigby had a cancellation, so win-win."

Studying the computer monitor for no real reason—she knew Holly hadn't meant to sound patronizing—Cora asked, "Can I get you anything? Water, coffee, tea…?"

"Ooh." Her bright blue eyes joined her mouth in roundness. "Coffee would be fantastic. Black, please. Thank you!"

"You got it."

When Cora returned to the front desk with her second-favorite mug, Holly was thumbing through the acrylic brochure tray.

"Here you go!"

"Thanks." Turning the gray ceramic to view the glossy gold painted heart, she said, "Pretty," then nodded at the textbook. "Are you taking Biology?"

"Mm-hm." Cora settled into the rolling chair. "Olivia had her baby early, and I wasn't supposed to start work this soon. Dr. Rigby said it's okay if I study as long as everything's done." She cringed. "It might be pointless since I'm probably going to fail this anyway."

"You've got this. How's Olivia? Boy or girl?"

"It's a boy. Six pounds, eleven ounces. That's why she dyed her hair blue."

"That's a cute gender reveal." When Holly sipped the coffee, her eyebrows dropped. Maybe it was bitter?

"Oh! She emailed a picture if you want to see."

"Let's hold off on that." Holly lifted the gray-and-gold mug. "I might need some of this lovely coffee first. I should let you study." Ambling toward the lobby chairs, she added, "Thanks." After she shuffled through the magazines Cora had just sorted before lunch, she took a seat.

Downcast over the magazine, her silky blonde hair, her shoulders, even her mouth drooped. Cora didn't think she had done anything wrong, but— *Wait a minute.* Holly had been asking Olivia about *in-vitro* fertilization; she must want a baby and not be able to have one. Her distant hand was ringless.

The phone rang.

"Fremont Women's Clinic. This is Cora." Listening, she stuck a yellow Post-it note in the margin of her Biology textbook.

HOLLY

TUESDAY, APRIL 26, 2016

Each step down the clinic hall was gross with the sticky edges of the panty liner clinging to her crotch. She shouldn't have slapped it on her thong so fast. Still, better than lubricant goo oozing into her pants.

Another silver lining: since IVF was more of a couple's thing, with a couple's salary and the daily ass injections, her vagina might catch a break and avoid the trauma of childbirth. Speculums and tampons could be its only visitors from now on.

Dr. Rigby's nurse ended their walk and opened the lobby door. "Have a nice day!"

"You too!" Holly forced a smile.

"Here you go." Cora was ready with a postcard. The nurse was friendly and all, but her helpful energy was tired whereas Cora was busting out in eagerness.

Wishing she had Cora's youthful exuberance, she said, "Thanks," and set the postcard on the platform above the desk.

"If you fill in your address, we'll make sure we get you scheduled on time." Plucking a daffodil-tipped pen from the pencil cup for Holly, she smiled. "Did Dr. Rigby give you the referral you wanted?"

"Yeah... That's not gonna happen." The flower top was supposed to make the pen pretty, or at least more fun, but the synthetic petals were shot out. Like artificial sweeteners, the fake frills left a bad taste in her mouth.

"I'm sorry." Cora offered her open hand. "I can write your address from the file."

"Oh, no, I've got it."

Holly Samuelsson

Cora's forehead was scrunched in concern.

"It's okay. I just didn't get the answer I was looking for…"

4502 Cherry St.

"…unless you have a millionaire friend who might want to take on a charity case."

Fort Herring, UT 84297

When she handed the card back, Cora looked deflated, slumped in her taupe cardigan.

"Sorry," Holly mumbled. Her jokes always flopped when she was bitter like this.

"Is it too expensive to be a single parent?" Cora paperclipped the reminder card to a file and frowned up at Holly.

It wasn't judgment in her green hazel eyes. She was spooked, a frozen kind of spooked. Why was she asking that? What had she been talking about with Olivia?

"Aren't you scared?"

Olivia shakes her head, flinty at first, but then she leans in and grins. "I'm terrified." She winks, nodding. "We can do this."

We? "Are you pregnant, too?"

Cora's eyes were big like a cornered animal's, desperate to find a way out and wanting to know what the hell just happened.

"Sorry." Holly repotted the daffodil pen. "Don't pay any attention to me. I'm in a funk."

"It's okay." Because Cora's eyes were calmer now, their beauty was more evident: explosions of gold bound by bluish-green bands. "I am."

A joke about borrowing the receptionist chair so she could get pregnant next came to mind, but instead, she said, "Congratulations."

"That's kind of you to say. But I have no idea what I'm doing."

"Welcome to adult life. Nobody does."

"I mean, I'm not sure I can keep her."

Holly pictured a cherub-faced toddler with Cora's curls, pictured brushing the little girl's red hair. *Woah.* It wasn't her baby.

"Not abortion. I can't do that." Her hand on her abdomen revealed a bitty baby bump under the floral sundress. "But this wasn't part of the plan."

"When are you due?"

"September 24th."

"Can you take a semester off?"

"I'm supposed to start University of Washington September 28th."

"That's tight. U-Dub's great for life sciences."

Cora nodded. "I was planning to go premed, but…"

"Fantastic!"

"I used to think so."

"What help do you have? Do you have a boyfriend? Can he move to Seattle with you?"

"Ex-boyfriend. I'm keeping my distance from him."

"I'm sorry. Do you have family who can help?"

"My parents want me to put her up for adoption. I just never thought… Life is so weird."

"Amen, sister."

Cora's breathy laugh bubbled into a smile. "At least I'm not carrying twins, I guess. The idea of adoption just…"

"What do you want?"

"I want what's best for her."

The beauty in Cora's eyes was more than aesthetic. Something sacred and attacked hid in there. Holly felt called to protect it but also a bit ridiculous for wanting to meddle. *Meh.* She could handle being ridiculous.

"Let's do lunch sometime. I'd love you to meet a couple of friends, a doctor and a physical therapist. Meena was with me the day we met."

"I think I saw her."

"How's Friday?"

CORA

FRIDAY, APRIL 29, 2016

The pocket-sized plates ticked by on the elevated sushi train like bullets for Russian roulette. Although the other diners were more in jeopardy by consuming the undercooked fish that was verboten for a pregnant woman. *How many laps around the restaurant do these take?* Cora selected a lime-green dish with seaweed-ribboned sweet egg and rice and lowered it to the bar.

"Don't tell me," a man said on her right. White-haired, tanned—maybe a fake tan given the orange glow—he scanned Holly, then Cora, then Holly's friend, Meena. "You're shooting a remake of *Charlie's Angels.*"

Meena was on the stool closest to him; she leaned closer and said behind her hand, "We could tell you, but then we'd have to kill you."

The old guy cracked up. "Shame. Good show. Enjoy your afternoon, ladies."

After he left, Meena turned back toward Cora and rested her open hand on the bar—not too far from the soy sauce bottle but too far to reach it politely.

"Sorry." Cora handed it to her. "Here you go."

Meena smiled and shook her head. "We often pray before lunch, but—"

"Oh!" Cora offered her hand instead. "I'd love to pray with you." When Holly took her other hand, she wished her dad could see them.

See, Dad? Intelligent people can believe in God.

"Beloved heavenly father," Meena's lilting accent fancied up the prayer. "We praise you and thank you for your abundance of grace. For what we are about to receive, may we be truly grateful. Amen."

"Amen," Cora smiled.

Holly poured soy sauce into her tiny square bowl. "What's your story, Cora? Do you have a faith family?"

"Do I believe in God?"

She nodded.

If Meena and Holly were Christian, they might not think it was completely nuts that she thought she had heard God, so to speak, and had been literally saved by Him. Maybe she could try to use humor: *"I want to go back to church, but my parents think believing in God is crazy and I used up my crazy quota when I ran away with my delusional sister and almost died. Want to see my scars?"*

"I do, but I haven't gone to church in a while. I used to love it, but I don't want to go without my family. My parents don't believe in God anymore."

"You should go!" Holly must have been a cheerleader in high school. "If church feeds your soul, you should go. I'm agnostic, but I'll go to support you."

"You're welcome to come to my church, Cora."

Having company wasn't the point. If she went to church, wouldn't it break her parents' hearts—again?

"Mom?" My face is warm and my eyes burn. Maybe from the golden onions and wormy ground beef I'm stirring.

"Mm-hm?" Mom says, making salad.

"Could we go to our old church for the Christmas service?"

Staring at the bowl, she pushes her wire-framed glasses up her perky nose and picks up a romaine lettuce leaf. "I'd feel like a hypocrite." She clasps the vibrant green thing and tears through its heart. "You can go."

"Pastor Beth is the bomb," Holly smiled, then told Meena, "One of these days, I'm going to crash one of your mission trips."

Cora stared at her plate while the two friends discussed Central America. Maybe it wouldn't break her parents' hearts to go to church, but it would feel disloyal and estranging. She wasn't sure when the anti-Christ sentiments started in the Martin home, but the final straw was when Julie moved back home and declared that church was sexist. Even sick, Julie had held court at the dinner table, apparently the boss of even Dad. When Cora looked up, Holly was studying her face.

"Most of my favorite people have faith in God," Holly said, then shrugged. "I used to be jealous, but faith is a gift. I'm okay with other people having gifts I don't." After inserting a hefty avocado-topped bite, she covered her mouth to say, "Same with babies," full-cheeked like an intrepid squirrel.

"What?" One of Meena's eyebrows rose as if trying to raise the bar for her friend's manners.

"Same with babies," she repeated, louder.

"Babies?"

Holly nodded, grinning like she wanted to blow her a friendly kiss.

"I'm pregnant," Cora said. "Holly didn't tell you?"

"Bravo! I adored being pregnant. Though I was wretched from morning sickness with my son." Her gaze landed on Cora's plate. "Oh! Thank goodness that's tamago. You know to avoid raw fish, yes?"

"Or smoked." Cora caught Holly frowning. "They have plenty of things I can eat."

"You sure?" she said, squinting at her. "We can ask the chef—"

"No need. This is perfect."

"Have you any questions for me?" Meena asked. "Mind you, my doctorate is in physical therapy, but I do work with doctors."

"I guess I need to figure out if it would even be possible to be a single mom in med school. My parents don't think so. But don't a lot of women work outside the home these days?"

"You might not keep your baby?" Meena's slack jaw seemed to realize it was being rude but was too sad to do anything above a pout.

"Adoption might be the right thing to do for her."

"It's a girl?" Meena's hand flew to her chest.

"Mm-hm." When Cora couldn't help smiling, Meena beamed back. "It's risky to try to raise her myself, but isn't being a student like having a job, in a way? Couldn't I just use daycare…?"

Holly grinned, too.

"By the time I get through undergrad, she'd be close to kindergarten age. I'd planned to go to University of Washington next fall, but I'd have more support if I stayed here." She shook her head. "But a B.S. from Mountaindale isn't even close to one from UW. MU doesn't even have a premed program."

"Medical school is competitive as a rule." Meena's eyebrows huddled.

Leaning in, Holly asked, "You're thinking stay at MU if you keep the baby, go to UW if you adopt?"

Cora shrugged. "I haven't talked to my parents about it yet, but they might be willing to help." *Mom won't help if tough love might make me go through with adoption.* Aiden being at University of Washington created more issues—issues for later.

"I can babysit!"

"Holly," Meena shook her head. "You'll be working. Even if you foster—or adopt—you'll need daycare."

"I'd like to help. Do you want kids?" Holly had the confidence of a fit fairy godmother, as if Cora need only articulate a wish—or three—and a magic wand would appear from Holly's Tiffany blue purse, flick with a happy spark, and make it so.

Cora positioned her rough wooden chopsticks around the sticky rice. "Someday."

"More than one?" Holly's big blue eyes confronted her.

Good question. Life goals like that hadn't even been on her radar. Maybe some women planned things like weddings and babies and house colors but that had never been her thing. Med school was it: one thing at a time.

"Being an only child sounds lonely," she decided. "I can't imagine not growing up with my brother and sister." The thought of Julie stole her appetite.

"When do you think is the right time to have babies?" Holly's interrogation was starting to give her a headache.

"Anytime but now?" She tried to smile.

Holly nodded. "After college?"

"After med school, for sure."

"When you have your M.D.?"

"Right."

"Don't forget about studying for your Boards," Meena said.

"Oh, right." *Crap.* "After? Pregnancy brain and licensure exams don't sound compatible. I'm having a hard enough time with work and school."

"There's residency, too," Holly said.

Cora sighed, pooped from the pep talk. "My dad told me about residency. He said they have regulations now, so doctors can't be worked to death like they used to."

Holly sipped her water. "Are you about nineteen?"

"I'm twenty."

"You're a freshman?" she said, plunking down the glass.

Cora nodded.

"You want a baby when you're 32, 33, then," she continued, adjusting her chopsticks.

"That sounds about right."

"Just please don't end up like me."

Meena scowled. "She would be lucky to end up like you."

"She won't." Holly turned to Cora and dunked a piece of sushi in soy sauce. "You won't. You don't have my issues. I'd just love to have a baby, and it hasn't worked out."

HOLLY

"Yet." Meena pointed her chopsticks at Holly before turning to Cora. "Do make sure it's an open adoption if you go that route."

The dragon roll's avocado topper melted like salty butter on Holly's tongue.

"The center I'm using specializes in those." Cora adjusted her plate. "I've met with an interested couple. They seem really kind. And I could visit my daughter—their daughter then, I guess—anytime. That won't be very often if I'm in Seattle, but on breaks. And they'd send pictures. They said we can video chat, too. It might be best for her to have two parents, stable ones who already have their careers."

"Single mothers can be great," Holly frowned. *That sounded defensive.*

Meena turned to her. "You needn't do it alone, babe. Say the word, and I'll reach out to Scott. Or Bobbie from my church."

When Holly stared at her plate, Meena redirected her coaching to Cora.

What's that saying about insanity—doing the same thing over and over and expecting a different result? The "good" guys didn't excite her. Did that mean Jacob was a bad boy? The memory of his irritated scowl when Vicki had asked about weekend plans still hurt, like he'd seen through Holly's socially acceptable veneer to how nasty she was, like her mom, and he wanted no part of her.

115

But single mothering could be responsible. Although the ones she knew co-parented with the dads in separate homes. She could be a dad, too. Her dad had been a fantastic example. Her mom, not so much.

HOLLY

If the hostess in the frilly tea house was offended by Holly's damp bun and flip-flops, she stifled it like a pro.

"Welcome. Do you have a reservation?"

"Samuelsson, for two." Holly limped closer. "My mother should be here."

After she consulted the calendar on the pastel turquoise pedestal, she said, "No one from your party checked in. May I show you to your table? Patio seating, yes?"

"Yes." *Mom texted she was here, though.*

"This way."

Tucking the folder with the green-and-purple double helix under her arm, Holly rooted around in her purse for her phone while trying not to plow into the hostess as they walked.

"Holly!" Her mother called. She gave a fluttering finger wave from the center of the room.

"Looks like she found another table." And it looked like she was naked in her nude-colored dress. Holly's sandals smacked with each step; the hostess followed.

"Hello, beautiful," Nanette called, rising from the lacy round table. Her ruched viscose bodycon would have been stunning at a dinner party with her high-rolling Vegas friends. But Mother's Day brunch in quaint little Mountaindale? And of course, she wasn't wearing a bra.

Holly yielded to a showy embrace and the subsequent arms-length inspection: wet hair, no makeup, an army-green tank dress, and ghastly flip-flops.

"One of us has outgrown playing dress-up," Nanette frowned.

"Sorry I'm late." Stepping back, she pointed toward the way out. "Our table's on the patio."

"You had a reservation? How thoughtful. Well, we're here now." Her mother smiled, scooting herself back in.

"We can move. The patio's adorable. It's sunny but not hot."

"Too much sun isn't good for either of us. You don't burn like I do, you lucky thing, but still. You don't want to get leathery. We must preserve our assets!"

Holly clutched the opposite chair and sat on her asset.

The hostess hovered. "Can I get you anything besides water?"

"We have mimosas coming," Nanette smiled. "And a pot of your narcissus tea."

"Coffee. Black coffee, please. Thank you." After she left, Holly said, "I'm glad you ordered drinks since you had to wait. My IT band started acting up halfway through my run, so the return trip took longer than expected."

"Are you stretching?"

Nope. "Of course."

"I remember when I used to do marathons. Your father was such a tremendous help massaging my legs when I would overdo."

She didn't dare look up from the menu. "Dad's an extraordinary human being."

"You take after him, you know."

The menu's edges wrinkled under her clenched fingers.

"Two mimosas?" The waitress's silver tray held svelte glasses and a peach-and-teal teapot.

"Perfect." Nanette placed her hands on her lap. "Thank you."

"And your tea."

When she left, Holly's mom raised her glass. "I'm so glad we're finally getting together. I've missed you."

"Yes." She tilted hers, too. "Thanks for making the drive."

"I needed to break in the new Beemer anyway. I made record time on 1-15 with the radar detector." She sipped without toasting. "And with Charles in Japan, it's a win-win!"

"How's the hotel? You could have stayed with me." That was safe to say at this point. She chugged the bubbly nectar.

"You might want to spend the night with me. They screwed up my reservation, so I got upgraded to a darling suite with a jacuzzi."

When Holly's gaze reached the end of the menu, she hadn't registered a single thing. So, she started at the top and said, "What sounds good? My treat. They have high tea, or we can choose whatever…"

A young waiter with a rolling cart stopped beside their table.

"We haven't ordered yet," she told him.

A silver-handled tower of three white china plates hung from his fingertips.

"No." Nanette flashed a brilliant smile and tapped the lace tablecloth. "That's our order."

Watching Holly, he eased down the first tray of tiered treats. "Cream cheese scones with clotted cream, orange marmalade, and raspberry jam." The second tower joined it. "Your savory items: cucumber sandwiches; mini quiches with brie, caramelized onion and cranberries; and mini éclairs with fresh mozzarella." Then the third silver-topped tier touched down. "And sweets for the sweet: raspberry tartlets, chocolate petit fours, and chocolate-covered strawberries."

"Charming." Her mother beamed. "Thank you so much."

"Enjoy."

As he turned, Holly raised her hand. "What's the spread in the cucumber sandwiches?"

"Cream cheese with fresh mint and watercress."

"Thank you." She stifled a sigh and dove back into the menu.

"Isn't this fun?" Nanette reached for a scone. "With so many tempting things, I couldn't resist. Dig in, dear." She nodded, spooning clotted cream.

Holly pulled her purse into her lap. *No Lactaid.*

"Is everything all right? You look exhausted. Oh! That reminds me." From her massive Louis Vuitton purse, she extracted a sparkly envelope. "Open it."

"You already sent my birthday present," Holly frowned.

"Don't begrudge me spoiling my children."

"I didn't even get you a card since we're together." After her mother waved her on, she tore it open: a gift certificate to Mink Lash Salon.

"You're going to love them. You don't need them like I do with my little blonde stubs, but a shot of confidence could be just the thing with you getting back out there."

"Thanks." The envelope went to the table's edge before she corked her mouth with a chocolate-covered strawberry.

"Come to Vegas when you have them done and we'll get lunch at the country club. The golf tournament is coming up. We'll reel in some nubile thing with your magnetic legs and set the hook with your bewitching blue eyes."

Holly studied the red stain on her fingertips.

"Your coffee?" The waitress was back.

"Oh, thank god." She clutched the cup. "Thank you."

"It's hot."

It was. She had to put it down.

"Tea?" Nanette poured.

"Could I add to our order?" Holly held a hand out to the departing waitress. "The seared tuna, tomato, and bacon on brioche?"

"Certainly. Anything else?"

"No, thank you. That's it."

The waitress disappeared.

"I thought I had gotten every delicious thing on the menu, but apparently, I missed one." Her smile was a simpering punishment. "Catch me up on your life, darling. Are you doing any work on your house? It has so much potential."

"It'll stay as is for now. I want to start a garden, but that might have to wait if I adopt a puppy. How's your remodel going?"

"That's a horrible idea. The dog, not the garden. A garden could improve resale value when you're ready to upgrade. If you do it right. My team can recommend someone in your area. It may not feel like it now, darling, but when you meet the right man, it'll happen fast. You won't be crammed in that bungalow long with your looks."

"Don't hold your breath. This old house is off the market."

"I know you're not selling it now." Jam slid off Nanette's discarded scone while she ogled the trays for some new delight. "You'd better call me when you're ready. I won't charge you a thing, and the distance is no problem."

"Me. I'm off the market."

"That's absurd. And you're not allowed to call yourself old. Your Keith was a perfect gem, but don't take it so hard."

"He wasn't perfect. Nobody's perfect."

"Not perfect for you, and that's what's important." She pressed her hand. "Don't lose hope. He's out there—the perfect fit for my precious girl."

"How's your remodel going?" Holly repeated, lifting the coffee cup to her clenched smile and blowing a rippling dent into its muddy brown surface.

"If I see another change order…!" Nanette shook her head. "There are perks. We've been eating out for a month while the kitchen's torn apart. And the crew is easy on the eyes. Yummy."

"Mom! Did you get into Charles' Viagra?"

"You're only confirming my theory." Waggling her finger, she said, "Lack of sex is turning you into a grouch. At the very least, you need a vacation."

Holly pinched the bridge of her nose.

"Look at all that stress you're carrying. You have to relax. You're young. You're beautiful. Go on a cruise, visit a foreign country. Have an adventure!"

"Like Barcelona?"

"Barcelona's spectacular. Your father and I enjoyed it very much. Even Brett had fun, although he couldn't appreciate it."

The plate's painted roses got hazy.

"Sweetheart. Don't be sad. Traveling alone can be thrilling. And you'll probably have a new boyfriend by the time—"

"Do I have relatives in Barcelona?" Massaging her temples with rude elbows on the lacy tablecloth, she stared at the flowering vines clinging to the edge of the empty dish.

"What? No. I don't have family there and neither does your father. We were only in Spain for his summer architecture program. But you can afford to stay in—"

"That's not what I asked."

Nanette's voice went flat and intemperate. "You have always been direct, like your father. Please don't—"

"HA!" blasted out of Holly, killing every conversation within a five-table radius. In the ensuing quiet, her creepy chuckle roamed free. "That's a relief."

The surrounding diners turned back to each other and resumed rumbling conversations.

"Here I was getting all worked up about being the illegitimate spawn of some rando." Holding out her hand to preempt interruption, she added, "A classy rando, I'm sure. Only the finest for my mother. But now! Whole new worlds of understanding are opening up for me. This mother fucker is direct. Fantastic."

The hue of Nanette's bronze-contoured face crept toward Addams family pale. "Get your blood sugar under control." She pushed the savory food pyramid toward her daughter. "You're being inappropriate."

"More news." She nodded. "I'll show you." From the glossy folder came colorful printouts. "Look, I don't have a genetic predisposition for Type 2 Diabetes. Isn't that fabulous? Not for Alzheimer's or Parkinson's either. Here's the ancestry stuff: 'Spanish: 19%.' Who knew, right? Besides you, I mean, and the cuckolding Barcelonian shitbird."

"I insist you eat something. We can discuss this, but not until you calm down."

Holly plucked up a chocolate-covered strawberry.

"Protein would be a better choice."

"In the spirit of being direct, I've gotta say this hurts, Mom. Your food choices here. Fourteen years. I found out I was lactose intolerant when I was 21."

She surveyed the lactose-laden goodies. "I forgot."

Not "I'm sorry." Nodding, Holly bit into the chocolate, and the strawberry squirted skunky, rancid acid. *Mold.* The cup of tea didn't deserve it, but she grabbed it and spat out the bleeding brownish mass.

CORA

"Emily was kind of pushy." Her mom scowled, either at the memory of Emily asking at lunch about coming to Cora's doctor's appointments or at the car that had pulled out in front of them. "I like that Gabe's job is secure here. Then you're not torn in two directions when you get time off. And a stay-at-home mother is rare these days."

"We'll see."

"You haven't decided?"

Cora shrugged. "It's a big decision." She hadn't even decided if she would go through with an adoption. As much as she wanted to confide in her mother, she didn't want to upset her on Mother's Day. Touristy shops passed by.

"Your dad thinks they might be religious nuts."

Gabe and Emily weren't snake handlers. She wanted her daughter raised to know God.

"You know what your father thinks about the religious indoctrination of children."

"Child abuse." "I know."

"If you're staying in the baby's life, dealing with people like that could be challenging."

Cora rested her head on the seat. Today was not a day for answers.

"Are you okay?"

"Mm-hm."

"You hadn't told me much about your checkup last week. I'm glad the doctor said you're healthy."

"We're both healthy."

"I'm glad it's healthy."

It. She had told her the baby was a girl.

"I'm proud of how well you're handling this."

"Thanks, Mom." When she rifled her purse for a tissue, her fingers hit the slippery ultrasound pictures she had almost shown Emily and Gabe at lunch. Dr. Rigby had encouraged her to start talking to the baby—the size of an avocado—since she could hear her now.

"You're going to be a wonderful doctor. Just like your dad."

"I don't know."

"You are."

"My brain is mush. I screwed up scheduling an appointment last week and double-booked Dr. Rigby."

"Maybe you should just focus on summer school and let something go."

"It'll work out."

"Don't worry about the patient. These things happen when you're pregnant. Mom brain." Her mother's eyebrows twitched before she composed her expression, erasing the regret if not the words.

Mom brain. Cora turned to face the passing homes. Her "mom heart" was broken, too.

"Honey. It's going to be okay. This will be over soon. The baby will have a good home and you'll be back on track."

The only track she felt on was a train track in a silent film, as the bound-up damsel in distress.

"Plans can change…"

"Cora. You're not going to throw your life away." The red light and her mom's eyes were piercing. "I remember being pregnant. The hormones wreak havoc. Please don't let your emotions rule your decisions. They won't steer you in the right direction." The car moved, giving her space to breathe.

"But I love the baby."

"That's why you're doing this, finding it an established home. The baby will be better off. I know you want children someday, but you want your career, too, don't you?"

Her temples throbbed. "I can't do this now."

"I want to understand."

"A job is a job, Mom. Theoretically, I could work at the clinic for the rest of my life. Sure, I'd rather be a doctor, but…" *It's not like love.* "Just, how would you feel if you…" *Didn't have Julie.* "Never mind."

At least Julie was safe now in an apartment with a job. Maybe soon her parents would call off that private investigator who checked on her every month.

When Julie had called Cora out of the blue a few weeks ago, she still sounded paranoid. The voicemail had only been weird because Julie hadn't left a number. But when she called back and asked if Cora had told their parents about the call, and then said she wouldn't be calling again because Cora had told them, that was weird. That was awful: holding the phone after Julie had hung up, abandoned by her again.

She didn't want to say goodbye to her baby.

Her mom might disapprove of the baby journal she wrote in every night. She would undoubtedly disapprove of how Cora would fall asleep cupping her hands around her belly, holding her daughter as much as she could—the closest thing she'd known to being whole.

CORA

Usually, when Cora was on campus near places Aiden used to hang out, she prayed for God to put him in her path if it was His will for her to tell him about the baby. She had yearned for an answer, a direction, some clarity about what God wanted her to do. All she'd gotten was silence.

Aiden would be leaving soon for Seattle, though. It had to be time.

So, she strode down the corridor where the teaching assistants' offices were and only prayed for strength, zipping up her yellow raincoat. But the closer she got to his office, the weaker she felt. And when Aiden's voice drifted into the hall, she almost walked past.

Cora hesitated near his doorway, and he spotted her from his desk chair, swiveled to face the little round table for students, where a woman sat. The student turned back, but Cora couldn't focus on her face. His eyes, shadowed, were all she could see.

"Why don't you start there?" He flipped the papers closed and handed them to the student, standing. "Check in with me tomorrow if you get stuck, okay?"

The woman left, glaring a little.

"Have a seat?" Aiden swung an arm toward the chair, moving closer.

"Sorry I'm interrupting." The office was too tight, and she stepped to the bookshelf while he fixated on the door he shut behind her.

"Please don't apologize." He waited for her to accept the vacated chair, then, back at his desk, he leveled his strained eyes with hers. "I'm the one who needs to apologize." Shaking his head and smiling a little, he said, "This is weird. I was just thinking about you yesterday."

Oh no. "This is a bad time." Cora clutched her purse handles.

Aiden raised his hand. "I'm not obsessing about you—anymore," he tried to laugh. "Sorry. It was about making amends to the people I've harmed. It's really good to see you. You look great."

"That's kind of you to say." To be polite, she wanted to reciprocate, but he looked haggard, and small talk didn't feel like an option. She also didn't want to encourage him. "Can I just be super blunt?" she sighed, bracing her spine against the hard chair.

"Please."

"But I need you to just sit there and not touch me."

"Shit, Cora." His voice cracked like a kicked dog's.

"Sorry. I didn't mean that like you're a bad person. I'm just trying to have healthy boundaries."

He swiveled to face his desk and gazed past it. Out the window behind him, tree branches popped with deep pink blooms. "Go ahead."

"I have a big decision to make, and it involves you. Us getting back together isn't part of this, okay?"

"Wait." Aiden spun toward her. "Are you pregnant?"

She couldn't breathe, swept into the undertow of his blue eyes. Was he excited? He looked hungry again, but not like he had in the hot tub. *This was a bad idea.* And he knew. *How? Had he meant to—?*

Knock knock.

"I should go," she said, standing.

"No, please." He almost touched her arm as he passed on his way to the door, but he didn't. "Stay?"

Because he hovered at a respectful distance, she nodded despite the hairs, like hackles, alert on her neck.

"Thank you." At the door, he spoke louder: "Sorry, I had to shut down office hours early. Can you email me, and we'll set up a time?"

The voice said, "Sure, no problem."

"Thanks. I appreciate it." And a pen squeaked while he scribbled a note on his whiteboard.

Cora tensed, anticipating his return. She needed a plan.

"We shouldn't be interrupted now." Sitting, sighing, he stared at the purse in her lap.

Her heartbeat drummed in her ears.

After a thick, awkward minute, his frown made her feel better. He couldn't have meant this to happen. He'd said it was an accident. And he looked the farthest thing from happy.

Voices laughed in the hall.

When their eyes met, his darted down again, and a breathy laugh fell out. "Anytime you want to put me out of my misery…"

"What?"

"You haven't answered my question."

"Oh. Sorry. Yes."

This time when he found her eyes, his were tighter and more haunted than she'd ever seen them. "Are you okay?"

A swell of something rose inside her: not nausea this time, not nerves, not desire. She was okay. *Now.* She would have liked to have heard that question, seen that concerned face when she learned she was pregnant— she hadn't been okay then. Then, they could have been scared together. If the pregnancy had been a consensual mistake, she would have even let him hold her. But this was her grim, frightening, lonely reality—and she was okay. No thanks to him.

Cora nodded. "Mm-hm."

"I'm so sorry."

She nodded again.

"What are you going to do?"

Fiddling with the straps on her lap, she said, "My parents want me to put the baby up for adoption. An open adoption."

Aiden nodded, slumped.

The vicarious gut punch curled Cora incrementally in. This was all wrong. It was his daughter, too, and she hadn't even—

"I haven't committed to anything," she blurted out. "I'm sorry I didn't tell you sooner. I just—"

His frown changed, and he looked stronger. "You have nothing to apologize for, Cora. I can't tell you how grateful I am that you've come to me at all. Okay?"

She nodded back.

"What do you want?"

"I want to do what's best for her."

Through his fist, he rasped, "It's a girl?" and his eyes welled with tears.

Glimmering like sun-kissed summer water on the lake, his eyes broke something in her. As she watched him take slow breaths through her own tearful eyes, she didn't feel selfish anymore about wanting to keep the baby. Her bond with her daughter wasn't something she could take or leave. It wasn't an emotion to ride out. Aiden sensed the connection, too, and he didn't even have the baby inside him.

Since the pregnancy test, Cora had felt like she was in a scene from a bad adventure movie, clinging to vines off a cliff. The idea of adoption broke off in her hand; that couldn't be a way out of this. Aiden's eyes made that clear somehow. The weirdest part was, instead of being weaker, she now had the strength to pull up.

She wiped her eyes. She opened her purse. And she found the slippery black-and-white ultrasound photos no one else had seen.

"Do you want to see her?"

CORA

FRIDAY, MAY 13, 2016

The tires squawked, scraping against the curb, so Cora straightened them, cringing, and shut off the Prius.

Holly's little ranch house was perfect, but not showy perfect. Its navy paint with its thick creamy white shutters and trim grounded the cheery yellow front door. The porch light shone unnecessarily in the bluish dusk. Two tall Tuscan pots with flowing plants framed the gateway to good tidings.

Cora was not in the mood. Her week had left her exhausted with school and work and seeing Aiden on Monday. She had half-expected him to text or call, but the ball was in her court to reach out when she knew how he could help. He wasn't crossing any lines.

Which made things more complicated. Last night, she had even dreamt about him and woke up longing and confused. The worst part was that her wishy-washiness about Aiden made her doubt herself. Her conviction to keep the baby was being gnawed at; fear and self-doubt had scuttled in like rats.

And now she was supposed to be social? Picturing Holly's confident smile, she white-knuckled the steering wheel. Maybe she would text— she was sorry but couldn't make it after all. Her stomach was upset; that wouldn't be a lie.

Headlights blasted her rearview mirror as a truck pulled up. When the door slammed, she scoured her purse to look busy and not like a loitering weirdo.

Tap-tap. A woman with glasses grinned through the window. "Cora, right?"

With no means of escape, she smiled, grabbed the pan of brownies, and opened the door.

"I'd shake your hand, but Holly will kill me if I drop these," the woman said, lifting her plate of deviled eggs. "I'm Paige."

"Hi." Something about her earnest smile made Cora feel at home as they ambled toward Holly's driveway.

"Sorry I got stuck in surgery and couldn't come to lunch."

As Cora opened her mouth, the front door vanished, and Holly appeared on the raised cement step, wiping her hands on an apron like a mother in a 1950s sitcom. The white apron's bib sported a Wendy's Old-Fashioned Hamburgers logo.

"My ladies!"

Paige let Cora pass first into her outstretched arms.

She's a hugger.

"I'm so happy you came!"

"Thanks for inviting me." Cora stepped in while Paige went through the hug turnstile.

"You brought them!"

"I wouldn't dare not." Paige grinned.

"Cora, you have to try one of these." When Holly peeled back plastic wrap and airplaned a deviled egg toward her, sulfur assailed Cora's sinuses.

Dodging back, she suppressed an urge to swat it away like a toddler. "Maybe later. Thank you, though."

Holly shrugged and bit into it. "Mm! Paige." She covered her mouth. "So good. Come in."

Cora followed them between the white farmhouse coffee table and the flat-screen TV on the wall.

"You brought brownies!" Holly reached to embrace the dish. "Yum! Thanks, Cora! Courtney's running late. Erica's in the kitchen."

Clutching the chocolate loot, she added, "Meena can't make it."

Paige followed her toward the source of a buttery, fruity aroma like piping hot pie.

But Cora's social anxiety and the distant bay windows drew her forward, past them. A silver briefcase lay on the dining room table. A glass door led to a darling deck with cozy colorful places to sit by a verdant backyard.

The trees on the periphery were too gracious to throw much shade. Their tops scalloped the edge of the darkening sky where ribbons of coral clouds had come to rest, mildly sunburned from their long day playing in the heavens.

The beauty pulled on her heart, blending something familiar and something new, precious and perfect and alien. She imagined a playground structure erected in the yard with a girl swinging. Holly was perfect mother material, and she wanted to adopt. Was Holly in her life for a reason? What if she adopted Cora's baby instead of Emily and Gabe?

The imaginary girl kicked skyward on the phantom swing set, and a ghost of Holly came onto the deck in her apron, wiping her hands as she'd done on the front porch moments before. There were smiles. There was happiness. It was home—a perfect home.

Queasy, Cora spun from the backyard vision, faced with Holly being a perfect hostess. *Holly would be a phenomenal mom.* Her daughter deserved a phenomenal mom.

"Hey, Cora!" Holly trotted from the kitchen, holding out pink and yellow soda cans. "Do you want some sparkling water?"

An hour or so later, sitting at the dining room table among friends who weren't hers, Cora felt better. Even though Holly and her home might look like an ideal setup for a happy child, it didn't mean Holly should mother her baby. Maybe when she was Holly's age, her life would be put together, too.

Erica, whose perfect balayage made Cora a little envious, played a third Jack—higher than Paige's three of a kind—and sat back with an extra gigantic smile.

"Nice one, E," Holly said.

Unruffled, Paige observed the cards for a moment. Then she moved forward and, with a smug side-eye to her presumptuous friend, laid down a second humble deuce: full house.

Erica's "What?" preceded a whoop from Holly. Laughter and mumbles—some accusatory, some incredulous—were interspersed with satisfied chuckling from Paige.

After the riot subsided, Courtney asked, "Why are men with the biggest dicks the biggest dicks?" Holly's lanky blonde friend was like a stretched-out fun-house version of Holly with sharper physical and emotional edges.

"Wow, Courtney." Paige reached across the table, claiming the heap of poker chips. "That's deep."

"That's what she said." Erica smirked into her glass of sparkling water.

Paige leaned toward Cora, "That may not sound very scientific, but Courtney's methodical about her sexual conquests. You have a spreadsheet, right?" She winked.

"Spread sheets?" Courtney asked.

The four friends exchanged a look, and their shaking heads established consensus.

Courtney's sigh sounded chagrined but not contrite about either her failed joke or her failed relationship. "I'm going to miss it."

"Him," Erica helped.

"Not Mack." She jabbed her toothpick into the lime wedge trapped at the bottom of her glass. "Just his cyclopean cock."

Holly gaped. "You were so excited about him."

She shook her head. "That 'love conquers all' stuff is a load of crap."

"If you love him—" Erica began.

"I'm over it." Courtney set the toothpick on the napkin, giving the poor lime a reprieve. "Some loves need space to breathe, or somebody dies."

"I call bullshit," Holly frowned. "Do you actually love him?"

"Call it whatever the fuck you want." Draining her glass, she stood and smoothed her clingy yellow dress on her way to the kitchen.

Holly whispered to Paige, "Do you know what's going on?"

She shrugged.

The cards fluttered and arced in Erica's manicured hands. "Your deal," she said, passing the deck to Cora.

Paige crossed her arms. "How did brunch go?"

"Not so well," Holly sighed. "Bull: 1; China Shop: 0."

"You're the bull?"

"My mom didn't appreciate being put on blast."

"I thought she was 'sex-positive,'" Paige sneered. "Doesn't she like being the center of attention? I wish your dad could help."

"He feels bad enough." Holly turned to Cora. "My mom's a hussy—a bigger one than I'd realized. I knew she'd cheated on my dad when I was eight. She left my dad for that shitbird, who dumped her later. Apparently, I'm a bastard."

"Holly?" Courtney's voice echoed from the kitchen.

"Uh-huh?"

"Where're your limes, love?"

Smiling at Paige and Cora, she said, "Be right back," and pranced over to Courtney. "I gotchu."

"You're the best."

Cora shuffled.

In the kitchen, Holly's voice quieted. "Can I mom you for a second?"

"Are you going to tell me to slow down?" Courtney teased.

"You're welcome to stay over. If you're driving, you could try one of these. They're pretty tasty. Or eat something."

"Bubbles do not make it tasty. But if you're asking me to sleep with you, that's the best offer I've had in a while."

"Then bottoms up. Please puke in my toilet if you have to."

Erica called to them, "I can give you a ride home."

"Deal," Courtney yelled back.

"That'll do." Paige nodded at the cards fluttering in Cora's hands. "What are we playing?"

"Texas Hold 'Em?" After Cora got a nod of approval, she flipped cards face up at each place.

Ambling back from the kitchen with Holly, Courtney asked, "Did you finish your paperwork?"

"Not yet. Thanks for getting that."

"Well, hurry up, lady." Courtney flopped down. "Get that shit in. We're desperate for foster parents."

Holly took her seat. "You've seen the application. It's huge."

That's what she said. Cora sipped her grapefruit-flavored sparkling water, which was pretty tasty.

"All in?" Paige and Cora were the only ones left since Erica had taken Courtney home and Holly was in the bathroom.

"Sure." Cora pushed her meager stacks of white, red, and blue chips to the table's center.

"You can take her, Cora," Holly called on her way to the kitchen.

Paige shouted over her fanned cards, "How long have we been friends?"

As the brownie platter clunked beside them, Cora tried not to take their abundance personally. How could anything compete with cherry pie?

"We can declare Paige the winner if you want to go to bed," Cora said, stopping Holly en route back to the kitchen.

"No way! I love having friends over. But are you tired? Have you decided about keeping the baby?"

Cora nodded, smiling back.

"Yay!" she cheered, bouncing on her toes, then clasping her hands at her chest. "I'm so excited for you. You can do this. When can I babysit?" She plunked down beside Cora. "Or are you going to UW? I bet you could swing the baby at UW if you can afford childcare."

Maybe Holly's optimism was contagious, but the world felt brighter, full of flawed but caring people, and she was ready to articulate a vague and impossible dream.

"I might have help from her dad, too."

"Your ex?" Holly's smile vanished. "Who you were steering clear of?"

Cora wished she had kept her mouth shut. She just nodded.

"Sorry." Holly touched her knee. "Catch me up."

"I told him about the baby on Monday. He was great about it, and he wants to help."

"Does he still love you?"

Did he? "He might, I guess. He said he did in January when we broke up and in February when I said I wanted no contact."

"Umm..." Paige grumbled, crossing her arms.

"Why did you break up?" Holly asked.

"Wait." Paige cocked her scowling head. "He got you pregnant right before you broke up?"

"It was an accident." Cora rearranged the cards in her hand in no particular order. "We drank too much on New Year's Eve. He even did some cocaine with his brother. I found that part out later."

The silence wasn't awesome.

"You want Captain Cokehead to babysit?"

Holly corrected Paige. "It isn't babysitting when it's your child."

"He might not be an addict" didn't even convince Cora as she heard herself say it; it certainly didn't persuade Holly and Paige. But she soldiered on. "Can't cocaine be a party drug that functional people use sometimes?"

Paige shook her head at her cards, but her frown looked more disgruntled than disagreeing.

Cora kept relocating cards and asked, "Do you think I should ask him to see an addiction counselor before he watches the baby—if I let him?" She didn't want to look at Holly, but she finally did.

Her big blue eyes were sympathetic, and her mouth was set and strong like a mother sending her daughter somewhere frightening but necessary. "Couldn't hurt, might help."

"Please be on guard with this guy, okay?" Paige said, softer. "It's not consensual if you're too drunk to consent."

"I hadn't consented. I'd told him I was waiting, but I put myself in a stupid position, and he lost control." In her hand, the king of hearts' sword skewered his head. "He's sorry, though."

"I thought—" Holly began.

Thwack. Paige's cards splayed on the table. "This asshole raped you?"

HOLLY

SUNDAY, JULY 3, 2016

Stupid autopilot. This was her lunchtime running route. Not the prettiest streets, but at least it went through the park. Kids buzzed around the playground structures while moms and dads chatted.

A new song whispered a minor note over the first drumbeat. The drum continued alone, slapping slower than Holly's feet until one solid misfit soldier, a low piano key, joined in doing double time beatdowns, inviting her to enlist. "Love Runs Out" picked up intensity. So did she.

Going full out was fantastic. Even dodging the woman with the stroller didn't hurt her heart. Flying past the buildings of Fort Herring Medical Center, she spied orange construction signs ahead. *That's right.* They were tearing up the sidewalk. *No problem.* Asphalt was bouncier anyway. As she veered into the parking lot, a classic white Jeep pulled into the far entrance. She glanced around for other cars.

Like that one. A sedan the color of old-lady-red nail polish inched into Holly's aisle. Not able to tell which side the white-haired driver wanted to park on, she smiled and jogged in place until the car crept into a spot.

Back on the sidewalk, an unfamiliar, muffled beat layered into the song and she worked back up to—

Someone tapped her bare shoulder.

Jolting away, Holly side-stepped into the bike lane and registered Jacob's face as he reached out for her, running at her pace. He pulled her away from the street. *Honk!* A car passed and they slowed to a walk. When Jacob's mouth moved, One Republic was still pumping promises through her earbuds, so she shook her head and extracted one.

"That went poorly," he chuckled. "You okay?"

Nodding, she tried to tamp down the tornado of butterflies he'd released in her chest.

"You should be more careful."

"I was fine 'til you showed up," she laughed.

"Sorry." He touched her arm. "Walk with me a sec? I dropped something."

The butterflies had spread to her brain, fluttering in her visual cortex so all she could see was flickers of color and him. She turned off her music and secured her earbuds in her shorts pocket while Jacob aimed for a sidewalk bench with a yellow-and-pink bouquet. *For a girl.* The gut butterflies plummeted into the pit of her stomach, stone dead. *Of course. He has a girlfriend.*

"Where's your habit?" he asked, nodding at her blue tank top and white shorts. "This is cute, but where do you hide the ruler?" At the bench, he scooped up the bouquet and smiled. "I refuse to call you Sister Holly. That would be weird."

Was he flirting with her? Jacob seemed like the farthest thing from a Keith. Jacob wasn't flirting. He was being playful. Nothing wrong with that. She could do playful. She loved playful. Playful was her jam.

"I took a hard pass on the nun idea." She braced her hands on her hips. "I want a baby."

"Really."

Shifting her weight between her feet, she said, "My brother and I are pretty competitive. He already has one, so I need at least two."

"As luck would have it, my sister just popped one out." His flower arm pointed toward the hospital. "Want to see if she's tired of it yet? I hear they're a ton of work, so you might score it for cheap."

Zombie butterflies rose, climbing over their undead brethren and clawing at her insides.

"Champ did the whole thing *au naturale*."

"Please tell her 'Congratulations' for me." Holly's smile faltered. That sounded like goodbye, which sounded awful.

"Tell her yourself. Our mom raves about you. I'm sure she'd like to meet you."

"No thanks." After Owen was born, Danielle bristled at anyone but family visiting. "I don't want to intrude."

"Let me buy you a coffee. The Starbucks mermaid's right there." Jacob nodded at the coffee shop across the boulevard. "A human can't resist the call of a siren," he said, then hummed a few bars of a melody, the enchanted vocal stylings of the Little Mermaid.

Holly tucked her grin into a humorless pout. "What was that?" She cupped her hand around her ear. "If it was louder…"

"Don't judge. My niece made me watch that last weekend." He tapped his bulky wristwatch. "Ten minutes. Then you can get back to your run. You'll be so jacked up on caffeine, you'll make up for lost time."

"Okay."

He smiled. "Now I don't have to come to Mom's appointment next week."

* * *

Holly fidgeted at the small square table while Jacob waited for their order. He looked so adorable in his short-sleeved button-down shirt and jeans. His shirt was untucked, which concealed his tight waist and cute ass. How did she—? The khakis at the clinic. She drummed on her bare thighs, inhaling roses, then leaned to the seat where he had left them. *What a thoughtful brother.*

When he arrived with their drinks, she let herself look at him again.

"Your triple venti, half-caff, sugar-free, non-fat yak-milk macchiato, extra foam." He slid the small white cup before her with a teasing dimple in his stubbly cheek.

"Perfect." She grinned at the 12-ounce Americano's steaming chocolate brown surface. "Thank you."

"So." Jacob pulled out the chair, which looked way too small for him. "You grew up in Colorado?"

"Mm-hm. You?"

He smiled across the table. "Here."

"Utah here or Fort Herring here?" The coffee was burning her hands, so she set it down.

"Fort Herring area. Mountaindale. Near Dugan Point."

"Your mom must be happy you've stayed close."

"My brother and sister are here, too. What brought you here? Utah here."

"I went to University of Utah for my master's in Nutrition and Dietetics."

"Ute, huh? That explains your hippie streak."

"Hippie streak?" She wasn't wearing any makeup. Was that it? *Shit.* She wasn't wearing any makeup.

He picked up his coffee. "Remember that whole bit you gave my mom about evolution?"

"That does not make me a hippie." She shook her head, examined her coffee, and crossed her arms. "This might give you a big head, but I have a confession."

"You're Catholic." Jacob sat forward with his forearms on the table.

Tugging her gaze from his beautiful hairy arms, she said, "I'm firmly agnostic."

His dark eyebrows scrunched. "Like a hard waffle?"

"Ew." Holly's face squelched.

"Right?" He propped his chin in his hand. "Where is this agnostic nunnery of yours?"

"The nun idea is long gone. Try and keep up."

Jacob looked enthused, not offended. "Yes, ma'am." He leaned back. "I'll take your confession, but I can't forgive you. I don't have that kind of authority."

Once she adjusted her napkin, she said, "If there is an authority, he'd like my confession."

"I'm intrigued." He sipped his coffee.

"Do you believe in God?" Steam was still rising from hers.

"I do now. Long story."

"Now I'm intrigued."

"I'm an intriguing guy. Tell me your thing."

"It isn't logical to give designer credit to a force without a mind to design with." Holly cupped the warm coffee in both hands and blew on it. "Thanks for challenging me on that."

"Glad to be of service."

As she sipped, the heat zapped her tongue and scalded a bit so the nutty, brothy flavor was only there when it was gone. "What do you do for work?"

"Law enforcement."

Pouncing on the opportunity for payback, she said, "You're a redneck."

"Only when I forget sunscreen." While he rubbed the back of his neck, his gaze fell on the newspaper left at the adjacent table. "Are you into astrology?"

"Not into it, but horoscopes are fun sometimes." She leaned back. "You're not. Are you? Is this a test?"

"Maybe." He winked, reached for the paper, and opened it. "What's your sign?"

"I'm an Aries."

"Aries, Aries…" He paged through.

"And yours?"

"I'm a cancer and a crab. See why I don't like the stuff? I am neither of those."

"When's your birthday?

"June 21ˢᵗ."

"Happy belated birthday."

"Thanks. Here we go." Jacob fanned open the newspaper, screening himself from her. After a moment, he pulled it down to his chest. "You have a secret admirer."

Holly laughed. "Not you, is it?"

"Woman, I hardly know you." He lowered his voice. "I think it's that guy in the corner. He's had his eye on you since we walked in."

After a beat, she elbowed her napkin off the table and, retrieving it, spied the gentleman: a man in his seventies reading a thick book. She rose and faced Jacob with her napkin and a smirk.

He smiled. "Write down your phone number. I'll give it to him. It would make his day."

"He is my type," she said, fingering the rim of her cup. "But I'm looking for a sperm donor, and I'm pretty sure he's out of the game."

"Can't that guy you were dating..." He fixated on the table. "What was his name? Bill? Bob? Billy Bob...?"

"How did you know?"

"You dated a guy named Billy Bob?" His delectable lips were solemn, but his joke was busting out his forest green eyes. "The Billy Bob? Thornton? You do have a thing for older guys. That's cool—"

"That I was dating someone when we met."

"I didn't." Jacob leaned back with a satisfied grin.

As she shook her head, her ponytail brushed the back of her neck. Then she put her elbows on the table and held her paper cup to her lips. They sat like that for a minute. The shadow of hair encircling his head and jaw was hot.

"You have intense eyes." His smiled. "You know that?"

"Who, me?" Holly's coffee tripped on the napkin. "That was all you, buddy."

"You're competitive," he shrugged. "If we were having a staring contest, I didn't want to forfeit. I did win."

"Really."

"You looked at the table when you put down your coffee. Now you have to give me your number."

"Fair's fair." She managed a straight face. "But I don't have anything to write with."

"Here." Pulling his phone out of his pocket, he swiped and tapped its screen and then slid it across the table. The new contact was named "Hot Jogger."

Holly laughed and typed in her number.

After he plucked the flowers from the empty chair, he stood. "Okay, bye."

"You're leaving?"

"See you later." He touched her shoulder. "What's your last name?"

"Samuelsson."

His eyebrows scrunched, then he smiled. "See you later, Samson."

"Samuelsson," she frowned.

"I heard you. Not a fan of nicknames?"

"Not if it refers to an arrogant manwhore."

Jacob's gut-busting laugh drew the attention of a green-aproned employee and a couple of customers before he reclaimed his seat. "This I have to hear." Chuckling more quietly, he added, "Granted, Samson had his issues."

Holly shrugged. "My dad dragged me to his church in high school. My mom and dad got a divorce when I was eight."

"I'm sorry."

"It's fine. My dad's better off. So, Samson. He was blessed by God, buff as hell, and he flaunted it. He knocked up women from the rival clan, even though they were at war. Genius move there."

Jacob beamed over his crossed arms.

"One of his trophy wives, Delilah, outsmarted him and got him to tell her how her people could overpower him—by cutting off his magic hair. Who does that?"

Instead of answering, his mouth squinched around a very distracting dimple.

"Wow," she continued, "I never caught the connection to *Tangled* before. Now that would have been a power couple: Samson and Rapunzel."

"He still helped his people during a rough time. Nobody's perfect. And you do have awesome hair."

She smiled.

"Rapunzel would be a shit nickname. And Samuelsson has a whole extra syllable."

"Fine. Call me what you want."

"I'll call you." He double tapped the table's edge and stood.

"Bye."

The window offered a last glimpse of him heading toward the hospital. After a moment of happily missing him, Holly found the Aries horoscope.

> **As the Sun moves through your solar fourth house, this week will bring a focus on home and family, dear Aries. Venus and Mercury are here as well, increasing feelings of domesticity. This is a propitious time to make memories with special people in your life. Focus on ways to have fun, break out of stale routines, and express yourself.**

Secret admirer, huh?

Marimba chords trilled, so she pulled her phone from her armband but didn't recognize the number. "Hello?"

"Samson. What's the polite thing to say if a baby's fugly? My first nephew was hideous, outdid his dad in the hair department. If this one's ugly, should I say he's 'striking,' or 'stunning,' or straight up lie?"

Her smile resisted speech. "Haven't you ever seen something so ugly it's cute?"

"Good call. I'll say he's cute no matter what. You women are so wise."

"Flattery will get you nowhere."

"Will flowers? There's one on the chair for you. It might be hard to run with."

In the seat where the bouquet had been, a yellow rosebud remained.

"And now you have my number."

Plucking up the rose, she said, "I thought you cops had to pass psych evals. You're clearly a stalker." The flower had a perfect poignant pungency, like prom silk and victory laps. "I'll be sending all future calls to the junk folder."

"Junk?"

"Fine. But you're not supposed to call a girl when you've had her number less than five minutes."

"Who made that rule?"

"It's common knowledge." Holly brushed the skin-soft flower on her lips.

"If you're dating. Don't get the wrong idea from the rose. Yellow is the color of friendship."

HOLLY

Courtney's left elbow knocked Holly in the ribs.

"Hey!" Her stride was thrown off as she pressed the sore spot under her green tank top, passing other runners with numbers on their chests.

"Sorry, love." Courtney twitched her head to their right. "Two o'clock. Glad I wore my good running bra." By "good," she meant a lacy raspberry red push-up and no shirt, so she'd pinned her number to her leggings.

Of course, Courtney had slept in and made them late to the fun run, and of course, she was now trolling for men rather than enjoying time with her friend, who might have news to share about a guy she's interested in instead of being an ear for Courtney's never-ending tales of—

"Dibs on the shaved one," she continued, lowering her voice. "I hope he shaves his chest, too."

The bald man with broad shoulders bobbed in a baby blue shirt beside a bearded man in a red shirt and baseball cap. The first man turned, searching the crowd. It was Jacob. Holly's lungs pinched with the shot of cool morning air. They were in his blind spot but coming up fast.

"You saw Lisa yesterday?" the man in red asked him.

Lisa?

Jacob nodded.

"How's she doing?"

"Holly," Courtney said. "Do you think we should—"

Jacob spun around. "Samson!" As Courtney jogged up between Jacob and Holly, he grinned around her. "Thought you might be here. This is my brother, Mark."

"Hi Mark." Holly waved from the left flank.

"This is Holly." Jacob's stride was easy. "Mom's dietitian."

"Thanks for helping Mom." Even through the beard, Mark's smile reminded her of Vicki.

"My pleasure. You two lucked out in the mom department."

"No argument here," Mark said.

"Courtney," Holly held out an open palm. "Jacob and Mark."

"Nice to meet you, boys." She extended a princess hand to Jacob as they jogged, and he gave it a quick shake. "We didn't mean to interrupt."

"No problem." His glance bounced off Courtney's bobbing cleavage before he said, "We were talking about our sister who had the baby."

That's Lisa. Of course. Sharing a smile, admiring Jacob's shadow beard, her heart did a little shimmy. The playground they were passing smelled of freshly cut grass.

"They're well?"

"Think she's keeping it. We'll have to find you another one."

"Holly told you she wants to adopt?" Courtney batted her eyes. "I admire mothers so much. But I like sex too much to settle down." She leaned around him to Mark. "Are you married?"

"Yes, ma'am." Mark held up his left hand.

"Do you have kids?"

"Two." He smiled, looking ahead.

"No more blow jobs, right?"

"Courtney!"

"They know I'm playing. Mark's not going to answer that anyway. He's way too respectable." To Mark, she said, "Forgive me. Your wife's a lucky lady."

Holly rolled her eyes. "Come on, Courtney. These nice men don't deserve this."

"We have thick skin," Mark said. "Feel free to leave us in the dust though. It's bad enough holding up my little brother."

Turning her face away from the men, Courtney said, "A little rest might be nice." After she raised one victorious eyebrow, the other joined it in a wiggle, her standard cue for a wingman.

Smoking hot friends suck. Was she going to have to watch Courtney shamelessly flirt with her crush? She could pull her aside and ask her to back off—

Jacob interrupted her brainstorm. "Did you two run this last year?"

"We did the 10K." Courtney's gaze lingered on him.

"Stay frosty, brother," Mark smirked. "These ladies are out of your league."

"True." Holly flew ahead and turned to face them, running backward. "Courtney, we'd better pick up the pace or we won't be able to respect ourselves in the morning."

"I'm good." She was probably shooting for a *double entendre* there. She should be good at sex with all the practice she'd had.

Seriously? Holly huffed, not happy she was being a judgmental hypocrite, but mostly not happy with Courtney.

"You go ahead." Her friend's perfectly shadowed eyes looked steely.

Hos before bros, huh? "See you at the finish line." Flinging frustration behind on the asphalt, she could go as fast as she wanted now. But she wished Jacob might catch up.

* * *

That afternoon in her kitchen, after Holly poured cucumber-lemon water into a glass while her washed hair dripped into her robe, she checked her phone, hoping for but not expecting an apology from Courtney. One missed call from Jacob. No voicemail. Sipping her water, she choked down the possibility that he might be calling for Courtney's number, then she typed:

Were you calling for bail money?

"That's stupid." She was deleting the unsent text when the phone rang, startling her. At least it fell on the table and not the floor. It was Jacob.

"Hello, this is Holly."

"Samson. Missed you at the finish line." His voice lit up her brain like dark chocolate.

"I had a Gingerbread Man thing going. I made good time." She paced to the front window and considered the yard that needed mowing.

"I'm sure you did." A chuckle bubbled under his words.

"I hope Courtney behaved better after I left."

"Not really. Mark decided not to press charges."

With a clenched gut, she said, "She's single if you want her number."

"No kidding. When I want a beautiful woman's phone number, I get it myself."

Awwww! Her smile almost broke her face.

"When you and Courtney get together," he continued, "does she do all the talking?"

"You must bring in tons of criminals with your Sherlock Holmes instincts." Holly paced to the dining room. "Hang on, you're not a detective, are you?"

"Well done, Watson. But sometimes, off-duty, I can be an idiot. Happy Independence Day."

"You too." She gazed at the backyard. "Your brother's cool."

"He's married."

"Dude!"

"That's not a thing we're doing, announcing people's relationship status?"

Jacob's voice made her stupid: no comeback.

"What's your 4th of July tradition? Go to big displays, have family picnics, light illegal fireworks?"

She smiled. "You'll have to grant me immunity first."

"That's a D.A. thing. You'll feel better once you get your crimes off your chest. Hold on. Record button's acting up again."

"What was the question? My 4th of July traditions?"

"The question is, do you want to come to my folks' house for their annual barbecue?"

"That was not the question," she said, and dropped onto her sofa. Her gratitude journal on her coffee table stared back at her.

"The one I was getting to."

"You're not asking me to meet your family." Running her fingers over the wide journal's leather cover, she hoped that didn't sound presumptuous. He had said they were friends. But he had also said she was beautiful.

"Just hang out with the ones you've met, plus my dad and some friends. Lisa's not coming, newborn and all. Do you have other plans?"

"Not really..." She stood. Meena wouldn't mind if she didn't join them for fireworks; she'd be mad if Holly turned him down.

"When can I pick you up?"

"But..." If Jacob was interested in her, this was a different kind of fast.

"But?"

She paced. "I'm washing my cat?"

"Samson. This is not a date. It's a party—a Davis 4th of July party. On a fun scale of 1 to 10, it's a guaranteed eight or above."

"Dang."

"Right?"

"Let me think about it." She wandered toward the front window.

"I respect that. Call you in 5 minutes."

"10? Actually—"

"Better idea—"

"Go ahead."

"No, you."

"What time is this thing?"

"Open house."

Mark's gravelly voice rang in the background.

"Are you there now?" she asked.

"It's no problem to come get you. I need to head into town anyway."

"For what?"

"Mom needs a couple of things."

"Beer!" Mark sounded close to the phone.

"And Mark's concerned about the beer supply."

It embarrassed Holly a little, like they were junior high boys calling a girl. "You shouldn't miss out on the party to come get me." She headed to her bedroom. "I can bring beer and whatever Vicki needs if you want to text me a list."

"You're coming?"

"I'll need the address."

"You're a triple threat, Samson. Logical, independent..."

"What's the third thing?" She eyed her closet.

"Speed. Obviously."

* * *

The lower number on the signpost registered as Holly sped past it, hugging the curvy wooded road.

"Shit." She scanned ahead for a space to turn around, inhaling fresh air from the open windows.

Finally where she was supposed to be, the driveway peaked at a canopy of trees shielding Vicki's sprawling home and a wide gravel parking area. Boy, they had a lot of friends. Holly parked on the periphery.

When her hands dropped from the steering wheel, her bare thighs made her reconsider her denim shorts. Would Vicki disapprove? Cleavage peeked out from the silky red blouse, so she pinched one more button closed, then took her purse from the passenger seat, pulled its strap over her head, turned out, and gasped.

A big dark thing was right there, skulking, with a huge hairy face, Holstein eyes under coppery eyebrows, a black nose, and a long lolling tongue.

Aww! With her hand on her chest, she smiled at the mountain of dog and gained control of her heart, which beat faster than the rhythmic crunching of gravel getting louder.

"Bernice!" Jacob called. "Sit." Bending down to the window, he smiled, "We won't bite."

Holly burst out of the car and crouched. "You are adorable!"

The hairy tail whipped.

"Thanks," he said, smoothing his blue-and-white plaid shirt.

"I'm not talking to you." She offered two open palms. "Can I pet you?"

The fluffy mammoth knocked Holly onto her ass.

"Bernice! Sorry."

"You gorgeous beast." While she rubbed her hands through the downy white chest, voices and music came from the other side of the house.

Jacob held out his hand. "Why am I having déjà vu? Off." He took her hand and zipped her up.

"Is she yours?"

"She's my folks' dog, but I'm her favorite. Or was."

"She's beautiful." Smiling up from the panting hound, she found Jacob grinning at her, then she retreated toward the trunk of her sky-blue Mini Cooper. "Got your beer."

"You're a godsend. Cute car."

"Thanks." She stopped and faced him.

He almost walked into her; she almost forgot what she was going to say.

"So ugly it's cute, or just cute?"

"Cute," Jacob smiled, standing really fricking close. "It suits you." His hand on the closest white stripe made her jealous. "How many tickets have you gotten in this thing?"

"Don't you have to read me my rights?"

"Do you feel free to leave?"

Free, yes. Willing, no. Resisting the urge to stay close, Holly resumed her short walk to the back of the car.

"Not until I give you your beer." The trunk door rose. "And the pie."

"Pie? You are not free to leave." His smile turned into a cringe. "Does it have cauliflower crust or something?"

After shooting him a disdainful look, she retrieved the shallow box with the pie in a nest of dishtowels. "Cauliflower can serve as a delicious substitute for many things."

"Great." He crossed his arms.

"Mashed potatoes, risotto…but never, ever pie crust. Or steak. Roasted cauliflower is tasty with enough butter and seasoning, but why call it 'cauliflower steak'? That's inviting disappointment." She handed him the cardboard box, proud of the close-to-perfect golden crust of scattered stars and wavy stripes that peeked through the plastic wrap.

"Tell me you didn't make this."

Holly grinned. "'You didn't make this.'"

"You made this." He raised the dish and inhaled. "Apple?" Bernice adjusted her hips to get him to notice how nicely she was sitting. "No beg."

When she dragged the box of beer bottles by its cutout handle, he stepped up and stacked the pie box on top of it, lifting both. He smelled better than the pie. She reached in for her red ice chest.

"Do you realize what you're doing?" he asked.

"What?" She grabbed her University of Utah cooler with the big white U.

"This house is full of Aggies."

Utah State Aggies. "Aggies who like pie?"

Jacob nodded.

"I'm willing to risk it."

"If it gets ugly, I'll throw the pie, and we'll make a run for it."

Holly nodded.

"Help me understand: paleo-touting dietitian by day, vigilante pastry chef by night?"

"Not every night."

"Does the mayor shine a croissant shape in the sky when the city needs you?"

She chuckled. "Stress baking."

Back to the trunk, he deposited the boxes and sat, ducking under the open hatch door. "I'm not going to break your car, am I?"

She shook her head.

"Why stress baking?" He patted the tiny space beside him. The dog planted her furry ass on the ground, but Holly stayed where she was.

"You get a lot of confessions, don't you?"

"It's the Columbo eyebrows." He waggled them and pinched an invisible cigar.

"Groucho Marx, you mean?"

He shrugged. "It's okay if you—"

"I don't know if I'm doing the right thing fostering babies."

Jacob froze, then twisted to peer into the backseat and said, "If you have one now and forgot it at home, then no."

"What if I fall in love with it and have to give it back?"

Standing and towering over her, he guided her to the back of the car, where he sat her down. "Didn't want you falling on your butt again." He circled a palm in her direction. "A lot going on right now."

"Or what if I get one of those drug-affected babies? There's a ton of them, you know. I could be horrible at figuring out what it needs. I've been taking the classes, but…"

"You're a perfectionist."

She consulted her sizable mental list of ways she failed on a regular basis. "Not really."

"Exhibit A," he said, sliding the pie into her view.

"That's just fun, decorating. It's probably prettier than it tastes. Don't start with a big slice. When I stress bake, I do things like forget an ingredient or measure wrong."

"How are you not in sales?" He had the cutest dimple.

"It's all about managing expectations."

Jacob braced his hand against the car. "What are the other fruits of your stress baking, besides attractive, inedible pie?"

"I'm only committing to short-term fostering."

"Smart. Build your confidence."

The long black fur on Bernice's back, warm from the sun, slid between her fingers.

"I haven't turned in the papers yet. I'm still thinking."

"No more thinking today," he said, pulling her to stand—an easy order to follow since his touch and his proximity overwhelmed her. "You've exceeded your quota."

"One last question."

"Walk and talk." He took the stacked boxes.

After she gathered her load and closed the hatch, her car beeped while they crunched over gravel toward the house.

"Do you think a person can love an adopted baby as much as their biological child?"

"Yep."

* * *

Vicki's kitchen had more of a Southwest vibe than Holly would have imagined. Jacob set the case of beer on the tan floor and lifted the pie to the terracotta tiled countertop.

"Quick." He waved her to the refrigerator and opened the freezer, so she passed off the quart of vanilla ice cream. "For the pie?" His fingers were toasty compared to the frosty tub.

"You can't have warm apple pie without ice cream," she said, rubbing her hands on her denim-clad hips.

"Genius."

"This is for me."

Before tucking the pint of lactose-free ice cream in the freezer door, he scrutinized the label.

"Can I put this in the fridge?" she asked.

"What is it?" Jacob's electric hands held hers over the foil-wrapped ramekin.

"It's a pie alternative for Mom—for your mom."

"I should probably test it." He had a million reasons to smirk at her;

she hoped it wasn't at how hard she was blushing.

"She'll need to heat it." Holly slipped away. "It's gross cold."

Tucking the dish in the refrigerator, he smirked, then closed the door and faced her. "Not sure how you knew you were coming over before I did. Are you a witch? Or is 'Dark Arts Worker' more politically correct?"

Holly smiled, resisting the urge to sit on the countertop. "It was for our receptionist. She has diabetes too. I have to bring her something when I bring treats for the team."

"You bring treats to work a lot?"

"When I want to bake, and I don't have friends over to help eat it."

"Did this coworker develop diabetes after you started working there?"

She scrunched her face at him; he held up his hands and backed away. The door to the back deck opened, and a dripping teen trotted through who smiled at them, clutching a towel, and disappeared.

Once he put the milk carton in the refrigerator, the ice chest was empty.

"Where does the beer go?"

"Outside. We should hide this first." He took the red cooler and moved away from the kitchen, offering his other hand behind him.

Holly's heart skipped, confessing it had wanted to hold that hand since last December when it had tried to help her off the clinic floor. She walked slowly instead of taking it, and his arm dropped as he entered a beige carpeted hallway lined with photos. A young Vicki smiled demurely in a sepia headshot.

"Your mom's so beautiful." Then Jacob's senior picture stopped her in her tracks. "Who's this with all the hair?"

He shook long imaginary locks over his shoulders.

"Between that and the Letterman's jacket, I bet you were quite the ladies' man."

"You have no idea."

In the rustic master bedroom, purses and bags littered the dressers, and a few jackets lay across the bottom edge of the king bed. While he opened the closet and stashed the ice chest, women's voices drifted in from the hall.

A massive, framed photo graced one wall: desert orange rock cut by a shadow. A cluster of violet flowers with furry leaves peeked from a crack in the desolate surface.

"What do you think?" Jacob asked.

"It's beautiful." Written in tiny architect-style caps in the lower right corner was:

J. DAVIS '15.

"Is this your work?"

"God made the rocks. I just took their picture."

"Damn."

"Not bad, huh?" A woman stood in the bedroom doorway: tall and French-looking in her black-and-white striped shirt and shorts, her dark hair in a wavy bob. "Vicki wanted to call it 'Hope,' but the artist formerly known as Jake calls it 'Purple Flower in Orange Rock.'"

"Holly, this is my sister-in-law, Faye. Faye, Holly."

Holly walked to her, extending her hand. "I owe you an apology."

"I doubt that." Faye's smirking blue eyes were gorgeous.

"Holly thinks she left Mark and me in an awkward spot this morning. We handled it."

"I'm sure you did," she said, finding a toy car in her purse. "My daughter is dying to meet you. Flag me down, okay?"

Holly nodded, trying not to read into Faye's comment which implied they'd been talking about her. While Faye disappeared into the hallway, Jacob gazed at the backyard below.

A framed photo stood propped on a smaller dresser—a group shot in front of a wide Christmas tree. Vicki stood dwarfed beside a man with Jacob's eyebrows. A young woman wearing thick-rimmed glasses smiled on their left. In front crouched a beardless Mark and Faye with long hair, holding a little girl between them whose eager smile was more of a tooth display. On the right, Jacob had receding hair, a goatee, and an attractive woman under his arm with wavy light brown spirals of hair and a tremendous grin. She looked a little young for him, but it was probably his hairline making him look older.

"Holly!" As Vicki entered her bedroom, her salmon-colored blouse billowed from her open arms.

"Hi! You have a beautiful home."

"I'm so glad you could join us!" She was a good hugger.

"Jacob said you're doing better off your metformin?"

"Thanks to you." Vicki patted her shoulders. "You're a better doctor than my doctor. But no shop talk. We have next week for that. Thank you for bringing the groceries. How much do I owe you?"

"Nothing. I'm glad I could contribute."

"Are you sure?"

"Of course. Before I forget, we put a dessert for you in the fridge— it's better warmed in the oven, but you can microwave it in a pinch."

"You're so thoughtful!"

Jacob stepped up. "You should see the pie she made, Mom. Don't let anyone cut into it 'til I get a picture." He held his arm toward the door. "Let's get you something to drink."

"Are you hungry?"

* * *

Holly's paper plate had become an open casket with the bones of a barbecued chicken breast. She tried to stay alert for Faye's story, but the nap-inducing late-afternoon sun and Grace's delicate fingers moving through her hair weren't helping. Sleepy bliss set in as she inhaled the smoky meat grilling and currents of coconut sunscreen.

"We're just glad Grace didn't need surgery."

"Looking good, Grace." It was a man's voice.

"Thank you." Grace was so sure of herself. Her attention to detail reminded Holly of Keith's daughter Keira, which had made her sad at first. She was also kind and confident like Owen and mature for an 8-year-old.

The man pulled out the chair to Holly's left. "I don't appreciate you trying to put me out of business."

Holly didn't appreciate this guy taking Jacob's seat. Trying not to mess up the second Dutch braid, she peeked out of the corner of her eye. "You braid hair?"

"Not Grace. You."

"Unless you're Ronald McDonald or the infamous Burger King, I have no beef with you. No pun intended."

"Just like a superhero to feign humility in the face of a nemesis." It was the slick guy she'd seen with Mark and Vicki earlier, dressed in an expensive-looking linen shirt and khakis.

"Hold still." Grace grabbed her head, twisting it to face forward.

"Sorry." To him, she said, "You realize you're casting yourself as the villain in your scenario."

"Captains of industry rarely have clean hands."

Faye laughed. "Holly, this is Chip, the family's favorite drug dealer."

"Pharmaceutical representative."

"Pleased to meet you, Captain Pharma." She held her hand over her torso. "I'm Holly."

"I know." His hand was baby smooth.

A tallish kid took a golf swing to a croquet ball across the yard. *Thwack.* Vicki stood from another table, put her hand on a woman's shoulder, and picked up plates, heading to the back deck where Jacob was manning the grill with his dad.

"And friend of the family. I still am, right?"

"Yes, Chip," Faye chuckled. "Our love for you is thicker than politics."

"Mark is thick-headed…"

"That's a good thing," she added, gazing into the sun-kissed grass, "having a solid skull. If you're too open-minded, your brains fall out."

Holly snickered.

"Women are so cutting," he sighed. "So, Holly…"

It was only a pause, and not a very long one, but even without seeing his expression, she recognized his type. *Ego the size of Kansas.*

"Where do you stand in our current political morass?"

"About ankle deep." She hated to ask since it would lead to more of him talking. "You?"

"I'm one of the few progressive minds here."

"A bit insulting to our hosts, don't you think?"

"No offense. Faye can back me up on this. Mark and I have frequent friendly debates."

"I need that hair band." Grace pointed to the center of the table, so Holly retrieved the elastic and held it over her shoulder.

"I'd prefer more friendly and less frequent," Faye said. "Or save it for your fishing trips so I don't have to suffer."

At the barbecue, Jacob's dad spoke with Vicki instead of Jacob, now absent from the deck.

"Done!" Grace sat in the empty chair between the two women, adorable in her red-and-white starred sundress.

"Thank you, Grace!" Holly patted down her head. "I feel so festive now." When she pulled the braids forward, blue and red ribbons trailed to her elbows.

"You're welcome." Her pert frown surveyed her handiwork around Holly's face before she smiled, nodded, turned to the pile of ribbons on the table, and then ran off.

"Mom, can you open this?" A boy of about five handed Faye a bottle of hard lemonade.

"For you?"

He nodded.

"Let's find you something better." Smiling at Holly, she asked, "Have you met Franco?"

She shook her head and waved. "Hi Franco. I'm Holly."

"Hi."

Dang, they make cute kids.

"Excuse us." Faye took her son's hand and the forbidden lemonade, leaving Holly alone with Chip.

Holly tipped up her beer bottle. Everyone else she had met had been lovely. This guy reminded her of Douchebag Dave, a title bestowed by Paige after he'd cheated on Holly.

"Come clean." Chip leaned in. "You're a fellow Democrat, right?" Before she could answer, he whispered, "I knew it," and held her arm. "Don't worry, your secret's safe with me."

Holly moved her arm, clasping the bottle in her lap. "I'm not." *Not worried.* She was a Democrat, but he could think whatever he wanted. The gazebo in the lawn looked like a great escape. Or she could make an excuse about Grace needing her help, doing whatever she was doing, scouting around a tree.

"Do you often party with your clients? Vicki was bragging about you."

"Vicki's sweet. Jacob invited me."

"Oh."

Grace galloped back holding a stick.

"You're back!" Holly smiled. "What's that for?"

"I'm making a toy."

"Cool."

After tying a white ribbon to the forked end, Grace called, "Uncle Jake!"

Behind them, a cluster of older men stood beside a table with their arms around each other. Jacob was squatting, pointing his camera at the group.

"Hang on." Holly touched her arm. "He looks busy."

"Pardon me, girls." Chip rose and rattled his plastic cup. "I need more ice."

Jacob was with Holly and Grace in a couple of minutes. "What's up, Bug?" He put a hand on Grace's shoulder.

"Do you think girlfriend will like this?"

Holly stiffened. He didn't have a girlfriend, did he?

He set down his camera and sat by Holly. "I'm sure she'll love it." The twinkle in his eye hinted at a secret joke.

"Is it too many ribbons?" Grace asked. "Do you have something to put on the end? Like a little mouse…?"

It's a cat toy.

"Let's try it this way. Do you want to give it to her?"

"I'm not sure I'm done," she said, studying her creation.

Holly eyed him. "You have a cat."

He nodded.

"Named Girlfriend."

"It's come in handy. When I'm at a bar, and strange women are falling all over me, I can say 'Sorry, ladies, I have to get home to my Girlfriend.'"

"You don't go to bars," Grace scoffed.

"Sometimes."

But she crossed her arms.

Jacob chuckled, "Even my niece knows I don't have game."

After a gasp and "A pinecone!" Grace was gone.

"Nice hair."

"Thank you." She touched the tips.

"Having fun?"

"So much fun." Her heart was so full it almost ached. *Did John Smith feel this way with Pocahontas, chilling with her tribe? A welcomed foreigner, possibly dangerous and inclined to defect?* "I'm not sure it's an eight or above, though."

"Ouch."

"Solid 7.5."

"Have you seen the creek yet?"

"There's a creek?"

"C'mon."

She followed him past the deserted slip-and-slide and croquet hoops. Music got louder as they approached the gazebo, which had a white railing draped with red and blue crepe paper like Holly's braids. Rihanna singing about lightning sounded less about hookups and more about sparks—or string lights, like the ones inside, flowering out from the ceiling's center point.

Jacob waited a few steps ahead until Holly joined him.

"I'm a sucker for string lights."

"Want to go in? There should be dancing later." His smile suggested he might want to, but it wasn't lechy.

She shrugged. "Do you think your parents would take a renter?"

"There is electricity. But no plumbing. And no kitchen."

"Worth it."

While they strolled toward a row of evergreen shrubs with thick trees behind them, the drifting music gave way to water tumbling over rocks. The blast of brisk air had the opposite effect of a cold shower as Holly tramped down the bank, her hand dangling close to Jacob's. The massive rhododendrons and the drop in elevation made it private. The burbling water beckoned to Holly's hot feet, so she plopped down and started unbuckling her sandals.

But above the creek bed came another noise: lusty moaning.

Jacob found the source before she did. "Noah Papanikolas!"

Two sets of bare legs lay beneath the leggy rhododendrons. Hands reached back for crumpled pants, covering the disappearing top pair. The shaved legs kicked at the dirt and scuttled under the bushes.

"Excuse me for a second." Tromping away through shallow edge water, he called, "Not gonna run, are you, Noah?"

A gangly curly-haired teen emerged from the space between the rhododendrons and stood, sullen.

"Good man. That's Trinity under there? Hi Trinity."

"Hello," the girl's high voice bleated, horrified.

"Noah, take Trinity back to the party and stay in sight." Jacob checked his watch. "I'll chat with your dad in 15 minutes. You should talk to him before I do."

"We weren't having sex." His indignant voice probably worked well when he tried to buy beer.

Holly smirked and fiddled with her sandal buckle, even more turned on by Jacob playing protective dad. Did he disapprove of premarital sex like Danielle and Meena, or was it only because they were too young?

"Really." Jacob clasped his hands behind his back. "What were you doing?"

"Just kissing."

He held a hand to his ear. "Pissing?"

"Kissing." Noah rolled his eyes.

"I thought you said 'pissing.' You can kiss fine in pants."

A giggle spewed out of Holly before she could cover her mouth.

"We weren't having sex."

Jacob stood firm.

Trinity crawled out the other side of the rhododendrons. She inched down her short cotton skirt, then scurried into the green expanse, veering toward the lawn's edge; Noah huffed as he walked past Holly. She offered a finger wave, but he avoided eye contact.

Splashing back to her, Jacob stopped beside her extended bare foot.

She grinned up at him. "His fun points just went way down."

"Nobody likes a cock blocker," he said, staring out at the yard.

I do. Her Jack-and-the-Beanstalk giant was back, looking bigger than ever above her. She was happy to have a chance to study him while he watched the strays return to the flock. "We need more cockblockers in the world."

He smiled and took a seat on the bank beside her.

"Were you channeling your dad there, or was that the Jacob Davis dad voice?"

"A little of Column A, a little of Column B."

"Do you have kids?"

He shook his head. "Never too soon to practice."

Holly wanted to practice making them. "Have you been married?"

"Engaged." Leaning back on his hands, he stretched his legs toward the creek. "You?"

"Not even close." She shifted to face him. "Help me with a theory?"

"Shoot."

"Do I emit some negative energy that only men can perceive?"

Jacob's smile was a Danielle smile, the kind she would give Owen after he said something adorable and ridiculous.

"You know how poisonous dart frogs are brightly colored to warn predators not to eat them?"

"Is that what these are for?" His hand touched her shoulder, clasping the red ribbon entwined in her hair.

Holly shivered.

"Cold?"

She shook her head. "Have you seen the show *Justified*?"

He nodded.

"Remember when the sheriff says, 'if you go through your day and everyone you meet is an asshole, you're the asshole'?"

Jacob had the sexiest little belly laugh. Her diaphragm pinged back.

"You're not an asshole," he chuckled.

"Do you know how many boyfriends I've had?"

Smiling at the creek, he said, "I don't ask questions I don't want the answer to."

"It's enough for a valid scientific sample. I'm the common denominator. I'm like a poisonous dart frog. Men sense it—eventually—and run. Self-preservation."

"Yours or theirs?"

A lumbering, tinkling thunder heralded Bernice, who came panting between them and greeted Holly with a slobbery sniff.

Jacob maneuvered the wagging rear haunches from his face and stood. "She's an emotional bloodhound."

Holly cooed at the dog's smiling face and ran her fingers through the toasty, silky fur.

"Hold still." Big hands braced Holly's head and a hot smooch landed on top. Then Jacob's face arrived beside her, lowering as he crouched. "If I drop dead in 5 minutes, you'll have your answer. Noah's dad is Pete. Be sure to report the love tryst to him if I die. Noah needs accountability."

Bernice plowed into the water.

"Thank you, Bernice! I lost track of what I was doing." She sighed through warm chills and undid the last sandal strap.

"Nice tatt."

"Can you tell what it is?" Tipping her knee, she smiled at the black flame outline between her ankle bone and Achilles tendon.

"It's a flame. I like the clean lines—just the essence of it."

"It was supposed to have a chalice. Unitarian symbol. But just as well since I haven't gone to church for ages. Did you know tattoos hurt like hell?"

Jacob smiled.

She shrugged. "I stopped there."

He gave her a hand up—she could get used to this—and she answered the call of the burbling water.

He called, "It's colder than it—"

Stepping in shocked like a wet burn.

"—looks."

Holly pranced over the round rocks, back to the grassy dirt. "Oh-dear-god," she laughed.

"Cold? Let's get you back in the sun."

Nodding, shivering, she plucked up her sandals and walked barefoot toward the sunny lawn. Jacob followed. His broad hands rubbed warmth into her arms.

Out of the shade, the grass loved on her soles, the pliable blade tips offering pleasant pokey resistance before yielding. Radiant heat bathed Holly's skin and opened her clenched muscles.

"Better?"

"Mm." *Much.*

*   *   *

"Just one song. Please?" Grace stood before Faye, who sat in the plastic lawn chair holding sleepy Franco's hand.

Holly squatted to her level. "I should go, too. I can walk you guys to your car?"

"Bedtime is overrated." Faye patted her lap; her young son climbed up and curled in. She smiled at Grace and Holly as she settled his head on her shoulder. "You girls go have a dance. Come here right after, yes?"

"Yes!" Grace grabbed Holly's hand and tugged her across the yard to the gazebo.

The dusky blue light made the vast backyard different. It smelled different, too. The evening air, cooling down after a hot day... She couldn't sniff out its ingredients, but it was soul food.

Entering the gazebo, she took in the ceiling. Against the bluish dusk, the tiny flowing golden lights summoned magnificent fairy-sized dreams, as if her heart had busted open from too much goodness and sprayed bits of forgotten hope everywhere.

Pink was venting between low guitar strums and clapping beats about being surrounded by clowns and liars, which was appropriate with Chip at the far end chatting up a twenty-something—probably someone's daughter—in a short sundress who was trying too hard. Holly grinned like a giddy George Bailey, glimpsing a wonderfully avoidable life.

As Grace's hand slid from hers, she beamed at her little dance partner who leaped to the center of the floor. Feeling like an 8-year-old with gigantism, Holly was about to chase after her.

"Hey." Jacob stood outside the gazebo's entrance with his camera around his neck holding two lit sparklers. His smile was genuine and kissable.

Grace zipped between them. "Thanks, Uncle Jake!" She grabbed the sparklers and handed one to Holly.

By the time Holly adjusted her grip away from the popping flame dandelion, he was gone.

"Dance with me!" Grace ran, twirling with her sparkler above her head, eyes only for the spitting flame.

Pink called it. "Just like fire..."

HOLLY

SATURDAY, JULY 9, 2016

The purring of the motor came first. When the engine shut off in her driveway, Holly was tempted to peek at what kind of car Jacob drove, but she kept lacing her hiking boot from her seat on the wood floor. She swiped the door's cheerful yellow exterior inward so only the screen door remained; his boots thumped closer on the curving path.

"Hi," said the best delivery her porch had ever seen.

"Hi!" Stretching up, she fumbled with the door latch. "Come in."

Her living room was smaller with the gentle giant there between the flat-screen TV on the wall and the white coffee table she'd made of stacked pallets. Jacob glanced at her legs—one boot on and one off—and shut the door, shifting her ice chest on his hip.

"Almost ready," she smiled. "New laces."

"Better hurry. Already behind schedule."

"What?"

"You would've called security if I ran after you."

"You did run after me! Almost got me hit by a car."

"We need to work on your situational awareness. I meant my mom's last visit." He shook his head. "Highly uncooperative. I appreciate you coming around, but you didn't have to leave your stuff at my folks' house to see me again. Where do you want these?"

"In the kitchen. Please."

"I like your house."

She liked his ass. And he clearly hadn't missed a leg day in a while. After he passed the tiny table with the black stool and disappeared behind the wall, she called, "Thanks." The ice chest thumped on the linoleum floor. The paper bag made a muffled clink against the countertop.

"Aww." He sounded sad.

"What?"

The first lip-trumpeted notes of "Taps" echoed as if a military funeral procession had started in her kitchen. Head down, he emerged, cupping the white ceramic pot that they'd given her with the tomato plant.

She grinned. And waited.

He stopped at her feet. "Going to let me hum the whole thing?"

"Please." She cinched a double knot.

"Tomato plant bit the dust?"

"Nope. She's out in the backyard in a bigger container. More room for activities." Holly hopped up. "Like root growth."

"She?" he asked, following her to the glass door in the dining area.

"Cute thing like that—" The baby plant perked up from its oversized pot on her deck. "Definitely a girl."

When Jacob stood close, gazing at it, the hairs on Holly's arms reached for him. She shivered and rubbed them down.

"If you're cold," he smiled, "you could try pants."

"You said we're doing something active outside. You're wearing shorts."

"I'll put this back before I get in trouble." He lifted the little pot on his way to the kitchen. "Interesting choice, decorating with dirt."

"It's going to hold herbs! I haven't decided whether I'll do basil or fennel."

"Do basil."

Frowning, she tried not to stare at his defined calves. "Have you ever had fresh fennel?"

"No." The ceramic pot clunked back on the windowsill. "Not a fan of the seeds."

"Do you like licorice?" she asked. "Black licorice, the real stuff."

"Are you dissing Red Vines?" Jacob stepped up, crossing his arms over his broad torso.

"Absolutely," she said, her hands on her hips. She wasn't trying to puff out her chest, although it may have happened reflexively, either out of assertiveness or the necessity of breath, which seemed short now. She seemed short now, play-fighting up at him when she really just wanted him to kiss her.

"Yes." He grinned. "I do."

Holly's heart galloped hell-bent out of reality—even though the present was pretty fricking fantastic—because "I do" on his edible lips was like a gunshot.

Daring him to read her thoughts, she stared back. "If I grow fresh fennel, will you try it?"

"Twist my arm."

She froze, staring at the swirling dark hair over his tan skin that looked like velvety Velcro.

"Did the rose hold up?" he continued. "I was trying to picture how you'd get it home—run with it in your teeth?"

Holly cringed. "It didn't make it home."

"Trashed it, huh? First and last rose."

"Remember the old guy?"

"Your secret admirer?"

"He said I was the spitting image of his wife at my age."

"He did hit on you," he smirked.

"His wife was in surgery, so I gave him the rose to take to her."

Jacob's smile vanished, but he didn't look upset.

* * *

A few minutes later, Holly belted into the old creamy white Land Rover, kicking herself for not accepting the hand he had offered, but gleeful that his ride wasn't a slick midlife-crisis-mobile.

When it revved awake, she asked, "Where are we going?"

"It's a surprise."

"I hate surprises."

Jacob raised a skeptical eyebrow.

She shrugged.

"All right then." With his hand on her seat, he backed out of her driveway. "Comment cards are in the center console. Fill one out at the end of our date if you have a complaint."

"I never said this was a date."

"It is." He glanced at her. "If you're going to jump out, let me know. I'll slow down." He accelerated down the residential street.

"Thanks."

"Sure thing." His deadpan profile made her stupid-happy.

She tried to lock it down. "Any excitement after I left?"

"I left right after you did. School night. Does a fistfight qualify?"

"You're kidding!"

He shook his head.

"Who?" Holly tucked a foot under her leg, turning toward him.

"Mark's buddy, Chip."

"Who with? Mark?"

"Hell no. Mark put an end to it. Even caught some friendly fire for his trouble."

"Is he okay?" She gasped, "Was it about the girl?"

Jacob did a double take. "What girl?"

"Never mind. He was just talking to someone who looked half his age. What happened?"

He shifted gears. "The Chipster called Dad's Army buddy a racist idiot for supporting Trump. In more colorful language. Got in his face."

"Uh-oh."

He nodded. "Effed around, found out."

"Is your dad's friend okay?"

"Oh yeah," he chuckled. "Mark said old Bill still packs a punch."

Holly inspected the bridge of his nose. Had he ever been hit before? Had he hit anyone before? And could he really be voting the way she assumed he was voting?

At a stoplight, he smiled, "What?"

She sighed. "Are you a fan of Trump?"

Jacob shifted gears. "Wouldn't say that."

Thank god.

"Voting for him. But I wouldn't hang out with the guy."

"Then why would you vote for him!"

He smirked, glancing from the road. "That's the first time you've yelled at me."

"That was not a yell."

It was a long drive, but Holly would have been fine if they were never there yet. She loved how Jacob told stories, depicting each one like a movie. The way he portrayed the lawn fire that had threatened to take down the gazebo and fighting it with hoses and buckets, she could almost feel the heat. And she loved that he didn't talk himself up too much or talk down about other people. Even when he criticized somebody, he was loving or funny about it. And she loved how he listened. In those 45 minutes, he gave her more eye contact than she'd gotten from Keith in the last month they'd been together. Driving, too.

When the "Wood Lake Resort" sign appeared, the Land Rover turned off the wooded two-lane highway.

"Oh, no." She shook her head, not having it, as they ground over the gravel. "I followed your cryptic instructions, and there was no mention of a swimsuit. I've only gone skinny dipping once, and I don't intend to do it now as a middle-aged woman—"

"You're not middle-aged. And we're not here to swim."

"Why are we here?"

"All in good time, grasshopper."

After they passed the rustic resort, he turned onto a dirt road she hadn't taken before. It went into the enormous pines up around the lake, which came in and out of view as they climbed, then dipped again.

Near a sign for a hiking trail, Jacob parked, then examined the thick watch on his right wrist. "Almost 11:30." He braced his hand on her seat. "On a scale of 1 to 10, how hungry are you?"

Gut butterflies were killing her appetite. "I could eat…"

"Not what I asked."

"…but I'm not really hungry."

"Great." He grabbed the door handle.

"But if I don't eat, and we're hiking for hours, I might turn into a whiny little bitch. I don't tend to have breakfast."

"A woman who knows her limits." Nodding in approval, he got out.

"We are hiking!"

"Never said that." He smiled through his open door. "Help me with the food."

"Don't you want me to wait here while you get everything set up for a perfect, romantic picnic?"

"This isn't romantic." Jacob pushed the driver's seat forward and handed her a tote bag from the backseat. "It's only our first date."

* * *

"You are a big fat liar." Holly smirked from her spot on the soft red-and-white checked blanket. Their view of the lake was idyllic with only an occasional buzzing boat. The sky was clear and sunny. The air smelled scrubbed clean by pine trees, just waiting for someone to light a barbecue.

"Rude." Jacob's grin-eating dimple gave him away.

"This is amazing."

"Apology accepted." He swatted away a bee as she held up the brick of almond cheese; he nodded and got a cracker. "I pay attention."

She cut a slice. "Want some?"

"I am not eating that," he said, taking a piece of smoked cheddar. "It's an abomination."

"It's not bad."

Jacob raised an eyebrow.

"For fake cheese."

He nodded.

Holly took a pull from her water bottle and drank in the view.

Extending his palm, he flicked his fingers twice like Morpheus inviting Neo to battle. "Let me see your phone."

"What sort of police state do you think we're living in? Don't you need a warrant?"

"Just consent."

"Why do you want it?"

"You don't want to be surprised?"

"We've been over this."

His open hand waited.

She smiled. "Two truths and a lie."

Jacob considered her proposal, then extended his thumb. "I need to check your downloads for cat photos. Deal breaker." He pointed his index finger. "I want to install an app." His middle finger went next. "I'm deleting all your other male contacts because I'm an insecure, jealous man. Even names that might be male," he said, counting again. "Jamie, Pat, Chris... What's your dad's name? He can stay."

"Dean. He's under 'Dad.'" Holly grabbed an apple slice. "Hard pass."

"Your loss."

"Why do you want to put an app on my phone?" She bit.

"Sure you want to know?"

Chuckling, she covered her half-eaten apple bite. "You're not getting it unless you tell me, creeper."

"Geocaching app. Thought you might want to race."

* * *

At a fork in the pine-needled path, Holly consulted Jacob's phone for guidance and called, "This way!" She walked backward. "This is so fun!"

"I thought you'd like it." He smiled with his thumbs in his backpack straps. "You and Grace have a lot in common."

"Are you saying I'm immature?"

"Trying to pick a fight? Maybe." He was nodding.

She squinted at him, holding back her smile as best she could until she faced forward. An open stretch without roots or rocks let her enjoy the surrounding trees, taking a slow spin.

"It's gorgeous out here."

"Not a bad view." Jacob's grin was so darn hot. He could be hiding a compliment in there, although he must find beauty in nature given his hobby.

On the map, the red dot was still a way off, but she realized— "I'm missing a golden opportunity." She waggled his phone. "Will this tell me all your secrets?"

He took the phone, tapped it, and gave it back. "Weapons free."

His home screen photo was a silhouette of a dark brown moose in a river surrounded by reflections of crisp evergreens. A Holy Bible icon perched in the upper right corner.

"That's pretty. Did you take it?"

"Yep. Guardsman Pass."

"He looks so close."

"I was sure he was going to run and wreck the reflection. I zoomed in some. And a slow approach."

The air was loaded with soul-scrubbing pine and clean sunny earth, and the early afternoon sun that streamed through the tall trees kissed Holly's skin. What a perfect day to be alive, on a perfect date with a perfect gentleman. Part of her didn't want him to be a gentleman. She wanted him to back her up against a tree and kiss the hell out of her, splinters be damned.

Seriously. When was she going to have her own back? What about Danielle's idea, Meena's idea: no premarital sex? *Right. Like that would happen. Unless...* Jacob was Christian. Would he want to wait until marriage? *Christian men want Christians. Remember Samson and Delilah?* Her toes hit a rock and she stumbled.

Jacob's hand flew to her elbow. "You okay?"

She nodded, breathing through the adrenaline dump and the fleeting contact. "I'm just gonna say it."

"What?" He hefted the backpack.

"Is this missionary dating?"

He laughed, "What?"

"You're Christian, so…"

"Catholics are Christians."

He thinks I'm Catholic? The thought stole her breath like a fox with its claws wriggling in her heart's hen house. *From my stupid nun joke?*

"Everything okay?" he asked, waiting a couple of steps ahead.

"Nothing against Catholics," she said, trudging toward him, "but I like my wine to stay wine."

"Sorry. I know. You're formerly Unitarian, firmly agnostic, and currently exploring the idea that a creator with a mind might have made all this."

Oh, thank god. Of course, he didn't think she was Catholic.

"You okay?"

"Mm-hm."

"I'm glad you didn't join a nunnery." He rubbed her back as they walked.

"Has anyone told you you're a good listener?"

"Sorry, what?"

"Goof." After Holly pushed his arm, all she could think about was his solid, springy bicep.

"Any recent developments in your hard waffling? A little polytheistic whipped cream? Some Buddha berries?"

"Good thing we ate, or you'd be making me hungry. The waffle's gotten squishier, that's all."

"Now I'm hungry."

"Got any snacks in there?" As she reached for his backpack, Jacob spun to defend it.

"Don't change the subject," he smiled.

"Hang on." She trotted backward ahead of him. "You've never explained your coffee comment."

"Why I like coffee? What's not to like?"

"Amen to that. You said you didn't always believe in God. What's that about?"

"You'll have to stop walking like that first. If you trip, I might not be able to catch you—again." After she fell in step beside him, he said, "I grew up in the church. Boy Scouts. Mark and I used to do some pretty stupid shit, but we never got hurt. Really hurt. Like we were in God's pocket. Until college Biology."

"Biology?" she smiled.

"Got handed a steaming pile of horseshit and gobbled it up like pudding." His eyebrows scrunched. "There was no questioning Darwin. People say Christians have blind faith… Look at this." He threw out his arms. "It's so fricking intricate. Like the eye." When he stopped, she stopped with him. "Are yours blue or green?"

"Blue." His were gorgeous, officially now her favorite shade of green.

"Thought so."

They hiked in silence. Holly checked the phone. The dot was closer.

"I can stop ranting."

"No, I'm interested."

He sighed. "Doubt got the better of me. I got depressed. Criminal Justice made sense, so I went with that. Want to talk about sports?"

"What made you have faith again?"

"Evil." His hand wrapped around the back of hers, turning her on while he turned the screen to face him. "Not much farther." Letting go, he asked, "Doing okay? Need any water?"

A cold shower. She shook her head.

"I had no clue how evil people could be until I joined the force."

"My brother says evil isn't a thing. He's Christian, too. He says it's the corruption of something good."

"Exactly."

Swallowing her fear that this would elicit an irreconcilable difference, she asked, "Do you believe in adaptation and natural selection? There's evidence to support it."

"Sure. That's how God designed life: 'Improvise, Adapt, Overcome.'"

Like what I told Owen.

"Your turn. Squishy waffle time." A breeze pushed his scent her way. Blue jays yelled at each other.

"I was raised Unitarian. After my parents divorced, my mom stopped going. My dad went full Jesus when I was in high school. He ruined UU church for me. Said it was a spiritual salad bar where people picked out the bits of religion they liked and left all the hard truth stuff behind."

Jacob grinned. "Your dad sounds cool."

"He's fricking amazing. When I was little, I believed in God—not the Christian God necessarily, but I prayed and believed in a higher power who loved me. But I also believed in Santa and the Tooth Fairy. At one point, I had an imaginary friend named Betty. She was a centaur."

"Go big or go home."

"Not sure when Betty jumped ship."

"College?"

She played an invisible drum kit. "Ba-DUM-dum TSSS. I used to be sort of jealous of people I know who have strong faith. You guys have, like, an aura. Not saying y'all are perfect."

"Crap."

"My brother Brett was insufferable. Then he found Jesus and his wife, and now he's tolerable. Most of the time. Mark reminds me of him. Not in a bad way."

Jacob nodded. "Mark straightened up in the Air Force."

The phone hung forgotten as they walked. The Christmas photo at Vicki's house came to mind, with Jacob's arm around that beautiful woman. Was that his ex-fiancée? Did she break his heart? An ex of Paige's once told her that his ex-girlfriend was his one true love—a downright shitty move on his part, but it could happen. Remembering how wrecked Paige had been—her rock-solid Paige—Holly was tempted to take off down the path and send Jacob a goodbye note.

But electric warmth encircled her hand. His hulky hand looked like a dream around hers.

"This okay? Your gears were turning like you were about to take off."

A gear. That's what it felt like—the hot, solid locking of it. She'd shaken his hand before, but this clicked into a familiar and freaky belonging. Of course she couldn't share that, so the proximity of their goal was timely.

"Hey." She showed him the screen. "We're almost there."

A zipping airborne thing whirred right in front of them and stopped her, then Jacob. The coppery hummingbird assessed them with its big black eyes, then buzzed away. Holly waited, willing it to come back.

"If you tell anyone, I'll deny it," Jacob whispered, "but you're crushing my hand."

"Sorry!"

"Just have to get the blood circulating before I lose a finger."

Around the bend, a cluster of Ent-worthy Ponderosas welcomed them to the red dot on the map.

"What now?" she asked.

"See if there's a clue."

Clicking on it, she read, "Get back to your 'blank.'" Instead of asking his opinion, she yelled, "Roots!"

He chuckled. "That's the fastest I've seen anyone solve one of these. Good thing there are only a couple." A meshwork of tree roots surrounded them.

"Let's split up. I'll take this side of the path. You take that one."

"Yes, ma'am." He trudged left.

Past him at a rise in the hill was a massive trunk, like the wrist and fingers of a hand that had gotten stuck reaching into the earth.

"There," she called, pointing to it. "If I were hiding something, I'd hide it there."

He surveyed the truncated-hand trunk, then turned and held out his hand. She jogged up and took it. This time, his touch was only happiness. Satisfying, present-day happiness. They walked over the uneven ground until they stood beside the giant.

"Dang." Holly craned her neck to find the top of the enormous thing. One space under a root finger—more like a thumb—was almost tall enough for her to walk beneath. She approached it and put her hand against the bark.

"You go ahead. I'll look out here."

"Okay." Ducking into the aboveground root bulb, she crouched inside and gazed up at the burly roots. *So cool.* The twisted tentacle was powdery. The tree-being seemed undecided, as if it had been waiting to be fossilized but might rather vanish into dust. Jacob's boots came in and out of view as she searched the interior.

In a crevice, her fingertips touched metal. "Found something!"

Jacob barely fit under the burled wood canopy.

An Altoids tin came easily from the gap, and she smiled, holding it out to him.

"Do I need one?"

Inside the open box lay a golf pencil, a penny, and a tiny booklet containing names and dates and scrawled messages. "Our names go in here?"

"First names or initials," he said, unzipping his backpack.

In the tight space, his sweet, musky scent overwhelmed her. As she let herself inhale—she did have to breathe—she hoped she didn't stink. She wrote at the end of the list:

JD + HS, 7/9/16

Blushing at the plus symbol, she checked the stubby pencil: no eraser. When Jacob held out his hand, she closed the miniature book and handed it over, hoping he wouldn't open it, but he flipped to the last page.

"Glad you didn't carve it in the bark. Bad for the tree." Winking, he reached into the backpack. "You usually take something, leave something, but that's tight." He offered two closed fists, fingers down. "Choose. But choose wisely."

She tapped the back of his right hand; he turned it over and opened his fingers to disclose a tiny plastic unicorn.

"Grace has outgrown these guys."

"She's so mature." Holly took it. "I was still into unicorns at her age."

"And centaurs. Ballsy imaginary friend."

"Seraphina, my Palomino, was an upgrade, even from a centaur."

"You had a horse?"

"Still do. She's with my dad in Colorado."

"Did you tell Grace?"

"She was telling me about her gymnastics competitions, so I told her about show jumping."

"That explains My Little Pony here." He revealed a horse figurine and nodded at her toy. "That's from her dad calling you a unicorn—a woman you don't find every day."

Crouched in the charmed root arch, Holly tried to keep her face in check, but she was sure her smile shot through her pores.

CORA

SUNDAY, JULY 19, 2016

Beneath the foyer's lofty chandelier, Cora waited for an answer, holding open the tall front door. "Bye!" she yelled again, hovering between the central air laced with pancakes and the fresh breeze pungent from roses.

"Enjoy your walk!" her mom called back from the kitchen.

Click. Outside the door of the palatial yellow Victorian, the ground was littered with candy apple red petals, like a bed ready for romance. Cora wanted to laugh, "Where are all my candles?" since this was probably the closest she would get to such a gesture. Trailing her hand over the delicate railing for balance, she waddled down the steps.

As much as she loved her brother, she did not want to have breakfast with him, even though she was kind of hungry. Wes had been an unmitigated twit. No, she was not going to marry Aiden. No, she would not be wishing their dad Happy Grandfather's Day. And no, she wasn't going to get rid of her apartment since she didn't need a hook-up place anymore.

Although that was a harder decision. It would be cheaper to move back home, and she was already spending weekends there. But babies are loud and disruptive; she didn't want to walk on eggshells. And it would be even more disheartening to live as a single mother in her parents' house when she clearly needed to start adulting.

It was fortunate that the childbirth class didn't start until tomorrow, with Aiden in town to see his dad. He was so interested in the birth plan—she still hadn't read the latest article he'd sent her about water births—that she might have let him come. Yesterday hadn't been too terrible. Aiden looked even better than when he'd left for Seattle: happy, healthy, and most importantly not flirty. Still intense and serious when he'd asked her to tell him if she changed her mind—about anything—but not flirty.

From the downhill slope of Beryl Street, she turned onto Frontier.

Was staying the right thing? Maybe Seattle could have worked. Aiden was striking the perfect balance of helpful and distant as if agreeing to her terms to dance holding the opposite ends of yardsticks. He picked up on every inch of resistance she gave.

It had just been too much, too much change, the idea of moving away, trying to make University of Washington work with a new baby. When she pictured struggling alone there with a crying baby—a fouled-up version of her old fantasies, first as an independent woman and then as Aiden's partner—even the imagined misery was an impossible weight.

After Frontier Street joined the wood-chipped hiking trail through Ashley Creek Park, the water burbled from below. Smiling, she breathed in the cool air loaded with negative ions. High voices of children in the playground sang over the sounds of the creek.

Staying home was the right thing. She could count on her family; she couldn't count on Aiden. She couldn't even talk to him really. Cora had prayed for God to create an opportunity to ask him about drug use, whether he'd be willing to get counseling before she would leave him alone with the baby, but so far, nothing.

When the path reconnected to Frontier Street at the park's end, a family in dresses and ties was clambering into a car, muttering about being late. *Church. Maybe another day.*

Cora's favorite shoe store was beyond the plaza. Bright sale signs plastered the window where an orange "Mephisto" sticker loomed large. *Were Julie's still in the cave—if there had even been a cave?*

Then, the smell of bacon and eggs announced a hip-looking couple sitting at a diminutive patio table outside a painted restaurant window.

"You want this, don't you?" the man smiled.

His table mate grinned. "Yes, please."

Shaking his head, he asked, "Why don't you order your own?" and handed her a slice.

The woman ripped off a bite with her teeth, pointing to her mouth and shrugging as if an answer would have to wait because she did not want to be rude. Her oatmeal smelled nutty. Past them, Cora's stomach grumbled over the man mumbling to his friend.

Or girlfriend. Or wife. Things she might never be. The thought or the man's low voice, which reminded her of someone, made Cora nostalgic and sad, tangled in a net of lost futures.

Beside her on Gersham Street stood a grayish robed woman of stone, cupping her cheek with one hand. Her other hand lowered a long torch. It wasn't a fountain anymore; the water had been disconnected, but at one time the torch had touched down into it. Like Moses with his staff, redeeming bitter desert water for the Israelites to drink. That would have come in handy in Cora's desert. *Maybe a deworming stick.*

Jacob. Her toe scuffed the sidewalk. That's who the bacon man reminded her of: Jacob. There were good men in the world. Jacob would be a good boyfriend. And husband. And father. She wondered how he was doing, if he was happy. Did he have kids?

Flashing to piggyback rides, she was on Jacob's back, clinging to his capable, broad shoulders where she felt safer than she ever had with Aiden. And she flushed. Passing an older man walking his dog, she hoped the lust on her red face wasn't too obvious. She hated how she blushed—all splotchy and bright and public.

Her hormones had mellowed to a reality-based equilibrium by the time she reached the intersection on Pinyon Boulevard. Women's voices drifted across it while Cora hit the "Walk" button.

Two Hispanic women traipsed up a gravel driveway beside a sign for Alchemy Hot Yoga. Their dark hair trailed from messy ponytails, maybe even dripping onto their tank tops.

"Flex. I'm serious," the teenager smiled, pulling the older woman's wrist.

"No!" She chuckled and reclaimed her arm.

The girl gripped it. "You've got biceps like Terry from *Brooklyn Nine-Nine*."

The woman laughed harder. "I do not!" Opening the back of a silver 4-door, she tossed in rolled-up mats and towels.

The teen called from the passenger's side, "Honey lavender iced tea?" and grinned over the roof like she knew her bright smile was a key to unlocking things.

"Yes, Isabel. You earned it."

HOLLY

SATURDAY, AUGUST 6, 2016

Drumming her fingers on the open driver's window, Holly squinted at the coffee stand menu. She wanted something different from her usual black Americano, but the featured drinks were too sweet. At least they weren't pushing pumpkin spice yet.

An image from *Parks and Recreation* flashed in her head: Tom and Donna sporting hedonistic grins asserting, "Treat Yo Self!"

"Can I have a 16-ounce latte, please?"

"Anything in it?"

"No thanks."

A few minutes later, she parked at her clinic. *Half an hour. That's it.* After that, she was going to enjoy the rest of her Saturday. Her latte was almost too hot to hold, but she slung her pale turquoise purse over her gray zip-up and beeped the Mini locked, walking with purpose across the asphalt.

She didn't usually let herself get this behind in her notes and filing. But at least it was from daydreamy distractibility and not disheartened doldrums anymore.

Back in her car in record time, Holly made the short drive to the mall. Pulling her phone out of its dash mount, she double-checked her conversation with Jacob to make sure she didn't owe him a text. And just because.

His last text was a GIF video clip: the bobbing back of an upright small brown dog with floppy ears. Its front paws clutched a baby gate, its back legs trotted up and down at ridiculous angles and then hopped twice on a loop above:

Can't wait to see you!

Inside the mall, the Victoria's Secret window was plastered with larger-than-life photos of almost bare-naked ladies with their duck lips parted as they stared blindly at people. Some goth teens stared back. As Holly crossed the threshold, a preteen girl with her mother approached, and she wished she were invisible. By walking in, she became complicit in all the lies society was telling this girl about the importance of being sexy.

"Welcome in." The loud woman in her twenties wore all black and a fuchsia tape measurer draped like an untied scarf. "Can I help you find something?"

"I'm just looking." Holly browsed the bits of satin and lace and checked a price tag, then moved to the clearance section. A pink corset with sheer sides and glittery bra cups was exactly like the one she had thrown away after breaking up with Keith.

The pile of pretties at the bottom of her trash can had asked, "Aren't you going to regret this?" Her wallet did.

In the black and silver fitting room, she hung teddies and babydolls on the wall hook and deposited a heap of silky colorful things on the padded bench. Unfastening the button on her jeans met with more resistance than when she put them on. She scrutinized her stomach directly, then reflected.

The full-length mirror showed her protruding belly, low and hard and round. Holly prodded her bloated abdomen. She hadn't had a huge dinner last night or a shit ton of sodium—*the latte*. She had forgotten to take a Lactaid. *Trick or treat.*

The sight of her pregnant-looking self sent a warm thrill up her spine and she imagined Jacob standing behind her, wrapping an arm around his wife. *No future tripping.* The present was already amazing.

As she grabbed a cluster of red ribbons from the bench, the crotchless bodysuit tangled like a messed-up game of cat's cradle. *How does this thing even—?*

Marimba chords chimed, muffled from her purse, so she dug out her phone. It was her dad. Holly held her jeans to her chest and turned away from the mirror before answering.

"Hi, Dad."

"Hi. I only have a minute. Seraphina's sick."

"What's wrong?" She paced in the glitzy changing room.

"She's been off for a few days. I didn't want to worry you. I'll keep you posted."

"Thanks."

In the background, a hinge creak preceded faint barking. "Vet's here. I love you."

"Love you, too." The call ended before she hit the red button.

When Holly faced herself again, her slumped and bloated reflection resembled a Debbie Downer with no business in a lingerie store. What was she doing here anyway? *Time for another relationship roller coaster? Really?*

Jacob might not even be thinking about sex—he hadn't even kissed her yet. But they'd been seeing each other a month now, and kissing could lead to other things. Her cheeks flushed, remembering the long look he gave her after the last time he hugged her goodbye on her porch, refusing to come in. She knew he was into her. Once he came in, the clothes might come off, and she wanted to be prepared.

A bruised-up part of her was waving yellow caution flags. *Think.* She considered what Danielle had said about overused tape. She trusted Jacob—she'd cling hard if she could. Meena's "sex goggles" came to mind, but her eyes were wide open. Objectively he was a fantastic guy. All the promise she'd seen in his eyes the day they met had come true in spades: he was steadier, more self-assured, and more selfless than she could have imagined. He was funny and he thought she was, too.

Picturing bringing him around her friends and family made her proud as hell. She wanted to introduce him to her people. *Not mom.*

The mirror reciprocated her rudeness by reflecting her mother back to her: in her turquoise bra and thong, she resembled a grainy photo of Nanette on a beach. Holly paced to the wall hook and fondled the deep purple corset. Her mother would tell her to go for it. She'd wonder why Holly hadn't locked him in already.

The red pile of ribbons on the fitting room bench tempted her. She could always try it on and save it for later. Some of the lingerie was on sale. The phrase "Treat Yo Self" came to mind again. Didn't she deserve to have a couple of things she felt sexy in?

The sight of her phone prompted her: she should move up her trip to the ranch. Seraphina wouldn't live forever, and if she passed before she could say goodbye… "Life is short" offered another justification for spending money on sexy little things.

Pacing faced her toward the mirror again with her baby-bump-like belly. She wanted a family, love—not just sex. *Sex isn't love.* How mad would she be at herself if she walked, eyes wide open, into the same stupid pain? She and Jacob were getting to know each other. There was no guarantee this would last. Didn't her heart deserve to be protected?

Keith's broccoli sits unwanted on his plate.

"I need to protect my own heart. I don't know how to stay in a relationship with you and do that. Having sex with someone who might not love me anymore seems seriously unhealthy."

Having sex with Jacob would be just as unhealthy as sex without love with Keith. Jacob might not love her yet—he didn't love her—he couldn't—he didn't really know her yet.

Sex bonds people. Jacob might not be "the one," and if he weren't, then what? Tear herself away from him like tired old tape?

Holly snatched up her jeans and stepped in.

HOLLY

SUNDAY, AUGUST 7, 2016

Stupid tape. Perched on her white sofa in her baby blue robe, Holly shook her hand at the wrist, but the sticky folds stayed. She peeled the Scotch tape off her pinkie, wadded the transparent strip into a boogery ball, and wiped it on the corner of her coffee table. The passive-aggressive wrapping paper triangles eased apart, revealing the box of binoculars.

The room was dim, with only the kitchen light on behind her and the bit of evening sun welcomed in through the billowy curtains.

Her phone chimed. She rose, tossing the flimsy tape dispenser which bounced and clattered through a slat. *Seriously.* The ringing led her around the sofa to the kitchen.

Jacob

She tried to think of something witty but drew a blank. "You pretty much suck at the hard-to-get thing," she said from the black metal stool.

"Holly?" It was Grace.

"I'm sorry, Grace. I expected your uncle. How are you?"

"Want to see Pete's Dragon with us this Saturday?"

"I would love to, but I'll be out of town." The calendar on her white refrigerator was clear on August 20th. "Can we go the week after?"

"I'll ask Mom. Here."

"Break hearts much?" Jacob's smoky voice made her want to eat his words.

"You're the one who put her on the phone."

"What's your excuse? Washing your cat doesn't fly."

"How about visiting my sick horse?" She meandered toward the window above the sink.

"Shit. Sorry. The Jackass Award goes to…"

"You're not a jackass."

"She must be old."

"Are you saying I'm old?"

"I'm not a stupid man, Samson."

"True." She fingered the feathery fennel plant in the white pot on her windowsill. "Both true."

"I need to get something to you before you go."

"What?"

"A thing for your dad. Thought I had more time before you left for his birthday."

He got Dad a gift? "You have an amazing memory."

"When do you leave?"

"Saturday morning."

"Quick drink Friday night?"

HOLLY

FRIDAY, AUGUST 12, 2016

Following the hostess through the darkish brewery, Holly dodged a darting busser.

"Sorry." As the young man scuttled past, Jacob's hand flattened on the small of her back, securing her close beside the island of him while two more black-shirted twenty-somethings flowed by.

Its warmth penetrated her silk blouse until they reached the rectangle of light where the hostess disappeared.

Holly only had a moment to miss his hand before she stopped inside the door frame, blinked against the light, and discovered herself in sweet, delicious radiance. Light glistened from the grid of square, lacquered tables enclosed by decorative fencing. Overhead, the vibrant early evening sky showcased flowering vines that twisted around thin beams, stretching as if they longed to meet in the center. Big round string lights had their own ideas for lines and ran diagonally from their wood counterparts. In the distant corner waited the hostess, not even trying to look patient.

"Where did you find this place?" Holly asked, stepping into the sunny sanctuary.

"Here."

She chose ogling over banter and walked past a group of diners at a line of joined tables. The stained wood tabletops glowed with white candles. Some summery honeyed scent evoked childhood.

At the corner table, Holly started to sit before Jacob slipped behind her.

"Did you want this one?" she asked.

But he gripped the chair's back, ready to push her in.

"Who says chivalry is dead?" she smiled, and accepted the favor, smoothing her black skirt.

The reserved sign took off. "Your server will be with you shortly."

"Thank you." Holly savored the trellised patch of sky until Jacob handed her a happy hour menu, pulled back his thin, olive-green sweater sleeve, and checked his watch.

"Seven minutes. Let me know if you want something. I'll hunt down a waiter."

She already had a full plate of happy. "I can't believe I didn't know about this place."

He smiled at his menu.

She ignored hers. "Speaking of pretty places, your house is adorable. I have a thing for red tiled roofs."

"Glad you like it. Next time, I'm driving." He was a little big for her Mini.

"When did you buy it?"

"December 2011. Still at Mountaindale P.D. Commute was great."

She did the math. That would be around the time of the Christmas photo.

"Nature trail's up the street," he smiled. "No geocache, but we could plant one."

Wanting to ask if he had lived in that house with his ex-fiancée, she pretended to read the menu instead.

"It's big for two—Girlfriend and me. And she's a big girl. I bought it with April, planning on kids. She didn't want the house when we called it."

"Did you two live there?" she asked the handsome, mind-reading open book before her.

He shrugged. "Couple months."

195

"What happened? Unless you don't want to talk about it."

"Not right for each other. April's great, married now. We both agree we dodged a bullet."

His ex is great? Not crazy, not a bitch, not all the horrible things her exes had said about their exes before her. Talking with Jacob reminded her of running over rocks in the stream near her dad's house: each solid step forward was exhilarating. But here, the stakes were higher than wet shoes.

"Is she in that Christmas picture in your parents' room?"

"Yeah." Jacob smiled, then nodded at the menu. "Anything look good?"

Besides him? "I haven't looked."

"No rush. Your options are limited. Most of the apps are cheesy." He set down the menu. "Dinner?"

The waning sun made the lights pop: beads of it swept overhead and around the fence, flames flickered on the tables, and red coils glowed in the coppery heat lamps.

"That's horrific." Holly's fork full of salad drooped.

"Stabby McStabberson's not the best dinner conversation. Victim made it, though. Your turn."

Letting the fork rest in peace, she clasped her hands. Was she really doing this? Dates should be casual, flirty. Enticing, not depressing. But she wanted to. Part of it was to wave him off, warn him that he might be in the presence of the new and not-much-improved version of her mother, Nanette 2.0, for his sake and hers. But he was like sunshine: he made her want to strip off things. Clothes, yes, but mostly—tonight—defenses.

"My worst day this year was finding out I'm a bastard."

"Doesn't work on multiple levels." Jacob pointed an accusing sweet potato fry. "You're a sweetheart for one thing. And your Adam's apple is way too small." He popped the whole fry in his mouth: case closed.

"My mom cheated on my dad. An earlier time I didn't know about. Her cheating's why they got divorced when I was eight. That's one we could do: Words That Make Your Skin Crawl. 'Affair.' That's mine. 'Affair' makes me think of a beautiful long-haired woman in a big-brimmed hat at a fancy horse race, and then she turns around and has a skeleton face."

His eyes were wide and sympathetic as he swallowed.

That went dark. She picked at her salad. "I don't know who my mom banged, but he has Spanish ancestry. I found out doing a DNA test to see if I had any genetic health issues besides my lactose intolerance."

"When?"

"March 31st."

Jacob's chair's feet scraped the polished concrete as he came and stood beside her. She studied his face, but he was looking toward her plate while his hot hand slid over the back of hers and grasped the fork she held. Smooth, rounded metal began to pull, slipping against her skin. Apparently, some wires got crossed in her somatosensory cortex because the sensation between her fingertips and her thumb transferred to other places.

Clink. Once she was deforked, his hand was back, enveloping hers and pulling her to standing. His eyes were so intense that she hardly registered his arms wrapping around her until she had to turn her head. Her arm glanced off something bulky above his belt. Jacob's warm hand cupped her head and held her in.

His heartbeat was strong and steady and beautiful, picking up its pace a bit while he stroked her back. When he kissed her head, she thought she was going to melt in a puddle right there in the restaurant. At least they were outside—a busser could hose off her remains. But seriously, the painful burn gripping her heart threatened to make her cry or come or explode somehow.

"The worst part is, I can't even roll my 'R's. Shouldn't that be a perk of Spanish descent?" Holly thought he might pull away, but he didn't. "If this whole detective thing doesn't work out for you, you should consider a career in professional hugging."

"Clientele couldn't afford me."

"It's a very nice hug, don't get me wrong, but…" She was about to joke about giving him a big head but caught the potential pun in time to be quiet, though not in time to avoid heat rushing to her face.

"I'm only willing to hug a handful of people. Have to charge a fortune if I want to pay my mortgage."

"Makes sense." She nodded up at him, straight-faced, her arms around the small of his back. When she realized the bulk was a gun holster, she found she didn't mind.

"Simple economics."

The waiter squeezed by them with drinks for another table.

"This is $75/minute. That's with the friends and family discount." His green eyes were like candy.

Crack candy. "Can I start a tab?"

"How's your credit?"

Holly tipped her head side to side. "On second thought, my neck already has a crick in it from the inferior quality of your service, so…"

His low laugh rumbled onto her.

"Excuse me." The waiter skirted by again.

Jacob tapped out. "You win that round. Let me know if you want a neck rub later," he said, pulling out her chair.

"Are all cops this forward?"

"Just trying to avoid small claims court." He smiled across the table.

Not the least bit hungry for food, she stabbed leafy greens and a chunk of chicken. "Most Bizarre Vacation." She scooped the smaller bits.

"Last July. Hands down," he said, and sipped his beer.

"Spill." Her bite of apricot and chicken and walnuts was surprisingly delicious. "Mm." The walnut crunched between her teeth with the chewy fruit sliver and the sweet, tangy…what was that juiciness, orange? Holly opened her eyes.

He was grinning.

She pointed her fork at her plate, chewing, and covered her mouth. "Real quick. Can you go back to the kitchen and flash your badge? Say you need this dressing recipe for a case you're working on?"

With a stern nod, he pushed back, but she reached and grabbed his hand, shaking her head.

"Last July," she smiled. "I promise I won't be too distracted by this paradise in my mouth."

When he pulled his chair back in, his face got closer, and his powerful green eyes locked onto hers right as she was wondering what he tasted like. He studied his beer, picked it up, and sipped it slowly, looking not at Holly. She drank some water. Chairs squeaked as a couple nearby got up from their table.

"Ever been to Hellfire Canyon Trail? A few hours south?"

She shook her head.

"Beautiful. Brutal but beautiful. That's where that picture at my folks' house is from."

"Right." *Conversation.* "Purple Flower in Orange Rock."

"I'd taken those shots earlier. I'm about ready to pack up, and I hear someone calling."

"Ooh." She settled in for a mystery.

"Keep in mind, that's not a popular spot. Hadn't seen another vehicle out there the whole afternoon. I turn around, and a girl's standing there."

"A cute girl?" She wiggled her eyebrows.

"Could've been cute under the dirt. Her hair got me first: orange, like a desert nymph had emerged from the rock."

"What was she doing out there?"

"Tagging along with her sister, who was having a bad mental health day."

"Yikes."

"Guess what she was wearing—or not wearing."

"Is this a romance or not?"

"Not."

"Pulling a Lady Godiva? Naked, without a horse?"

"No shoes."

"What?"

"Barefoot. She'd given her shoes to her sister, who'd ditched hers."

"Shit."

He nodded.

"That's love right there. I think you win."

"Not done."

"Oh."

"I get her into town for medical care. Her feet are all effed up. Next morning, I tag along with Search and Rescue for the sister. Not every vacation ends in a helicopter ride."

"Ooh."

"We're up there. I'm showing the pilot where I think she might be. And we see her."

"Yay!"

"Not yet. Guess what she did?"

"She had antiaircraft weapons."

"You're good at this game." Jacob grinned.

Holly flourished her hand, bowing. "Thank you."

"She ran."

"From rescue?"

He nodded.

"Did you save her?"

"After a while."

"You should call up your old Boy Scout troop leader. There has to be a badge for that."

The sky had darkened, brightening the lights. Resting her elbow on the mostly empty table, Holly propped her chin in her hand and savored the glittering view. When she shifted to smile at Jacob, he was already smiling back.

"Thanks for cheering me up. This was amazing."

"Dessert's coming. Don't forget, your dad's gift is in your backseat."

"What is it?"

"A surprise."

"I won't tell him."

An elongated triangle of chocolate truffle cake drizzled with caramel landed between them. The waitress set down two spoons before leaving.

"Is it a book?"

He smiled.

"It's a book."

He loaded his spoon with a bite of torte.

"What kind?"

"You tell me," he said, lifting the bite to her mouth.

Holly wrapped her fingers around his hand and overturned the spoon, so her tongue wiped it clean.

When he stared at it, she gulped down her bite without tasting it and offered him her clean one. "You can have mine."

But Jacob tucked it to his breast as if it were Gollum's ring. "Good work." He turned it in the dim light. "This stuff's sticky as hell. How is it?" he asked, carving a bite for himself.

"You tell me." She smirked while he inverted his spoon to eat it.

"It's no Samson's apple pie. It'll do."

"The pie was okay? I'm glad I didn't switch salt for sugar or anything." Holly shaved off a bit of torte.

"Wouldn't say that."

She frowned.

"Better than okay. Grace is excited about the movie playdate. Let me know if you want her to leave you alone at some point. I'll let her down gently."

"No way. I've been jonesing for kid time, and so far, no hits on fostering." Caramel and chocolate lit up her nerve endings. "It's my fault. I said I only want to foster babies."

"Tag me in if you need help with that."

Thank god he was looking at the dessert and not at her. She covered her mouth to say, "Seriously?"

"Not volunteering to move in." He chased a toffee nugget with his spoon. "But I could help you get a decent night's sleep once in a while."

* * *

Shifting gears as she drove him home from the brewery, Holly's arm brushed against Jacob's black jacket. The smell of leather and the scent of him was too much. She tasted lingering chocolate on her tongue and wondered if he tasted like chocolate, too.

Poor guy was slouched in the Mini Cooper's passenger seat so that his head didn't skim the hardtop.

"Are you sure you're not cutting off your circulation? That does not look comfortable."

"It's not," he chuckled. "Next time we're taking my car."

Cringing, she sucked air through her teeth. "About that."

"I thought you had a good time. Dump me anywhere off this road, then." He pointed out the windshield. "Good-looking ditch up ahead."

"It's not you." She maintained the firm-but-sympathetic front. "It's just, I met someone else who I really click with. She likes Disney movies, I like Disney movies. She likes animals, I like animals…"

"She acts like she's 12, you act like you're 12."

Holly gave the side of his denim leg a baby backhand and then rubbed it in apology.

"Oh my word." She squeezed his thigh—or tried to. "Why can't I get ripped like this? I work out."

Jacob's hand slipped over hers. Her heart rate was alarming, and she caught her speed and pulled up from the gas pedal. Getting into a wreck—that's where she was heading. It could be a forbidden fruit thing; he might only feel like the most mind-blowing guy she'd ever dated because she'd decided not to have sex with him yet. Was she really going to hold herself to that? *I mean, come on.*

Ice cream. He's ice cream.

That made her think of chocolate on his tongue again, and she burned to taste him.

Nope. What do we do with ice cream?

Keep it out of the fricking house.

Right. She didn't usually have trouble making small talk, but the rest of the drive was hot and quiet.

"Right up here." He pointed to his driveway.

After she pulled up to his tidy stucco on the hill, she left the Mini's motor humming since hers was redlined.

The seatbelt zipped off him with a click. His door opened, triggering the dome light, and he hung his leg out to the cement.

"Come meet Girlfriend." Jacob's warm hand rested on her thigh, and he rubbed the slick material of her black skirt. "I have a lint roller if she gets you."

"I have an early flight." Holly blinked at the dash clock, then her wristwatch. That was reasonable, right? She wasn't being too cold. He had to know she liked him.

When she dared a glance at him, he was studying her face.

Please don't ask why I'm not getting out of the car to give you our standard (amazing) hug.

His gaze dropped to her lap where her hands were, and he pulled her left palm to his mouth, imprinting his lips like a branding iron, a burning rose. As he exhaled, his breath feathered over her skin, sparking a new rush of heat, and reminding her that her brain really needed some oxygen.

Her sharp inhale skimmed her taut vocal cords in a happy sigh so loud it startled her. It sounded like sex.

And those eyes she'd seen across the table were back. They stayed with her as he pulled his leg back into the car, slammed the door, and reached his hand around her neck. As his long fingers bloomed up through her hair, and her eyes closed, he kissed her—cheek.

The dome light dimmed off. His fingertips trailed, tracing her left clavicle, and lifted off at the horseshoe gap between the opposing bones. Holly was frozen, hot, and blind.

"Why is it—" Jacob kissed her ear. "—that on patrol—" Behind her ear. "—I could get people—" Her hairline. "—to step out of their cars—" The side of her neck. "—no problem." He kissed her right collarbone. "But you—"

Her lips were aching. She flipped toward him, kicking the gas pedal, and the car revved.

"Oh!" She gasped, inches from his face.

"Good thing this was on." He patted the erect handbrake between them, then reached to the steering wheel and turned the key. "Safety first."

The car went quiet. Her body was screaming. His smile dimmed to something sweet and serious as he brought his hand to touch her chin, watching her eyes and then her lips as he closed in for their first kiss.

So much better than chocolate.

HOLLY

"Here's a bathrobe. Sorry I don't have a smaller one."

Holly hugged the plush, navy terrycloth mass and smiled at her dad—such a cowboy with his big mustache.

"It's perfect." The creamy shag rug of the guest bedroom was silky beneath her feet.

"I put fresh towels in the bathroom. Need anything else before you tuck in?"

She shook her head, scanning the room. The deep brown wood of the walls, the square frame of the bed canopy, the floor, and the raised ceiling complemented the clean white of the comforter, the lamp shades, and the cushion on the button-accented bench that spanned the foot of the bed. Her suitcase sprawled out on the taupe armchair in the corner.

"No, that should…" The package from Jacob, wrapped in twine and simple paper, sat on top of her suitcase. "Oh!" She brought it to her dad. "This is from a friend of mine. You can wait to open it with your other presents, but I'm dying to know what it is. You're okay celebrating a week early, right?"

"Of course. I'm glad we can all be together. Which friend?"

"Jacob. You haven't met him. He's a cop."

"Not weed then."

"Dad!" she laughed.

He shrugged and said, "I should try it for my glaucoma…"

"Open it." Sitting on the padded bench, she added, "Please."

Her dad put the parcel on his lap. Unfolding the paper revealed the back of a masculine mahogany picture frame. He turned it over.

It was a black-and-white photo of Holly. The contrast made the sparkler and the string lights pop, vibrant. She hadn't known he was taking a picture when she was dancing with Grace on the 4th of July. It seemed vain to stare at herself, but she couldn't help it. It was somehow Jacob she was looking at: Jacob seeing her. Her dad was smiling.

"Jacob, huh? Please tell him 'Thank you.'" His eyes tightened as he lifted the photo from his lap. "I haven't seen you smile like this in a while."

Holly hadn't seen her dad smile like that in a while. She slipped her arm around his rough flannelled back, his wrapped around her shoulder. Her brain had known nothing had changed since the Barcelona reveal, but her heart was late to the game. It had been telling her, "Fine. It's fine. Everything is fine." But apparently, her heart had been a deceitful little bitch, because now it was sucking in love like love was air and it had been drowning.

Breathing deeply, she smiled, and her dad squeezed her shoulders. It was good to be home.

That night, Holly stirred, restless through no fault of the very cozy bed. Throwing on her white puffer jacket, she tiptoed to the back door and slipped on her dad's rubber boots.

The stable's faint funk welcomed her home: clean wood chips, musky horse body, and mucky horse poop. The brisk night air cut the usual harsh hints of ammonia. It helped that there was only one resident, with Astrid and Abba staying at a friend's during Seraphina's quarantine. As Phina's pained wheezing got louder, Holly's chest got tighter.

She put on a brave face and peered over the stall gate to the beam of light shining on the haunches of her golden horse lying on her side. "There's my girl." Making a quick stop in the tack room for a couple of heavy blankets, she left the light on and the door cracked. The hinge creaked as she passed through the gate. "How's my sweet Seraphina?"

Slow raspy breaths answered.

Not well. She unfurled a blanket behind Seraphina's head, then sat and used the folded one as a pillow.

"That's my girl. Easy." Holly stroked the huge neck and heaving chest. "It's okay." A rattle in Phina's lungs drove a tear down her cheek. "I'm here."

Laying with her front pressed against the horse's back, mane hair tickled her nose. At first, she draped her arm around Seraphina's side but then moved it onto her own hip so she wouldn't make breathing any harder than it was. Eventually, she slept.

HOLLY

Clack. Creak.

Holly blinked awake to the gate closing and her dad's footsteps. She smiled into the dark pre-dawn light and held a straight arm up toward the stall entrance over Seraphina.

"I thought I'd find you here."

No more labored breathing. "Dad! I think Phina's getting—" She placed her hand on her withers: cold. "No." Jumping to her knees, she planted her palms on Seraphina's side. "No no no no no." She threw her arms around the dead horse and buried her face in her mane.

Seraphina's body was there—where was the rest of her? Holly wanted to run after her sweet feisty spirit, yelling, "Hey! You forgot something!"

Her dad's hand hugged her shoulder.

The rooster's crow hurt.

* * *

The morning birds were gentler and more understanding when she finally sat on the front porch, huddled in her puffer jacket and plaid PJs. Leaning back in the teak armchair, she listened to the dawn chorus.

Her gratitude journal splayed open, offering two big blank pages to hold her grief. Her spine stung a bit against the hardwood, but pain was unavoidable today. The door creaked.

"Glad to see you're using that. Here you go." Her dad held two steaming coffee mugs, extending one.

"Thanks. I love it." She set her leather-bound journal on the side table, hanging it slightly off the edge to leave room, and brought the hefty mug to rest at her chest and raised knees. "Definitely an upgrade from my last one. Don't tell Brett, but it was my favorite birthday present."

"I got non-dairy creamer. Can I bring you some?"

"No thanks. It's fantastic as is."

He pulled his Bible from beneath his arm, cozy in the flannel coat.

Holly blew on her coffee and then surveyed the valley, green and pink, serene, and full of slow, steady life.

"I think she was hanging on to say goodbye."

"Thanks for calling me." She sighed. "I'm glad I got to be with her."

Birds zipped through the rosy glowing sky.

The valley was brighter and her coffee was colder when her dad set down his Bible and got up from the big wooden chair. On the page in Holly's lap, Seraphina's head was taking shape.

"Want a warm-up?" He lifted his empty mug, smiling through his bushy mustache.

"No thanks."

Instead of going in, he planted his free hand on her shoulder and studied her sketch. "I've always said you have my artistic talent."

"Does your heaven have horses in it?"

"Heaven has all God's creatures. Or the New Earth. They're part of His creation, which was good before we let sin in."

"Why do humans have to take the fall for that?"

"For The Fall?" he smirked.

"If God made us and he knows everything, he'd know we'd screw it up. So, it's on him."

Her dad stepped back, eyeing the porch's wood ceiling.

"See? No lightning. Maybe he knows I'm right."

"Brett said you're reconsidering whether creation is a myth."

"It's worth thinking about." In her lap, the slope of Seraphina's nose, her pointy ears, her mane conjured up the fluid power of Seraphina's muscled grace beneath her. "I see some evidence of a creator, but that doesn't mean I believe in God—your god."

Her dad's crinkly eyes twinkled. Holly admired him, tan and happy, while she waited for him to argue.

Finally, she shrugged. "I might be Jewish."

"You should enjoy the Old Testament then." Stepping to the end table, he slid his Bible close to her. "My favorite book's Ecclesiastes."

"What's the shortest book?"

"Third John. That's New Testament. I don't know the shortest Old Testament book offhand."

"How many Johns are there?"

"See for yourself. You could try a chronological reading plan."

"How about alphabetical? Is that a thing?"

"You can figure it out." His bristly smooch on her head tickled her scalp. Then he patted her shoulder, going in.

Holly breathed in the cool, fresh air. Jacob would like it out here. It was so wonderful, having him to miss. There might be something to Meena's "sex goggles" theory. Knowing his lips were hundreds of miles away helped her ratchet down her lust a bit, freeing her to think about the other things she loved about him.

Did she love him? She'd already told Keith she loved him by this point, over a month in. Of course, she and Keith were having sex and Jacob hadn't ventured past first base. He was incredible at first base. *Easy there, Lusty.* She inhaled more cool, clean air. She loved how slow he was taking things—now that she was away and not aching for him.

Brett's "Lust-aid" packet came to mind, so she doodled a rectangle in the bottom right corner of her gratitude journal. He had said love was putting the team before the self. Was she taking her brother seriously? A block "L" formed in the sketched outline.

She didn't want to be selfish like her mom.

Be kind.

Fine. She didn't want to be selfish. Could she be a good partner if she and Jacob became a team? She was a good cook. She had a decent work ethic. She was thoughtful. She liked to help. She would pop out babies and love on them, change all the diapers if she had to, and raise them to be good little girls or boys or both—

Like Owen? Christian, like Owen? Would Jacob be okay with her sharing her doubts if she supported them exploring Christianity? Would she be okay raising kids to respect a Christian father who held fast to an old book that got a lot of bad press? How bad was it?

The front door creaked. "Stay out here as long as you want, but I could use your help with some blueprints. My new neighbor wants a treehouse for his grandkids."

"Treehouse?" She was up. "I want one."

HOLLY

Having a little human in Holly's kitchen felt incredibly right, like the vegetables in their places in the white ceramic tray.

"What was your favorite part?" Grace poured ranch dressing into the center bowl.

Whisking the peeler around the carrot spindle, she said, "That's a tough one."

"The part where you cried?" she asked, capping the bottle.

"You saw that, huh?" Holly smiled. "Hey, can you put those napkins on the table for us? I'm almost done with the—"

Jacob walked into the kitchen and clomped up to her, removing first the peeler, then the carrot from her hand.

"Can I help you?" she laughed up at him.

He pulled her into a hug.

"You okay, buddy?" Holly patted his back. "Grace, what's wrong with your uncle?"

Craning her neck, she examined him. "Did the movie make you sad, too?"

"I'm being selfish," he said. "Can Grace smell your head?"

"What?"

"I should have asked, too. Sorry."

Holly smiled a bewildered nod-shake.

After he scooped up Grace, he placed a hand on Holly's shoulder.

"Hold still or we'll break her nose. Smell that?"

Poking her perky nose onto her head, Grace said, "I smell summer."

"I'm with you." Holly plucked up a carrot. "It's coconut. Reminds me of suntan lotion. Why your uncle is obsessed with it…"

He shook his head. "Wrong."

"It's my shampoo—"

"It's brains."

"What?" Holly laughed.

Grace considered it, then pushed off her uncle's hip. "You're silly," she giggled as he eased her down to standing. "'Brains.'"

"Good call, Grace." She resumed peeling.

Jacob frowned matter-of-factly. "Some people with enormous brains smell like coconut. It's science."

"What is going on?"

"Nice journal." He grinned.

"What? Oh."

"Sorry," he said, taking her hand. "I thought it was fair game like a coffee table book. Then I couldn't look away."

"I want to see!"

"That okay?"

After Holly shrugged, he led them from the kitchen to the light gray sofa beside the front window, putting Grace between them. On the white pallet coffee table, the broad open pages of her gratitude journal displayed a sketched horse head and scattered bits of writing.

Grace pulled it onto her lap, but Jacob kept a hold of one corner, covering the tiny "Lust-aid" packet she'd drawn. His other arm stretched over the back of the sofa.

"Is that Seraphina?" Grace's finger hit a tear-drop stain by the biggest sketch.

"Mm-hm."

"You're a very good drawer." Sunlight from the window lit up her smile.

"Thanks. I drew a lot of horse heads as a kid."

"What's this?" She pointed to a block of writing:

The Matrix of Existence

In the beginning | God | created | the heavens | and the earth. – Genesis 1:1

TIME | FORCE | ACTION | SPACE | MATTER
– Herbert Spencer, physicist

"I copied that from a wall hanging my dad carved."
"What does this mean?"

Second Law of Thermodynamics = Sin?

"What's thermodynamics?" Her little mouth had no problem with the big word.

"Complicated." Holly laughed.

"Why things in the world get disorganized." He had hit the essence of it with zero mansplaining.

Grace nodded. "Will you show me how to draw horses?"

"Sure."

Jacob smiled, rubbing Holly's shoulder.

CORA

"She has your hair." Cora smiled at Aiden, which was easier than yesterday since he was looking at Naomi and not at her. And because she wasn't in labor. And because her mother wasn't there staring murderously at him until he handed over the hot rock the doula had recommended for Cora's lower back and finally left the hospital room.

Naomi was so tiny cradled in his arms. He looked overcome. His dark, draping hair obscured his eyes, but even from her partially reclined bed, Cora could tell Naomi was rocking his world. Maybe even as much as she had rocked hers.

She reluctantly let her eyes close. *Joy.* Naomi was joy. She brought joy. Like that verse in the book of James.

"I hoped she'd have your hair until I saw her," Aiden whispered from the chair. "She's perfect."

The nurse in pink scrubs was back with the flowers he had brought. "Sorry, folks. I couldn't find a vase, but this should do for now. Here by the window?"

"That's perfect," Cora smiled. "Thank you."

After the older woman deposited the giant plastic mug with the bouquet, the morning sun lit up the budding peach roses and the broad pink lilies.

Turning, she surveyed them and said, "You're such a beautiful family." Then she marched out calling, "Congratulations!"

The awkward silence broke with Aiden's nod at the gift on the tray table. "Do you want to open it? It's for Naomi."

"Sure." Inside the pink and white paper was a thick, dark blue book with a full moon holding the words: "Under the Same Moon: A Story for Loved Ones Near and Far." A small fox and a big fox gazed up at it.

"It's recordable, so she can hear my voice."

Cora turned it over, blinking.

"Is that okay?"

She knew what he meant: did she mind having him invade their space? It was his eyes that sometimes hurt her, not when he smiled, but occasionally if they were serious.

"This will be great for her. We'll video chat between visits, too." Because his eyes were too much—longing and sad—she studied the back of the book. "Thank you."

"You'll tell me if you change your mind about Seattle?"

"It's just best for us to be close to family right now."

Aiden bowed over Naomi, cradled and tiny in his arms. "The *Fort Herring Gazette* is looking for a reporter."

"What? No. You can't leave *The Seattle Times* for that!"

He shrugged.

"No. Please, don't."

Finally, he looked at her. "When are your parents coming back?"

Her mother's last text had read: **Let us know when he's gone.**

"Later."

"Do you think they'll ever forgive me? Not that I blame them. If I were your dad, I'd kill me."

Cora glanced at the open door and said, hushed, "Please stop apologizing. Remember, they don't know everything."

HOLLY

The creamy silk of the wedding dress was absolute paradise. After Holly removed it from the rod and hung it over the others, she brushed her fingers within the plunging halter top. It was just as smooth inside.

"I think I found the one!" Paige called.

Tucking the silky treasure between its racked sisters, Holly strode to the area reserved for bridal parties. She smiled at Paige's mom in the chair across the furry white rug as she sat beside Meena on the low sofa.

"Courtney isn't coming?" Paige's mom asked.

"She was called in to work," Meena said, as the curtain to the changing room whooshed open.

"Here she is!" The smiling salesgirl stepped aside.

It looked like a sexed-up Sleeping Beauty dress with a thick below-the-shoulder band waving inward toward a plunge in the center where Paige's magnificent breasts peeked through.

"You look gorgeous," Holly smiled.

Meena nodded. "It's perfect."

"Classy, but hot," Holly added. Any joke about Paige finally showing some skin had to wait since her mom was there.

Paige evaluated herself in the mirror. "Not too much air for the twins?"

"On your wedding day?" Holly settled into the sofa. "Weapons free."

"Mom, what do you think?"

"I thought you wanted something with more lace."

Paige's smile faltered.

"Are you wearing a veil?" the salesgirl asked.

"I was thinking just some white flowers or beads or something in my hair."

"What about a lace wrap?" the young woman asked. "Let me show you a couple."

After she left, Paige studied her reflection, turning and smoothing the A-line skirt. "Do you think this will hide the baby?"

"Let's see." Meena stood, then pinched the loose material at her back. "Paige, you look so beautiful. Seriously."

The salesgirl returned holding an armful of holes and smiled at Paige in the mirror.

"Can we go up a couple more sizes and tailor the heck out of it for the baby belly?" Paige asked.

"You got it. We'll have you come in again two weeks before the wedding and take it in. Here's the wrap."

Paige's mother sprang from her chair and took it, covering her daughter's pearly shoulders and chest. The lace acquiesced to gravity voluntarily, possibly out of respect. While she fought to get the thing in line, over Paige's cleavage, Holly spaced out, reminded of last weekend.

I unzip my hoodie, baby-wipe my pits, and put on more deodorant. I start to zip back up at my bathroom mirror, but sports bras are clothes. It's my fricking house. And I want Jacob to kiss me again like he did in his driveway.

He's standing in my living room in his running gear, looking out my front window while he chugs his water.

"I could make us breakfast if you're hungry."

When he turns, I swear he almost does a spit-take. He smiles and dabs his chin on his shirt. Then he finds a coaster for his glass (thoughtful man) before he comes closer.

Damn, I love his smile. I want to dive into his eyes and hang out there all day. And I want to run my hands over his stubbly cheeks. Not just my hands. He steps so close I think he's about to touch my waist. I can't breathe—and not just because I'm flexing my stomach a bit.

"You'll have to show me how you got those sometime." He zips up my hoodie, all the way up to the middle of my neck.

I'm surprised he doesn't pull the hood over my fricking head and tie it around my nose. "These?" I clutch my boobs.

He laughs. I love his laugh.

"Your abs. Your workout routine."

"That makes more sense. Your chest is perfect the way it is— without boobs." I pat it with both hands and let them stay.

"I don't want those. On me, I mean." He sighs and shakes his head. "I'm gonna go." He rubs my shoulders.

"Pilates. For your core."

"Are you calling me fat?"

I can't stop rubbing his chest. "You do have man boobs."

"Wow."

"Nice firm ones."

He's shaking his head and killing me with that smile. "Pick you up at 6 o'clock for dinner?" He kisses my frustrated forehead. "Go shower, you stinky woman."

"I'm not stinky! I just—am I?"

I'm about ready to sniff my armpit when his hands are on my waist, and he's picking me up. I squeak. All I can do is brace myself on his shoulders and clamp my legs above his hips. I'm looking down at him for once.

I grin. "You're early."

He would do fine carrying her across a threshold. *Hypothetically.* It scared her how much she wanted him—forever-wanted him. This time had to be different. She had to make it different. She liked that Jacob hadn't told her he loved her yet. Of course, part of her yearned to hear it but the waiting made it mean more.

What would it be like to wait for sex until a wedding night? The back of Paige's dress had a marathon procession of old-school buttons. Holly imagined herself in the dress with Jacob behind her, giving his attention to each deliberate undoing. She shivered.

The smooth goddessy thing on the distant rack would come off faster. Her face roasted, imagining Jacob's hands sliding between the silk and her skin. She wanted that. She wanted him, but she also wanted that: the earning it, the waiting for it, the having and holding when the decision to unite has already been made, and it's not just because it feels good, not just for the present, but for as much of forever as you can get your hands on.

"Holly." Meena stood behind Paige, holding the train, jerking her head from the direction of Holly's chair.

Holly jumped up and joined them, careful not to step on the train. The salesgirl was showing Paige two bustle options.

"Please tell me we won't be stuck in taffeta," Meena murmured.

"You'll look ravishing," Paige gave them deadpan eyes in the mirror. "Your dresses are from the Pink Tutu collection."

HOLLY

"Say cheese!" Paige called from the tripod in her gray hoodie dress. Her neckline was a lower jaw of white shark teeth. The hood with the eyes and upper fangs flopped back.

"Emulsifiers and food coloring!" Holly grinned under Jacob's arm, hugging his burgundy-and-gold damask Burger King mantle.

Click.

Between shots, she rested her head on his thick fur collar. One of Meena's guests in the dining area turned from the chatting crowd in smeared Harley Quinn makeup.

"Crap!" She had forgotten about her red hair dye and freckled makeup for her Wendy's costume, which was sexier than the Old Fashioned Hamburgers logo.

Jacob's collar was still clean. He smiled at her while she stroked his silky jaw.

"I'm glad you decided against the wig and beard. You look more like Yul Brynner this way."

"I'd have to lose the shirt," he said, and tugged the ruffles around his neck. "You do have the red hair." Then he nodded at her red-and-white striped tights. "Deborah Kerr would never approve of all that leg." His mischievous smile said he did.

He had seen *The King and I?* Grace was no excuse for that.

Paige swirled her Jolly Rancher green punch and waited at the tripod.

"Spy pose." He held up an imaginary pistol and turned his back to Holly.

She put her back to his, mirroring him.

Click.

"Lose the guns." Paige lifted her head above the camera. "Cross your arms."

Click.

"One more?"

While she hesitated, Jacob spun toward her, flicked his velvet mantle behind him, and dropped to a white-stockinged knee.

What the—

It looked like a proposal, but he extended an arm and clapped his crown to his heart. Recovering her breath, she put out a ringless hand for him to kiss in allegiance.

Click.

"Take his crown."

He stood and placed it on her head. Holly crossed her arms and tried to look haughty until his warm pucker on her cheek goosed her eyebrows.

Click.

"Not fair!" she laughed.

"One feisty redhead coming up." Grinning, Jacob removed the crown and offered his arm. "Queen Wendy? Shall we proceed to the chocolate fountain?"

"That does sound good."

"I can take camera duty after I feed this one," he told Paige.

But she waved them off. "I'm shutting down soon." She pulled up her shark hood and emptied her drink.

"Can we get you a refill?" Holly held out her hand until a bleeding surfer with a ragged hole in his shirt approached, carrying a paper plate. "Rob!" She smiled.

"Dude!" Paige's fiancé's eyes were glassy.

Paige must be DD. "Aye Carumba? No, that's Bart Simpson."

"Cowabunga."

"Right." She patted Jacob, enjoying his clear sober eyes.

Rob wrapped a red-splattered arm around Paige and held the plate while she took a stuffed mushroom.

"Gnarly."

"How about a picture of dude and his catch?" Jacob asked.

From Meena's decked-out dining room table, draped in purple spiderweb lace, Holly smiled over at the Jaws-inspired photo shoot.

"Holly!" Batman had a higher voice than in the movies.

When she tilted her head to take in the grayish-blue eyes and thin lips in the black-horned mask, her braids moved: one up, one down.

"Cute costume," he said, sidling closer.

She shifted her weight away from him.

His black glove planted on his chest. "Scott."

"Scott!" She shook her head, laughing. "Of course. Sorry."

"Being on call Halloween weekend sucks. How've you been?"

"Doing well," she smiled. "Was there an emergency?"

"Typical drunk shenanigans. Fortunately, the kid who brought his friend in with the broken wrist didn't actually have an arrow through his head." He checked his watch. "I'm technically on call for another hour, so we'll see."

Across the living room, Rob had Jacob's attention demonstrating a photo idea with one arm tucked back.

"Are you okay?" Scott peered around into her eyes.

"Mm-hm." She held up her cup. "Hydrating always helps."

"I should get something. Water, because call." He tapped the pager on his Batman belt.

"Clever! It blends in. Non-spiked punch is another option. I haven't tried it, but Paige likes it. Meena does everything perfectly, so…"

Scott smiled. He didn't move.

Holly sipped. "Right over there." She pointed to the beverage dispenser.

Beep-beep-beep. Beep-beep-beep.

"You've got to be kidding me." He pulled his pager off his belt and sighed, reading a message. "Listen. Meena said you like poker. Do you want to drive out to the casino sometime?"

Her empty water cup froze over her face like a dog muzzle before she took it down. "I'm sorry, I—"

An arm slid around her waist: Jacob's.

"Scott, meet my boyfriend, Jacob." *Oh crap. He's never called himself my boyfriend.*

Jacob's eyes twinkled at her.

"Jacob, Scott. He works with Meena and Paige at the hospital."

The men exchanged a handshake.

"Duty calls. Excuse me." Batman vanished without a cape flourish.

Holly searched Jacob's face—happy, not jealous. She expected him to tease her about jumping to the boyfriend label before they'd had a Define the Relationship talk, but he just held out his arm.

"My queen?"

If she was his queen, him being her boyfriend must be okay. Holly curtsied. Before they moved, she had to kiss him. She was grateful he bent down in consent.

*   *   *

Holly checked herself in the mirrored wall above Meena and Gary's bathroom sinks for chocolate remains. She couldn't help smiling at her fake freckles. She couldn't help smiling, period.

After the toilet flushed, the interior door opened, revealing Courtney—a lot of Courtney. Her tattered Kelly-green skirt had hiked up around her hips, and the tiny Peter Pan hat drooped, cocked on its headband.

Holly went to close the door just as Deadpool entered the master bedroom.

"We need a minute," she cringed. "Wardrobe malfunction. There's a half bath down the hall."

While she closed the door on the masked man, Courtney shimmied, hiking up her nude fishnets and smoothing down her slanted miniskirt.

"How you doin' there, Pete? Need a ride home?"

"I'll get a ride on a Lost Boy." Slumped over, she sneered at her torn stockings. "Fucking nail." Then she joined Holly at the adjacent sink and slurred, "I forgive you, you know."

"What?"

"You're supposed to save the tall ones for me."

"Nice try, Hunty." Chuckling, she got soap. "I never agreed to that."

"He's too wholesome for me. You guys need to get a room. Feeding each other chocolate strawberries like you're at your fucking wedding."

"We were goofing off." She hoped they hadn't been inappropriate.

"So, it's good? The sex." Her tone implied, "Dummy."

Courtney used to be her confidante, but no way was she going to let her be a virtual voyeur with Jacob. She meditated on the bubbles.

"Oh my god!" Courtney's hand slammed over her smirking mouth until she cringed and swiped her sputtering lips with still-soapy hands, then doubled over the sink.

Holly handed her the hand towel she wasn't quite done using.

Rising tall and tipsy, she lowered the towel. "He's gay!"

"He just isn't a manwhore." She dried her hands on her little white apron. "We're still getting to know each other, for goodness' sake."

"'For goodness' sake.'" Fondling Holly's red braid, she smirked, "Miss Goody Two-Shoes here. With her gay boyfriend."

"We can talk when you're sober." She went for the door. "Let me know if you need a ride."

"Oh, sweetie," Courtney lunged, stumbling in her sparkly sandals, and knocked her into the door. "Don't be a beard. I mean, I wouldn't mind sitting on that face." She studied her eyes as if trying to see sex in there. "But don't be a beard." Patting Holly's cheek, she pushed against her shoulders to stand, weaving for balance.

As Holly got the hell out of there, she almost bumped into Deadpool waiting outside the door.

Down the hall, she glanced back: no Deadpool. No Courtney, either.

Oh crap. She doubled back to the bedroom. Meena and Gary had nice friends, so he probably wasn't the kind of guy who would take advantage of a frisky, drunk girl, but…

A gentlemanly Deadpool was escorting Courtney out of the bathroom, depositing her on the elegant king bed.

After Holly said, "Thank you," he nodded and closed the bathroom door behind him. "Courtney, love, I'm going to get you some water, okay?"

She stared toward the headboard.

"Stay—"

Apparently tempted by the pillows, Courtney flopped down just short of them.

"—here."

* * *

"How you doing over there?" Jacob shifted gears and planted his hand on Holly's striped knee.

"Well," she nodded, pulling her jacket tighter beneath the seatbelt. "You sure you don't want to go to your friend's party? I feel bad we stayed at Meena's so long."

"I didn't commit us. I said we might swing by."

"Next…" Would they be together next Halloween? "Next time we have to choose, let's do something with your friends first."

"Deal." He squeezed her hand before he had to shift.

When he parked the Land Rover in her driveway. Holly couldn't decide whether asking him to come in would be smart, to talk and lay down some boundaries, or extremely fricking dangerous.

Jacob turned off the engine.

"Do you want to come in for a minute? It's late, so—"

"I'd like that." His eyes smiled over something serious, which put her into a full stifled panic. If "that" was sex that he thought was being offered…

While they walked up the cement path, she rooted around for her keys.

"Get many trick-or-treaters?" he asked, tall beside the jack-o-lantern, surveying the front yard and surrounding homes.

"My neighbor said it's dwindled. I've only been in this house for a few years. I haven't been home for Halloween yet."

Inside, she hung her coat and purse on the coat tree by the door.

"You look ready." He ran his tempting fingers through the plastic cauldron of candy on the end table by the sofa. "Peanut M&M's, Three Musketeers, peppermint patties...?"

As she passed him, she touched his fuzzy mantle and muttered, "Lesser evils."

"I'm taking one of these." He rustled open a dark chocolate square.

"Do you want a glass of wine or something?"

"No thanks. I'll take off soon here."

Standing alone in her bright kitchen, Holly faced the rows of glasses in her open cupboard. She didn't need water. She needed a miracle. *Zero trust.* That's what she had in herself. At the sink, she watched the water level rise.

Jacob joined her, crinkling the metallic paper. "Trash?"

"Hm?" Her racing pulse was making her slow. The glass overflowed before she shut off the tap. "Under here." After clunking open the cupboard beneath the sink, she moved away, cupping her dripping glass.

When he stooped, she remembered a dream: she was standing at the sink, he came up behind her and pressed against her back, wrapping his arms around her—

Thump. The cupboard door closed.

Holly turned tail to the tiny table at the counter's end and sat on the metal stool. She hoped he couldn't read her mind today as he approached and stood before her.

"Remember that morning at your clinic when you looked like a pufferfish and said you wanted to be a nun?" He lifted a red braid over her shoulder.

"Pufferfish?"

"Sexiest pufferfish ever."

"Hmph."

"Someone who had eaten pufferfish and was deathly allergic to seafood?" he smiled. "That have anything to do with Billy Bob?" Jacob's warm hand stroked her arm. "I know the news from the genetic test sucked—"

"Sort of. His name isn't Billy—"

"I don't want to know his name." His raised hand almost looked authoritative in the gold buttoned sleeve, but the ruffled cuff ruined it. "If I meet him, I won't know whether to shake his hand and thank him or knock him on his ass."

"It had more to do with me," she said, toying with the lacy edge of her Wendy's apron. "I need to talk to you about something."

"Okay if I go first?"

Holly nodded.

Jacob cupped her shoulders. "If I ever hurt you like that, I'd have to eat my own gun. And I'm not in a hurry to take the room temperature challenge."

She cocked her head.

"Dead bodies, ambient temperature? Sorry. Anyway. You know I don't believe in fortune telling—"

"Really," she smirked.

"—but I see potential here."

Her chest pinched, and she couldn't look away from his eyes. If he expected a response, that was too bad because her brain was in a land far, far away where beautiful babies were being made. Jacob's gaze dropped to her mouth, and his fingertips sizzled along her jaw. When his electric thumb stroked her lips, she lost power to her eyelids.

"What's your thing?"

While Holly blinked, he moved to stand beside her, wrapping his muscular arms around her shoulders. Her head reeled from whiplashed expectations, so she leaned on him.

"Sorry." She closed her eyes again, no longer anticipating a kiss, but to compose herself.

"Take your time."

A mental image invaded the darkness: the two of them in her bed, just a short walk away. It sounded like perfection. She didn't have the discipline for this.

Jacob's thumb brushed her face. "Hey. You're leaking."

She rubbed the liquid between her fingers, staring down.

"It's okay. Whatever it is." He guided her to stand and held her.

Pressing her face on his furry chest, she whispered, "I can't do this."

He tensed. "Us this?"

"No!" Holly squeezed him. "I love this."

"Shit, woman." He laughed, hugging her tight.

"I need your help."

"You got it."

"Unless this is a dealbreaker for you." Her cheek took refuge in his fur collar.

"Cat photos?" He stroked her back. "I'll make an exception."

"Sex."

Jacob chuckled. "I guess if we're quick about it…"

"The next time I have sex should be with my husband."

Pulling back from the hug, he said, "You're married?" and held up her naked ring finger. "Give a guy some warning."

Holly stared, sort of nauseous.

"Sorry." He captured her in a bear hug. "Not funny. That's a perfect plan. I wholeheartedly endorse your position and would like to subscribe to your newsletter."

Oh, thank god. It was out, and he was still in.

Jacob's eyes were sweet as he brought her hand to his lips and planted a warm kiss on her ring finger above the knuckle, watching her eyes like a deposit on a promise, and then held her.

"I have a confession." His words wafted through her hair.

"Hm?" She took recovery breaths from her comfort zone.

"I kinda figured."

"What?"

"I'll explain." He held up a finger. "One thing, real quick." He pulled her into a kiss.

After she kissed him back, she threw her arms around his ultra-cozy waist and said, "You have a brilliant future as a hostage negotiator. Explain yourself."

"Your journal. 'Lust-aid.'"

"You did see that!"

He kissed her again. "Can't help it. This angry-troll-woman thing is superhot. I'll help. Step One: No more showering."

"Don't do that." His pheromones would get the better of her.

CORA

Cora stared into the sterilized waiting area. She was cried out. When a man in pale blue scrubs gawked at her as he passed, she realized she must look sketchy sitting there in her jammies with her hair in a frizzy ponytail. Maybe that's why that nurse, Shelly, had been so hateful.

In the unforgiving chair, she reread the article on her phone. It said babies were extra sensitive to radiation, so X-rays could cause cell mutations, cancer… Maybe she shouldn't have brought Naomi in. The impact wasn't that hard.

The silence before Naomi's cry thundered in her memory while her gaze blurred over the blinding floor. It was a no-win situation. Even if her dad had been available to consult, she wouldn't have been able to sleep without getting Naomi checked out. *She'll be okay.*

And something would work out with Child Welfare. Holly or Aiden would text back, or someone in authority would realize she wasn't the monster that the nurse and then the caseworker tried to make her out to be. Who would do that—hurt their baby on purpose?

A text from Wes popped up:

Can't I be a Safety Service Provider?

She wrote back:

You have to be at least 18.

That Vanessa woman had scared her so badly, talking about foster care or needing a supervisor…

Did you try their hotel?

They can't help from Maui. No point ruining their trip. Go to sleep, Wes.

"Cora?"

Even though the voice wasn't Vanessa's, she was afraid to look up.

An ivory-haired woman towered above her. "May I sit?" She did. "Cora, my name is Frances Carvey. I'm Vanessa's supervisor. I'd like to talk to you about your daughter."

Cora's phone vibrated. Hoping it was Holly, she checked: Wes.

That sucks. Want me to ask Eli's mom?

"Your baby's going to be okay," Frances said. "They're finishing up the X-rays now."

"Thank you."

"I understand you hit her with a weighted tape dispenser?"

"The tape stuck to my finger instead of breaking off." Cora sighed. "It was the end of the roll, so when I moved my hand, it slid across the changing table and bonked her head. I should have bought new diapers with functional tabs. I was trying to save money."

As Frances stared, Cora wondered if she should explain how she had tried to use a regular disposable Scotch tape dispenser, but that required both hands. The old-school dispenser had worked for a while.

"Has Naomi had any other injuries?"

"She isn't even five weeks old. We hardly leave my apartment."

"This happened in your apartment."

Cora dabbed her nose with the Kleenex, shaking her head.

"Has she had any other injuries?"

"No," she said, fixating on the tissue ball.

"The doctors are doing a skeletal survey, so if there—"

"What?" Cora sat up.

"Don't worry. It's only an X-ray."

"But they're only supposed to X-ray her head."

"She won't feel a thing."

"Naomi doesn't need other X-rays. Submitting babies to too many X-rays can cause cancer. I didn't say they could do that."

"We'll see any historical injuries from those results." Frances paused. "Is there anything you want to tell me?"

"I told you I don't want her to get unnecessary X-rays. Can something please be done about that?"

"If your baby has been hurt before, it would be better if I hear it from you."

Sniffling, Cora shook her head and crushed the tiny wad.

"Vanessa," the supervisor called.

The caseworker stood tall and spidery, rising from her distant seat. When she arrived at their chairs, her shadowy eyes glinted cold behind her cat eye frames. Her cropped brown hair was like Julie's.

"Could you find more tissues for Ms. Martin?" Frances asked. "Cora, I need to take some pictures of where this happened."

"I need to be here."

"Your daughter will be in good hands." Standing, Frances glanced at a frowning police officer stationed against the wall.

The officer stood with her legs apart and her arms back like a navy hourglass. Her dark hair was slicked back in a low bun. *Is she here to arrest me?* When Cora regained her feet, she wobbled, and she could have sworn the officer gave her a tiny, encouraging nod.

Vanessa returned with tissues trailing.

Before Frances took Naomi's diaper bag off the chair, she said, "This should stay with Naomi. Don't you think?" She handed the paisley bag to Vanessa, whose burgundy-tipped fingers formed a pincer hold around the strap and guided it to the linoleum floor.

Extending her long arm toward the bank of elevators, the supervisor smiled at Cora. But her smile of encouragement was different than the officer's: it spurred compliance, not hope.

Cora followed.

Ding. The elevator door slid open, revealing a gray-haired woman in a white doctor's coat chatting with a woman with cherry red braids and firecracker-striped tights. *Isn't Halloween tomorrow?*

Turning, Pippi Longstocking stared at the floor number display. "This is me." It was Holly. Her blue eyes locked on Cora; she startled. "Cora! Did you get my voicemail?"

CORA

Naomi. Cora bolted up to darkness. Blinking, fumbling into the empty air beside her bed, energized by adrenaline or the rare deep sleep, as her foot hit the floor, she remembered: Naomi was out with Holly. Covers off, she felt her way out while her eyes adjusted to the dim light coming around the blackout curtains, and she grabbed her robe from the door hook.

The short hallway was brighter.

"You are the most beautiful thing," Holly whispered.

Superhero colors: that's what hit Cora first. The cherry red of Holly's costume hair and the royal blue of the couch framed the woman who had come through when no one else had, who was now holding the most important person in the universe and giving her a bottle.

The second thing that came to Cora's sleepy head was how the morning sun had teamed up with the frizz of Holly's red locks and given her a peculiar halo, turning the two of them into a weird and wonderful Madonna and Child portrait—this Mary lounging without a meek bone in her body. Holly's feet were propped on one of Cora's white pillows, now on the coffee table near the heap of blankets trailing to the floor.

With a big smile, Holly said, "Mornin,' pretty mama. You sleep okay?"

"Good morning." Her breasts ached, engorged. Naomi looked content. The bottle was almost empty.

"I'm sorry. Is this okay?"

"It's fine. Thanks for feeding her. I'll pump."

"Here." She scooched over.

Cora grabbed a swaddling cloth from the bassinet railing and sat, taking Naomi. When she kissed her head, it smelled like a ripe love melon, lighting up receptors in her brain of connection, family, and home.

"Imma go pee." Holly tromped to the hallway while Cora switched Naomi's milk source.

Cora liked her even more when she wasn't holding her baby—who looked so perfect. Almost perfect. Tracing the tiny scratch of dried blood on her forehead, she whispered an apology and kissed it better. When Naomi's sucking slowed, she wasn't ready to put her in the bassinet, waiting by the white armchair.

"Please tell me you have coffee," Holly said, wiping her hands on the yellow pajamas.

"There should be a bag in the freezer," Cora answered as softly as possible. "The coffeemaker's in the cupboard above the stove."

"There is a god!" Opening the freezer, she asked, "Can I get you anything?"

"Actually, if you don't mind, I should drink some water."

"Of course!"

"Thanks!"

Cupboards thumped. Water ran in the sink. "Your place is adorable."

"It's the best I could do with my budget."

"You did a fantastic job with Nessie last night." Holly padded to the couch with Cora's glass, clunking it onto a coaster. "How are you so patient?"

"You mean Vanessa? Thanks."

"Loch Ness Monster." Grinning, she turned to the kitchen.

Seeing the back of red-haired Holly in her yellow pajamas was surreal, like looking at a cartoon version of herself. Cora sighed at her sweet bundle and eased up from the couch.

"I sort of wanted to cut her."

Cora froze. *She can't be serious.*

"To see if she has acid for blood—or motor oil. No way that bitch is human."

Once Naomi was settled in, Cora felt lighter, relieved that Holly wasn't crazy, and that Naomi had slept through her joke.

"Coffee filters are…?"

"I'll make it." Cora joined her in the kitchen.

"Thanks. You remember Courtney?" Taking a seat on the countertop, she said, "She's emailing me links to the law we need to keep them in line."

"Please thank her for me."

"I have a favor. Totally fine if it's a no. Could I take a quick shower? I'm nasty, and I'm dying to wash my hair."

"But what about…" The safety plan demanding line-of-sight supervision spied on them from the counter.

"Right. What if we put the bassinet in the bathroom?"

While Holly was in the shower, her phone buzzed on the coffee table. Cora could barely hear it over the hum of the double breast pump: *znnn-sht, znnn-sht, znnn-sht.* She leaned forward in case it was Child Welfare checking on them.

The screen read: **Jacob.**

Cora sat back, holding the suction cups to her breasts, and tried to relax.

Knock knock knock knock.

It couldn't be trick-or-treaters yet. Sighing, she pressed her forearm against the plastic cones, picked up the Medela bag, and waddled to the door.

The peephole showed Vanessa's cat eye glasses.

Oh no. "Hi Vanessa. If you can give me just a minute, I'll get decent."
Znnn-sht.

"That's a violation of the safety plan, Ms. Martin. Open the door." The sucking hurt. Milk dropped into the squatty transparent bottles.

"I'm pumping. I just need a second."

"If you don't open this door immediately, I'll have to assume the worst."

"One second," she called, grappling with the bag strap and the suction cups. *Znnn-sht.*

"Do you want to keep your—?"

Clacking open the deadbolt, Cora pulled the door ajar and faced away, clutching her robe over the pump tips. "My parents don't fly back until tomorrow morning. Frances said that's when we'd need to talk again."

"I'm aware." She slid past.

Before following her, Cora checked the sporadic drips, turned off the yellow dial, and barely stopped in time to avoid hitting the caseworker, who had braked where the hallway joined the main room.

After her cropped head swiveled left to right to center, it aimed at the bassinet. "Where is your safety service provider?"

"Holly's in the shower." Closing one side of the nursing bra and trying not to drop the pump, she wished Vanessa would move so she could get to the kitchen.

"Good thing I dropped in, isn't it?"

"I'm sorry." She cocked her head, adjusting the second bra cup. "What do you mean?"

Beside them, the bathroom door opened, and Holly appeared, securing a peachy orange bath towel under her armpits with her soggy blonde hair trailing over her shoulders.

"Ness! I thought you were coming tomorrow for the changing of the guard." Scanning the walls for a clock, Holly said, "My shower wasn't that long, was it?"

"Long enough." About-facing in the hallway, she goose-stepped to the bassinet. "Ms. Martin, I have to take your daughter into protective custody."

"What are you talking about?" Cora followed, frantic, depositing the pump and wobbly milk containers in the kitchen. She circled to face her. "No."

Vanessa bent toward the bassinet, then straightened. Her eyebrow rose and her mouth opened, but sound came from behind her instead.

"Improvise, Adapt, Overcome." Standing at attention in the orange towel, Holly had one arm slung through the handle of Naomi's car seat with her other hand supporting the base. "Bassinet wouldn't fit."

Her lips smiled, but her eyes burned as she stared down the caseworker. It was probably good that she was soaked, or she might have burst into angry flames like one of those sad Buddhist monks.

"Can we get you anything?" Holly came dangerously close, almost shoulder checking her with no concern for her precarious towel. Once she transferred the car seat to Cora, she braced her hands on her hips and asked, "Coffee, water, the tears of your enemies?"

Vanessa scoffed.

Because Naomi was sleeping, Cora set her car seat near the couch.

"You haven't seen those mugs?" Holly marched into the kitchen. "They're hilarious. My friend has one, a metal one for camping. She's a social worker, too. Courtney Wakeman. Do you know her?"

"We work in different units," she said with a judgy raised eyebrow.

"Ah." Holly opened a cupboard. "Now that you're here, Ness, I'll go change. That's okay, right?" she asked, filling a glass at the sink. "You can be trusted to supervise?"

Beside her, Cora tucked the extra full bottle into the refrigerator.

"You can go."

"Cool." She strode to the white armchair and slung her gym bag over her shoulder.

"Cora, can I change in your room?"

"Sure." Even though that would leave her alone with Vanessa, she made herself smile.

When Holly was down the hall, her phone buzzed on the coffee table—an incoming call: **Jacob**.

"Holly, could this be urgent? It's the second time he's called."

Trotting back, she clamped her phone to her ear while assessing Vanessa's face. "Detective?" she smiled. "I'm just playing." She turned her back to them. "What's up, handsome?" Ambling into the hallway, she said, "That sounds fun. What time? … One sec. Vanessa, there's no way we'll get the green light for these two to be on their own today, right?"

"Correct."

Holly shook her head and proceeded toward the bedroom. Naomi fussed, so Cora took her out of the car seat, bouncing and pacing.

"Can you tell Grace I'm sorry? I'm helping a friend with her baby today, so I won't be able to go." She stopped in the hallway. "Paige isn't due until April."

Cora shuffled around the kitchen table to be as far as possible from Vanessa.

"All night, too. You don't know her." Holly lowered her voice. "I want to respect her privacy. … Okay. I lo—'ll talk to you later." She froze. "I'm practicing my Southern drawl. … Wendy is too Southern. … You're not my accent supervisor. … Okay, bye."

"Ms. Samuelsson, come back, please."

She returned to Vanessa but so did a snarl that only kind of tried to hide under her smile.

"When you approached my supervisor with this plan, you indicated you were acquaintances. Does this close friendship you failed to disclose interfere with your ability to be objective?"

"We aren't that close," Cora said.

"Cora!" Holly almost sounded offended, and she peeked around the caseworker. "I'm right here." Then she winked.

"I mean…" Naomi's diaper smelled foul. When Cora looked up, Vanessa was backed into the living room with Holly's gym bag between them.

"That's better." Holly nodded, giving her a smug, "drop dead" smile and extending an arm toward the couch. "Do you need to take notes?" After a beat with no response, she smiled bigger. "Okay then. I met my friend Cora when she started working at my gynecologist's office." She asked Cora, "That was, what, spring?"

"Around finals. Late April. I'm so sorry, but can we relocate so I can change Naomi's diaper?"

"You can do it there." Sneering, Vanessa pointed at the pad on the floor.

"Her changing table is in my room." Since the caseworker just stared, Cora explained, "That isn't as padded," while she supported Naomi's thighs to keep from smooshing poop everywhere.

"So, you prioritized your own comfort over your child's?"

Holly groaned. "I insisted. Cora was exhausted and deserved to get a decent night's sleep in her own fricking bed."

"No need to escalate, Ms. Samuelsson. If the floor was good enough last night—"

"Okay then." Holly stepped between them. "After Cora took a job at my doctor's office, I introduced her to some friends in the medical field since that's what she's studying. She's hung out with me and my friends a few times."

Cora brought Naomi down to the changing pad.

"I started dating a guy and got all wrapped up in that. I consider her a friend."

Holly's strong smile hit home. Cora hadn't had a friend she could count on since Thalia moved away during their junior year of high school.

"Thank you for your transparency."

"Here to help," she nodded. "You okay there, Cora?"

"Mm-hm."

"Okay. I'm gonna change." The bedroom door thumped shut.

On her knees, Cora changed Naomi while Vanessa stalked in their periphery. The dirty diaper sat in a sealed wad as she fastened the new one over Naomi's soft little Buddha belly. Once she kissed it, she snapped the monkey onesie closed.

"Those tabs work fine." The caseworker snaked to the kitchen. "You do have a fan, don't—never mind."

Click. The fan hummed. Cora let her eyes close for a moment, breathing before speaking.

"We went to a 7-Eleven after Frances left last night. I'm throwing out the defective ones."

"That's evidence!"

Cora flinched. Naomi cried.

"Shh." She tried to be quick about wiping her hands with a fresh baby wipe.

"You haven't disposed of them yet, have you? Your dumpsters are on-premises—"

"They're in my room." Lifting Naomi to her shoulder, she picked up the wrapped poopy diaper.

"I'll take those when I leave."

Please let it be soon.

"You took Naomi out last night?" Vanessa finally moved aside so she could access the kitchen trash.

Nodding, sighing, she tossed it.

"Where was your safety service provider?"

"We went together. Holly wanted to treat me to working diapers so I wouldn't be triggered by the tape dispenser."

"Where was the baby?"

Knock knock knock.

"Excuse me." Cora hesitated, trying to walk through the kitchen past Vanessa.

But the caseworker puffed up in her path. "Where was the baby?"

"Sleeping. In the car. Excuse me, please. There's someone at the door."

"You didn't leave the baby unsupervised in your vehicle?"

"No."

"So, you violated the plan."

"What?"

"Your safety service provider left you unsupervised with the child."

"No! Holly paid for them." Naomi fussed in her arms. "Excuse me."

Knock knock knock.

"Cora?"

Aiden.

"Are you expecting someone?"

Cora backtracked through the dining area, but the door opened before she could get through the living room. Aiden had come in, and Vanessa was a step ahead.

"I'm Vanessa Dix—"

He slipped past her and wrapped Cora and Naomi in a hug. "I got here as soon as I could. Are you okay?"

Cora nodded. Her heart pounded backward out of fear into something else. His arm around her was such a blessing. When he kissed Naomi's head, she wanted to tell him "Thank you" a million times. His eyes didn't hurt to look into, even though they were serious, diving into hers.

Something sad flickered in them before he smiled.

"I assume you're the father?"

Holly's mutter drifted from the hallway: "Where'd I put my coffee?" In gym clothes with her hair in a wet messy bun, she spotted Aiden with his arm around Cora and froze.

Her eyes were like a mirror: Cora was not standing beside a boyfriend but a fiend.

"Your name, please?" Vanessa demanded.

"Aiden Walsh," he said over his shoulder. He released Cora and offered his hand to Holly. "Thank you for helping last night."

"Sure thing." She shook his hand but didn't really smile.

When he extended his hand to Vanessa, she focused on Holly.

"Ms. Samuelsson, could you describe how the new diapers were purchased last night?"

Beside Cora again, he whispered, "You sure you're okay?"

She gave him a quick smile, distant and distracted, shifting away.

"Cash?" Holly said.

"You bought them," Vanessa said.

"Over protest. It didn't come near to balancing out the shitty part of Cora's day, but it was one thing I could do."

When Aiden touched Cora's arm, it wasn't comforting anymore. "Be right back."

"The baby was where?" Her raised hand warned Cora not to speak.

He disappeared into the bathroom.

"In the car with me," Holly said. She scanned the kitchen and the tables, then turned to the hallway. "I must have left my coffee in the—"

"Ms. Samuelsson."

"Yes, ma'am."

"Who's your certifier?"

"Debbie Ellsworth." Her head tilted. "Why?"

Vanessa peered in her Coach bag.

"Why?" She repeated, louder, stepping up.

The caseworker pulled out her phone. "I have concerns with your honesty."

"My honesty?"

"Your stories don't make sense."

"The diaper thing?"

She nodded.

"Cora, do you have any paper?" Holly squinted at the refrigerator. "Got it." In the kitchen, she yanked off the magnetic pad that read "Faith – Hope – Love." She plunked down the pad, drew a box, and wrote "7-11." "Here's the store." Next, she drew a cute VW bug profile. "Here's the car." Three circles went inside. "Cora. Me. Naomi." Above the car went a dollar sign. "I gave Cora some cash." Holly swooped an arced line from the car to the box. "Cora took the money and went in." The pen reversed course. "Cora came back." Holly jabbed the VW and slammed the pen down. "Are we clear?"

When Aiden arrived at Cora's side, she stopped bouncing with Naomi.

"As I said…" Vanessa poised her pickled-beet talon over the phone. "I have concerns with your honesty."

That evening, Cora and Aiden stood beside the bassinet in the darkened living room. Naomi slept peacefully, unscathed, Cora hoped, from the day's drama. Naomi had startled when Holly yelled at Vanessa, but the shouting didn't last long.

Aiden's hand on the railing wasn't far from hers. Now that Naomi was asleep, Cora's body alerted to his; she was almost afraid to move. How awkward was this going to be, him sleeping there?

"You should go to bed," he whispered, holding out his hand. "I've got this." It took a second before she registered his gaze on the baby monitor.

"Bottles are in the fridge," she whispered back, setting it in his open palm, careful not to touch him. "Are you sure?"

"I can't let you have all the fun," he smirked.

"When you put it that way…"

He nodded, accepting the victory, with a delighted smile that cut like a knife. But not one he was wielding.

"Thanks again for coming," Cora managed, retreating to the kitchen. "Can I reimburse you for your plane ticket? At least part of it?" Her hands grounded her on the counter between them, but her mind took flight to his room.

> *"I'll pay for half your plane tickets." His breath ruffles my hair by the roots. His arms pin me to the hot seat of his lap, so I can't help but face the merciless monitor and the slick, shiny loveseat where Aiden will be tangled up with some other female—a more convenient love.*
>
> *I'm out. Trying to.*
>
> *But he's standing tall and holding me. "Who am I kidding? I'll pay the whole thing. Maybe I should invest in a private jet." His smile is still sexy. But I don't trust it.*

Aiden's smile was flattened, either because he'd remembered too, or just mirroring her. "No way," he said, hushed. With his long legs, it was two steps to the kitchen counter. "I still have that check to give you for child support. I'm happy to stay longer. I know your parents will be back tomorrow, but I can probably work from here, and my friend

Rachel offered to host the Monday night meeting for me."

"Meeting?" *Rachel?*

"AA," Aiden smiled. "Alcoholics Anonymous."

"That's great." She tried to think through her goosebumps. "How long have you been doing 12-step groups?"

"Leading meetings? Just a few months. I started working the steps during treatment, in February."

His text:

I'm going to earn your trust back, even if you can't see it. At least become a man who comes closer to deserving you.

"You like it?"

"I don't do it for fun," he whispered, tracing the edge of the peeling vinyl counter. "I go because it's important for my recovery."

CORA

MONDAY, OCTOBER 31, 2016

Being in Julie's bed was weird. So was being this tired in the middle of the bright day. Cora tried to enjoy the comfort of it and push past the sickening slipping-backward sensation. The view was still phenomenal with three ginormous windows framing majestic pines and the radiant blue sky. This forced admission to the treasured tree house was all sorts of wrong, like being plunked on the tricycle you had coveted as a kindergartener when you're 16 and ready for a car.

Naomi looked so perfect and peaceful sucking at her breast. The abrasion on her forehead had formed loose dots, about to fall off. Cora stroked the violet cap and her soft wisps of deep brown hair.

Nestling her head on her bent arm, she kept one hand on Naomi's milk source. Beneath them, the swaddling cloth was spread like a picnic blanket. She pulled the comforter over her shoulder, cold since her unbuttoned red shirt furled behind her. She shouldn't be missing class, but Naomi was more important. Maybe she could make it to Calculus in the afternoon.

A knock on the door startled her; she turned her head when it creaked open.

"Vanessa's here." Her mom looked tense.

"She's early."

"She was in Mountaindale for another home visit and wanted to see us before she drove back to Fort Herring."

"It's a 20-minute drive."

"We're in no position to argue."

"Please tell her I'll come down when Naomi's done nursing."

"You can nurse her while we talk?"

"I'll come down soon." Cora took a breath. "It's not my fault she's early."

"Do you want me to close the curtains?"

"No one can see in. Thanks, though."

The door creaked closed.

A warm hand pressed Cora's bare shoulder.

"Wait! Please!" hissed above her.

Mom? She blinked awake and turned.

Her mother's arm pointed arrow straight at the entering caseworker.

"Oh my gosh," Cora whispered. "I must have fallen asleep." Clutching her shirt together, she crawled off the bed, propped the long fluffy sham pillows around Naomi, grabbed the baby monitor's mobile unit, and nodded toward the door.

Vanessa snaked past under the Berkeley pennant, surveying the room and Naomi. "They look so peaceful while they're sleeping," she said in a loud, almost monotone voice.

At the doorway, Cora said, hushed, "Let's talk out here."

Instead, slinking between the bassinet and the bay of windows, she peered into the crib, then made a calculated visual sweep of the room. As her gaze passed over Cora, she remembered Holly's acid-for-blood theory.

Does she see through a robot screen with white block letters scrolling like the Terminator? The red and orange human-shaped blobs the Predator saw before it devoured its victims came to mind. *Probably more like that.*

* * *

Downstairs, Cora took her father's armed chair at the head of the table in the sunny open kitchen. Her mom sat across from Vanessa with scrap paper and a pen to take notes like she did to keep score when they played Scrabble. The caseworker crossed her legs, keeping her notepad out of sight.

"As I informed your mother, there will be a shelter hearing tomorrow at 11:00 a.m. There are—"

"Why? Naomi's with me now."

She waited, glaring: interruption penalty. "When an infant suffers a suspicious injury, a petition is filed with the court to ensure safety and cooperation. As long as you and your parents cooperate with the assessment, a removal may not be necessary. Depending, of course, on the results of our investigation."

"I don't understand."

"An attorney will be present at the hearing to answer your questions."

"You…" She sighed. "Abuse is nonaccidental harm to a child. This was an accident. And the X-rays were fine."

"A five-month-old infant's skull is extremely fragile." Vanessa raised an eyebrow.

"That's why I took her to the hospital."

"You said you were concerned about the blunt force from the tape dispenser."

"Yes," Cora breathed. "That's why I took her in."

"You're minimizing the impact now."

"What? No. I'm going by what the doctors said. From the X-rays."

"X-rays only show injuries to bones."

"What are you talking about? They didn't—"

"If you can't lower your voice and calm down, I'll have to end this conversation."

"Did the doctors tell you something they didn't tell me?"

"I wasn't present for every interaction you had with the medical team, so I'm sure I don't know." Vanessa studied her watch. "We need to get through these questions, if you don't mind."

Cora stood. "Please go ahead. I'm listening." While she got a glass from the cupboard, the distance helped her breathe.

"On average," she said, entranced by her own flowing pen, "how many alcoholic beverages would you say you consume every week?"

"I'm breastfeeding. I don't."

"During your pregnancy?"

"Zero." Taking the filtered water pitcher from the refrigerator, she studied her mom. "I could have had a glass of wine with dinner before I knew I was pregnant?"

"When did you discover that you were pregnant?"

"Mid-February." She poured.

"Before mid-February, what did your alcohol use look like?"

"Just that—maybe a little wine at dinner sometimes." When Vanessa caught her glancing at her mother again, she flushed. "And when I got pregnant, I'd had champagne. New Year's Eve. But I don't think that would affect Naomi." While the caseworker scrawled, Cora brought her water back to the table. "I'm not an alcoholic."

"Your mother said you sought the help of a mental health professional regarding some trauma involving your sister?"

"Ms. Dixson." Her mom lowered her pen. "Our family suffered a tragedy with my eldest daughter. Getting counseling is to Cora's credit."

"I'll need the counselor's name to corroborate this."

Aiden. Dr. Fairbanks had said he could go to prison for rape. "No."

"No?" She sneered.

"Correct, my answer is 'no.'"

"If you refuse to cooperate with the assessment, you will be out of compliance with our safety plan. Further legal action will be taken. That could include placement of your child in foster care."

"What?" Her mom hardly ever raised her voice.

She knew her mother had grown to love Naomi, but she hadn't known quite like this. They were a team again, but she had hurt her again—this time by bringing the danger into their home instead of following it out.

Scooting away, Cora strode to the counter where her parents kept the cordless landline, the family calendar, and desk supplies. After extracting her blue spiral notebook from the vertical letter holder, she folded back its slick paperboard cover. Her heart pumped outrage.

"Vanessa," she said, returning. "I need your help with something. Is this legal authority found in the Utah Code or the administrative rules? Nothing supports what you're saying in the Rules of Juvenile Procedure. Your questions are supposed to be limited to factors that impact child safety."

Behind the cat eye glasses, her eyebrow twitched up, unyielding. "Unfortunately, we see many cases where mentally ill mothers are unsafe for their children."

"You think I'm mentally ill?"

"This line of inquiry is a necessary part of the assessment."

"I'm not mentally ill."

"We will need to corroborate that." Stick-straight with her pen hovering over her paper, Vanessa was the Queen of Entitlement.

Her haughtiness helped. Maybe even more than Holly's pep talks or Aiden manning up to be a better human and father, or her mother fighting for a being who she'd once considered disposable.

"Do you also need to corroborate that I'm not a registered sex offender?"

"Cora!" Her mother paled.

A twitch behind the cat eye glasses preceded cool, calm collectedness—a face reminiscent of Paige's when Erica thought she'd just made a cunning play and only Paige knew the outcome.

"That is a simple search of a database." Vanessa's satisfied smirk was much uglier than Paige's smug mug when she'd displayed her full house.

But Cora wasn't done. "How about corroborating that I'm not a meth dealer or...a bank robber?"

Her mom sighed.

"When we receive a report of concern," she said, feeding off Cora's anger like a cold-blooded reptile with a warm meal, "we must determine whether that issue presents a threat. Your mother told me you sought mental health help. If someone reported that you deal methamphetamine, that would be another conversation."

"Perfectly sane people seek counseling."

"Ms. Martin."

Her mollifying tone made Cora wonder if she had raised her voice for a second.

"A reliable answer to the question of your mental health—"

No, she's just a bitch.

"—one on which the agency could legally rely, must be given by an expert in the field. Mental illness can be a fluid, subtle disease. The report that you needed professional intervention needs to be investigated. Especially considering the totality of the evidence, which includes physical injury to a vulnerable infant." She rummaged in her flowery tote. "If you have that name, we can fill out a Release of Information." Raising her pen over a form, she simpered. "Perhaps this can all be put to rest."

Cora nodded. "You can leave that with me."

Vanessa's head twitched back like a snake before it cocked. "I'm sure you'd like this to be over with as soon as possible."

You're my buddy now, huh? As she reached her open hand for the forms, her fingers almost touched Vanessa's water glass.

"When I return to the office and report to my supervisor, if she decides that the conditions of this safety plan are no longer being complied with, this could end today. Police could knock on your door within the hour and place your daughter in community foster care."

"Ms. Dixson!"

"Relative foster care is preferred, but your daughter needs to know the potential consequences."

We weren't friends for very long. That was Cora's left brain talking. Her right brain was zooming in panicky Chicken Little circles. She tried to imagine Frances's reaction to such a report. *This can't possibly be legal.* Was Vanessa's mouth lower than usual? She wasn't happy, that's for sure. *That's a good thing.* Still haughty, and that eyebrow wouldn't quit—but her smirk was gone. And what was with her escalating, bringing in the big guns? *She isn't feeling omnipotent anymore.*

When Cora fidgeted her outstretched hand, the caseworker seized the glass and relocated it to a distant placemat.

"Leave that form with me," Cora said. "Thanks."

Standing, she spoke as if Cora weren't there. "Thank you again for your cooperation, Ms. Martin. It could save your grandchild from placement with strangers. Please contact your certifier immediately so the process can be expedited."

CORA

WEDNESDAY, NOVEMBER 2, 2016

"Good morning." The security guard had a compassionate smile—weird for a greeter at the gates of hell.

Cora gaped at the X-ray machine. She didn't have to put Naomi through that, did she?

"Step through and stop at the other side, please."

As she walked through the tall gray doorframe, which must be a metal detector, she cupped Naomi's cotton-capped head and held her close. Was this such a dangerous place that people might bring weapons?

"You're good." He turned to her parents, who were putting their belongings in round plastic tubs.

"Cora?" A Hispanic woman in a brown suit and dark-framed glasses approached from the wide corridor lined with benches. Cora nodded, so the woman extended her hand, then dropped it since Cora's hands were full of baby. "My name is Renata Ochoa. I'm the attorney here to help you today. Have we met?"

"I don't think so." But something about her face was familiar; Cora studied it while Renata introduced herself to her parents. "We can talk in here." She gestured to a hallway, then led them into a windowless room with a round table.

Rummaging in her black bag, the lawyer pulled out a yellow notepad and her phone. "How are you holding up?"

Cora shrugged from her chair. She should smile back, but any

254

emotional response risked opening her Pandora's box of feelings, which harbored howling witchy ghosts.

"For shelter hearings, there is an 'attorney of the day' on rotation to help parents. An attorney from the Department of Justice represents the Department of Children and Family Services. Today, I am your attorney, so anything you tell me is privileged. Having third parties present waives that privilege—your parents could have to testify about something you intended to tell me in confidence."

"I want them here."

Her mom looked as terrified as she was, and her father still had his permafrown.

"Support is always welcome." Renata nodded. "Today's hearing has two parts. The first part is the arraignment on the petition, which we will go over in a minute. We usually enter denials, get an attorney appointed, and get court dates. You have a right to contest the allegations at a trial, which will be in 60 days."

Two months? She clung tighter to Naomi.

"Foster care?" her dad barked.

Cora flinched.

"That's what they want here?" he demanded.

"Russell." Her mom touched his arm.

The lawyer sat back a little.

Dad. She's trying to help.

"It's an in-home plan," Renata said. "The caseworker didn't tell you?"

The next few minutes blurred while Cora fought tears of relief and paced to soothe Naomi. At least Naomi was too young to pick up on the swear words her father was spewing about Vanessa.

After her dad settled down, Renata said, "Let me see if the court worker is here with the documents we need to review." The door swung closed momentarily before she returned empty-handed. "We can talk without them for now." She scrolled on her phone. "They have alleged two things: that your mental health interferes with your ability to safely parent—"

"What the hell!"

"Russell."

"—and that your child has suffered a physical injury that does not match your explanation."

"That's…" Her dad sighed, leaning back in the metal chair to make more room for his lungs.

"We are going to enter denials so you can fight those claims at trial." Renata smiled at Cora.

"Sounds good." Nothing but getting out of there really sounded good, but if Naomi wasn't being taken, she could survive this.

Knock knock knock.

Renata waved to a gray-haired bespectacled man peeking in through the door's thin rectangular window.

"Sorry to interrupt," he said. "Do you know if the dad's coming?"

When Renata looked at Cora, she said, "Aiden's back in Seattle. He doesn't live here. Does he have to be here for this?"

Propping open the door, he braced a pad of paper against his pinstriped suit. "Can I get his phone number?"

While she pulled up Aiden's number and read it aloud, her father's eyes burned into her.

* * *

About half an hour later, Cora paced in the back of the courtroom, wincing at Naomi's cries. Vanessa sat at the rectangular table on the right, vindicated as if Cora were, even now, hurting her infant. Her mom turned back from the front left pew beside her dad and gave her an encouraging smile.

Through the double doors came muffled snatches of Renata's conversation with that other lawyer, who she'd asked to speak with in the hall. Although Cora felt guilty for eavesdropping, she was grateful when her pacing brought her closer and when Naomi stopped crying.

"Vanessa is turning it into a witch hunt. She started off on the wrong foot, and she's doubling down on her mistake."

"It might be your vision that's clouded, Renata. We both know you're a bleeding heart, especially when it comes to young moms." The door cracked open. "I know my client is more risk-averse than you." Her icy tone was clearer, louder. "But that way, no one gets hurt."

The woman powered through, flinging the door behind. She made resting bitch face look good. Even her hair seemed afraid of her in its sleek auburn bob clipped within an inch of its life.

Bouncing her squalling bundle, Cora smiled in apology, preparing for the inevitable eye contact. But with her head high and turning, the dour and polished lawyer marched by as if Cora were a transparent thing. Then she roosted at Vanessa's table and whispered.

Cora didn't notice her mother until she was close, holding out her arms. "Why don't you let me take her? That way you can concentrate."

"Thanks."

Her mom opened the double doors, and Renata was standing there, staring as if she'd seen a ghost, with the photo of the tape dispenser dangling by her side.

"I know, Naomi," her mom cooed, "I know." She nodded at Renata and pushed through the second set of doors. The first one closed over the lawyer's belated recovery, thudding like a distant bomb.

A moment later when Renata came in, she looked like herself again. She waved for Cora to follow her to the table on the left and pulled out a padded chair beside the pinstriped man helping Aiden, who sat by the wall.

"Here." Placing a legal pad and a pen in front of her, she said, "In case you want to take notes. If you need to tell me anything during the hearing, press that mute button. They will be recording." Her wedding ring glinted as she touched the spindly microphone that stretched up like a black dandelion bud.

In a minute, a door opened to the left of the judge's elevated bench, flanked by the American and Utah flags.

"All rise," a woman in a cardigan said, stepping inside the door.

Everyone stood while a man in a black robe entered. His thick white hair was slicked back in an Elvis wave.

"Franklin County Juvenile Court is now in session," she continued. "The Honorable Thomas Palmer presiding."

Judge Palmer took the tall black chair behind the Utah State seal and surveyed them. "Good morning, everyone," he said, booming and baronial. "Please be seated."

Renata's eyebrows pinched down behind her glasses.

"Your Honor." Aiden's lawyer sidled up to the woman by the judge. "Could the court get Father on the phone? He lives out of state."

"By all means," the judge said.

The lawyer handed over a sheet of yellow paper and returned to his seat.

"Good morning, Your Honor." Vanessa's lawyer smiled with her hands on her lap, obedient like a Doberman.

"Are you here for the State?"

"Lindsay Schmidt," she said, standing. "Assistant Attorney General for the Department of Justice, Your Honor. It's a pleasure."

"Thank you, Miss Schmidt. Judge Bronski fell ill, and with Judge Hager on vacation, they pulled me over from Circuit Court to assist."

"Hello?" Aiden's voice came through the speakers.

"This is Judge Palmer from Franklin County Court—juvenile court today. Is this…" He squinted at the papers in his hands. "Aiden Walsh?"

"Yes, sir."

"Excellent. Glad you can join us. We're just getting started here, so if you could, please mute your phone, and I may have some questions for you." Then he smiled at Vanessa's attorney. "What do we have today?"

"The shelter hearing for Naomi Martin."

"Very good. Miss Martin?"

Cora stood with Renata.

"This is about your baby?"

But Renata spoke first. "Your Honor, if I may?"

"Please. Nice to see you again, Mrs. Ochoa."

"You as well, Your Honor. I have reviewed the Petition and the

Protective Custody Report with Ms. Martin. She and her daughter are correctly named. Their dates of birth, address, and phone number are correct. The Indian Child Welfare Act does not apply. We waive formal arraignment and advice of rights, enter denials to allegations 3A and 3B, request court-appointed counsel, pretrial and trial dates, as well as a permanency hearing. Ms. Martin may retain an attorney, but in the meantime, we would request that FCPD be appointed. We also need to be heard as to disposition."

"Go ahead."

Renata paused.

The judge's assistant peeked out from behind her computer and handed him something. "Denials need to be entered on the record," she whispered. "Here are the dates."

"Very good. Denials are entered to—what was it, Mrs. Ochoa?"

"3A and 3B."

"3A and 3B. Miss Martin, you will be appointed an attorney. Your court dates will be as follows..." He held the papers at arm's length. "Pretrial conference November 17th at 9:00 a.m., Trial December 29th at 9:30 a.m. And a permanency hearing on November 2nd, 2017, at 1:30 p.m."

"That's only if your case is still open," Renata whispered as they sat.

Aiden's lawyer stood. "Your Honor, Father will proceed in the same manner—enter denials to C and D, that he lacks sole custody and cannot protect from mother's abusive and/or neglectful behaviors."

Could Aiden just agree that I'm abusive?

"He supports the in-home plan." The pinstriped lawyer smiled.

Nodding, the judge stared at the far wall. "Did you write down those court dates, Mr. Walsh?"

"Yes. Thank you."

Cora wished she could see his face.

"What about you, Miss Martin?" His gaze flicked to the blank notepad before her.

Startled, she grabbed the pen, but Renata's hand stopped her while the quiet woman who'd been sitting in the back slipped through the half wall, offering a piece of paper.

"We have the dates now," Renata said, passing it to Cora. "Thank you."

Judge Palmer nodded. "There should be a phone number for your attorney, who should be appointed in two business days."

The assistant whispered.

With a furrowed brow and a warning tone, he said, "That is the number for the court." Then he recovered his smile. "Call in two business days. They will give you the name and number of the appointed attorney." Addressing his audience, he said, "We do things differently across the street. So, the child can stay with her mother?" The last question was for Vanessa's lawyer.

"Your Honor." Lindsay stood tall. "My client has been working diligently to keep this baby with her mother."

Does she know that's a lie?

"As you can see in the Protective Custody Report," she continued, "Mother's refusal to sign Releases of Information for her mental health records brought us here. Given the suspicious circumstances around the head trauma to this vulnerable infant, compounded with Mother's history of mental health issues, my client would be remiss not to review these records."

His nod was like a death knell.

Lindsay heaped more dirt on Cora's grave. "My client is eager to maintain the current placement with Mother, but we need the court to make certain orders."

Judge Palmer flipped through the papers.

"The conditions of the in-home plan are on Page 4. Namely that Mother reside in maternal grandparents' home with line-of-sight supervision, that the family cooperate with the assessment, and that Mother sign releases for her mental health records and complete a psychological evaluation."

At the end of the enemy's table, Vanessa's hissing voice caught Lindsay's attention. She pointed at something.

After reading from the legal pad, Lindsay said, "Also, my client would like Mother to submit to a urinalysis. Mother's behaviors at the hospital were concerning for substance abuse, and she admitted to using alcohol."

Renata pressed the mute button and whispered, "I am objecting to that." The coppery flecks in her dark eyes glowed like embers. Her righteous anger was like Holly's, facing off against Vanessa in her orange towel: *"Improvise, Adapt, Overcome."*

Cora sat up straighter. *What would Holly do?*

Lindsay droned on, "In addition, Your Honor…"

Almost smiling, Cora whispered, "Couldn't hurt, might help? A drug test would be clean."

"…my client would like the Court to order…"

"Are you sure?" Renata frowned.

Cora nodded.

"…Mother not to co-sleep with the baby to avoid a fatal accident."

"Thank you, Miss Schmidt. Miss Martin? You're willing to comply with these conditions to keep your baby with you?"

Standing beside Renata, she couldn't track what the conditions were anymore, but even if they included swimming with sharks or a transorbital lobotomy, she was ready to agree.

"Your Honor, I need to be heard regarding disposition," Renata said, motioning for Cora to sit.

As Cora obeyed, she wondered if the sharks were disappointed.

"First, the Protective Custody Report is fraught with errors and misrepresentations. It implies that Ms. Martin intentionally hit her baby out of anger and frustration. That is not what happened."

When Renata pulled out the photograph of the tape dispenser, Cora twinged, reliving the thudding impact after the burly thing slid into Naomi's sweet head, and the moment of silence before she cried. She couldn't look up from her lap until Renata had walked from Lindsay, who hissed to Vanessa for a second, and then to the judge.

"Ms. Martin had not torn the diaper in a fit of frustration," Renata said. "She was trying to salvage a bag of defective diapers. The tabs had fused, so she was using tape. The accident happened when the tape failed to cut. Because it was the end of the roll, the dispenser slid to her daughter's head. The injury was very slight and has already healed."

The judge squinted back at Naomi.

"After the accident, Ms. Martin put ice on her daughter's head and brought her to the hospital to make sure she was okay. There were no conflicting reports about the accident from Ms. Martin, as the report tries to suggest—only what appears to be confusion, suspicion, or both on the part of one nurse and one caseworker. Ms. Martin's words were twisted and taken out of context. She said she was 'in a daze' and 'trying to wake up' during the diaper change—not at the hospital.

"Caseworker Dixson described Ms. Martin as agitated and hostile in the hospital, but some emotion would be expected from a distraught first-time mother of a newborn. Especially if Ms. Dixson was prodding Ms. Martin in an unprofessional, accusing manner. Ms. Dixson was the only person at the hospital who reported Ms. Martin being angry, which included hospital staff and Ms. Dixson's supervisor.

"Ms. Dixson made exaggerated, erroneous claims in her report. For example, during her visit to maternal grandparents' home, she noted fear that Ms. Martin might injure her with a water glass. My client and her mother can only surmise that Ms. Dixson experienced this unwarranted fear when my client reached for forms near a water glass. If Ms. Dixson imagined that my client would start a bar-fight-style brawl in her parents' home, that was not based in reality.

"Furthermore, the comment that Ms. Martin was 'sluggish, consistent with coming down' is complete speculation. I am sure Your Honor is familiar with the problem-solving principle of Occam's razor."

Cora wasn't. The judge smiled with his mouth but not his eyes.

"When faced with two competing theories," she continued, "the theory with the fewest assumptions is generally correct. Here, Ms. Martin appeared tired because she was sleep deprived, being the sole caregiver for a newborn. There is no need to search for another explanation. There is certainly no factual basis to jump to substance abuse as Ms. Dixson has. At the home visit yesterday, Ms. Dixson was fishing for evidence against Ms. Martin."

Fishing isn't a violent-enough analogy. Maybe whaling with a harpoon.

"Maternal grandmother shared that my client proactively sought counseling when the family was grieving after the disappearance of her older sister, Julie Martin. If the State is trying to imply that Ms. Martin must share her sister's mental health issues because they are related, that would be wild speculation.

"Ms. Dixson even turned maternal grandmother's words against her, alleging that she has memory issues or was feigning them to protect her daughter. She only said she wanted to take notes during their conversation since her daughter had not yet joined them."

Renata consulted the scrawled notes on her yellow pad, checking off items.

"As to the State's recommendations, we support Naomi being placed with her mother. We stipulate to them residing in maternal grandparents' home. And we stipulate to Ms. Martin not co-sleeping with her infant; she does not make a practice of that, regardless. Those are the only lawful conditions. The remaining conditions are not legally or factually warranted, and we object to them. Line-of-sight supervision is unnecessary to ensure child safety and would be unduly burdensome on the family."

"The drug test," Cora whispered.

Renata muted the microphone. "Are you sure?"

She nodded, so Renata released the button and said, "The requested UA need not and should not be ordered because the facts do not support it, but Ms. Martin will voluntarily complete one today."

Judge Palmer made a note.

"Your Honor." Renata waited for him to look up. "I can't stress this enough. If the Court were to order Ms. Martin to sign releases of information, that would be reversible error. Conditions of an in-home plan must be tailored to increasing protective factors and promoting child safety. Any condition designed to assist with the State's investigation is an unlawful end run around a parent's right to due process of law.

"I also move the Court to amend the condition that Ms. Martin and maternal grandparents cooperate with DCFS's assessment. To be a lawful order, the condition should read that they will cooperate with the safety plan, not the assessment—their investigation. Thank you, Your Honor."

Lindsay hopped up as if they were on a teeter-totter. "Your Honor."

The judge bowed his head.

"Thank you," she simpered. "I'm sure the Court can see through Counsel's defense tactics."

Truth isn't tactics.

"Rather than addressing each of Counsel's claims, I will let the Protective Custody Report speak for itself. My client is trying to protect a vulnerable infant who has already suffered head trauma at least once in her mother's care. That's why these conditions need to be ordered. Cora Martin's sister suffered a schizophrenic break. Schizophrenia is genetic in origin, and it manifests around Mother's age.

"The baby's head trauma is concerning. Mother's mental health is concerning. The agency needs to do its due diligence. If, after a thorough investigation, we determine this was indeed an accident and that Mother does not have mental health issues, we will be happy to close this case." Lindsay settled her hips into the seat like a satisfied socialite chicken. A man-eating chicken who consorted with snakes.

Judge Palmer scrutinized the papers before him. The paneled courtroom seemed relieved to have peace and quiet, but Cora needed it to end so she could breathe.

"May I say something, Your Honor?" It was Aiden.

His lawyer stood. "Mr. Walsh, just a moment. Your Honor, Father supports the in-home plan with Mother, but we were not able to discuss all the conditions, so if he could be heard on that."

The judge nodded. "Go ahead, Mr. Walsh."

Cora stared at the table while Aiden spoke.

"I'm glad to hear this can be over once they can see Cora's a safe mother. She doesn't need supervision. And she doesn't have a drug or alcohol problem. Cora is one of the sanest, most grounded, kindest people I've ever met. Naomi couldn't have a better mom."

Her vision blurred.

"Thank you, Mr. Walsh. Miss Martin."

Using the table for balance, she stood with Renata, swiping a tear.

"You have an opportunity here, and I hope you take advantage of it—for your daughter's sake."

She nodded.

He waited.

"Yes, Your Honor."

"You have an excellent attorney, but I hope you understand that everyone here wants to ensure your daughter's safety."

You don't understand. "Yes, Your Honor."

"I'm happy to order the following: placement with mother, conditioned on her continued residence with maternal grandparents as safety service providers." He smiled at Cora's parents in the front pew. "I am not ordering line-of-sight supervision. Mother will sign Releases of Information for all mental health records."

"Your Honor," Renata said.

"I am not ordering a psychological evaluation. I am ordering Mother and grandparents to cooperate with the safety plan." He surveyed everyone. "I thank the attorneys for their advocacy and presentation of the case. Cooperation is the key to getting this little family back on its feet. Best of luck to you, Miss Martin. And thank you, grandparents, for making this in-home plan possible. The agency needs to do its job." He flashed his Hollywood Santa smile.

Renata stood. "Your Honor."

His smile fell off like a mask. "Mrs. Ochoa?"

"We should be able to gather information helpful to the Court by early next week. I would request a review shelter hearing as soon as the Court has availability."

Recovering his preferred magnanimity, he said, "I won't be here. You'll have Judge Hager or Judge Bronski."

Renata stood stiff.

"What is the first opening for a review hearing next week?" he asked the assistant.

Reading her monitor, she whispered to him, "If parties are available, the Court could hear this on Monday at 11:00 a.m. with new shelter hearings."

"No, I'm sure that won't give Mother's attorney enough time for her investigation. How about Wednesday? Would a week from today be too soon, Mrs. Ochoa?"

"Monday would be sufficient, Your Honor."

His brow furrowed. "Wednesday, November 9th. 11:00 a.m. Court is adjourned." He stood.

While his black robe billowed behind him, Cora stood with the others, and a chill flowed over her. The man who had judged her was leaving: the white sheep of the Death family.

* * *

Back in the small conference room, her dad pulled out a chair for her mom, holding Naomi. Unable to pick a chair, Cora had a pinched, spinning headache; she was probably dehydrated on top of everything else. Renata opened her mouth as the door closed behind her, but it sprang open before she could speak.

It was Vanessa, waving papers like a white flag—for Cora's surrender, not hers. Her smile looked sincere for once. Blocked at the doorway, her face soured.

"Now that Ms. Martin is represented," Renata said, standing in her way, "you will need to go through me." Tugging the forms from Vanessa's grip, she pushed the door wider. "You can go."

"Failure to cooperate with the safety plan—"

"Right," the lawyer smiled. "We need a copy of the new safety plan."

"They already have a copy, so you can get that from your client. The terms are the same other than the conditions the judge ordered."

"Exactly." She adjusted her foot, bracing open the door. "I am sure you will update the plan with the judge's modifications when you get back to your office. If you could email the updated plan to Ms. Martin and me by the end of the day, I would appreciate that." Lifting the forms, she said, "You have one in here for the UA, right?"

"Yes."

"Perfect. I will email you scanned copies. Have a good day."

"The UA needs to be done today, or it will be considered dirty."

"I know."

"And those releases need to be signed immediately, or your client is in contempt."

Renata smiled. "Are you trying to give me legal advice? Unlawful practice of law is frowned on by the Utah State Bar, unless you have a law degree?"

"I do not." Vanessa's eyes narrowed to almost nothing behind her cat eye glasses.

"That's my *pro bono* tip of the day for you: don't give legal advice. You can go."

The caseworker leaned around her to Cora's parents. "I would strongly recommend—"

"Vanessa!" Renata's volume startled Cora and her mom. Naomi stirred.

The wide-eyed caseworker arched back like an affronted house cat who had found a she-wolf occupying her favorite couch.

Renata's smile was gone. "As I said, you are not to speak to my client without my permission. Do you have a question for me?"

"I was speaking," she sneered, "to the safety service providers."

"Now is not a good time. Thank you."

A smirk oozed over her face. "Tell your client that unless I have those releases today, that baby will be in foster care tonight. You have a nice day, Ms. Ochoa. Let's hope your client can, too." The door started to close behind her.

But Renata jerked it open and called through the hallway, "Lindsay! I'll email you the releases next week, okay? I need an office appointment with my client."

"Okay," Vanessa's lawyer called.

Back in the conference room, Renata shoved the door, but the soft-close hinge wouldn't allow it to slam.

"Sorry about that," she sighed. "I will give you the address for the treatment center so you can get the UA done when you leave."

Naomi fussed.

"Here, Mom, I'll take her. Dad, can you hand me that blanket?"

"Here?"

"Yes, Mom, here." Cora turned to Renata. "You don't mind if I—"

"Please, go ahead."

"Thanks." She spread the swaddling cloth over her shoulder and helped Naomi latch on.

Renata shook her head. "What the judge did is not legal, ordering you to sign releases for your mental health records. If we can get your case before one of our regular judges, they can undo this."

"If I don't sign them, aren't I risking Naomi going into foster care?"

Her mom patted her arm. "She'd be with us for a few days. We could make it work."

"We don't know that." Her dad glowered. "They only have to say we're uncooperative to take her. We can't even keep our private life private."

CORA

MONDAY, NOVEMBER 7, 2016

"Have a seat wherever," Renata said, sweeping her hand from two chairs at her desk to a couch beneath a wall of windows. The top blinds stayed wide open, letting in the blue sky and the tips of power poles, but the lower ones were slanted.

Grateful for the privacy considering the sidewalk right outside, Cora rolled out a chair at the mahogany laminate desk. "I like your office."

"One of the perks of staying at Franklin County Public Defender for eleven years." On the credenza behind her sat an upright black block with white flowing script:

Do not be overcome by evil, but overcome evil with GOOD

"Isn't that a Bible verse?"

Nodding, Renata asked, "How are things going?" and lowered her standing desk attachment with her computer.

"Fine. No drama. No sleep," Cora laughed, "but no drama."

"I remember those days when my daughter was a baby. And I had my husband to help. Can your parents help with night duty? The first night I got 8 hours, I woke up a new woman."

"I'm sure they would." But the sleeplessness wasn't about that. "I hate to bug them."

A photo behind Renata showed a preteen girl in a basketball uniform standing beside a handsome man, probably Renata's husband. He appeared happy and confident with one arm around the grinning girl and one arm pinning a basketball to his hip.

"Is that your daughter?" *Wait a minute.* Scrutinizing Renata's face, she imagined her without her thick glasses, with her hair in a ponytail… "I have seen you before! You do yoga, right? With your daughter?"

"Oh! Do you go to Alchemy, too?"

She shook her head. "I just saw you and your daughter on a walk." Nodding at the photo, she asked, "Is that your husband?"

"Mm-hm."

"Is he her coach?"

"He was."

"How cool!" Cora smiled. "He doesn't like hot yoga?"

"I only started this year. Hugo passed away in 2015."

"I'm so sorry."

"We miss him." Sighing, Renata refocused. "How much time do you have? I am sorry my hearing took longer than expected."

"As long as my mom is doing okay with Naomi—I'm sure she is—I don't have any time limitations. But don't you close at 5:00?"

"I can stay past 5:00 if we need to." Flipping open a pale green legal file, she made a note. "Dr. Fairbanks has not faxed me records regarding your Effexor prescription and your work with him, or the hospital in Sego. But I only sent those releases Wednesday, so not surprising."

"Those are still confidential with you, right, since you're my lawyer?"

"Certainly. We will decide together whether to share them with DCFS."

"Can we just send parts of it? There's information I need to keep private—about someone else."

"That might be possible, if we can limit their release to the assessment and a summary from the doctor. Who are you protecting, if you don't mind?"

"Aiden." Cora sighed. "I've forgiven him, but the sex wasn't consensual. Dr. Fairbanks knows. Date rape. He recommended I have no contact with him."

"I am so sorry."

"Aiden's sorry, too. He had—this is confidential, right?"

Renata nodded.

"He said he'd done some cocaine with his brother, and that's why he lost control and took things too far. After their mom died, he said he and his brother started partying. He mostly drank and smoked pot, but Neil got into cocaine and Aiden would do it with him sometimes, like a bonding thing." Cora shook her head. "But he did drug treatment on his own, after he... after we broke up. He's still doing 12-step groups. He's even leading a meeting up in Seattle." She shrugged. "That's what he told me anyway."

"Wonderful." The kindness in Renata's face reminded Cora of how she pictured Jesus: seeing evil clearly like the tar pit it was, having the merciful discernment to spot stuck souls, and having the strength to help them out. "If you like, we could wait on the releases until Wednesday. It is very likely our regular judges will fix the illegal order so you would not have to sign them."

"That's safest, I think. Would Naomi stay with my parents if I got in trouble?"

Renata nodded. "Can you tell me more about what the Sego psychiatrist said? Your father mentioned *folie à deux*."

"That's when one person develops a mental illness and someone close to them gets wrapped up in their craziness because of the relationship. They said my sister, Julie, and I shouldn't be alone together."

HOLLY

MONDAY, NOVEMBER 7, 2016

"Beetlejuice? Like the movie?" Holly crossed her arms over her tan moto jacket.

The moon was the brightest thing in the night sky, almost half-full and waxing. They hadn't reached the crest of the hill yet, but the break in the trees allowed for stargazing.

"Different spelling." In the semi-dark, Jacob's black leather coat and the yellow leaves were cast blue. He came behind her, pulling her close and pointing up. "Look down and right. See that blue star?"

She followed the trajectory of his finger. One star looked a bit bluer than the rest.

"I think so." It was utterly unfair, asking her to use her brain when his inviting body pressed behind her.

"That's Rigel. Orion's left foot."

"Huh."

"You're hiking. You're lost. It's nighttime. Where's North?"

"The North Star."

"Right. Where's that?"

"North."

Jacob's chuckle rumbled onto her back. "I'm getting you a compass for Christmas."

"I'd rather night hike with you anyway."

"You can do this." He patted her hip. "I'm pinned under a tree—"

"Ouch."

"Hurts like hell. Find help. North." Turning her hips, he pointed her in a different direction.

Her running shoes shuffled through the leaves. "This way?" she asked, gazing upward.

"Mm-hm." His hands slipped beneath her jacket, back on her hips.

Holly wished his hands were under her sweater and her jeans, too. His warm mouth planted on the crown of her head. She tried to get into the spirit of the challenge, focusing on the cold sky instead of her hot date.

"The Big Dipper's there, right?" She pointed.

"Mm-hm." Jacob's breath was steady on her scalp.

Holly spun around, breaking the connection between his lips and her head. "You're not even looking!"

"I trust you." His breathy laugh breezed through her hair as he docked her back against his heavenly body.

"You're a horrible teacher."

"Did you say something?"

"Whatever. Big Dipper's there." Her left cheek vibrated.

"Thought your ass of steel was lopsided." He grabbed it. "Clang!"

She slipped her phone from her back pocket: **Cora**. "It's my friend with the baby."

Can you still foster?

"What's wrong?" he asked, holding her shoulder.

"I need to make a call." Stepping away to protect Cora's privacy, she said, "You can tell me my horoscope when I get back."

Click. A round patch of path lit up. "Not astrology." The beam of light moved as Jacob held his stubby flashlight to her.

Holly shook her head and waved it off.

Click. Darkness again. While Jacob returned to looking at the stars, she held her phone to her ear and ambled up the path.

After a ring, Cora said, "Hi Holly."

"Is everything okay?"

"We're still with my parents, but we're fine."

"Oh thank god."

"Sorry! Not for Naomi. Did your certifier get back to you today?"

Holly picked up her pace, heading up the wood-chipped trail. "I told her not to bother."

"What?"

She shrugged. "Screw those jerks."

"No! I feel terrible. You wanted to foster, and you'd be such a good mom. Some baby needs you."

"You're sweet. I'll think about it." She did need to think about it—and think about how much her hope in a family with Jacob had contributed to her faded interest in fostering. Gunshots or explosions were popping on Cora's end. "Are you calling from a war zone?"

"It's movie night." Then her volume dipped as she told someone, "Go on without me."

"I can let you go." She stopped, gazing into the trees.

The noise faded. "I'm going to bed anyway."

Holly meandered down the trail. "My mom and I used to watch old classics. Stayed up all night once. Doesn't that sound fun? We could make popcorn..."

"I'd be lucky to stay awake for one," Cora laughed.

"Hey, I should probably keep my big mouth shut, but are you and your ex back together?"

"We're just friends. Co-parents, I guess."

She frowned. "I couldn't forgive someone who'd taken advantage of me like that. I get that he was high, but how fricking reckless is that? It's like that movie with Denzel Washington as the cokehead pilot. They should both be in prison."

The dark hillside was quiet.

"Sorry."

"I was reckless, too. And I couldn't forgive myself if I kept Naomi from knowing her father, so…"

"Can I mom you for a second?"

"Sure."

"He looks at you like you're a cheeseburger and he's starving."

Cora's laugh sounded tight.

"I dated a guy like that once. He was intense—and hot! It was like junk food—fast and cheap, and I sort of wanted to puke afterward. Junk love. Your ex reminds me of him. Be careful, okay?"

"Aiden might be dating someone else now. Co-parenting is going well, actually."

"That's fantastic. And you're amazing."

"Hardly. I should let you get back to your night. Thanks again for everything. I owe you."

"Movie night. Then we'll be even." She surveyed the spot where Jacob had been.

"That sounds fun. Maybe when Naomi's older and I'm not so sleep-deprived. Have a good night!"

"G'night!" Jacob was not in sight, only trees and shadows. "Oy! Boyfriend!"

"Wow."

Click. A spot of light came through a stand of pines, beaming to a fainter glow on the path before him. She smiled and followed the dim spotlight, which moved a step ahead of her until she found Jacob sitting on a stump like a sexy Lorax.

"Did I miss the conversation about this being an open relationship?"

"What?" Holly walked closer.

"Movie night?"

She stood beside him and stroked his silky head. "Are you jealous? The flashlight clicked off. "No."

"Darn."

"Unless it's a dude." He clipped the tiny tool back on his belt.

"That friend I had to help on Halloween."

Drawing her to his lap, he asked, "Can I do anything?"

She hesitated, shaking her head, and put her phone in her jacket pocket before she sat.

He patted her hip. "This zips, right? Don't want to lose your phone."

"Does it get old being right all the time?" Holly searched for the zipper until his hands were on hers.

He found the tab and pulled. She could hear it more than feel it, the itsy metal pieces threading together, uniting, bonding, holding fast. It sounded so fricking much like unzipping, which was really what she wanted... She tried to be content. Jacob's warm lap under her ass was paradise. His gentle-giant arms surrounding her made everything right with the world. And even though the fallen autumnal leaves were on the downhill side of life, the air around Jacob was spring.

"What do you want for Christmas? Besides a compass."

Your hands on my body. "I'll have to think about that," she laughed, and draped her arms over his shoulders. "What do you want for Christmas?"

"Hold on. You thought of something."

Holly shook her head.

"I have ways of making people talk." His dark eyebrows dropped, mock-threatening.

"Trained at Guantanamo?"

"You don't have to tell me."

"Reverse psychology!" She smirked. "I am all over you, mister."

His smile went limp as if her all over him sounded fantastic.

Oh, help. She filled her lungs with cool air, but the scent of leather and soap and him came with it. "What happened to you not showering?"

Jacob brushed his fingertips below her chin. "I have a proposal."

Not a marriage proposal. Calm down. "What's that?"

When his lips coupled with hers, she was back at the ranch one teenage summer with her mouth around the sweetest summer peach. The memory would have been a better match if she'd sat on an electric fence.

He hovered just past the smile she was trying to contain in case he wanted to kiss her again. If a massive meteor ended it all right now, she was good.

Bullshit. The kiss was like the first bite after a long fast: perfect and satisfying for a moment but waking an insatiable beast. Why, in the name of all that was holy, did she have that talk with him? If they broke up, she'd regret not having sex with him. Losing him would hurt like hell regardless.

"Safer out here." His close, playful grin made the aching worse. "I'm not an outdoor sex guy."

What was he saying? She found her game face. "That might be a deal breaker. What's your policy on tents?"

"Tent I could do. Remind me to take us camping someday."

"Take us camping someday."

"You are a huge help."

"You're welcome."

"What would you say to a little reconnaissance mission?" The silkiness of her white cashmere sweater couldn't compete with the bliss of his calloused hand sliding underneath. "Tell me when to stop."

"Nope." Holly told her head to move, and it responded, pivoting on her neck.

"Good call." His hand pulled away from her belly.

She held it there. "I might not tell you to stop."

"What about 'hashtag vagina goals'?"

"You're all sorts of kryptonite. Did I tell you how hot I thought you were when we met?"

"Sorry I've let myself go," he said, grinning in the moonlight. "Weren't you with What's-His-Face?"

"Don't judge."

"Wouldn't dream of it. Speaking of..." His warm fingers slipped under the waistband of her low-rise jeans. "This six-pack you have going. Fair game? Always wanted one, but I like food too much."

"I don't have a six-pack."

"Right here." He traced the ridge of muscle forming her Adonis belt from her hip toward her crotch. "You even have a 'V.'"

"I do not." Her heart was flying, pushing blood through her veins like a treadmill on way too high. She put her hand on his and braced it there, bracing herself there.

"Too far?"

She pulled his hand onto her breast over her bra.

He chuckled. "If I have to…"

"Ass," she smirked.

"I'll get there." His fingertips touched her skin, taking her breath despite the stupid padded push-up blocking his palm. He closed his fingers around her like a farmer considering whether a beloved tomato was ripe enough to separate from its vine. Her breast was dying to be dinner, but all she could do was grab his jaw and shut his mouth with hers. Cradling her neck, he kissed her back.

Once she mustered the brainpower to unzip her jacket, she tossed it off, and his hand trailed down to her lap. His lips were gone. She blinked.

His bright smile kept her from going in for another kiss. "You okay?"

Holly nodded, breathing fire. "I hope you don't do this with all your suspects. What I want for Christmas is your hands on my body. That's my confession, what I was thinking. But that's so five minutes ago." She fingered his waistband. "Now I want to go back to your house and get naked."

A switch had flipped, knocking Jacob's smile offline and disconnecting his features from the grid of sociability. His intense eyes dropped from hers as he bent to her neck.

Instead of kissing it, he whistled.

Squealing at the stream of air, she leaped off his lap. As he continued, looking up at her, she registered the first bars of "You Can't Always Get What You Want."

"Not a fan of being serenaded?" His voice was deeper than usual.

"That wasn't a serenade. That was a sneak attack. You know I'm ticklish."

"You're right." Standing, he lifted her onto the stump.

"What's this for?"

"Lady should be up high for a proper serenade."

"This just makes us even."

"Even's good." He kissed her. "See?" They kissed again, holding hands.

"It's okay, I guess." She rubbed her thumb over his hand. "I have another confession."

"Sure you're not Catholic?"

"Positive." Holly slipped off her sweater and dropped it, cold but thrilled in just her bra.

"Um…" Jacob backed up a step.

"Women's fashion isn't fair to men. It's all lies: the makeup, the Spanx, the push-up bras…"

"I've seen you without makeup. Spanx would be pointless."

"This, though." She slid her thumbs under the straps of her bra and pulled forward like a geezer with suspenders. "I've got to be honest. These are not my boobs." Locking eyes with him, Holly unclasped her bra, held it dangling beside her, then let it fall. "These are my boobs. Sorry."

He stared in the moonlight. "Damn."

From the trail, leaves rustled beneath quick footsteps.

Jacob turned, his left hand flying to his waist. Holly jumped down and snatched up her sweater. Tinkling metal joined the rapid footfalls as she clutched her cashmere to her chest, getting jabbed by the pine needles clinging to it.

A Rottweiler ran into the grove of trees and straight at Jacob, who offered open palms. It sniffed him and trotted to Holly. She put a low hand out, too, and the dog gave her a long snarfle. Her other arm went into her jacket with Jacob's guidance.

"Molly!" a voice called.

Holly slipped her second arm in, spinning to keep her back to the trail.

"Molly!" the woman called louder.

Holly struggled with her zipper. Jacob searched the ground, and the dog scampered toward the voice.

"There you are. Come on." Footsteps headed away.

Jacob wrapped his arm around her shoulders, and they just listened. Then he offered her bra. "Want to get naked again and put this on?"

She found the zipper, but he took her hands, shaking his head.

"Bad idea. Have to ticket you for lewdness if a witness showed up. Class B Misdemeanor."

"You wouldn't have my back?"

"Can't risk losing my job."

His coltish eyes were infinitely lovable.

"I have my wife and kids to think about," he smiled.

"Current or future?" She looped her sweater around her bra.

"Future." He hugged her shoulders. "Might be you." Papery leaves crinkled under their feet as they rediscovered the nature trail.

"Don't I get a say in this?"

"If you got pregnant, we'd have to get married."

"There's good." She pointed to a shrub. "Nice and private."

"Respect the process, Samson. I know you like everything fast—"

"Not everything." Holly smirked.

He chuckled. "Are you Samson or Delilah? Repeat after me."

"'Repeat after me.'"

Jacob squeezed her hand. "I, Samson…"

"'I, Samson…'"

"Don't want this mook's hands all over my gorgeous body."

"Aren't oaths supposed to be truthful?"

"Looking for blind obedience here."

"Not really my thing."

* * *

The trail dropped them onto the asphalt uphill from Jacob's house. Between his hot hand and the frigid air free-ranging under her jacket, popping her nipples against the leathery material, the night was a stupid kind of young.

"Want to watch old movies and stay up all night?"

"Dammit, woman. I'm taking my blue balls and going home."

"Fine." Holly smiled, disappointed and grateful. They thumped down the hill past charming houses.

"I figured out what you're doing."

"Trying to seduce you? Because if you don't touch me, or look at me, or get within a five-mile radius, I can be good. Mostly."

He shook his head. "Different thing."

"Giving you wildly mixed signals?"

"Knowing's half the battle, but no."

"What?"

"Sabotaging my vote. Get me sleep-deprived so I forget to vote tomorrow."

"See how red my hands are?" Walking backward down the slope, she put them up.

Jacob kissed her palm. "Tastes guilty."

"I might as well come clean. Have you heard of the 'Him Too' movement? Promise not to tell anybody."

"You have my word."

"Patriotic women across the country are giving their bodies to conservative men tonight to keep them away from the polls. I was relieved when I got you as my assignment. You're not entirely disgusting."

"That's my girl." He squeezed her hand, surrounding it in electric warmth.

In a house with big windows, a light behind a darkened room cast a silhouette of a man with a baby on his shoulder. She wanted that so much. She wanted that to be Jacob so much. And it seemed close, like if the hill was a little steeper and she could get some momentum, she could fly to that place.

"About your Christmas list." He brought their hands to his mouth and kissed the back of her hand. "Before I volunteer for the 'Him Too' movement, we need some rules of engagement."

"Okay."

"You're not stepping foot in my house tonight. I grab your purse, you leave. Agreed?"

"My heels are there, too."

"And your heels."

Holly sighed. "I see how it is. Let a boy get to second base—"

He stopped in front of her. "Hi." The hill put them closer to eye level. When he braced his hands on her hips, his thumbs on her abdomen sent fire through her veins. "Do I have your attention?"

"Mm-hm."

"You're getting in your car when we get to my place, yes?"

"Deal."

"And you're not going to let me tear your clothes off in my driveway."

"Aww."

He looked stern—sort of.

"Fine. No." She didn't mean to grin so hugely, but she couldn't help it. "You have a wife and kids to think about."

CORA

"You okay?" Wes was sitting, not helping, and not being lectured about not helping.

"Mm-hm." Cora held aside the serving bowl of mashed potatoes to see where she had scuffed the dotted rug. She nudged its upturned corner with her foot.

The dusky central window in the nook behind her dad reflected her crazy hair and her mother following her with dinner rolls. She took the tall, upholstered chair near her father; her mom sat by Wes.

"Pass the potatoes?" Wes asked.

As she did, the red-eyed raven looked askance at her from the gold *Tree of Life, Stoclet Frieze* print. Unfurling the cloth napkin, she kept her eyes down for a stealth prayer. But it was only *Help.*

Her mother offered the green beans.

"Thanks." Cora spooned them onto her gilded plate. Silverware clinked against china.

Wes prodded his Cornish game hen. "How much trouble will I get in if I pick this thing up and make it dance?"

Laughing helped. "Five bucks if you do," she said. "And sing. Let me get my phone first."

"What song? Ooh! Ba-by chick, doo doooo doo-duh-doo, ba-by chick doo doooo doo-duh-doo, ba-by—"

"That's enough, Wes." Only the corner of their dad's mouth smiled.

"Mom." Wes turned to her. "You've outdone yourself as usual. I don't think I can eat little ladybird, though."

"Once you cut into it—here." She moved her plate to the side and lifted his. "Let me—"

"Terry! For heaven's sake, you're not going to cut the boy's food for him?"

"My bad." Pulling his plate back, Wes plunged his fork into a potato pile while their mom sank into her seat.

Their dad salted his dismembered chicken and scrutinized Cora. "I know your attorney thinks today was a win, but I hope you know you have nothing to hide. The psychiatrist at the Sego hospital saw right away you weren't mentally ill."

"A lot of people take antidepressants, too," her mother said.

The fragrant flaky roll absorbed the pat of butter as it left the knife.

"It's no different than the drug test." Her dad studied her. "Aren't you concerned at all that Naomi's father isn't volunteering to UA?"

"He probably smokes pot."

"Wes!" Cora said.

"Everybody does."

Their mom recoiled. "You don't."

Wes shook his head, skewering green beans.

Before Cora could decide whether it would be helpful to share that Aiden had completed treatment and was now an active member of a 12-step recovery community, her father said, "It galls me that Child Welfare had him supervising you," sawing white breast meat. "You need a custody order. That petition is ludicrous. He shouldn't have sole custody—you should. Be careful. He might try to get custody when you're vulnerable."

"Aiden isn't trying to take Naomi from me, Dad. He's trying to help."

"He can't be trusted."

"Dad." She set her fork on the plate's deep blue rim. "I know he made mistakes. I did, too. If you got to know him…"

He shook his head, chewing.

"His parents asked if we could come for Thanksgiving dinner. It would be so great if—"

"Who you choose to have in your family is your business." Her dad pointed at her with his empty fork. "He will not be part of mine."

HOLLY

"What do you think, Girlfriend? Would you two get along?" Holly showed her phone screen to the Maine Coon sprawled across her lap.

The mega cat rubbed her whiskers against the corner, pushing back her upper lip and exposing sharp teeth.

"No eating the puppy."

The cat's tawny eyes stared; she was making no promises.

In the photo, the puppy's big dark eyes were magnified in black fur diamonds, and her coppery tan ears perked up and sloped out. Her head was cocked, pointing one ear higher. Holly beamed at the picture once more before opening her Bible app.

Thank god she was done with Deuteronomy. Ecclesiastes had to be better; she was excited to start her dad's favorite book. Resuming the requisite rubbing of Girlfriend, Holly settled deeper into Jacob's espresso-brown leather sofa. Rachel Maddow's lips were moving on TV, but she'd muted her. Girlfriend purred like a motor idling.

For everything there is a season, and a time for every matter under heaven.

Isn't that a '60s song?

Was this a new season? She did look like she belonged there: her charcoal leggings complemented the dark gray edges of Jacob's rug, and her cranberry zip-up matched the rug's deep red center. The season of Jacob? Of starting her family? Or just a season of Jacob, another boyfriend in her long line of boyfriends? *Seasons end.*

A text from Cora popped up:

Thanks for checking in. We got what we asked for, but I'm still at my parents' house.

She typed:

If you see Nessie, tell her to eat a bag of

As she scrolled for an eggplant emoji, Holly had second thoughts, so she deleted it, typing instead:

Stay strong!

She almost added, "I'll be praying," because she had. She'd been praying for Cora and also for herself, for faith. But she preferred to keep that private like when she'd applied to colleges—her friends didn't need to know about the rejections.

I should pray for Mom.

Holly stared at the coffee table. *Where the hell did that come from?* Her phone in her lap answered: the text about Thanksgiving. That's why Nanette was on her mind. She went back to reading, picking up the last line she'd read:

For everything there is a season, and a time for every matter under heaven.

Was it time to make amends with her mother? It wasn't that she didn't love her; she just didn't trust her. *And the thought of being like her makes me want to run to a deserted island.* When keys scraped in the front door, she was laughing at herself, picturing a failed attempt at running on water.

Jacob's feet plodded inside in a moment, so her guilt for not getting up to open the door was short-lived.

"Hi!" she called.

"Sorry that took so long." His footfalls rang through the house.

"I'd come help," she said, lounging her head against the sofa. "But I'm trapped under your Girlfriend."

"Cat!" Plastic bags rustled in the kitchen. "Get off my girlfriend."

About to turn off her phone, the heading below distracted her:

The God-Given Task

What gain has the worker from his toil? I have seen the business that God has given to the children of man to be busy with. He has made everything beautiful in its time. Also, he has put eternity into man's heart, yet so that he cannot find out what God has done from the beginning to the end. I perceived that there is nothing better for them than to be joyful and to do good as long as they live; also that everyone should eat and drink and take pleasure in all his toil—this is God's gift to man.

Well, thanks.

"More 'research'?" He stood beside her, grinning.

Air quotes and everything. Punk. "Mind your own business." Smirking, she put down her phone and searched for the TV remote beneath the feline overflow.

"Never tried an alphabetical reading plan," he said, then nodded at the TV. "MSLSD?"

"What?" She pointed the remote like a magic wand and turned it off.

"Your news. Food's getting cold." He scooped his arms under the mass of fluff and relocated Girlfriend.

Holly pressed her palms on her toasty lap. "She's better than an electric blanket."

Jacob gave her a hand up and a peck. He started to lead them to the kitchen but kissed her again instead.

"Didn't think that would take so long. The deep fryer Dad wants was on sale. Checkout line took forever."

She loved that Jacob let her hug him as long as she wanted. "It's okay," she said with her cheek on his chest. "I still love you. Even if you did vote for Trump."

They hadn't used the "L word" yet. *Crap.* Clamp went her mouth and then her eyes.

Once she released her squint of regret, she caught a flash of his smile.

"Sorry," she laughed, pulling away. "You know what I mean."

"Yeah." He hauled her back. "You love me."

Channeling her embarrassment into the most portentous scowl she could muster, she said, "I mean, your questionable political beliefs haven't made me hate you."

"Aww. Your questionable political beliefs haven't made me hate you, too." He joined his hands in a heart shape and placed them on his chest.

"Brat."

Chuckling, he clasped her hips at close-talking distance. His eyes got sweet and earnest as if he might profess his love because she'd accidentally started it.

"Don't you dare!" Her fiery eyes locked with his. "Look," she said, retrieving her phone from the sofa. "Here's something else I love." She held up the screen like a mirror; she was Perseus, and he was Medusa. "Look at this face! She's a German Shepherd mix."

After he took the phone, she put her hands on her hips.

"The shelter isn't sure who the dad is, might be an American Bulldog. Look at her little Flying Nun ears! The mom and siblings are spoken for. She's the runt. She's why I bought a house with a fenced yard. She's the one."

"The one, huh?" His face flickered with some private thought as he handed her phone back. "If you love her, you should bring her home. Make her part of your family. Food's getting cold."

"Really?" Holly wanted to ask how Girlfriend got along with dogs, but that felt presumptuous.

She followed him into the kitchen and boosted herself onto the countertop, which was speckled like Keith's except the base was brighter and the spots were more substantial. As transparent plastic warped beneath Jacob's fingers, the container made low, bubbling clicks.

"Make her feel at home." He opened the second one. "You're invited to Thanksgiving dinner at my folks' house," he said, hovering his hand over the shrimp in black bean sauce.

"I'd love that. My mom asked if we wanted to have Thanksgiving with her, but it's a long drive."

"We could do that."

No.

He stuck his finger in the beef and broccoli. "Maybe we should nuke these. How starving are you? The shrimp will hold up better if we heat it on the stove."

"That's fine. What can I do?"

He fed her a piece. "If you want to put some plates and forks out…"

"Mm." The garlicky meat sent happy signals through her body and cooled her jets a bit. She dismounted and went to the silverware drawer.

Pans clanged as he set two on the range.

C'mon brain. Forks. A road trip with Jacob would be fun, but…her mom. *Knives.* Holly placed napkins and utensils in the breakfast nook. With the three craftsman windows surrounding the table, it was almost out in nature, like a masculine version of her dining room. The gas stove click-click-click-woofed on and he turned on a second burner, centering the pans over the flames.

Back on the countertop, she faced her fear. "Please don't think less of me. I'm afraid to have you meet her."

"Your mom?"

She nodded.

"We'll do Thanksgiving wherever you want." He left his post to rub her thighs. "You're not your mom. And you're not a poison dart frog."

Glancing at the pans, she asked, "Do you want me to stir that, so it doesn't burn?"

"On it." He returned to the range.

"Either way, I'd like to give your folks a pie for Thanksgiving." Holly hopped down and took two square plates from the cupboard.

"As long as you're not stress baking." He dumped the shrimp dish into the second pan. "Last time Mark may have gotten food poisoning."

"You said it was good!" When she only got a wink, she said, "You're feisty tonight," and rubbed his hulky back while the green florets and beef slices swirled in the shallow pan. The savory aroma was almost as tempting as he was.

"Just happy to have my girl with me. What about two Thanksgivings? There's the weekend. Vegas could be fun." His lips opened, then sealed over something with a smile.

"I'll think about it." She hugged his back.

"When do you want to pick up your little ankle-biter?"

Seriously? "The shelter's open tomorrow…"

"Stay here tonight. We can go in the morning."

Holly's heart hiccupped.

"I'll be a gentleman."

"I don't have a change of clothes. Or a toothbrush."

"I've got toothbrushes."

"From your string of broken hearts, no doubt."

"New ones."

"I forgot you're a Boy Scout."

"'Be polite, be professional, have a plan to kill everyone you meet.'"

"The Scouts have gotten dark."

He winked. Then he smooched her.

Half an hour later, Holly cracked open a fortune cookie, raining dust on her mostly empty plate. She read the tiny strip: "'You have a secret admirer.'" Waving it, she smirked from the memory of Jacob asking for her number. "Bit late, isn't it?"

"Show some respect. These things transcend space and time." In the high-backed bench seat across from her, Jacob studied his slip with red lottery numbers on the back. "The first cookie was poisoned." Then, grinning, he read, "'Something wonderful is about to be happy.'"

"In"—Holly regretted the words as they came—"bed." She shook her head. "Doesn't work there."

"'You have a secret admirer in bed.'" He popped a hunk of cookie in his mouth. "That could work."

Standing with her plate, she reached for his. "Movie time?"

They were on the sofa two hours later. Holly lay with her head in Jacob's lap while he massaged her IT band, his long arm effortlessly spanning the distance from her hip to her knee. It was almost as nice as the ass rub had been.

Katharine Hepburn and Humphrey Bogart were paddling down the Nile, singing like drunk sailors. She wished an alligator would pop up and eat them, and not only because Humphrey Bogart was an unbelievable romantic lead with anyone but Lauren Bacall. Didn't they know they were in dangerous territory?

"Hey." Jacob smoothed her tight forehead. "You know this isn't Mission Impossible, right?"

"Tom Cruise wouldn't appreciate that."

"You staying over. We can do it. Not do it. I have a plan."

She stroked his stubbly jaw. "Of course you do."

* * *

In bed, waiting for Jacob to brush his teeth, Holly pulled the navy comforter over her t-shirt and leggings and nuzzled into the smell of him on the pillow.

"Light off?" He stood in the doorway in white striped pajama pants with no shirt.

Payback's a bitch. "Sure."

His gaze flicked to her bra on the bedside table before he clicked off the light and turned into a silhouette. A bluish glow filtered through the curtain as he climbed in and slid his arm toward her. She nestled her shoulder into his armpit and rested her head on his firm bare chest.

Breathing him in directly was hugely different from inhaling what had lingered on his bedding, different as pizza out of the oven and the ghost of a scent from its cardboard box. This she could eat. She rolled into him and kissed his chest, which made her mouth tingle like she'd used musky mint lip balm. Holly planted her lips there again, longer, then licked them. *Holy hell.* He was luscious.

"You seem tense." She sprang to her knees and straddled him.

"What are you doing?"

"Shoulder rub." Her hands moved down to his pecs.

Jacob chuckled. "Dietitians don't take Anatomy?"

"Chest rub, then. It isn't 'undercover activity.'" She smiled, relishing the power and the view, stroking his ridiculous arms.

"Uh-huh." His raised eyebrow dropped as his eyes closed.

She was glad he was enjoying it—though not too much since she couldn't feel a thing under her hips.

"Sorry," he frowned. "This is really uncomfortable."

Holly sat up while he adjusted what she assumed was a wedgie.

"Okay," he said.

Her hands went back to his chest, and her hips onto his. Touching down, she twitched into frozen stillness. He was enjoying it—a lot.

He reached for her as she was bending down to kiss him. Sparks seemed to fly from two sources—his hypnotic lips and breath and tongue around hers and the irresistible length of him tickling her lower abs, promising something impossibly better. It was really hard to pull her mouth from his. She positioned her hips over the base of him and slid glacially forward. His. Heat. Was. Beautiful. Holding at the top, she fluttered like a pinned bird, wanting to never ever move while also wanting to, badly.

Jacob clasped her arms. "Don't move." He lowered her, flattening her chest onto his.

"I thought I wasn't supposed to move."

He sighed a chuckle into her hair.

Like an addict, she was twitching and trembling and mouth hungry. She tugged up her shirt and eased backward, skimming her nipples over his slick, sparking, barely prickly chest.

But he pulled her up. "Holly." His arms were a very nice vice.

If she couldn't move, at least her breasts were splatted against his come-hither pecs.

"Hold still 'til I can get up," he said, planting his hands on her back. "Please."

"That's the problem. You could put an eye out with that thing." She rode his laugh like a surfer paddling over waves.

She was drifting off when Jacob patted her back again.

"Be right back."

Once she moved off him, he went to his dresser, slipped on a shirt, and climbed back under the cozy comforter.

"Turn around. I'll spoon you."

Smiling obedience, she flipped over, and his chest met her back. His breath on her neck gave her a thrill, so she scooched her hips back. But his retreated. Even though it wasn't really a rejection, she felt sort of pouty before his hand slid down her leg to her bare foot.

She twitched. "What are you doing?"

"Checking for running shoes."

"What? Goof," she laughed. "Darn, I was hoping for a foot rub."

"We can do that." Jacob kissed her temple, and then sat cross-legged, placing her foot in his lap.

"Ew." She tugged it away. "You don't have to do that."

He repossessed it. "Woman, let me rub your feet."

"Please stop if they're nasty." She rolled onto her back and melted, letting her eyes close. "Mmm. Thank you." Trying hard to relax, she reined in her thoughts about how amazing his hands would be other places.

"I love you" came out of the dark.

Holly's eyes shot open, and she shot up. "Please don't say that because of my slip earlier," she said, knee-walking toward him, sort of terrified.

Jacob pulled her close, so she wrapped her legs around him and sat between his crossed legs.

"It's true." His basketball hands held her hips.

She couldn't see his face as well as she needed to. In his hands and off-balance, she couldn't think straight. He wouldn't say it if he didn't mean it, but… His kiss, consuming and long and deliberate, should have cured her terror, but it made it worse.

"I vaulted it," he said, "so you wouldn't freak out and go full Gingerbread Man on me."

"Really?"

While she settled for another kiss as an answer, her mouth apologized to his tongue for wanting any other body part. Her ass succumbed to gravity, and central heat shot up through her PJs and leggings. Her breath caught. Then she cradled his head in her hand, wrapped her other arm above his shoulders, and nestled her lips on his neck.

"I love you, too." Holly flickered like the center of a flame. The terror wasn't gone, but she didn't feel alone in it. Somehow it was more real than anything she'd known, like true happiness *should* scare the ever-loving shit out of you. She never wanted to let go of him. Not even to have sex. This was what she needed: tight, hot holding. She was loved and home and the best, unsafest kind of safe.

After sitting for a small eternity in kinetic stillness, he chuckled. "My legs are officially asleep."

"Sorry!"

"Don't be. It's a good idea, sleep. Let's get some." They resumed spooning, closer this time.

While she breathed through the temptation of him, he wrapped his arm around her and rubbed her belly.

After a minute, she had to ask. "Did you and April wait?"

"No," he said, squeezing her. "This is better. Never thought I'd win the Woman Lotto, but here I am. Gorgeous girlfriend with an iron will."

"Iron will, my ass."

"Clang!" He grabbed it.

"You know I'd totally do you."

"Not tonight." His enormous hand smoothed her hair. "Get some sleep. Gonna have your hands full of puppy in the morning."

HOLLY

FRIDAY, NOVEMBER 25, 2016

"Everything was delicious, Mom. Thank you."

From Holly's seat across the modern black dining table, Nanette's coiffed blonde head was showcased against the massive painting behind her of flowering multicolored bushes surrounding a garden path. The round bushes weren't the problem. Her mother's free-range breasts, though, perky beneath her translucent white cold-shoulder dress... Those were horrifying.

"Not bad for two-day-old catering." Nanette smiled through still-perfect lipstick.

"Some flavors improve with time." The round frames of Charles's glasses complimented his bowtie and spiky gray hair.

Even sitting directly across from her mother through dinner, Jacob had been oblivious to the excessive show of mammary force. After Holly clasped his warm hand on her thigh, she got up.

"Finished?" She took his plate, still not knowing what to make of them. Each Fornasetti porcelain dish featured a big black-and-white ass. If her mom was trying to look worldly and daring, fine, but it was more like she was mooning them.

"I'll help." Jacob pushed out his chair.

"I've got it."

Nanette clipped to the end of the table, hovering her breasts near Charles's face. "Pie now? Or later?"

Charles wiggled his eyebrows, sliding his hand over her hip. "A little later?"

Holly widened her eyes at Jacob, who was managing a straight face, before she clomped to the open kitchen in her strappy black heels.

The modern white kitchen had almost enough lumens to burn away unwanted mental images, but not quite. Recessed lights in a rectangular hollow of the slick wall on her left shined on the gas range and a bowl of purple pomegranates. She paused at the sink, hidden in the countertop.

Nanette's heels clicked around the marble slab island. "Shame the sweet potato crostini got eaten up." Setting two stacked ass plates between the sink and a black platter of chrysanthemums, she said, "Those were divine!"

"Do you have a garbage disposal?"

"Do I have a garbage disposal." Smirking, she shook her head. "Leave those."

"That crostini could be great for my diabetic clients," Holly said. "I should find a recipe."

"I don't know, they're very rich with the blue cheese." She about-faced and cat-walked to the table, stopping beside Jacob, who stayed facing Charles.

Charles was telling the ice fishing story. Nanette sailed around the chunky black table, sheer billowy material trailing behind while she gathered first Holly's wine glass, then her own, and ran her fingers over Charles's shoulders.

Returning, she extended her Greek goddess arm. "Let's give the boys a minute to chat."

Holly accepted her glass. "The salads held up well. This Sauvignon Blanc is amazing."

"I had them keep the dressings on the side." Tipping back, Nanette drained her glass, then tapped it with a pointed, glossy beige nail. *Tink tink.* "New Zealand. They have a low-cal Sauvignon Blanc, too. In fact…" She glided past the white monolith partition into the kitchen's secret workspace, bright and compartmentalized like a luxury Ikea showroom. "Want me to open it?"

"This is plenty." Holly followed her.

"Suit yourself."

"What was in that dip with the parsnip pizza pockets?"

"You mean the pigs in a blanket?"

"It tasted like mint and cilantro."

Nanette laughed. "That is not my wheelhouse."

"Did you get the pie out?" *Like I asked?*

"Port," she muttered, and then smiled at Holly. "That's still in the refrigerator. How about some port?"

It would have been better at room temperature, but cold chocolate pecan pie would have to do. After she retrieved it, she eyed the electric mixer beneath her mother, who stretched up from the tips of her heeled toes to pull a bottle from a cupboard.

"You should have seen this place on Thursday." Nanette set down the bottle. *Clink.* "Wall-to-wall people. Everyone had the best time." Flicking open a handleless white cupboard, she said, "Susan asked about you. We still haven't forgiven you for not marrying Michael after high school. You were so cute together. Are you Facebook friends?"

"No."

"You should see his kids." The raisin-colored liquid glugged. "Cutest things! Michael's daughter just placed in a gymnastics competition. First grade! She reminds me of you at that age." She braced a hand back, tits out. "He looks better, more filled out. *Salud.*"

A stack of square dessert plates waited past the leftovers. Black-and-white mannequin hands faced off like a brainless attempt at a handshake—possibly mocking the Sistine Chapel painting of man and God touching fingers. Holly hoped the art didn't offend Jacob and hoped her mom wasn't trying to. With a slice of pie between the hands, they could look cute.

"Not as big as your new boy. Is that your type now? Tall, bald, and burly?"

"Mom!"

The men's voices were busy enough, but sound bounced everywhere. "I don't have a type."

Nodding, Nanette raised a penciled eyebrow. "Your boyfriends have run the gamut. You even dated that Asian boy in college."

Holly was without words.

"He seems genuine. Must have been a heartbreaker before he lost his hair. If you two have a son, he won't go bald because that gene…" Her eyes stared blankly into Holly's, then she shook her head and recovered a tight smile. "Never mind." She strode farther into the alcove as if she were looking for something.

Right. That gene's carried through the mother. Since Holly's dad had a full head of hair, she bet the Spanish sperm donor didn't.

Nanette ambled back to her and took a purple swig. "Jacob's handsome—how do you put it?—'as is.'"

"He's amazing as is."

"He voted for Trump, didn't he?"

"Let's not talk politics."

"Jacob isn't as whacked-out as some Republicans. You'll tell me if he gets controlling or wants you to quit your job."

"Mom? You know that thing about assuming?"

"As long as he doesn't brainwash you."

"Want me to put the food up?"

"We'll throw all this out." Nanette waved at the dishes. "Aren't my new plates fun? They're from Italy." She'd already said that, talked about the whole fricking trip.

"The whole house is elegant as hell."

"You didn't have to get a hotel." Grinning and waggling her finger, she approached. "Didn't I tell you that you needed to get laid? Look at you. Vibrant." She fondled a tip of her hair. "Let me know if you've changed your mind about the lashes. It warms my heart to see you enjoying life again."

"We didn't get a hotel to have sex. We're waiting."

"Waiting for what?" Her mother brought the two sides of her hair together like she was making sure they were even.

"I'm waiting until marriage."

"To have sex?"

She nodded.

"You're hardly a virgin, dear."

Holly stepped back. "That's not the point."

"Is this his idea, some traditionalist thing?"

"Do you think I'm a puppet?"

Nanette finally lowered her voice. "Darling, you are gorgeous. Any red-blooded man wouldn't be able to not do you. Don't end up in a passionless marriage."

"If anything, I'm too attracted to him." She got out the sugar.

"Passion isn't bad! I know I've hurt you, but—"

"Mom. Sex is a beautiful gift. But things that powerful need containment."

"Did he say that?"

"I'm ending this conversation if you can't be respectful. He's better than I deserve."

"That's impossible. I love your outfit. Hottest-girl-at-the-funeral look. It works for you." She touched the sleek black material on Holly's arm. "Of course, you'd look sexy in a garbage bag. He's clearly enamored with you. He's just a different breed."

A galloping horselaugh careened off the walls like slalom gates.

"Charles laughing like a college boy." She squeezed her hand. "Jacob will fit in fine. Don't worry."

Holly checked her watch, not worried. "I'm going to start the whipped cream."

"Do you have what you need?"

"Just need your bourbon."

"That's right." Nanette strutted to the high cupboard and returned the port while Holly set heavy cream and a jar of vanilla paste by the mixer. "Charles and I have been talking about moving someplace a little less…Vegas." She flailed her hand in circles. "Just when we're getting things the way we want them. Here, dear."

"Thanks."

"Before you two get serious, see if he'd move to a bigger city."

Holly poured the cream.

"I'd love to play with all the babies you'll be popping out. And no 'Grandma.' 'Gigi,' like Owen calls me." The mixer hummed. "Take some bathing suit pictures now. The body never fully recovers."

The spinning whisk was more interesting than whatever her mother was saying about stretch marks and creams. It was time. "Mom."

"Don't even bother with that brand. Not worth the money."

"Do you have a picture of my biological father?"

"God, no. Charles would destroy it."

"He knows about him?"

"Charles was very understanding."

"What's his name?"

"Let it be, darling. The man has a family."

Holly flicked up the mixer speed, so it hummed higher pitched at a higher volume.

"We already broke one home."

"Mom! I'm the product of the fricking homewrecking. Wouldn't you want to know if you had a child you hadn't met?"

"He knows about you. Don't ruin the man's life." After a disapproving frown, she strolled to the other side of the alcove. "Do you know how Keith's doing since your breakup?"

All Holly could do was seethe and watch the sweet cream froth in the silver bowl. A slight pressure moved from the small of her back to her hip and she recognized the feel of Jacob's hand.

Smiling thanks, she registered his maroon merino sweater: the one he'd worn the day they met. She slipped her arm around his waist, avoiding the bump of his holster.

"Chuck's tired of my bullshit and wants pie." That was directed to her mom. His look was only for her—sweet and concerned and asking if she was okay. "I'd rather hear about Keith. Billy-Bob?"

Nodding to both questions, Holly smiled at him.

"Can I get his address? For a thank you card: 'Sorry not sorry for your loss.' That reminds me, Nanette, I wanted to get a pic of you two in your Japanese garden, but we missed the light. What's another good photo spot?"

"Charles and I do need one for our Christmas card. Thank you, Jacob."

"Chuck's a doll, but I was thinking mom-and-daughter pic."

"Let's do both. We could show off my new kitchen?" She extended an open hand to Holly, who pretended she didn't see, staring into the fever-pitched spinning.

"It's beautiful," he said, "but all this white…"

"It might wash us out." She nodded. "I'll find something while you finish up. Just a sliver for me."

The two of them were alone in the bright, whirring space.

He shrugged. "Maybe I'm wrong."

Shutting down the mixer, Holly went in for a full-frontal hug. "It would look like a passport photo," she whispered.

"Exactly." His breath was sweet by her ear. "Give me the signal when you want to get out of here. Sometime after pie and before you kick your mother's ass."

* * *

In the hotel bed that night, Holly moaned beneath him. "Right there."

"Here?" Jacob's thumbs rotated in perfect little circles under her shoulder blades. He approached knots perfectly—slowly, so they didn't even know they were being undone.

"Mmm. You're too good to me."

"Never eaten off a woman's butt before."

She smirked into the pillow. "Could've been a man butt."

"Nah. Too pretty. Hold on. That was your butt! You never told me you modeled in Italy."

"I might be able to get a deal if your mom wants a set."

"Samson, you're a genius. Can you get them by Christmas?"

"Expedited shipping." Another knot succumbed to his magnificent hands. "I wonder what they'd think of each other."

"We should have a big party and get them together. Next year. Summer?"

Holly smiled until her mother's words returned. *"He knows about you. Don't ruin his life."* She sighed.

"Want to talk about it?"

"No. Thanks."

"How's Komi?"

"Meena's kids want a dog now. They're sleeping on the floor with her, so she isn't lonely."

"Cute. Sleepy?"

"Mm-hm."

Jacob gave her hip a double pat and dismounted. She turned away from him and held up the hotel pillow as he slid his arm beneath it and fit himself around her back like a Lego.

"The man has a family." A tear made a slow trek over the bridge of her nose and down her cheek. *And I'm not it.* The first tear started a trend. She sniffed.

He stroked her face. "You're leaking. What can I do?"

"This," she said, and snuggled back against him.

"Copy that." Her head got a smooch. "I liked the chandelier in the kitchen." His fingertips tucked under her waistband. "Like an antler lamp and string lights had a baby."

She breathed into the heat of his hand on her belly. "My mom said antler lamp doesn't want to meet me."

"What?"

"My biological father, the Barcelonian shitbird. He knows I exist, but I'm not supposed to contact him. Might upset his real family."

"Do you want to contact him?"

"Sort of."

He rubbed her belly. "Tag me in if you want help with that."

304

She nodded. "Thanks."

"I think Charles likes me."

Smiling, Holly said, "I think so, too. They're a funny couple, but they work."

"He offered me a couple of Viagra."

"No!"

"I'm saving them for later."

"What?" She flopped over to see him. "Tell me you didn't take them. I mean, you didn't take them from Charles."

"'You didn't take them from Charles.'"

She grabbed her pillow.

Jacob took her hand, grinning. "I'm messing with you."

"Goof."

"He did offer."

"Seriously?"

He nodded.

"I'm so sorry."

"Don't be. I had fun."

"Really?"

"Yeah," he smiled. He patted her spot on the mattress, so she scooched back to spooning position. "Smart to see the mother of the woman you're dating. Get a rough idea what you're getting into."

"She's very well preserved. I won't be that hot at her age."

"No?"

"Nope. Injecting artificial crap into my body has no appeal for me."

"Well, shit."

"I'm already getting gray hairs."

"You do not."

"Around my temples."

"Never seen 'em."

"I pluck them."

"Ah."

"But soon, there'll be too many." She flourished her hand over the covers. "All this is super temporary."

"Promise me one thing."

"Depends what it is."

Grabbing her breast, he squeezed out a giggle. "Never get implants."

"I won't."

"Thank you."

Holly held her hand over his. "Twenty bucks these are knee height by 2030."

"I'll take that action."

Even with his hand on her breast, the bliss of his still body was enough. As they drifted toward sleep, she was full. It wasn't satisfaction, although there was that. He saw her. Even in the dark, even given the parts she was ashamed of—her mother and all the ways she was like her. And he loved her.

She smiled.

He snored—breathy rhythmic rumbles.

> *Mom's kitchen is too bright. I squint at the recipe book.*
> *Jacob swipes a finger in the mixing bowl and cringes.*
> *I taste the frosting, too: sour. What did I do wrong?*
> *But I can't read the words.*
> *"It's your home wrecker," Dad says from behind me.*
> *What? I turn.*
> *Dad's holding out my gratitude journal.*
> *"It's your record keeper."*

HOLLY

SATURDAY, DECEMBER 3, 2016

Meena waved Holly forward into the sanctuary of the synagogue. Although Courtney had dubbed the French twists "old lady buns," Meena was sexy as hell in hers with her tawny chest and shoulders capping the gray satin gown.

"What's going on?" Following her from the main hall, Holly hugged her crocheted wrap tighter. The swooping halter top dress was really too cold for winter.

"Bridal party photos are delayed." Meena led her farther into the sunlit room of dark wood pews. "One of the boys is completely trolleyed," she whispered, "A bit of vomit on a tux. Courtney's spot cleaning, the darling. You'll tell Jacob?"

When Holly nodded, Meena glided out. Her swirling henna-inspired tattoo peeked over the back of her gown. Past her, Gary read his phone. Probably their babysitter again. He and Holly exchanged a wave before he put his arm around his wife and they strode away, talking.

Sunlight streamed in from a grid of tall windows with arched tops. Craving warm sun on her skin, Holly walked to the light and trailed her fingers along the smooth wooden pews. Then she stood in a sunbeam and waited.

Nope. Still cold. The podium nearby had a round crowned tree carved on its base. Squatting, she traced the engraved tree's edge. It made her think of Adam and Eve and what the beginning was really like. She breathed. *Roses.* The white open flowers on either side of the lectern smelled sweet, fresh, and mature. They reminded her of the yellow rosebud from Jacob.

Her grateful gaze climbed the walls, taller from her position crouched by the carving. The gratitude was too big to keep in, and this was a perfect place to say "thank you" to whoever was in charge of the universe. She held her hands and bowed her head.

But an uninvited memory popped up: her eight-year-old self kneeling beside her bed, praying, *"Dear God. Please don't let Mommy and Daddy get divorced. Amen."*

Frowning at her adult hands, she rose, catching a trace of toxic wood finish. She turned to leave.

Jacob stood between the pews at the sanctuary entrance, striking in his black suit.

"Yay!" She marched up the aisle. "I get to see you!"

"Come here a sec," he mumbled, pulling her around a corner. "What do you think of this spot for pictures?" He opened the door to a walk-in closet.

"Love the backdrop." She locked down her grin and followed him inside. "Soft lighting," she said, fondling a coat's fur collar.

"How attached are you to that lipstick?" With a tug of a string, an exposed lightbulb illuminated overhead, and he shut the door behind them.

The bulb was begging for an "idea" joke, but Jacob's idea seemed better, so Holly just said, "Depends who's asking."

"That was your warning," he said, taking her hands. "You are stunning."

"Hairy-baby stunning?"

His dimple flashed, mismatched with his earnest eyes. She loved their staring contests. But when his thumb feathered over her jaw and his fingertips roosted below her ear, she had to forfeit. A second after her eyes closed, the light clinked off.

Somehow Jacob's exhaled breath had more oxygen than she could get straight from the atmosphere. When his teeth clasped around her bottom lip, he hesitated, then dragged away until it popped out like she'd bit it deep in thought.

After a few minutes, Jacob's mouth vacated hers and she was squished into his arms.

"You're it," he said, warming her scalp.

Her breasts wanted to slice away the impudent material between them. "I'm loving the tonsil tag," she whispered into the dark, "but we should probably—"

Clink. "I'm serious."

Holly blinked in the sudden light. "I—"

"Ball-and-chain serious." His toasty thumbs tickled her bare back beneath the wrap where the plunging halter top ended. "If the 'M word' freaks you out, tell me. Thought I was going to stroke out when I saw you up there."

She smirked, "Did you smell toast?"

Smelling burned toast after a stroke was a myth and not that funny, but damn, she loved his smile. Holly inhaled all the happiness she could handle, braced her palms against his black lapels, swan-dived into his deep green eyes, and discovered a treasure of words. Words from a sunny July day beside a sidewalk bench, spoken by a beautiful man holding flowers that weren't all intended for her.

"As luck would have it," she said, "my friend is about to get married. I hear it's a ton of work. We could see if she's over it yet. We might score the venue for cheap."

* * *

"Come on!" Courtney's ringlets boinged while she tugged Holly's hand.

"You go. Better odds."

Courtney scanned for another single lady, then gunned for Erica.

The DJ's voice boomed. "Tick-tock, ladies."

Holly leaned on the gift table and beamed across the banquet room at Jacob, who held his camera at his hip, chatting with a couple of Rob's friends. She didn't need a bouquet. When he caught her eyes, his expression changed, exuding cozy, admiring warmth. He felt close. They seemed close—to marriage. Would he wear a suit like that? She wanted to etch him in her mind. As her mental camera clicked and his smile grew, she wondered if he was doing the same thing.

Jacob twitched his head toward the gathering women.

Scrunching her mouth, she answered with a slight head shake.

He nodded and then smiled at her before Rob's friend asked something.

Turning, Holly caught Rob and Paige frowning, interrupting each other, in a corner past the DJ. *Fighting already?* Holly's temples tightened.

Sitting at a round table, Meena's back was turned to their friend's first argument as a married woman, and her head was bowed, while Gary rubbed her sexy shoulders. When she raised her head to whisper something to him, the look they shared was precious. A smile flickered on Holly's face. Meena and Gary weren't perfect, or perfectly alike, but they had something.

From the hall behind Holly, a strange female voice said, "Look at Samson."

No one else calls me Samson.

"Unbelieving partners destroyed him. Or Solomon—"

"Rob isn't going to lead Paige to worship other gods," her companion answered. "Unless it's the wine god."

While the women chuckled in the doorway, Holly flushed. Paige had said he'd cut down.

"They flew in a rabbi from California," the first woman said.

"I thought our synagogue was too conservative for an interfaith marriage."

Holly glanced at Paige, heading to the front table alone, and then at Meena. Was Meena's marriage happy because she and Gary shared the same faith?

When the women from the hall stopped near the gift table, Holly recognized Paige's aunt.

"I hope they don't do the garter toss," the aunt told her friend. "It's so demeaning." She glanced at Holly's bare hand and smiled. "You should be up there."

Faking a smile, she shook her head.

Courtney and Erica had joined the cluster of women on the dance floor. They were all so different and so beautiful, like flowers. As Erica laughed at something Courtney said, her wide grin and highlighted brown waves matched an image in Holly's brain: the Christmas photo in Vicki's house. Her friend bore an uncanny resemblance to April, Jacob's ex-fiancée.

A swirl of something sinister churned in Holly's gut. *The white sauce on the chicken?* She knew she shouldn't have eaten it without a Lactaid. *Erica's Christian.*

The two older women were still gossiping but too far away to hear, which was fine with Holly, who was already poisoned. Were they right? Holly knew she wouldn't destroy Jacob as an agnostic partner—but would they make each other miserable?

She tried to shake it off. Jacob knew she wasn't Christian; he'd gone into their relationship with his eyes wide open. The vulgar gurgle from her gut sounded like a sound effect from a monster movie. *The white sauce.* She'd chosen that, knowing it might make her sick, just because she wanted it and didn't take the consequences seriously. A lurch of nausea hit, and she bolted. The bathroom was just down the hall, but her legs started to quake as hard as her insides.

Turning the corner, Holly flattened herself against the first private wall. *Jacob might be happiest with a Christian woman.* Like that first date in the woods, the fox was back in her heart's hen house, wriggling its claws, ready to pluck her heart out of its nest and devour it.

After hobbling to the bathroom, she clutched the peach tile beside her and doubled over, trying to breathe. A blonde girl walked in, about eight years old.

Holly straightened and tried to smile. "Go ahead."

The girl didn't move.

A thirty-something relative of Rob's came in next. "Are you hiding, too? You're dating the photographer, right?"

The girl had disappeared.

All she could say was, "Mm-hm."

"Hang on to him. It's hard to find single men our age—good ones, at least."

He's a good one. She smiled and got the hell out, turning down the empty hall toward the emergency exit.

The DJ's voice boomed from the ballroom. "Okay, beautiful people, let's get all the single guys to the dance floor. Rob, can you bring your bride a chair? Or—there you go. Highly trained best man stepping up."

The slow beats of the next song guided her down the hallway while she tried to unspook herself. *Easy.* Her pulse thundered, unresponsive. Was that Freddy Mercury? Her pace slowed as the tune became familiar: "Another One Bites the Dust."

No. Her feet stuck in the thin industrial carpet as if it were impossible mud.

A flicker near the bathroom caught her eye: the little girl, staring at her like a twin in *The Shining*, but she looked angelic, not demonic. When the girl sped away, her blonde hair trailed, reminding Holly of herself at that age—the age when her world ended.

The first time.

Spinning, she staggered toward the emergency exit.

"There you are." Jacob had entered the hallway behind her.

His voice. Tears rolled down her cheeks.

"You missed the flower toss. Now Erica's going to hold up our wedding. We should get her into online dating. Tinder? Match dot—hey." He hurried the last few steps, braced her arms, and turned her to him.

"Shouldn't you be taking pictures?"

A flicker of "That's ridiculous" flashed over his face. "You're more important."

"Paige is counting on you."

"Plenty of cameras out there. What's wrong?"

Holly sighed. "Am I your Delilah?"

His handsome head tilted. "You're my Samson. What's wrong?"

"Do you think Paige and Rob shouldn't be married? He's not Jewish."

"That's their business," he frowned.

"Don't you think having different faiths can be hard on a relationship?" She couldn't see him clearly anymore, only a sweet, fuzzed-up version of him.

Jacob pulled her into a hug, saying, "Oh, Holly," and brought her head in before he moved his warm hand to her neck. "Don't want to mess up your hair."

"I don't want to mess up your life."

"Wow." He shook his head and kissed the top of hers.

A bobby pin pushed in. "The Bible warns men like you against women like me."

He chuckled, "Sorry. Sounds like a country song. Where does the Bible say that? Song of Solomon is about a woman like you, but it's a celebration, not a warning." Rubbing her back, he asked, "When did this start?"

"Paige's relatives were talking."

"Ah."

"Samson and Solomon. Christians have the same problem, right? You're not supposed to hook up with people who don't share your faith?"

"Do your beliefs tell you not to marry me?" His thumb stroked her wet cheek.

"Of course not."

"Then mind your own effing business," he said with a bittersweet grin.

"You're my business. What if you're blinded temporarily? Love does that. And later, you regret choosing me."

"Not gonna happen."

She shook her head. "Even if your love didn't fade, it still wouldn't be right."

"According to whom?"

"The Bible."

"You pay a lot of respect to something you claim not to buy into."

"I respect you, and you believe it. I don't want to drag you down."

"'Drag me down.'" He sighed, squeezing her. "If we're unequally yoked, you're the one who's held back. You're much faster."

"I'm serious. I've been praying for faith, but it's not coming." The tears did, hard. It hurt even more to say it, to hear it, like she had empowered a demon she hadn't known was eating her heart out. *God doesn't want you.* "I can't share your faith."

His eyes pinched while he wiped her tears. "Once, I didn't either. You read the Bible more than most of my Christian friends. It's a matter of time."

She tensed. "You're banking on that."

"No. I predict it. I see you growing."

"If I stayed as is, would I be the person you'd want to raise kids with?"

"Yes!" Jacob brought her lips to his, but the soft touchdown was like goodbye.

Holly's heart lurched.

When he pulled back, his eyes were wide and sad. Cheers from the ballroom rose and faded.

"I don't think you're being honest with yourself."

"Holly." He held her arms. "I love my mother. I don't need another one." Jessie J started belting out her favorite running song, muffled from the ballroom. "You either trust me, or you don't."

"I trust you completely."

"Good. Then—"

"I don't trust you not to sacrifice too much for me."

"Holly."

"In Ephesians, it says faith is a gift from God." Tears fell. "If God is real, he hasn't chosen me."

"You can't know that." He wiped her cheek.

She wanted to shake him for making her say it again. "I don't have faith."

Jacob shook his head. "I choose you," he said, pulling her into his arms. "Let's table this for when we have clear heads. Okay? It's been a long day. We'll get you home to Komi. Get some prescription-strength puppy cuddles. I suggest a sleepover." He held up three Boy Scout fingers. "As much as I want to get you naked and kiss every worry out of your body, I promise to be a gentleman."

"I don't think that's a smart idea." Another tear slid cold down her cheek.

"How about this: I draw you a bath, make you a cup of that weird herbal tea, and get out of your hair. Your beautiful, jacked-up hair. Stop worrying. We're good."

"I'm not. I'm a Delilah like my mom."

"Hey."

"Why would God want anything to do with me?"

"Holly." He took her hand. "We're taking you home." And he pulled her toward the ballroom.

She pulled back. "I'll keep praying for faith, but you shouldn't wait—"

"What?"

"If you want to...find a Christian..."

"What the—no. Stop. We're good."

Suffering the horrible distance of him at arm's length, she turned away, her shoulders shaking.

"Hey." He held her trembling head. "Shh."

"If you have space," she sniffed, wiping her gross nose on her gross arm. "You might find the woman God has planned for you."

"She's. Here." He squeezed her. "No more God talk. The foot is down. We need to get you out of this funk."

"If you had some space from me—"

"Space?" He stiffened. "Do you want to be with someone else?"

She shook her head.

"Did someone hit on you tonight while I was taking pictures?"

"No! Why would you—"

"Wouldn't be the first time. Chip?"

"What? Oh."

"Batman?"

Holly grimaced.

"Third time's the charm?"

"No!" She put her hands on Jacob's chest. "No one hit on me. If they did, I wouldn't be interested. You're my dream guy. I love you."

"Why are you running?"

"I don't want to hurt you."

"Then don't run. Easy."

HOLLY

"Take it easy, Mom." Holly extracted herself from the charcoal suede sofa and held out her arm, directing her mother to stop. "You need more water?"

"I can get it," Nanette said. "I'm feeling better."

"It's what I'm here for." She wanted to move anyway. Unlike her mother, getting over her cold, Holly was feeling worse.

The one-week time-out with Jacob was excruciating. It had made sense the night of Paige's wedding to give him time to think about having an agnostic partner. Now, it felt presumptuous, as if she were so fricking magnetic that her presence could turn him into an idiot. On the other hand, she was scared as hell it would work.

Sunday had been a sob-fest. Monday was a shit show. So, when Nanette had called Tuesday afternoon, asking if Holly could play nurse since she'd gotten a nasty stomach flu and Charles was away, she had jumped at the chance.

"Thank you." In the black jumpsuit, her mother appeared to be part of the leather recliner. "Vodka this time, please." Her face was softer without her makeup.

"Probably not great with your cold medicine."

A thundering collapse startled Holly. House flippers were doing demo on the massive flat-screen TV, which she usually enjoyed. But instead of satisfaction with every wall they busted through, she got queasy and mournful, so she hurried out of the room.

"Holly, dear," Nanette called after her.

"Yeah?" As she arrived back on the shag rug, its black-and-white cowhide pattern made her wonder if her mom missed her dad sometimes.

"I think some canine therapy could be just the thing."

"Seriously? Komi could eat your furniture."

"I'll keep an eye on her."

She sniffed the glass. "Was this vodka?"

Nanette had a beautiful laugh when she wasn't trying to impress anyone. "Things can be replaced."

That evening, back in the "theater," as they called it, Holly sat on the floor beside Komi. The air raid sirens and exploding World War II bombs didn't disrupt Komi's sleep; her oversized paws twitched rhythmically. Holly hoped it was a happy dream, chasing something fun and not running in fear, not in a nightmare like her new normal. Did Komi dream about Jacob, too? She sighed. Waking up from life without Jacob would be fantastic. *Anytime now.* While Komi woofed whisper barks, she boosted herself up onto the sofa.

"Even though I wouldn't have picked Jacob for you, there's something lovely about how you fit." Nanette turned down *Mrs. Miniver*.

Holly unfurled a throw blanket she could barely see.

"You can't make other people's choices for them. That's something I learned raising you, you know." She smiled. "I had a harder time with you than your brother because I thought we'd see eye to eye more."

Refolding the blanket, she hoped it wasn't very expensive because she might have to puke in it. Jacob fit her perfectly in every way but one, a big, dream-crushing one. Marrying him, having kids with him… The pounding sounds of destruction from the black-and-white movie were a fitting soundtrack for her life.

"Sweetheart? Holly. What's the matter?"

"I need a Kleenex," she said, darting to the bathroom.

When she returned, tissue box in hand, Nanette was sitting beside a sleepy-eyed Komi on the shag rug.

"We're worried about you."

Holly plopped down on the other side of Komi.

"I'm sorry," her mom said.

"Thanks."

"I'm sorry I cheated on your dad."

Which time? She couldn't take any more emotional hemorrhaging. "It's okay."

"It's not. I'm truly sorry. Is there anything I can do to help fix my mistake?"

I'm a mistake? was her first thought, but she shook it off and shook her head, burying her nose in a tissue.

"This isn't about me, is it?"

"Nope." Trying to smile, Holly reached over Komi and patted her mother's leg.

"I hope you can forgive me someday. I'm here if you want to talk about it."

"I do forgive you, Mom."

"Really?"

"Mm-hm." Holly stroked Komi's back, grounding herself in goodness. She was grateful for Komi; Komi wasn't going anywhere. *I'm grateful for Mom.* She wasn't going anywhere—and for the first time in a long, long, long time, that was comforting. Holly thought about what she'd said about not making other people's choices for them. Jacob would have agreed with her.

But then Keith came up out of nowhere, Keith and his counselor's comment about love being a choice. Jacob choosing her was utterly different. She wasn't Jacob's broccoli. Jacob choosing her was like being welcomed home: an open-armed, running-at-you welcome home.

The tissue box moved—it was her mom's hand pulling one out. Her mother's disfigured face was almost unrecognizable. Agony mangled it like a masochist Picasso. But it was familiar: Holly's 8-year-old self had seen that tormented face before the divorce.

Leaping over Komi, she threw her arms around her mom's shuddering shoulders and brought her in.

* * *

That evening, in the sumptuous guest bed, Holly's arm was getting tired. Another snuffle warmed her knuckles through the mesh of Komi's portable crate.

"I'm here. Go to sleep."

Komi shuffled around and around, then flopped down with a harumph.

Holly plucked up her phone and scrolled to Meena's name. But it would be rude to call after 10:00. On the ceiling, stars of reflected light flickered from the pond in the Japanese garden, romantic and hopeful. Tears came. *Crap.*

Needing a distraction, she opened her Bible app. Haman had just been hanged on his own gallows before dinner; Esther's drama might get her mind off her own.

Hang on. Why was she doing Bible research now when her relationship with Jacob might be over? In high school, there had been a time when she'd been curious to see if she might be blessed with a Eureka moment, a flash of faith, a key to the house of her dad's faith family. But wasn't she reading it now because of Jacob?

Kids. Kids with Jacob. That was the real motivator. When this all started, her question at the ranch was whether she could raise kids to respect his belief in the Bible, regardless of her own. *Or whether the Bible was bullshit.*

Jacob didn't know that.

He lifts my chin. "You read the Bible more than most of my Christian friends. It's a matter of time."

"You're banking on that?"

"No. I predict it. I see you growing."

Was she growing? Was he seeing something blooming in her, not just the Bible reading? Jacob might be making her a better person; she didn't think the Bible was. Was it?

She scrolled to the "Highlights" section of her Bible app. And scrolled. And scrolled. *Dang.* There were a lot. She liked this one. 1 Corinthians 13:4-7:

Love is patient, love is kind. Love does not envy, it is not boastful, is not arrogant, is not rude, is not self-seeking, is not irritable, and does not keep a record of wrongs.

It felt good to forgive her mom.

Love finds no joy in unrighteousness but rejoices in the truth. It bears all things, believes all things, hopes all things, endures all things.

The words felt like a beacon guiding home. She had a long way to go to embody that kind of love, but having a goal like a mile marker always helps.

But the verse listed below it, 13:2, was in orange, her code for questions:

...and if I have all faith so that I can move mountains but do not have love, I am nothing.

What's the reverse of that—having love but not faith? Lonely, that's what.

She hadn't asked Jacob her God questions, not wanting to get his hopes up or to be influenced by him. Even so, if she did have some kind of spiritual moment now, how could she trust it? She'd take any kind of leap to get to Jacob. She hoped she wouldn't lie to herself like that, trick herself, but she'd done dumb—done it well. *Solid performances in Dumb. World-class.*

He deserved to be warned. In his experience, Bible reading must have accompanied his growing faith, so he assumed the same was happening for her. He probably thought her "research"—picturing his air quotes brought a lovely kind of hurt—was prompted by something pure and good. Not a selfish, doubting, "how bad is this thing" motivation.

Truth is ugly. Her truth, anyway. She saw wisdom in the Bible, flickers of truth, a better way to live. From what she'd found so far, she'd be okay raising kids in a quasi-Christian household, as weird as that would be. But how would that work, with Daddy thinking Mommy was going to hell? She had to call him and confess what was behind her Bible reading.

No. It was late. And that was breaking the rule. Just because she'd made the rule didn't make it fair to break it. But he needed to know. *Informed consent.* Holly groaned and rolled over, barely able to find their texts and add one:

Are you awake?

Why am I doing this? Her finger hovered over "Send." She wanted to connect, to hear his voice, to have him tell her he still loved her and that everything was okay. Jacob wouldn't care why she started reading the Bible. Didn't that just show how future-trippy she'd been, thinking about raising babies with him in August? When they'd only been dating for a month?

Selfish. As usual. Tearing up, she tapped the screen to delete, but the text bubble floated upward. Sent.

Crap. Lurching upright, her heart raced. *No.* She scrambled to wipe her eyes and typed:

Sorry, I

Her phone vibrated. Between seeing Jacob's name and bringing it to her ear, a black cloud of terror stormed in: *What if he's already decided?* He could have thought long and hard and might have even realized he was attracted to someone else, and besides didn't his parents want him to marry a Christian girl like April or Erica or probably any of the girls he'd ever dated since his days as a varsity football player, and this might be the last time she would hear his beautiful, rumbly voice—the voice that made her diaphragm twitch and her heart smile and sometimes incited more lustful reflexes—because he really deserved someone better, and although he would never think of it that way because he was too good of a human being, he probably realized—although it hurt him, she was sure—that they weren't meant to be together and it was best to rip off the Band-Aid and end this now.

"Hi," she whispered.

"Please tell me it's over." His voice was like a cello. "The time-out, I mean."

"I need to tell you something."

"K."

"I've only been reading the Bible to see if I could raise kids to respect it since you do." She left out when she'd started; he had only caught her reading later.

"That's it?"

"Sorry, I shouldn't have bothered you. I thought better of it, but it already sent."

"Okay."

"I don't want you to give me credit where credit isn't due. If anything, the fact that I've been reading the Bible and still don't have faith should be a tick against me."

"Can I be a tick against you? Wouldn't bite, just snuggle."

Holly's laugh was a groan. She smiled and lay on her side, pulling the comforter over her shoulder.

"Make up something else to tell me," he said. "I miss your voice."

"I can tell you what my mom said. But you should think about the Bible thing."

"What's to think about?"

She scoffed. "My weird motives! My lack of faith. We're still where we started. Don't you think you need a Christian woman?"

"Would you call me an arrogant manwhore if I told you I want you no matter what?"

Holly giggled into the fluffy pillow, wishing it was him. "I thought I was Samson. Besides, if you were a manwhore, you'd put out."

His laugh was heaven, and she breathed, grinning, picturing his smile through the phone.

"Wow." His chuckle burbled to quiet. "What'd your mom say?"

"She told me I can't make your choices for you."

"Me choosing you?"

"Mm-hm."

"You're shitting me." His voice was springy, smiling.

"Nope."

"I take back every mean thing you've ever said about her."

Holly grinned.

"You should always listen to your mother."

"Really?" The glimmering pond lights danced on the ceiling.

"Be there in 20 minutes."

"I'm at my mom's. And I don't always listen to my mother. Although we did have a nice moment."

"Your independent thinking is one of the 10,879,256 things I love about you."

"You're impossible."

"I can do impossible. Want to see me pull an Ethan Hunt and get to Vegas in two and a half hours? If I use my siren…"

"Don't!" she smiled. "Before you go Team Nanette on me, you should hear the other thing."

"Listening."

"She got sick, and Charles is away on business, so I'm helping out. Upshot is, tonight she compared Christianity to a physical disability."

"Nice," he laughed.

"My mom said if I marry you—"

"When."

Komi whimpered.

"No!" Holly reached toward Komi's crate. "*If* we got married, I'd need to make accommodations."

"I do have special needs."

"You're not offended?"

"She's on my side. I'll take it. When do you get home?"

"I head home tomorrow after Charles gets back."

"Red eye?"

"Not sure. He is coming from Japan." She tucked her arm under the warm duvet. "Why?"

"Mark rented a cabin to get some friends together. Think I freaked him out. We're calling it 'Bros-Ski-Brewski.'"

"Freaked him out?"

Komi sighed, lying down.

Jacob sighed, too. "He doesn't like seeing me down."

"I'm sorry."

"Don't be. Thanks for the rule violation. Are we done with this bullshit? I mean, this really clever idea you had, which has fortunately run its course?"

She smiled and smoothed the fluffy comforter.

"Holly...?"

"Sorry. I guess? You're free to break up with me if you decide I'm right."

"Deal. Text me when you're 20 minutes out. Meet you at your house."

"No! Your boys' weekend. Bros-Ski-Brewski." Turning on her side, she wished the pillow were his chest.

"Won't be back 'til Sunday. I'll tell him, 'Toughski shitski.'"

"You should go! We can spend time together after."

"I'm holding you to that."

Holly smirked. "You can hold me to anything you want."

"That's just mean."

HOLLY

FRIDAY, DECEMBER 9, 2016

In the rearview mirror, Komi was antsy, getting tangled in the leash.

"Lie down."

Marimba chords chimed from Holly's purse. Wishing she'd put it in the dash mount after the rest stop, she glanced from the straight stretch of interstate to find the Mini's phone button.

"Hi, this is Holly."

"Hey." It was Courtney. "You still at your mom's?"

"Hey, you! I'm on my way back. Want to go out tonight?"

"Can't."

"Hot date?" Was Courtney dating someone? How long had it been since they'd talked?

"Maybe. Nina said you know him. Scott?"

"No way!" Her grin was in full force, gaping a bit. "What are you doing? Drinks? Dinner?"

"No drinks."

"Right! I forgot about your No Alcohol November. But it's December now…"

"Nah. I'm taking the rest of the year to detox. We'll see from there."

"Wow. That's fantastic!"

Courtney chuckled. "I can finally take a turn being DD."

Laughing, she asked, "So, dinner…?"

"And a movie, unless he's lame, and I bail. Either *Arrival* or *The*

Girl on the Train."

"You don't sound excited." Holly was. She loved love. How cool would it be if Courtney and Scott found it, too? He might be perfect for her.

"I am, a little," she said, not sounding like it. "But that's not why I'm calling."

Komi whimpered in the backseat.

"What's wrong?" She groped in her purse for a chew toy.

"Vanessa's been busy."

"What?" When her fingertips brushed the firm rubber, a Porsche flew past, so she grabbed the wheel, startled.

"I shouldn't be telling you this. Don't mention me when Debbie calls."

"My certifier? Can't I just supervise? What about Cora's folks?"

"Don't push it, Tiger. Debbie barely got you approved after Diapergate."

"Seriously?"

"I know. It's bullshit. Don't rock the boat, okay? How far out are you?"

"Just outside Beaver. I'll come as fast as I can."

Courtney paused before: "That's what he said."

Holly shook her head, chuckling.

"I can watch the kiddo for a few hours. When Debbie calls, have her ask me, like you're not sure."

CORA

Znnn-sht, znnn-sht, znnn-sht. Only the flaps of her nursing bra held the greedy plastic cones to Cora's breasts. Her helpless arms, her head, her twisting red hair, and the translucent rubber tubing all succumbed to gravity.

Her tears had dried up. Her milk had dried up. Each clenching suck yielded only pain. Only physical pain, though, and Cora would have had to be in her body to feel it.

It was a watching more than a feeling, registering the percussive pulses like heartbeats. The extending tubes confirmed her new status as an android. It made logical sense that this thing might be keeping her alive now: a robotic pump to replace the fleshy heart she'd been born with—missing.

Her heart was still on Holly's front porch—in her mind, anyway, where Holly had cradled her while she waved goodbye like a movie heroine. Naomi would be in her bassinet now in Holly's room. Or she might be having a bottle. Holly would take good care of her. Maybe better than Cora could.

Aiden's poem came to mind:

> *Mi Corazón*
> *Is gone*
> *I'm not sure how I'm breathing*
> *Death is slower than I expected*

Now, they had that in common. Or they would have that in common if Aiden weren't fine now. *Different time zones.*

A buzz broke through the *znnn-sht, znnn-sht, znnn-sht,* and her phone lit up on her glass coffee table. *I'm not home. Go away.* Whoever it was couldn't help. The shuddering phone skimmed away from the wilting houseplant and a pile of bills toward the table's edge to do itself in.

Cora read the screen despite herself: **Aiden.**

The clenching on and in her chest lurched like a miserable hiccup. Had he sensed her thinking about him? *No.* That was magical thinking. Like in the desert when she and Julie had been surrounded by rustling, wispy tufts of tall, tiny flowers, and Julie said, "The bees are telling us to go this way." Magical thinking was dangerous; Aiden calling was just a coincidence. But it reminded her of the physical world, and she turned off the pump. He could leave a voicemail.

Raising a plastic cone, she scraped up milky moisture by its edge. The robot apparatus had to come off before she poured her labor into one container; it almost reached the 4-oz. line. *It might be enough.*

Putting it in the refrigerator took all her strength, so when she tripped coming back to the couch, scuffing her cork-soled scuff on a pacifier she hadn't seen in the dark, Cora didn't have the heart to pick it up. Beyond sobs, she kicked off her house shoes, flopped onto her back, propped her feet on the couch's arm, and pressed her palms against her eye sockets.

Buzz.

She held still and hoped it would stop.

Buzz.

Dropping her hands to her chest, she turned and observed her phone skittering at the table's edge, hanging off a little. She was curious. Would it go over?

Buzz.

It moved a little more.

Buzz.

It moved a little more.

Then nothing. Tucking the throw pillow under her head, she turned to her side and watched the phone be still.

After a minute, she closed her eyes.

Buzz.

She grabbed it: **Aiden.** "Hi."

"Cora? Are you okay?"

Letting her eyes close, she sighed. *Of all the asinine questions.*

"Sorry. Of course you're not."

Her ears pricked at his insight. The shadowy ceiling was pinstriped by persistent light cutting through the blinds.

"Did you have a good visit with our girl?"

"Mm-hm."

"Why is Holly being the foster parent so different from her being a safety service provider? You can't be there at night?"

She shrugged even though he couldn't see.

"Cora?"

"The caseworker said they got a new report of concern. We have court tomorrow."

"11:00 like before?"

She nodded, then said, "Mm-hm."

"Should I call in? I'm scheduled to be in the field doing interviews, but I can try to swap assignments. I can say it's a family emergency."

Family? Aiden was Naomi's family, even if he wasn't hers. "That's okay. It won't make a difference."

"Are you going to be able to sleep?" His voice was sweet.

"We'll see."

"Do you want to talk?"

"No. Thanks."

"Do you want my folks to call in?"

"They can."

"Only if they can help. They don't want to upset your parents."

"They're already upset."

"I feel bad about Thanksgiving," he sighed. "Would they meet my parents if I wasn't there?"

"I don't know." She didn't know anything. She didn't know why Child Welfare insisted she was a terrible mother; she didn't know if they were right. She didn't know why Aiden was still in her life, being sweet and supportive and apparently healthy and normal, or why her heart still ached for him sometimes, like when she was trying to sleep the night before Halloween knowing he was out here on the couch. She sat up.

"Sorry. We don't have to figure that out now. I wish I could be there with you."

"I have to go," Cora muttered, sliding her foot into her sandal.

"Do you have one minute?"

Where was her other Birkenstock? She knelt, feeling under the coffee table. "I guess." When her fingers hit the strappy shoe, she dragged it out.

"Have you heard of the serenity prayer? 'God grant me the serenity to accept the things I can't change, the courage to change the things I can, and the wisdom to know the difference'?"

Frozen, she wasn't sure if she was putting on the red slide or taking it off.

"Cora?"

CORA

SATURDAY, JULY 11, 2015

Alone in the orange Utah desert, Cora felt abandoned and maybe watched. Not watched by the stalker that Julie had insisted was chasing them, but maybe by Julie. Unless her sister had kept going without even looking back. It could just seem like someone was watching her because the rust-colored rock walls surrounded her like giant hands around a bug.

She cupped her hands at her mouth. "Julie!"

Her echo sounded desperate. As she wiped her eyes, the tips of her matted red curls prickled her arms like frayed electrical wires. A feverish shudder rolled over her skin, pooling in her swollen hands and feet.

Should she turn back? Even though Julie had been walking in this direction when the echoes of distant gunshots ricocheted in the narrow ravine, she could have turned around. Her big sister could be back at the car right now, even driving out of this hell. She wouldn't do that, would she? A tear slid down her cheek.

She must be this way. Cora plodded along the trickling stream in her black closed-toe sandals. Did lab rats feel like this, going through mazes to determine their intelligence? Smart or not, she needed to get to her.

The murky flow finally meandered to a clearing above a ridge the water must have cut years ago. She stepped up the bank and surveyed the sandy expanse littered with boulders and spindly trees. Getting out of the narrow ravine had been a goal, but now that Cora had emerged, no relief was in sight. The new hilly frontier was so far-flung, something like agoraphobia seized her throat. Her chest ached as if her lungs were bricks. Her heart rapid-fired like a rabbit stomping a warning. Julie could be anywhere.

One of the scraggly bushes speckling the terrain had something under it like a heap of clothes. *Julie's plaid shirt?*

Running toward her, she called, "Julie! You're o—"

The body didn't move, even to breathe.

Cora's fingers pressed her mouth. "Julie?" Her vision blurred as she crept forward and stooped. Her hand dangled above what might still be her sister. "Julie?" Meeting heavy resistance from the dead air, she touched the frail arm.

Julie stirred.

"Oh, thank God!" She dropped to her knees and embraced the sharp shoulder.

When Julie turned her head, her boyish light brown hair a matted mess, Cora sat back on her heels. Tiny red spots and something less visible cloaked her sister's gaunt face.

"Are you okay? Thank God you're okay."

She stared through her as their grandmother used to after her memory had gone. Her dark eyes were like holes. Her feet were bare.

"It's me, Cora. Where are your shoes?"

She rasped, "He told me to take them off."

"Who?"

"The stalker." Julie didn't seem like Julie anymore. What were those brown eyes seeing?

"You talked to him?"

"In the cave."

What cave? "Why were you in a cave?"

She propped up on her elbow. "The FBI—they're coming for all of us."

"We haven't done anything. Why would—"

"You shouldn't have yelled. I thought you'd been shot." She had all the emotion of a weatherman.

Maybe she had imagined her little sister had been killed because she thought she deserved punishment, yelling for help after Julie had told her to lie by the bush and be quiet. But she'd had to try. Whoever was shooting could have heard and helped.

"Here," Cora sniffed, unbuckling her Birkenstocks. "Take my shoes."

"I can't wear those."

"I'll be okay." She set a sandal in the whitish dust beside her. "I have socks. That's something."

Julie shook her head. "The cork's shaped to your feet."

"They might not be comfortable, but they're better than nothing." She sighed. "Just try them, at least."

Once she put on the shoes, Cora offered her a hand, which she didn't take. Cora reached instead for the mustard yellow hobo bag on the ground—her purse, which they had been sharing since they left the car the first time when it got stuck. "Can I carry this for you?" The car keys clinked against the hollow can of sunscreen spray and Cora's dead cell phone.

Julie snatched it away. "I have it."

"Why don't' we go back to the—"

"Shh!" She stared over Cora's shoulder, squatting. "Get down. Down." She pushed until Cora lay flat.

Hopelessness weighed as heavy as her sister's insistent hands. *Not again.*

Julie was backing away.

"Where are you going?"

"The bush is too small for both of us."

"Don't you think we should—"

"Shh! Don't move. I'll be right here."

Promise? The view of her big sister blurred. "Don't leave this time."

"Be quiet. We'll go when it's safe." Julie glanced around and moved to the scraggly shrub behind her.

Her neck hurt as she craned to see Julie tucking into a ball.

"Your head's sticking up," she hissed.

Cora didn't want to make her mad again, so she tucked her head in. Julie had to know she was on her side, or she might leave her. *How can I get her back to the car?*

A couple of minutes ticked by in mostly dead silence. The sand itched Cora's cheek. *We have to get moving.*

"Julie?" she whispered.

CORA

SUNDAY, DECEMBER 11, 2016

"Cora? Are you there?"

"I'm here."

Aiden sighed.

"I wish I could be there. Are you okay, really? I mean, you're not thinking of doing anything crazy, are you?"

Crazy? Her shoulders pinched. "What do you mean?"

"Like hurting yourself? I know you don't really drink. Or hurt yourself, I guess." He sighed. "Sorry. I'm just worried about you. Probably transferring my own shit."

Cora slid off her slip-on and tucked her bare feet up onto the darkish blue couch, pulling the throw blanket over her lap. "I'll be fine."

"Yes. You will. And tomorrow, this might all be over."

"We'll see."

"Shit," he mumbled.

"What's wrong?"

His "Nothing" was cut by a moment of dull silence.

"Are you getting a call? We can go." Ironic that they might have to end the call now that she wanted to talk.

"Sorry. I forgot I was supposed to see a movie with a friend. Shit. I'm so late. Hey, if she decides to just go without me, can I call you back?"

"Okay. Have fun."

"Thanks. Sorry. And call me if you change your mind and want me to call in. Please."

"Sure."

He sighed. "Take care of yourself, Cora. Oh! Have you tried listening to music? You should put some on, like that jazz you like."

Rather than sitting in her dark, shabby apartment, she was transported to Aiden's kitchen, dancing barefoot on the earthy wood floor.

"Text me if you can't sleep. Or if you need anything. Or if you want me to call in—or fly in. Okay?"

As she nodded, tears fell.

HOLLY

After Naomi's midnight bottle, Holly couldn't sleep. She was overwhelmed by all the lovely life in her unlit bedroom: the delicious pile of man softly snoring under her chocolate brown comforter, the sweet-tempered baby in the bassinet, and the unconditional love fluff in the crate in the corner. Like her heart, her room was so crammed full of goodness that it might burst.

It was like a dream she didn't want to wake up from, and she was afraid to fall asleep and miss it. It was Naomi's last night with her, hopefully. The thought of poor Cora—her eyes were so desperate when she'd left… Jacob wasn't going anywhere, thank god. She resisted the urge to spoon against him and risk disturbing his sleep. Komi wasn't going anywhere. Two out of three was pretty great. She could sleep. Life was good, amazingly great.

"I love you, Holly Samuelsson."

Jacob. What? She must have drifted off.

He bent over her, his shadowy face adoring but sad in the dim light like he was snapping a mental picture before goodbye.

Holly tried to blink herself awake in the dark. "Where are you going?"

"Work." His kiss on her forehead was warm and soft and bristly. "It's early. Go back to sleep. I'll call when I can." Backing away from the bed, he whispered to Komi, "Keep Mom safe." His silhouette disappeared from the doorframe, and his heavy feet trudged to and out the door. It thumped closed.

* * *

That morning in her bright kitchen, Holly decided that huffing baby head might be better than drinking coffee. *Cucumber.* Naomi's scalp exuded a similar creamy mildness. She sniffed again, luxuriating in the soft, dark wisps of her hair. *Grapefruit?* Picturing a server at a wine bar comparing babies to varietal blends, she laughed at herself.

"Well, you are intoxicating," she smiled, taking in Naomi's dark lashes and her tiny bulb of a nose.

More out of habit than from any real interest, she plucked up the TV remote and turned on the news, stepping around the kitchen wall.

The blonde anchorwoman's talking head frowned, austere beside the photo of a familiar building: the DCFS office. "…in an armed standoff at the Department of Child and Family Services."

Holly froze.

"The incident began at about 2:40 a.m. when the suspect drove through the glass entry doors and barricaded herself inside the building."

Jacob.

The TV screen filled with grainy video, zooming in past yellow caution tape and police cars through an empty parking lot to the front steps. The tail end of a car poked out where the glass-walled front used to be. As the camera panned out, it passed an olive-green armored truck with a star on its passenger door and SWAT in dark letters over the front fender. There was only one SWAT team in the county—Jacob's.

Something clattered on the linoleum floor. Her hand was limp. Faint, clutching Naomi, she fumbled for the black metal stool. Sitting, breathing, not dropping the baby, she surrendered to the newswoman as she would to a nurse administering a sickening shot of truth.

"The bomb squad has responded to the scene, and police have evacuated the residents of nearby homes."

Komi whined at the back door, but Holly was afraid to stand. She couldn't lose Jacob. That couldn't be the last time she saw him. That scared, nightmare-savvy part of herself, warning her the bliss was fleeting, to stay awake—it was right. She should have listened.

CORA

Cora held her arms in a T-shape as the young security guard waved the wand over her.

Down the lobby corridor, Renata faced off with Vanessa's lawyer, Lindsay. "Your client is asking to be sued."

After nodding at her boot buckles, the guard smiled at Cora. "You're good."

So, she proceeded to the end of the X-ray machine's conveyor belt.

"Get in line." Lindsay flipped through a thick stack of papers. "Not a great day to threaten my client. I thought you had better taste."

The round gray tub holding her purse emerged.

"Victim is not a good look for you, Lindsay." Renata's eyes flashed fire as she approached.

Behind her back, Lindsay's disdainful look morphed to something uglier, sneering as if Cora were a stray that had wandered in smelling like wet dog.

Renata led Cora and her parents into the familiar windowless conference room. Cora's text conversation with Holly hadn't changed since Cora had assured her:

No problem. See you soon.

"Are we still doing this?" her dad asked. "Having a hearing when there's a bomb threat at the Child Welfare office?"

"Fortunately, the office was empty when the woman drove into it." Renata set her notepad and documents on the table. "And almost everything is electronic these days."

He nodded, frowning.

"Let's get Naomi home," Renata smiled.

"Holly's here." Cora's mom waved her in through the vertical strip of glass in the door.

Holly backed in, holding the car seat, and Cora stood. As she reached to take her daughter, her relief was tainted by her friend's ashen face. Renata studied Holly, too.

"Oh!" Cora unbuckled Naomi to get her in her arms as soon as possible. "Renata, this is my friend—"

"Holly." She smiled with an outstretched hand.

"I'm sorry," she said, taking it. "I can't remember your name."

"Renata. Renata Ochoa. You helped with my pre-diabetes and my celiac."

"Right." Her smile was broken.

"I never did schedule that follow-up," she chuckled. "The advice you gave me already helped... Please have a seat." Her smile dropped and she asked, "Is that okay, Cora? It might be—"

"I want her here."

When everyone was seated and Naomi was back at Cora's chest where she belonged, the lawyer said, "The good news is, as you know, there is no reality-based reason for DCFS to be bothering your family. As soon as we can get a judge to see the truth, this should be over. And today we have a judge who knows what she's doing."

"What's the bad news?" Cora asked.

Renata lifted papers and locked eyes with her parents. "It is about Julie." She glanced at the tired shell of Holly and asked Cora, "Do you want to talk alone about your sister?"

"It's okay." Cora told Holly, "My sister has mental health issues."

Holly nodded, looking sleep deprived.

The quiet was too long, so Cora turned to Renata.

Her brown eyes were somber. "She is saying you do."

"Julie?"

"Apparently, Vanessa tracked her down Friday morning. Julie told her that Cora has the history of delusional behavior. She flipped the whole desert story." Renata's face pursed in a sad shrug for Cora's parents. "And she said that you two are physically and emotionally abusive."

HOLLY

MONDAY, DECEMBER 12, 2016

The conference room door hadn't closed behind Cora's dad yet when her mom followed him, saying, "We'll be back."

Holly had only seen her own dad cry that hard a handful of times, like all the muscles in his gut and face were in the most excruciating cramp.

Naomi was the only content one, asleep in Cora's arms.

Holly hoped Renata could comfort Cora. She was tapped out. *They'll be back. Will Jacob?* Her fears about him getting hurt or killed were gaining the upper hand. She wanted a hug, a Jacob hug. Like that first long, supportive hug at the brewery. That kind of hug.

While Renata and Cora started reading paperwork, her mind stayed in the brewery since she could be with Jacob there. She remembered sitting down after the epic hug and sharing stories. This time she would hold his hand over the table. If he survived this thing, they needed to go somewhere to make their own most bizarre vacation memories.

Naomi fussed, so Cora discretely clamped her to her breast, checking her under the draped blanket. Her red hair trailed in frizzy ringlets.

Jacob's voice was in her head, still at the brewery: *"Her hair got me first: orange, like a desert nymph had emerged from the rock."*

What did Renata mean by "Julie had flipped the desert story"?

"Hey Cora?"

They turned to her.

"I don't want to pry, but your sister didn't run from rescue helicopters in a desert, did she?"

"No." She frowned. "I don't think so."

"It just reminded me of a story."

"Knock knock!" The bitchy prosecutor cracked open the door and graced them with a pearly smile. "Renata? Judge wants to see us in chambers."

* * *

In a crowded burger joint about half an hour later, the closest flat-screen TV showed that same shot of the breached DCFS doors above the anchorman. It was too far away to hear, but she could read:

STANDOFF ONGOING WITH ARMED SUSPECT AT DCFS OFFICE

"Avo-cobb-o chicken salad, gluten-free?"

"Here." Renata leaned back against the red upholstered booth.

The waitress reached over Holly's bottomless broccoli to the space by the wall, depositing the massive plate. "You must be the 'shroom burger." The smaller dish slid in front of Cora, across from Holly.

She hadn't told them why she wanted the aisle seat, but she was pretty sure she was going to puke if she didn't hear from Jacob soon. She checked her phone on the table—nothing. Since they entered Red Robin, she had been picturing him in his Burger King costume. A gut gremlin was dead set on convincing her that would be their only Halloween.

"Can I get you ladies anything else?"

"I don't think so." Renata smiled at the waitress from below a goofy picture of Albert Einstein sticking out his tongue.

"Enjoy."

Holly stared at the steamed green florets in their little white bowl, like a smaller, squattier version of the pot with the tomato plant from

Jacob: his first gift to her.

"Would you pray for us?" Cora asked.

"Certainly." Renata clasped her hands and lowered her head. "Father, thank you for the food we are about to receive from thy bounty through Christ our Lord. Please strengthen us, protect Cora and her family, and protect the officers trying to keep us safe and bring a peaceful end to the standoff. We pray that you would calm the heart of the hurting woman there and heal Cora's sister if that is your will. Even our suffering is filtered through your loving, all-powerful hands. We thank you for your sustaining grace. In Jesus's name, Amen."

"Amen. Thank you."

Holly wanted to say something but couldn't open her eyes yet. Her heart was knocking, and she tried to listen. A ringtone jolted her eyes open, shooting her hand to her phone right as Cora picked up hers.

"Hi, Mom." She glanced at Naomi, asleep in her car seat on the red upholstered bench by the wall. While the happy birthday song broke out at a nearby table, she adjusted the baby blanket.

Holly made sure her ringer was on. It was.

"Let me see." Cora tucked her phone to her chest. "Do you need my parents for anything?"

Renata held her fingers over her full mouth and shook her head, so she went back to her mom.

"1:30's fine." The singing got louder, so she covered her ear, squinting. "No, I'm fine. Holly's here, too. Wait a minute. Mom? Julie didn't run from rescue helicopters, did she?" Her eyes grew wide and rose from the table, meeting Holly's. "Okay. Thanks. Love you, too." Cora set down her phone. "She did."

Holly couldn't say his name without tears. "Did a big, beautiful man rescue you and your sister?"

"Jacob! Your Jacob?"

CORA

Her heels throbbed on the folded blanket on Jacob's dashboard. Peanut butter from the granola bar stuck to the roof of Cora's mouth, but her arms felt like lead, so she only picked up the crinkly plastic bottle for a drink when her throat threatened to cramp against the goo, tripping a memory from almost three days ago.

> *The water bottle warps in a crunchy burble in my hand. Julie turns the rental car away from the ratty convenience store, and the bag with Julie's water smacks my leg. The sun coming up blinds me for a second as she pulls onto the road.*
>
> *Looking out the window feels like being in a plane, which would be fun if I didn't think my pilot was losing it. At least we're back in Utah, heading in the general direction of home.*
>
> *There's nothing around but desert until a brown Forest Service sign comes up: HELLFIRE CANYON TRAIL, it reads in yellow letters. She turns onto it.*
>
> *"Shouldn't we stay on the road?"*
>
> *She says, "The road's too dangerous."*
>
> *No, this is too dangerous. But there are tire tracks, so cars have gone here. Maybe she wants to pull off and wait. Maybe she'll sleep. She maneuvers into the ruts, then straddles them. Potholes pop up like obstacles in a video game. The dodging and weaving goes on for miles.*

"Shouldn't we turn around?"

She stares forward like a soldier in a tank. The trail turns, but she doesn't. I'm holding on, bouncing. The car's lurching up and down.

"Julie?" Brush screeches against the car. "Julie?"

A drop-off looms ahead, right in our path.

"Look out! Stop!"

My head flies forward, and the shoulder seatbelt digs into my chest. Then it's quiet except for the motor, running high as the engine revs. Julie has the gas pedal floored.

Jacob's ominous black bag invaded her thoughts. *Why carry extra weight?* She was safe with him, right? He was a police officer.

He said he was a police officer.

A stack of business cards in a binder clip faced down beside the Betadine water. Touching his stuff was an invasion of privacy, but she peeked.

Dutch Bros. Coffee
Buy 10 cups get your 11th one FREE!

After Cora dropped the clipped cards back in the console's cup holder, her peanut buttery fingerprint remained. She always got caught when she did something she shouldn't. The glove compartment under her elevated legs had a silver keyhole and a rectangular Tuffy emblem. What was in there, a gun? Fear triumphed over manners, so she leaned forward and reached just as a muffled metal clunk came from the back and the rear window whirred up.

"You still here?" *Thump.* The SUV trembled. *Thump. Clack. Thunk.* "Doin' okay, Champ?"

"Mm-hm."

Jacob took the driver's seat, and his bulky arm almost touched her across the console. Cora shifted away and tucked the blanket tighter as he slammed the door, startling her. When he clicked the door lock, she stared down and inched her hand toward the door handle. Reclining with her feet on the dash was not a good defensive position.

He reached into the cup holder, pulled out the bound cards, and inserted his water bottle. When his ginormous hand appeared above her lap, she flinched.

"Here." The white card displayed a familiar tricolor logo: a forest-green peak, a purple plateau, and a lime-green bottom layer. The block letters read:

Mountaindale Police Department
Officer Jacob Davis

"Don't talk to strangers." He winked.

"Thanks." *Thank God.* Breathing deeper, she pocketed the card.

"Hand me a couple of napkins?" he asked, pointing to the glove compartment. "Sweating like a pig. No cop jokes, please."

The compartment door dropped open, revealing a stack of brown paper napkins on a Land Rover manual. She handed over a few.

"Thanks." He flung his hat in the backseat like a Frisbee and patted his bald head. Jacob had her dad's hairline but dark stubble instead of red hair. "How about those feet?"

The Betadine rinse sent shockwaves through her body as the disinfectant lit up every cut. Cora tried not to twitch too much or cry when he sprayed them, standing outside her door while she held out one foot at a time. After it was finally over, the gauze caught and pulled on her torn skin, even though she could tell he was trying to be careful.

"That'll have to do for now."

Her bandaged feet returned to the folded blanket on the dash, and he went back to the driver's seat.

"Buckle up, Buttercup."

The Land Rover climbed, jostling over rocks beside the drop-off. He drove slower than Julie had, but Cora could still picture them careening off the cliff.

"If my sister's there, she won't trust you."

"Figured." They lurched over the bigger rocks.

"If she acts fine and says she'll follow you out, can I still ride with you?"

"You got it."

"What if she won't come?"

"If my Jedi mind tricks don't work? That's a big part of police training." Smiling, he studied her. "Will you be okay if I have to put the hooks on her? Handcuffs. Got my battle rattle in the back. SWAT officers are always on-call. At least in Franklin County. Small crew. I wouldn't hurt her."

"Was that the black bag you took with you?"

"Good situational awareness. It was either that or make you sit in the dirt. Leaving unsecured weapons with a minor…"

"I'm nineteen."

"No offense. You seem like a good kid."

The navy Ford sedan came into sight before the giant gray outcrop, offering a clear view through its dusty windows. *Julie could be sleeping— or hiding.*

Jacob stopped the Land Rover. "Stay here." Rocks crunched under his hiking boots. He circled the sedan, peering in and pulling the door handles. "Nobody's home."

Her stomach sank, threatening to empty in solidarity with the vacant car.

"You okay?" he asked, standing at his open door.

She nodded, shivering.

"Cold?"

How is Hertz going to get their rental back?

"Hey. You were right. She's not here. We'll get help to find her. Okay?"

Cora nodded.

"Do you have the keys?"

She shook her head.

"Any water or food in there?"

"No."

"Okay. Sit tight." He tromped away, calling, "Julie!" His echoes returned, then the replies of chirping insects.

Could she hear him? Would it scare her?

"Here," he said, holding out a blank notepad and a pen. "Write her a note."

While he tramped to the rental car with water bottles and granola bars, she tried to grip the pen in her sausage fingers.

Dear Julie,
I'm okay.

Cora hoped she cared.

A photographer is giving me a ride out.

No way was she going to tell her he was a police officer.

Please stay here at the car. I'll send help.

She tried to see it from Julie's perspective, but Julie's mind was a terrifying place. Maybe she should have made up a fantasy that she might buy into. Maybe her sister would never see the note.

When Jacob crunched back, she offered the pad. "I don't know what else to write. She might not even think it's from me. My hands are just…"

"It'll do." Walking away, he wrote something and tucked the note under the rental car's windshield wiper.

Cora took a mental picture of the vehicle as he returned to his place behind the wheel.

"She has food and water now if she comes back. Even if critters take the food, they shouldn't mess with the water."

The engine revved. The gearstick stuck and then jerked into reverse. He braced one hand on the back of the passenger seat and turned, driving backward. She closed her eyes and took slow breaths, counting against her carsickness and fear of heights. After spinning around at an open space at the foot of the hill, they finally faced forward and rattled over the ATV trail, leaving the ravine behind.

In the rearview mirror was only dust. The orange cloud cast a fog over her eerie reality. Instead of pure relief, a sick gravity tugged her back. Her lungs cramped like she was drowning, making Jacob her lifeguard, pulling her toward a sunlit surface. But she was reaching back, searching the dark water below for Julie, anchored.

"Pronghorn antelope." Jacob's arm stretched in front of her, pointing out the passenger window.

Graceful silhouettes leaped through the sagebrush-peppered landscape. The sky behind the dancing deer-like creatures radiated pink. The beauty, the movement, and the twilight clouds eased hope into her soul. There was life in this harsh place.

She's alive.

"We should have service soon." He swiped the screen of his phone, mounted on the dash. "Then Search and Rescue can get a jump on finding your sister."

HOLLY

MONDAY, DECEMBER 12, 2016

The salad, the broccoli, and the burger sat untouched. A commercial on the restaurant's TV showed two teddy bears walking hand in hand in an airport.

"What did he tell you about Cora?" Renata's dark eyes sparkled behind her tortoiseshell glasses.

"He said he found a barefoot girl in a desert when he was out taking pictures." Holly tried to focus on Cora. "He said your sister was having a bad mental health day, and she ran from the rescue helicopters."

"Can he come to court at 1:30?" Renata's voice rose like a kid's ready for Santa.

"Holly!" Cora's hand flew to her heart. "He's in that standoff, isn't he?"

Nodding, she hoped the empathy and fear in Cora's eyes wouldn't make her lose it.

"I'm so sorry." Cora reached over the table and held her hand while she told Renata, "He's on the county SWAT team."

Did I tell her that?

Renata winced. "Shoot."

He'd better not get shot. Or blown up. Gripping her lifeline, she said, "I'll call him. At least leave a voicemail." With each ring, stupid hope rose and crashed. Of course he couldn't pick up. He was busy. The news would say if anyone were hurt.

"You've reached Jacob Davis."

No, she hadn't—but it was heaven to hear his voice.

"Leave a message, and I'll call you back." *Beep.*

"Hi. It's me. I'm at the salon to cover up all the gray hair you've given me today. I wondered if you'd like me as a brunette. Or a redhead?"

Cora's eyebrows scrunched.

"Sorry. First standoff jitters. When you're done saving that world, I need you back in mine. Remember your desert nymph? The girl you picked up last July? Not this July, that was me." She sighed. "Your barefoot redhead is my premed friend with the baby. Her sister is spouting lies that Cora is the problem child. We need you. At 1:30. At the juvenile courthouse. Please. I love you. And if you dare get yourself killed, I'll murder you. If you have plans tonight, cancel them because you owe me a huge hug. Huge. Okay, bye."

CORA

Renata and Aiden's attorney stood from their table on the left as the front courtroom door opened for the judge. Cora stood, too, like a lagging member of a cuckoo clock with doors opening and people popping out.

"All rise." The same assistant who had helped the substitute judge waited at the open door; her cardigan was turquoise today. "Franklin County Juvenile Court is now in session, the Honorable Maureen Bronski presiding."

If the courtroom was a cuckoo clock, the teeny tiny woman with short salt-and-pepper hair and a sliver of green shirt peeking out of her ginormous black robe could have been the elf who made it. A grumpy elf perhaps, but a smile flickered behind her glasses.

"Please be seated."

They did.

"Ms. Schmidt, are we still having a contested shelter hearing?"

At the table on the right, Lindsay sat beside Frances instead of Vanessa. Frances scrutinized her cell phone and reached out to her attorney but missed her arm as she stood.

"Yes, Your Honor. However, as discussed in chambers, parties have stipulated to entry of the exhibits tendered before the noon hour for judicial efficiency."

"Judicial efficiency." She smirked. Her voice wasn't particularly deep, but it carried authority. She multitasked, clicking her mouse and reading something on her monitor. Maybe she hadn't read all the documents yet?

Cora hoped she didn't think poorly of her from her psychological evaluation. Renata said it was good, but it was awfully personal. Also, she didn't like that she had lied to Dr. Williams—and gotten away with it—telling her the parent-friendly version of Naomi's conception instead of the whole truth.

"Yes, Your Honor." Lindsay smoothed her lilac skirt.

"I appreciate the early Christmas present. No argument or witnesses, then?"

"We believe the concerns outlined in our Protective Custody Report are sufficient for a finding that a community foster placement is necessary, Your Honor. However, Ms. Ochoa notified me over the noon hour that Mother may have a surprise witness."

Renata stood. "Officer Jacob Davis would be a rebuttal witness to refute some of Julie Martin's statements in the agency's report."

"He's at my client's office dealing with that mentally ill mother with the bomb," Lindsay said.

Cora turned back to Holly, who looked awful; she was pacing in the back of the courtroom, holding Naomi close.

"We have time," Judge Bronski said. "I've read the documents."

Aiden's attorney stood. "Father is aligned with Mother, Your Honor. No additional witnesses or exhibits."

"After receiving the late notice of Mother's witness," Lindsay said, "my client was able to secure telephone testimony of Julie Martin, if the court will allow."

Julie? On the phone?

The diminutive judge pivoted her cropped head from Lindsay to Renata as if it were a lovely day for a tennis match. No longer like a wise, friendly elf, she was like a Roman emperor in a gladiator stadium, watching while Cora was dismembered below.

Renata stood. "We object to telephonic testimony. Her credibility and mental health are at issue. The Court would need to assess her demeanor, which is virtually impossible over the phone."

"Your Honor," Lindsay lobbed back. "Counsel opened this door. If Officer Davis weren't being called to impeach her, we would have relied on her statements in the report. Any relevant evidence is admissible in shelter hearings, and the Court can discern, to some extent, the witness's credibility by phone. Ms. Martin, Julie Martin, should have an opportunity to defend herself."

"Father joins Mother's objection, Your Honor."

"I'll allow it. You have the number?"

Nodding, Lindsay handed a slip of paper to the assistant as she spoke. "The State calls Julie Martin, maternal aunt."

The judge read something on her computer monitor.

Ring.

Cora startled at the phone amplified through the courtroom's speakers. Holly continued pacing with Naomi in the back, looking waifish. Her parents hadn't arrived.

What would she sound like? The raspy alien voice in the desert? Or the weirdly normal voice on the phone months ago when she had said goodbye like they would never speak again, just because Cora had dared to tell their parents that she had called, and Julie didn't even sound sad about it? Which voice would claim that Cora was the crazy one, that she had gotten them stuck in the wilderness and was so obsessed with imaginary dangers that the real ones almost killed them?

Cora moved the yellow pad to her lap and stared down. She hoped it might look like she was reading. She wanted to pray, but tears threatened when she tried to find words and she did not want to cry.

In the dark, her mind filled with desert, planting her under the scraggly tree where hope had found her. Instead of a protective invisible hand on her back guiding her, something like a calming hand pressed her shoulder. Maybe God wanted her in this chair.

On the other side of Lindsay, Frances studied her phone, then reached out to her attorney, holding the screen toward her.

Ring.

"It's over," the judge smiled, nodding at her monitor. "The standoff." She kept reading. "The bomb squad is going in to clear the building now. The suspect is in custody."

Lindsay nodded, passing the cell phone back to Frances.

Ring.

"Hello?" came through the courtroom speakers.

Julie.

"This is Judge Bronski from Franklin County Juvenile Court. You're on speakerphone in open court. We're calling for Julie Martin?"

"This is she." She sounded normal.

"You've been called by the State as a witness in the matter of Naomi Martin." The judge raised her hand. "Please raise your right hand."

"Who? Cora's daughter? I didn't know her name. Is my sister there?"

"Ms. Martin, please keep in mind this is a court proceeding. I understand you can't see us, but we're in the middle of a hearing. Your sister is here with her attorney, and there is a caseworker, a supervisor, here with the attorney for Child Welfare. Are you prepared to testify?"

"I'm at work. Can I call you on my break?"

The judge peered over her glasses at Lindsay, who stood.

But Julie's voice continued through the speakers. "When is the commitment hearing? My sister needs help."

"Ms. Martin—"

"My boss is coming," Julie whispered. "I'll call on my break. I have Vanessa's number."

Click.

"Ms. Schmidt?" The judge sighed.

"I apologize, Your Honor. The State would like to recall her if she becomes available."

"Why not." She shook her head. "You can reopen your case. Ms. Ochoa?"

"Thank you, Your Honor. May I have a moment to see about my witness?" She turned to Holly, who was now sitting in the pew behind them with Naomi asleep in her arms.

She frowned at her phone, swiped the screen, and then shook her head.

"Oh." The judge was reading on her computer again. "There's an injured officer."

Cora spun back to Holly. Blood was draining from her face, and Naomi's head dropped in her sagging arms. Cora pushed back from the table, hoping she didn't need to vault the half-wall to catch Naomi.

"Dog bite," she added. "Not a gunshot, at least. Although dog bites can be ugly…"

Holly tucked Naomi to her chest, staring at the judge.

"That's Officer Clark, Your Honor," Frances said. She lifted her cell phone.

The judge cringed. "Don?"

Frances nodded.

"Must have been friendly fire." She shook her head. "If that was Kreiger again, they might need to retire that dog." Sighing, she asked Renata, "Any word from your officer?"

Holly's face turned into Christmas, and she extended her phone toward them:

OMW

"My witness is on his way."

"Excellent. Let's get going."

"Thank you, Your Honor," Renata said. "The Court has ample evidence that Naomi Martin is not endangered in her mother's care. Mother's Exhibit 101—the November 17th psychological evaluation conducted by Dr. Williams—shows her only diagnosis is Generalized Anxiety Disorder, and her mild anxiety does not impair her functioning.

"On Page 12, Dr. Williams notes that Ms. Martin's anxiety is situational. The environmental factors driving her anxiety began with chronic illness, her sister's and her own, then Ms. Martin attempting to protect her sister, which led to the desert incident, followed by an unplanned pregnancy, and now this.

"Ms. Martin's legal involvement with DCFS is her primary stressor now. That includes having her infant daughter taken from her care. Secondary factors are Ms. Martin's college coursework, concern for her older sister's welfare, and even the presidential election results.

"Mother's Exhibit 102 contains medical records from Fremont Women's Clinic detailing the prenatal and postnatal care Naomi Martin received and the absence of any concerns for substance abuse by Ms. Martin.

"Mother's Exhibit 103 is the entire medical record from Fort Herring Medical Center after the accident with the tape dispenser on October 29th. The facts are clear. The event that prompted Ms. Martin to seek medical care for her daughter was an accident.

"Only two individuals noted suspicions of abuse." Renata raised a finger. "Emergency Room Nurse Shelly Fuller..." Her middle finger joined it. "...and intake caseworker, Vanessa Dixson. Ms. Fuller retracted her statement after consulting with the radiologist. That retraction is noted in her case note on Page 32."

Judge Bronski nodded, looking bored.

One extended finger remained. "Only one person—who isn't here for me to call to the stand—thinks this was not an accident: caseworker Dixson, who is not a medical expert."

Lindsay rolled her eyes and rose. "Your Honor, Ms. Dixson needed to take a personal day. She had previously worked with the mentally ill mother who attacked the DCFS office."

The judge did not look impressed.

"Caseworkers have a difficult job," Renata said. "We appreciate the agency's goal: to keep children safe. But accidents happen. In this case, the agency's hypervigilance crossed over into fantasy.

"Cora Martin is a protective mother better suited to keep her daughter safe than anyone. There was an accident on the night of October 29th. Ms. Martin sought professional help to make sure her daughter was okay.

"One suspicious mind—granted, a mandatory reporter, and I'm not trying to slander Ms. Fuller—smelled blood in the water, so to speak. Ms. Fuller's misguided call to DCFS started a chain reaction that has eaten away at Cora and Naomi Martin's fundamental right to be together as a family without unlawful State interference.

"Mother's Exhibit 104 is the UA Ms. Martin voluntarily took after the shelter hearing—negative for all substances.

"The latest report of concern came from Ms. Martin's older sister after Caseworker Dixson reached out to her. It is remarkable," she sighed, "that the agency would consider Julie Martin's statements credible when her mental illness was documented by law enforcement and known to the agency before they filed the petition against my client.

"This is from Ms. Dixson's initial Protective Custody Report." Renata pulled stapled papers from her pale green file and read aloud: "'On Saturday, December 12, 2015, at 1:31 a.m., San Francisco police received a report that a woman in her late twenties was loitering on the Golden Gate Bridge, appearing suicidal. Julie Martin told officers she did not plan to jump but was waiting for her sister, Cora, to meet her there. Julie Martin stated that Cora had told her to meet at that location and time. Law enforcement believed she was experiencing auditory hallucinations, and she was placed on a mental health hold at San Francisco General Hospital.'"

The papers fluttered in her hand. "Now, when this poor delusional woman makes slanderous claims about her sister and their parents, DCFS takes it as fact and runs with it? Removes an infant from her mother?"

Renata looked a fiery kind of radiant, like an angel. She knew about Cora's weird past, yet she believed in her. Holly knew some of it, and she believed in her, too. And Jacob. Renata kept talking, but Cora tuned out, listening to the internal symphony blossoming: separate instruments with their distinct melodies uniting, making something beautiful that had been planned from the beginning.

"The Court will hear from Officer Davis—"

"Objection, Your Honor." Lindsay was up. "It would be improper for the Court to accept Ms. Ochoa's statements in lieu of the officer's testimony, should he not be able to speak for himself."

"I know the difference between argument and evidence. Proceed, Ms. Ochoa. We'll take a recess if needed until your witness gets here. I'm not going to penalize him for protecting the public."

Lindsay sat.

"Thank you, Your Honor. Officer Davis will refute the claims made by Ms. Julie Martin regarding Cora Martin's mental health."

Bass notes rumbled through the courtroom walls, happy ones: men laughing. Quick heavy footsteps and a booming thump of double doors made Cora turn.

Holly was up, shifting the bundle of Naomi to her shoulder.

The courtroom door opened, and Jacob came through. Holly sped toward him, but he was faster. He had thicker hair crowning his head, joining a short rough beard.

With Naomi sandwiched in their hug, they looked like a perfect family. Something strained inside Cora, like an off-key note or a whisper from a gossip who isn't truly your friend. Instead of the courtroom, she pictured them in the *Tree of Life* painting in her parents' dining room: she was the bitter, lonely woman, and all the love, even her baby, was two golden frames away.

Holly pulled out of the embrace and trotted to her. "Can you take her for a second?"

Cora reached over the half-wall. As soon as she had Naomi in her arms, all was right and clear again. Jacob winked at her above Holly's blonde head, and Cora smiled back. She was happy for them, but she realized she didn't want a man. This love—mother love—was pure and safe and bigger.

"Your Honor—" It was Lindsay.

"Sit. Down." The judge softened her tone, waving at the couple. "Not you two. Take all the time you need. Well, another minute or so. If you need more time to hug your wife, we'll take a recess."

HOLLY

"Thank God you're okay." Hugging Jacob was like hugging a tactical pincushion. Despite being jabbed by his utility belt, radio, and even the pen in his breast pocket, Holly still squeezed.

His baby beard pricked her scalp as he whispered, "I don't like this game anymore."

She laughed, "What game?"

"My 'Worst Day This Year' has changed twice now."

"This one's on you for volunteering to be on the SWAT team. And Angry Bird." Her cheek bounced on his chuckling chest. "Hardest. Day. Ever."

"Not bad for your first standoff," he said, stroking her head.

Holly groaned. "No more standoffs."

"Only one new gray," he smiled, smoothing the hair at her temple. "Don't ever dye your hair."

"Don't tell me what to do." She grinned back at him.

CORA

"Thank you, Your Honor." Jacob released Holly and waited at the central opening in the half-wall. He smiled at Renata, then Cora.

Renata turned to the judge. "Mother calls Officer Davis."

The assistant stood. "Step forward and be sworn."

He took a few long strides and stopped before the judge's bench, then turned toward the woman and raised his palm.

"Do you swear or affirm to tell the truth, the whole truth, and nothing but the truth in the case now pending?" The back courtroom door closed. "I do."

"State your name and spell your last."

Renata put a hand on Cora's arm, nodding at her parents settling in beside Holly.

"Jacob Davis. D-A-V-I-S."

"Thank you. Please have a seat in the witness chair." The assistant sat behind her computer.

Renata let him get situated. "Officer Davis. How are you employed?"

"I'm a detective with the Fort Herring Police Department."

"Detective. I apologize."

"No problem."

"Detective Davis, are you familiar with my client, Cora Martin?"

"I am." He smiled at Cora.

"How do you know her?"

"I met Cora in July of 2015. Mid-July."

"Where did you meet her?"

"Hellfire Canyon. A few hours south."

"What brought you there?"

"Providence? I like to get out in nature. Photography's my excuse. Pretend I'm doing something productive."

"You were taking photographs?"

"Yes."

"Do you know what Ms. Martin was doing in the canyon that day?"

"Objection." Lindsay stood. "Calls for speculation."

Judge Bronski's eyes definitely rolled this time.

"I'll rephrase the question. Detective Davis, could you please tell the Court what you observed when you met Ms. Martin?"

"Heard her first. She called for help."

"Then what did you observe?"

"She wasn't wearing any shoes."

"Did she explain why?"

Lindsay popped up again. "Your Honor. I realize that the rules of evidence are relaxed at shelter hearings; however, if Ms. Ochoa could ask these questions of her client instead of—"

"Are you objecting?"

"No, Your—"

"Then sit down. You may answer the question, Detective."

He nodded. "She had given them to her sister, who was hallucinating about a stalker and the FBI."

Lindsay twitched but stayed seated.

"Did Cora Martin mention her sister's name?"

"She did." Jacob stared down, frowning, then snapped his fingers. "Julie."

Renata nodded. "Then what happened?"

"We drove to their rental car and left a note and some food and water. Julie had the keys."

"And then what happened?"

"I took your client to a police station where an ambulance picked her up. Then I started working with their local rescue operation. Couldn't go out until the next morning."

"In the time you spent with Cora Martin, what, if any, opinion did you form about her mental health?"

"Objection. Detective Davis is not a mental health professional."

"I am asking for his lay opinion."

"Overruled."

Cora's shoulders tensed until Jacob gave her the tiniest of winks. His smile was so generous and so much like when he saved her in the desert, she felt rescued all over again.

"You may answer my question," Renata said.

"Right. Sound as a pound. I have some training in mental health as it relates to law enforcement. Ms. Martin, in lay terms, struck me as a selfless young woman who was trying to save her sister. Her affect was appropriate for the circumstances. She spoke in an organized, coherent manner, and she was an accurate historian, based on what—"

Lindsay stood, shaking her head. "Your Honor. This is sounding more like expert testimony."

"I understand his opinion, Ms. Ochoa. Is there something you need here, or can we move along?"

"What, if any, opinion did you form about Julie Martin's mental health?" Renata asked.

His mouth opened and shut before he spoke. "That young lady was not well."

"How so? What did you observe?"

"What I remember most was her running from the rescue helicopter."

"Did she know who you were?"

"We announced. Helo had a loudspeaker. Didn't help."

"Do you recall anything else about her demeanor?"

Tilting his head, he stared down and then looked at Renata. "She didn't fight. Once we put hooks on, you could see her wheels turn. She refused to drink water or eat anything. She was…" He sighed. "Like someone who might have been brilliant but got her wires crossed."

"Is there anything else you think the Court should know?"

"Don't think so."

"No further questions, Your Honor."

"Ms. Schmidt?"

Lindsay nodded at Judge Bronski. "Thank you, Your Honor. First, Detective, thank you for your assistance with the bomb threat at my client's office today."

"Part of the job."

"You had some difficulty remembering the name of Cora Martin's sister and then you were confident about your answer. Why is that?"

He hesitated before saying "Julie Andrews."

The lawyer frowned, "Yes?"

"I'd rather not upset the family."

"Please answer the question, Detective."

"You know the opening scene in *The Sound of Music*? Julie Andrews spins on a mountaintop and sings 'The Hills Are Alive'?"

"I'm sure the Court is familiar."

"In the helo, I made a stupid joke. Occupational hazard. We started calling her Julie Andrews."

She cocked her head.

"First because she was circling, and then ran back and forth like... Like the hills were coming after her." He frowned.

Lindsay whispered to her client, then addressed the judge. "No further questions."

"May the witness be excused?"

"Yes."

"Yes," Renata agreed.

Judge Bronski nodded at Jacob. "Thank you. You're free to leave."

"Thank you." He strode to the back.

"Anything else, Ms. Ochoa?"

"No other evidence, Your Honor."

"Very well. Ms. Schmidt? Has your star witness reported for duty?"

After huddling with Frances, Lindsay stood. "The State will rest on its exhibits, Your Honor. We may have maternal aunt testify at trial on December 29th."

The judge asked Renata, "Closing argument?"

She nodded, standing. "Detective Davis's testimony should put to rest any concerns the Court may have about whether Julie Martin's accusations against my client are credible. The facts do not support State intervention. Placement should be with Mother, Cora Martin, with no restrictions. Furthermore, I move to dismiss the petition and terminate protective custody, as there is no probable cause to believe that Naomi Martin's welfare is endangered in her mother's care. This needs to end today."

Aiden's attorney stood to say, "Father joins the motion."

"Your Honor!" Lindsay rose. "I was given no notice of counsel's motion to dismiss. My client has a right to present its case in support of its petition."

Judge Bronski peered down. "Do you have additional evidence?"

Frances touched Lindsay's arm and pressed the microphone's mute button.

"Why don't you consult with your client for a minute?" Propping her chin in her hand, the judge waved at them. "We can take a five-minute recess if you need time to discuss the merits of your case." A sideways smile crept up her wrinkled cheek. "Shouldn't take that long."

While they whispered, Naomi stirred in Cora's arms and opened her bright blue eyes. She would need to be fed soon.

"Hi," Cora said softly, smiling.

"Your Honor?" Lindsay was up.

Judge Bronski turned to her assistant, who nodded.

"We're back on the record," the judge said. "Ms. Schmidt?"

"My client takes no position on Mother's motion to dismiss."

"Motion granted." The elf judge's side-smirk was bigger than ever. "Best of luck to you, Ms. Martin. I hope your sister gets the help she needs. Court is adjourned." *Smack. Clunk.* Her gavel popped the cuckoo-clock people up again. Only her head and shoulders were visible as she glided to the door.

* * *

"Well done, counselor." Jacob stretched his hand to Renata as the glass exit door shut behind Lindsay.

"My star witness helped."

"Could you email me a subpoena?" He handed her a business card. "For the boss."

"Certainly," Renata said, smirking at it. "Did Cora tell you the name we were looking for?"

Holly wrapped her arm around his waist. "They thought you were whiskey."

"Jacob Daniels." Cora cringed. "I could have sworn your card had the Mountaindale logo."

"It did. Transferred to Fort Herring after that. Your photographic memory will serve you well in medical school."

"I completely botched your name!"

"Half-right's not bad for a half-dead person."

Even her father laughed before he turned to Renata. "Why didn't they fight us harder after all this?"

"The motion to dismiss?"

He nodded.

"I would like to say once they had all the evidence, they realized they had no case." A modest smile curled up. "The five-page email I sent to the Program Manager documenting Vanessa's unprofessionalism and poor judgment with multiple families may have helped as well."

"That's why," Cora's dad said.

"I do believe the agency tries to do the right thing," Renata frowned. "With the wrong people wielding all that power, though..." She shook her head. "I tried to warn their attorney. There is more than one kind of liability."

After Holly and Jacob had left and Cora's parents finished asking

Renata a million questions, they exited the glass door. Renata went on ahead, down the courthouse steps. Cora stopped on the cement platform carrying Naomi and her mother followed.

"You two wait here." Her father passed them with the empty car seat. "I'll get the car."

Three. There are three of us, Dad. Her head was suddenly killing her and she really needed to go study for her Chemistry final.

Down the stairs, he turned right toward the parking lot.

"Can I have my water, Mom? It's in the diaper bag."

"Here. I'll take Naomi." Holding her close, her mother sat on the planter's edge. "You're coming for dinner?"

When Cora lowered the bottle, her mom was beaming at Naomi. She smiled, "Sounds great."

The deciduous trees filtered her view of the sidewalk on the next block, where her dad ran into Jacob heading their way. She had hoped it might not have been "goodbye forever," that maybe she would see Jacob again with Holly, like at one of her poker nights, but this was sooner than expected.

Her mother sniffed at Naomi's bottom with a sour face.

Cora stepped up. "I can go change her, Mom. Can you tell Dad when he gets here?"

"No, I'll do it. Tell your dad I'll be right out." While she took Naomi and the diaper bag inside, Jacob and Cora's father shook hands by the street.

Jacob approached the courthouse in his knit cap, picking up something near the sidewalk. Smiling at Cora, he reached the courthouse steps and trotted up.

"Apple doesn't fall far from the tree." Naomi's hand-knit red bootie was extra tiny in the palm of his giant hand.

"Thank you!" Cora slipped the bootie into her coat pocket.

"Need a ride? Piggyback?" He squatted with his back to her.

"No thanks," she laughed.

He turned, towering above her again, and grinned through his short scruffy beard.

She had already thanked him. She had already said goodbye. It was nice to be with him, but also weird.

"Naomi's a good name," he said.

"Thanks."

"Family name?"

Cora shook her head. "It means 'joy.' There's a Bible verse about counting trials as joy because of what they produce, so—"

"Steadfastness. James 1. Sorry. You were saying?"

"No, that's it."

"Feel free to tell me to butt out, but does Naomi's father need some friendly encouragement to step up? He's missing out."

Cora flushed.

"You can't get these first years back."

Naomi. He's missing out on Naomi.

"Sorry. Not my business."

"No," she smiled. "Aiden is a great dad when he's around. He asked me to go to Seattle with him, but I wanted to be close to family. He's even talked about moving back, but I don't think that's a smart career move."

Jacob stared up the street. "Holly would love to babysit. Don't be shy about asking for help."

Cora wanted advice more than help. "Can I ask you a question?"

"You just did." He winked. "I'll give you a mulligan. Shoot."

"How do you know if you can trust someone?"

"Still hitchhiking?"

She smiled.

"Gonna need some context."

"About Aiden."

"The guy you were just saying was a great dad?"

"I don't want to be naïve. My parents hate him."

"Ah."

"Holly doesn't even like him."

Jacob gazed in another direction and smiled. "You think they're smarter than you?"

"They're all smart."

He stepped his feet apart, facing her. "God didn't short you on brains."

She smiled.

"I get it." He nodded. "You're gun-shy. You trusted your sister when she didn't deserve it," he said, sticking out his thumb. Then he straightened his index finger. "And you trusted your ex when he didn't deserve it. That about right?"

"Exactly. I keep making the same mistakes."

"Riddle me this. If you take a back seat to your parents' judgment…" Extending his middle finger changed the incidental finger gun to a three. "Or Holly's." He added his ring finger. "Wouldn't *that* be making the same mistake?"

As he clasped his hands behind his back, Cora's gaze blurred on his uniform, equipped for battle, which she was not.

"Hey." He nodded, smiling empowerment, like the encouraging nod the female police officer had given her that awful night in the hospital. "You get very far in the book of James?"

She shrugged.

"Try verse 5." He nodded at the Volvo pulling up, then held out his hand to say goodbye. "Keep in touch, okay?"

"Definitely." When Cora pulled her hand free from her pocket, Naomi's red bootie fell out.

Jacob stooped to retrieve it, chuckling. "You Martin women and your shoes."

CORA

This was a terrible idea. Granted, she hadn't really invited Aiden; he'd asked if he could join her. And when he'd asked if his friend could come, Cora couldn't say "No." Although she might have made an excuse or faked a cold at the last minute if she had known his friend was a girlfriend. A beautiful girlfriend, who even Naomi was making eyes at. And, of course, if Cora would have realized that Sunday was New Year's Day.

But Cora had survived the pre-church chatter with a couple of the congregants asking Rachel if Naomi was her baby, and Aiden raving about what a wonderful mom Cora was and touching Cora's shoulder as he guided Naomi back into her arms. And now everyone was singing. Except for Aiden, who had insisted on changing Naomi's diaper.

After the last verses of "It Is Well with My Soul," the man with the acoustic guitar left the platform with the singer, who looked like his daughter. A bespectacled pastor in a green polo shirt approached the stained wood podium toting a thick Bible with multi-colored tabs.

He smiled at the people in the sunny sanctuary. "Please be seated."

Cora did, smoothing her pale blue dress. She placed the song sheet on the padded bench to her right, away from Rachel, who was one space over. A woman with tight white curls and big round glasses sat a short distance away.

"For any visitors joining us today, I'm Paul, one of the elders here.

Pastor Tom called me last night and asked me to preach this morning."

I guess he's not the pastor.

"Pastor Tom is fine. He just had to take care of some family business. This is going to be more of an open devotional than a sermon. I didn't have much time to prepare a message. So, please bear with me." Smiling, he adjusted his glasses and said, "Please open your Bibles to Psalm 91."

The Bible in the wooden pocket in front of Cora came out easily. While she thumbed through its pages, she listened.

"'The one who lives under the protection of the Most High dwells in the shadow of the Almighty.'"

"Dwelling in the shadow" plunged her back into the desert, their first night.

The moon's so bright against the bluish-black sky. The whole desert is blue, darker in the shadow where we are, lying beside the gigantic rock wall. I can't stop shivering even with Julie's body pressed to mine and the sand heaped over our legs.

Cora shivered.

"'I will say concerning the Lord,'" Paul read, "'who is my refuge and my fortress, my God in whom I trust: He himself will rescue you from the bird trap, from the destructive plague. He will cover you with his feathers; you will take refuge under his wings.'"

A mental image of a colossal dove's wings surrounding her, protecting her, brought tears to her eyes. One dropped onto the open Bible, and she wiped it with her finger.

"'His faithfulness will be a protective shield. You will not fear the terror of the night, the arrow that flies by day, the plague that stalks in darkness, or the pestilence that ravages at noon.'"

More tears came as Cora recalled the mountain lion's terrifying scream through the darkness. Snot threatened to drip. While the man continued to read, a feather touch alighted on Cora's arm.

"Here, dear." The white-haired woman held out a tissue.

"Thank you." Cora pressed it to her nose.

"'For he will give his angels orders concerning you, to protect you in all your ways,'" Paul continued. "'They will support you with their hands so that you will not strike your foot against a stone. You will tread upon the lion and the cobra; you will trample the young lion and the serpent. Because he has his heart set on me, I will deliver him; I will protect him because he knows my name. When he calls out to me, I will answer him.'"

"I'm sorry." I squint through the twiggy branches to the blinding blue sky. A breeze kisses my skin.
    In my heart, I hear, "Get up."

"'I will be with him in trouble. I will rescue him and give him honor. I will satisfy him with a long life and show him my salvation.'"

Click. A man in a slouchy hat stands on a ledge just ahead near the bottom of the orange rock wall. He's hunched over, facing away from me.

Cora's vision blurred. She wasn't abandoned. She never had been. She was loved.

The warm tears rolling down her cheeks were interrupted by a hand on her left shoulder. Blinking, she smiled up at Aiden, seeing well enough to take Naomi.

"Are you okay?" The diaper bag went on the floor, and he sat on the other side.

Nodding, Cora whispered, "I'm glad we came," and kissed Naomi's head. "Thanks for changing her."

"Thanks for letting me. And for inviting us," he whispered back. Then he took Rachel's hand and turned forward, listening.

HOLLY

"Finished?" Holly reached for Jacob's mostly empty plate on his coffee table. Beside it sat white paperboard take-out containers with red Chinese symbols and a white paper bag.

Komi lay at his feet beside the brown leather sofa. Her front half sprawled onto the rug where she had strategically placed her head between her paws for maximum cuteness. Girlfriend gazed up from the space that Holly had just vacated. Jacob looked up, too, but his eyes were friendlier than the tawny tubby cat's. He pulled Holly onto his lap.

"I thought you were in a hurry to hike." She smiled, hoping for a kiss. "I'm fine skipping again."

"It's warmer tonight." He reached around her to the coffee table, folding her forward, and pulled a cellophane-wrapped cookie out of the bag. "Forgot your fortune cookie."

"You know I don't eat those."

"Open it. For fun."

"Since when...?"

Jacob smiled, stubborn.

The wrapper was an improvement. Lucky Dragon was becoming more hygienic. As she cracked the cookie, it was lighter and spongier, too.

"'A golden opportunity is in your future.'" Flipping over the slip, she said, "No lottery numbers?" When she tossed the strip of paper toward the table, it flitted to the floor. "What does yours say?" But the paper bag only had a couple of soy sauce packets left.

"I'll eat yours." He popped one half in his mouth.

"You know that fortune goes to you now, right, since you're eating the cookie?"

"I like golden opportunities."

"Selfish."

"You turned it down. You should always say 'yes' to a golden opportunity."

"You have one coming now, so be prepared."

Jacob shrugged. "The universe is full of surprises."

Holly held the back of her hand to his forehead. "What is wrong with you?"

"We're late for our Friday night hike," he said, and kissed her palm.

"You're the one…" She shook her head and took his plate.

Behind her, Jacob lobbed a chunk of chicken to a suddenly sitting Komi. Her little alligator yap snapped it up.

* * *

The evening sky was turning deeper blue at the crown of the hill above Jacob's house. Treetops framed the emerging stars. While Komi took off after something, her retractable leash whirred, vibrating the plastic handle in Holly's thin gloves.

"Remember how to find Orion's belt?" He stared skyward.

"I didn't bring my compass."

"You don't need it."

"I'm not going to get lost." The leash jerked her arm. "I always have my phone with me when I hike alone."

"What if your phone dies or breaks, or you, I don't know, lose it behind a couch cushion?"

"I found that within a couple of hours."

"Mm-hm."

When she tried to give him a playful shove, he caught her.

"Nice telegraph, Western Union," he said, pulling her close.

As Komi trotted up, Holly said, "Bite him for me."

But Jacob turned her into a human shield and nommed on her neck.

"Hey!" she laughed. "Don't. Stop. Don't stop."

"Back to work." He squeezed her shoulders. "Find Orion's belt." With an encouraging pat, he released her to stand alone in the dark.

"Seriously," she groaned and braced her hand on her hip, arching back. Actually, the night sky was breathtaking. Tiny points of twinkling rays shining from light years away. Time was such a funny thing. The moon was bright, full but for the left third still in darkness.

"If you can't find Orion's belt, how about Samson's ring?"

Holly turned. "That's not even a—"

Jacob was on one knee, holding out a black velvet box. Like an oyster with a pearl, something sparkled inside the white interior.

Her gloved hand clamped over her mouth as she squatted down to him.

"Pretty sure this is it, but you're the expert." The moon lit his lovely face. "Will you marry me?"

Komi's head inserted between them, and her cold wet nose sniffed Holly's mouth.

"No!" she sputtered, laughing. "Komi!"

"No?" Jacob lifted Holly by the arm to stand with him. "That's your answer?"

"Yes!"

He grinned. "Yes, no is your answer?"

"No, yes is my answer."

"To marrying me?"

"Mm-hm."

Snap. He flipped the box shut with one hand and held her.

After some time with them kissing and Komi darting back and forth, being curious but mostly exceptionally good, Jacob gave her a slow peck and tucked a strand of hair behind her ear.

"Thank God." His warm thumb stroked her neck. "Didn't save the receipt for this thing."

Holly beamed. "Yes, you did." Her lips sparked with the memory of his.

"Didn't think I'd need to since you practically threw yourself at me." She waited.

He smiled. "I did."

When he opened the little black box and pulled out the ring, she half-stifled a squeal, ripped off a glove, and stretched out her fingers, bouncing just a bit on her toes. The ring nestled by her knuckle: one cushion-cut diamond with tiny diamonds trailing down the white-gold band.

"I love it!" She threw her arms around his waist again, exclaiming, "I love you!" and squeezed hard.

His sexy belly laugh preceded a warm smooch on her head. "We can exchange it for another one if it isn't exactly what you want. Danielle tried to help me—"

"That's why she acted so funny at Christmas! Asking Brett for an anniversary ring isn't her style."

"I'm supposed to tell you she knows good dress shops in Salt Lake City."

"You all are so sneaky." She gasped. "Did you ask for my dad's blessing when we were there?"

He smirked.

"That's what you were doing!"

The dimple made him look suspicious.

"What? What else were you doing?"

"Might be a surprise."

"Christmas is over. What? You know I hate surprises."

* * *

While they held hands walking down the hill to Jacob's house, Holly kept trying to look at her ring without tugging Komi's leash.

She smiled up at him. "Sleepover?"

"I should have you go home." He brought their clasped hands to his lips and kissed her knuckles. "My willpower is tapped out."

They continued down the hill.

"Want to borrow some of mine?"

Jacob sighed. "No making out."

"Deal."

"If you could cover up that hot body of yours, like the first night you stayed over ..." In a Lumbergh voice he added, "'That would be greeaat.'"

She shuddered, then grinned at his *Office Space* imitation. "I don't know... That night was pretty hot."

"Every minute with you is hot."

"Aww!" But her flattered face turned into a scowl. "If you can't stop saying romantic shit like that, I won't have any willpower either. How's a girl supposed to keep her pants on with all this happening?" She circled her palm at him.

"You know your angry-troll-woman routine is a huge turn-on. Yuge," he winked.

"You brilliant man! Lust quenched!" Like a baseball referee over a safe baserunner, she threw straight arms out. "Next time I start grinding on you, pull out a Trump imitation." Slipping her arm into his, she asked, "How can I be your lust quencher?"

He shook his head. "My desire for you is unconditional."

"Aww."

"Shonk!" Jacob cupped his hands like he was landing a football at his chest. "Right on the numbers."

They strolled home as a unit, with Komi trotting ahead and coming back to check on them, perky ears flapping.

"How does summer sound?"

"For the wedding?" *Their wedding!*

"Unless that's too soon. I know a lot of planning goes into these things."

"I have a system pretty well dialed from helping Paige." Her heart was sprinting, gleeful. "The venue could be a problem."

"We could use my folks' place. String-light the hell out of it."

The gazebo on the 4th of July came to mind, radiant in the bluish dusk, smelling like cooled-off sun and fun and family, peppered with glimmering bits of hope. And dancing.

The cells in Holly's body hummed like captive fireflies.

EPILOGUE

HOLLY

If that Belgian Malinois didn't ease up on Komi, Holly would have to say something. The black beast had gone straight for her when it entered the dog park. The owner hadn't even made half a lap around the perimeter yet—she was strolling, talking on her phone like she owned the place.

Komi yelped.

That's it. "Hey!" Holly barked at the woman and sprinted toward the dogs.

The brunette looked up.

"A little help with your dog?" she called, pissed.

"Krieger!"

Why was that name familiar?

The black, horse-eared specimen was at the stranger's side in a moment. Krieger sat at attention while she murmured into her phone, then slid her hands into her trench coat pockets.

Meanwhile, Komi rolled over in the muddy grass—probably nasty with poop residue—whipping her tail like a windshield wiper. Her tongue lolled out of her panting mouth as if to say, "Hi, Mom. Where'd my new best friend go?"

The brunette frowned from a distance. Holly faced off with her, bracing her hands on her hips and standing above Komi until Komi bounded up and away.

The woman's mouth curled into a cocky smirk as she called, "This is your girl, huh? I get it now."

Behind Holly, Jacob was jogging up with the ball that had gone over the fence. While the woman walked toward them, her dog heeled off-leash. Chuckling, Jacob handed Holly the slobbery ball.

"Ew."

He smiled and planted a kiss above her ear, whispering, "This may be the answer to our wedding party problem."

In a few more militant steps, the woman stood before them, beaming and way too fricking beautiful. "Nice to finally meet you, Holly. I'm Dawn."

"Officer Dawn Clark," Jacob said. "She's kind of a big deal."

"Hero, you might say," she winked at Holly and extended a hand in a fingerless glove.

"Easy on that hand," he said as the women locked eyes.

Dawn smiled at him. "Just a flesh wound," she said, suddenly British.

"'Tis but a scratch," Jacob answered, smirking back at her.

What. The. Hell.

ACKNOWLEDGMENTS

Thanks first to my Heavenly Father and my family for enabling my labor of love here.

Tiffany, your encouragement and guidance in the early days meant the world to me—thank you! And to the other lovely women who sampled this at various stages—Vicki, Audrey, Sarah, Amy, Paula, and Meg—with a special shout out to Shala, who agreed to a second helping. You are all such a blessing!

Thanks, too, to my editor, Ema Barnes, who caught when I was trying to be funny and helped me put my darlings in their places. Lastly, thank you to artistic geniuses Mark Karis and Cornelius Matteo for creating the cover and the author photo that not only captured but improved the visions in my head.

ABILENE

Dear reader friend,

If you'd like to join us back in Fort Herring for *Junked Love* and *Over Love*, please subscribe to my mailing list for weekly blog posts, publication updates, and deals: www.abilenepotts.com.

To help spread the love, please rate or review *Junk Love* on Amazon, GoodReads, or wherever.

SOURCES

From Grace Community Church's "Fundamentals of the Faith" Lesson #1, "Our God-Breathed Bible," at www.gty.org/fof (2009):

The Matrix of Existence
In the beginning | God | created | the heavens | and the earth.
– Genesis 1:1
TIME | FORCE | ACTION | SPACE | MATTER – Herbert Spencer, physicist

Answer to the Second Law of Thermodynamics = Sin

From The Holy Bible, available at www.bible.com:

Trials and Maturity
Consider it a great joy, my brothers and sisters, whenever you experience various trials, because you know that the testing of your faith produces endurance. And let endurance have its full effect, so that you may be mature and complete, lacking nothing. *James 1:2-4, Christian Standard Bible (CSB), © 2017 Holman Bible Publishers*

For everything there is a season, and a time for every matter under heaven.
Ecclesiastes 3:1, English Standard Version® (ESV®), © 2001 Crossway

The God-Given Task
What gain has the worker from his toil? I have seen the business that God has given to the children of man to be busy with. He has made everything beautiful in its time. Also, he has put eternity into man's heart, yet so that he cannot find out what God has done from the beginning to the end. I perceived that there is nothing better for them than to be joyful and to do good as long as they live; also that everyone should eat and drink and take pleasure in all his toil—this is God's gift to man.
Ecclesiastes 3:9-13 (ESV®), © 2001 Crossway

Do not be overcome by evil, but overcome evil with good
Romans 12:21 (ESV®), © 2001 Crossway

Love is patient, love is kind. Love does not envy, it is not boastful, is not arrogant, is not rude, is not self-seeking, is not irritable, and does not keep a record of wrongs. Love finds no joy in unrighteousness but rejoices in the truth. It bears all things, believes all things, hopes all things, endures all things.
1 Corinthians 13:4-7 (CSB), © 2017 Holman Bible Publishers

If I have the gift of prophecy and understand all mysteries and all knowledge, and if I have all faith so that I can move mountains but do not have love, I am nothing.
1 Corinthians 13:2 (CSB), © 2017 Holman Bible Publishers

For you are saved by grace through faith, and this is not from yourselves; it is God's gift
Ephesians 2:8 (CSB), © 2017 Holman Bible Publishers

Testing of Your Faith
Count it all joy, my brothers, when you meet trials of various kinds, for you know that the testing of your faith produces steadfastness. And let steadfastness have its full effect, that you may be perfect and complete, lacking nothing.
If any of you lacks wisdom, let him as God, who gives generously to all without reproach, and it will be given him.
James 1:2-5 (ESV®), © 2001 Crossway

The Protection of the Most High
The one who lives under the protection of the Most High
dwells in the shadow of the Almighty.
I will say concerning the LORD, who is my refuge and my fortress,
my God in whom I trust:
He himself will rescue you from the bird trap,
from the destructive plague.
He will cover you with his feathers;
you will take refuge under his wings.
His faithfulness will be a protective shield.
You will not fear the terror of the night,
the arrow that flies by day,
the plague that stalks in darkness,
or the pestilence that ravages at noon.
Though a thousand fall at your side
and ten thousand at your right hand,
the pestilence will not reach you.
You will only see it with your eyes
and witness the punishment of the wicked.

Because you have made the LORD — my refuge,
the Most High — your dwelling place,
no harm will come to you;
no plague will come near your tent.
For he will give his angels orders concerning you,
to protect you in all your ways.
They will support you with their hands
so that you will not strike your foot against a stone.
You will tread on the lion and the cobra;
you will trample the young lion and the serpent.
Because he has his heart set on me,
I will deliver him;
I will protect him because he knows my name.
When he calls out to me, I will answer him;
I will be with him in trouble.
I will rescue him and give him honor.
I will satisfy him with a long life
and show him my salvation.
Psalm 91 (CSB) © 2017 Holman Bible Publishers

Printed in the USA
CPSIA information can be obtained
at www.ICGtesting.com
JSHW012103130124
55371JS00006B/19